PRAISE FOR THE COOKBOOK NOOK MYSTERIES

"[A] delectable page-turner with a tasty mix of characters, crime, and cookbooks, blended beautifully in a witty, well-plotted whodunit that will leave you hungry for more."
——Kate Carlisle, *New York Times* bestselling author of
the Bibliophile Mysteries

"There's a feisty new amateur sleuth in town and her name is Jenna Hart. With a bodacious cast of characters, a wrenching murder, and a collection of cookbooks to die for, Daryl Wood Gerber's *Final Sentence* was a page-turning puzzler of a mystery that I could not put down."
——Jenn McKinlay, *New York Times* bestselling author of
the Cupcake Bakery Mysteries, the Library Lover's
Mysteries, and the Hat Shop Mysteries

"Readers will relish the extensive cookbook suggestions, the cooking primer, and the whole foodie phenomenon."
——*Library Journal*

"A mystery featuring a cookbook bookstore is completely irresistible, especially when the author combines it with complex and very well-developed story lines."
——Kings River Life Magazine

"You really can't go wrong with a cozy by this author whether she is writing as Daryl Wood Gerber or Avery Aames. All her stories are completely captivating and very entertaining."
——as into a Good Book

T0176267

Grilling
the Subject

DARYL WOOD GERBER

BERKLEY PRIME CRIME, NEW YORK

BERKLEY
PRIME
CRIME

An imprint of Penguin Random House LLC
375 Hudson Street, New York, New York 10014

GRILLING THE SUBJECT

A Berkley Prime Crime Book / published by arrangement with the author

ISBN: 9780425279410

PUBLISHING HISTORY
Berkley Prime Crime mass-market edition / August 2016

PRINTED IN THE UNITED STATES OF AMERICA

10 9 8 7 6 5 4 3 2 1

Cover art by Teresa Fasolino.
Cover design by Jason Gill.
Interior text design by Kelly Lipovich.

This is a work of fiction. Names, characters, places, and incidents either are the product of
the author's imagination or are used fictitiously, and any resemblance to actual persons,
living or dead, business establishments, events, or locales is entirely coincidental.

PUBLISHER'S NOTE: The recipes contained in this book are to be followed exactly as
written. The publisher is not responsible for your specific health or allergy needs that
may require medical supervision. The publisher is not responsible for any adverse
reactions to the recipes contained in this book.

Penguin
Random
House

To my husband.
You will always be in my heart.

Acknowledgments

*"Flaming enthusiasm, backed up by horse
sense and persistence, is the quality that most
frequently makes for success."*

~ Dale Carnegie

Thank you to my husband, Chuck. I am so blessed to have been loved by you. You fill my thoughts constantly and you always will. Your enthusiasm and support were without bounds. I could not have accomplished so much without you as my team partner.

To my family and friends, thank you for all your love and support. I cherish you.

Thank you to my talented author friends, Krista Davis, Lucy Burdette, Julie Hyzy, and Jenn McKinlay for your enthusiasm for writing. Thanks to my brainstormers at Plothatchers, Krista, Janet, Kaye, Marilyn, Peg, and yes, another Janet (we all have aliases, I think!). Thanks to my blog mates on Mystery Lovers Kitchen: Cleo, Krista, Leslie, Mary Jane/Victoria, Roberta/Lucy, Linda, and Sheila. Love you all! Thanks to the Delicious Mystery group and the Cake and Dagger crew (you know who you are)!

Thanks to those who have helped make *A Cookbook Nook Mystery* series a success: my fabulous editor Kate

Seaver as well as Katherine Pelz and Roxanne Jones. Thank you to my fabulous artist, Teresa Fasolino. Another superb job!! And thanks to my copyeditor Amy Schneider for your terrific attention to detail.

Thanks to John Talbot for believing in every aspect of my work. Thank you to Sheridan Stancliff, you are an Internet and creative marvel. Thank you to Kimberley Greene, I appreciate everything you do for me.

Thank you, librarians and booksellers, for sharing the delicious world of a culinary bookshop owner with your readers.

Thank you, readers, for allowing Jenna Hart and her family and friends to join you in your imagination. Thank you for sharing your love of my books with your family and friends. An author's story cannot come alive without readers!

Chapter 1

I DIDN'T MEAN TO. It was an accident. But as I swooped past one of The Cookbook Nook's display tables while carrying a stack of cookbooks in my arms, my elbow nicked a spine. That set off an event that would make a domino-chain-reaction physicist proud. Every book that I had carefully placed upright fell. *Smack-smack-smack*.

All the customers in the shop, a few still dressed in their Sunday finest, spun to take a peek. My cheeks burned with embarrassment. *Slick, Jenna, real slick.* Why was I off my game? I had been on edge since I'd awakened this morning. I took a tumble over a log on the beach during my morning walk, and then I burned the toast, broke a glass, and snagged my favorite lacy white sweater on the door latch. Each time I blundered, I felt like I was being watched—judged—by an unknown someone.

"Shoot," I muttered under my breath. I didn't mind the mess. Ever since I'd quit working as an advertising executive in San Francisco and returned to Crystal Cove to help my aunt Vera open a culinary bookshop—nearly a year ago; how time flies—I had arranged and rearranged The Cookbook Nook multiple times. I had assembled books by chefs, by theme, and by difficulty of recipe. Customers seemed to enjoy the rotation. I think they secretly liked the personal attention the staff at the shop provided when they asked for help locating a title.

"Eek!" Bailey Bird, who was my best friend and also my employee, shrieked at the top of her lungs, which sent my already pinging nerves into overdrive. She was at the back of the store near the children's table, trotting in place. Her multicolored bangles jangled; her summery skirt flounced up and down. "Jenna, help!"

I rushed to her, my flip-flops flapping. My hair caught in my mouth; I sputtered it out. "What's going on?"

"Eek!" she shrieked again.

She wasn't on fire. I didn't see a mouse.

"Are you practicing the flamenco?" I asked in an attempt to lighten the mood.

"Spiders. You know I hate spiders!" She tap-danced, trying to nail her prey with the toes of her espadrille sandals. "Help!"

I pushed up the sleeves of my second-favorite lacy white sweater, hiked up the knees of my trousers, and crouched to inspect. Afternoon sunlight highlighted two spiders: one, including its legs, couldn't have been the size of a pea; the other wasn't much larger. They must have materialized from the box of books Bailey had brought from the stockroom. I rose to my full height, nearly a head taller than my pal, and said, "They're itty-bitty."

"Jenna Hart, dagnabbit, do something! Or are you too old and feeble?"

"Ha!" I was an official thirty-something now. I had celebrated my birthday a couple of weeks ago, not with a big bash, just a May fling with friends. I didn't feel older, but I was definitely looking at life differently—in decades rather than in years. Weird. Maybe that was the thing that was bothering me. Age. Life. Zipping by.

"C'mon," Bailey pleaded.

Tigger, the darling ginger kitten—now *cat*—who rescued me when I first moved back to Crystal Cove, darted from beneath the children's reading table and pounced at one of the spiders. He didn't catch it. His quarry fled to safety under a floorboard.

"One flew the coop," I quipped.

"Get the other one," Bailey cried.

I wasn't a fan of spiders, but I would never make such a ruckus about teensy creatures. Wait. I take that back. I might— *might*—squeal if I saw a black widow spider.

"C'mon, Jenna! Pronto. Puh-lease!"

"Okay, hold your horses. Calm down. You're going to drive away customers," I quipped, if my antics over by the display table hadn't already scared them off.

A number of customers, their arms filled with cookbooks to purchase, were backing toward the exit.

"Don't flee, folks," I said. "She's overreacting. Everything is fine." To Bailey, I said, "Stop it. You're yelling so loudly, you'd think we've encountered an onslaught of bugs worthy of a Steven Spielberg movie!"

"I'm s-sorry." Her teeth were chattering, her eyes as wide as saucers. She didn't like bugs. Any kind. Her fear stemmed from a time, way back in grade school, when a trio of boys dumped her in a woodpile. Her hair at the time, unlike the short hairdo she sported now, had been long and quickly became a nest for a horde of creepy-crawlers. Over the last year, my aunt Vera, who for the past forty of her sixty-something years liked to dabble in alternative methods of coping by telling fortunes or doing hypnosis and aura readings, had tried all sorts of sense therapy with Bailey to help her overcome her dread, but nothing had worked.

Hmm. Maybe I should consult my aunt about the weird vibes I had been experiencing all day.

"Swat it," Bailey pleaded.

I snatched a piece of construction paper off the children's table—the table was always set with artistic goodies so kids could have fun while their parents shopped—and I flailed at the teensy spider. I caught it with one blow and glanced at my buddy. "Feeling better?"

"I will if I'm able to nab one of Katie's delicious barbecue muffins before they're all gone."

A half hour ago Katie Casey, my other best friend and the inventive chef of The Nook Café, an adjunct of the bookshop, had set out a tasty display of barbecue muffins for our customers to snack on. People had been flocking into the store ever since to taste the savory delights. Sure, they intended to purchase cookbooks, too, but the cheese-and-ground-beef-stuffed muffins were fast becoming legendary. Katie promised to cook all sorts of yummy ranch-style food throughout the week, like mini cups of baked beans, cornbread, and even a cake decorated to look like a cactus. I'd begged her to include her finger-licking-good, dry-rub ribs, but she said they would be too messy for the shop. I agreed, but I craved them.

Why was she hooked on a barbecue theme? Because this week and on into next week, Crystal Cove was hosting the Wild West Extravaganza. The WWE promoted family-friendly, animal-friendly events all over the West Coast. Sure, there would be rodeo events, but no steer wrestling and no bulldogging. There would be horse races, rope jumping, stunt fighting, and more. To get ourselves in the mood, we had rimmed the front door of the shop with the image of an old jail and decorated the shop with all sorts of western doodads.

"Jenna! Bailey!" Ava Judge, one of our regular customers, flew through the front door in her typical designer suit and smart high heels. *Spitfire*. That was how people would describe her. She had a sizzling personality and high-octane energy, all wrapped up in a raring-to-go athletic body. She played tennis two to three times a week—great for a forty-something—and most often won. As she always did, she flourished a real estate flyer. She never missed an opportunity to promote her business.

Ava scooted to a stop and thrust the flyer at me. I accepted it. A million-dollar home in the hills was for sale. "Where's Vera?" she asked.

"On a date. With the deputy." I returned the flyer to her. "Why?"

"It's so sad." Ava's voice caught. I took a closer look at her perfectly made-up face. Tears pressed at the corners of her eyes. She fished in her oversized, crammed-to-the-gills tote; her hand came out empty.

Realizing she was searching for a tissue, I dashed to the sales counter, fetched a tissue from a box, and returned. I handed it to her. "What's got you so upset?"

"Haven't you heard?" She dabbed her eyes, then stuffed the tissue in her bag. "The promoter for this week's event . . . died."

"Oh no."

"Was he murdered?" Bailey asked.

I whacked her. "Not every death is suspicious."

"Some are."

"Not this time." Ava shook her head. Her long, high-lighted tresses swayed back and forth. "He was bucked off a mechanical bull last night. His second-in-command is going to take his place. Shane . . ." She snapped her fingers. *Snap, snap, snap.* "His last name is . . . oh, help me out . . . what was that TV western called, with the darling gambling brothers?"

"*Maverick?*" I suggested.

"That's the one."

"I know Shane Maverick." He had worked with me at Taylor & Squibb Advertising in San Francisco. "Bailey, you know him. Remember, he worked in sales and had the gift of gab?" Bailey and I had lost touch during college; we had reconnected while working at Taylor & Squibb. She had been in charge of monitoring all the campaigns—on air, in magazines, and on the Internet. However, city life isn't for everyone, and she, like me, had moved home recently to switch up her future.

"Yeah," Bailey said. "Shane. Sort of pudgy and out of shape."

"Not anymore," Ava said. "He's quite a hunk."

I nodded. "He sure is." At one time Shane was a good sixty pounds overweight; now he was ultra fit. I knew because he was the person who had opened my husband's gym locker in San Francisco when I was trying to solve a mystery about his death. My heart snagged at the memory. *David.* Once the love of my life, gone over three years. *Buck up, Jenna. No tears. Not at work.* "I didn't know Shane was involved with the Wild West Extravaganza. The last time I saw him, he was managing a chain of workout centers. One site is located in Santa Cruz, just about thirty minutes from here."

"He's not doing that anymore," Ava said. "He did, while the Wild West Extravaganza group courted him and relocated their headquarters to Crystal Cove. He was in and out of town a lot for interviews and training, but now that they've snatched him up, he's moving to town."

"The WWE relocated here?"

"Sure did. I sold Shane a place in your dad's and my neighborhood."

I laughed. "And you couldn't remember his last name?"

"We haven't closed escrow yet."

"Ava, give me a break. You're toying with me." I gave her a long, knowing look; she obviously liked Shane. "Are you two—"

"No." Ava cut me off. "He's engaged and living with the piano teacher. The very *pregnant* piano teacher."

We only had one piano teacher in town: Emily Hawthorne. She was a regular in the store. She preferred organic food cookbooks, although, come to think of it, she hadn't visited for quite a while. How could she be *very* pregnant?

I wondered, then blushed. She and Shane must have hooked up months ago on one of his many trips to town.

"By the way—" Ava snapped three times again; I got the feeling she was a habitual snapper. I had seen her snap at service people, like a gardener or a housepainter, and I'd caught her snapping at her clients, too. Nobody seemed to mind. She got things done. On time. A rarity in the real estate business. "Shane is an animal safety buff, so no horses or animals will be hurt this week. Also, he has some new ideas how to drum up tourist interest, and the mayor is on board. She thinks Shane is wonderful. I think she wants him to run for city council in the future."

"Wow," Bailey said, "talk about jumping into a new town with both feet. Are you sure he didn't kill the other guy to get the job?"

"Stop it," I said.

"Murder happens." Bailey plucked at her coppery hair and threw me a pert look. "You and I know that all too well." She was referring to the fact that we had been acquainted with a few people who had died under suspicious circumstances. All that sadness was behind us now. A few months had passed without a single incident. To a former advertiser like me who understood flow charts, Crystal Cove was on an upswing statistically.

"Shane is a good guy," Ava went on. "Promise." She hoisted her tote higher on her shoulder. "Mind if I browse the shelves?"

"Be our guest." I made a sweeping gesture and then remembered I hadn't fixed the arrangement I'd destroyed on the display table. I hurried ahead of her to reset the dozens of barbecue- and grill-themed cookbooks.

Without asking, Ava placed a stack of flyers on the sales counter and then moved to our display of Wild West–style aprons. I'd ordered a half dozen fashioned out of bandana material and another half dozen made out of cute cow-print fabric with red-checkered borders. "Are any of you partaking in the festivities this week?" she asked while holding a cow-print apron in front of her and inspecting its length on her body.

"Tito and I are going to the pole-bending event," Bailey said. Tito Martinez, a reporter for the *Crystal Cove Crier*, is Bailey's fiancé. "Have you ever seen that? It's sort of like slalom racing for skiing. One horse, one rider, weaving around poles. I hear it's exciting."

"What about you, Jenna?" Ava asked.

"I plan to take in the horse race."

"Down Buena Vista Boulevard?"

"Is there going to be another?"

Our fair city, which was set on the coast of California below Santa Cruz and above Monterey, was one long stretch of gorgeous territory, marked by an age-old lighthouse at the north end and a public pier filled with shops and fun things to do at the south end. The weather was beautiful year-round, with the occasional splash of rain or drift of fog. The hills to the east boasted wondrous vegetation and beautiful homes. The crests of the mountains sparkled as the waning sun cast its rays on them at sunset. Buena Vista Boulevard, which is what we called the section of the Pacific Coast Highway that cut through town, was populated with shops and restaurants. A main portion of the street would be closed off and traffic detoured for the horse race.

"Don't miss the rope twirling," Ava said, "or the chuck wagon race."

The rope twirling would take place on The Pier. The chuck wagon race would be held on the beach. In addition, in the parking lots joining the community college and the aquarium, there were going to be live bands and food trucks. The Cookbook Nook had lots of activities planned over the course of the next ten days, too. For our first specialty event, Katie would lead an adult gingerbread-making session where customers could learn how to construct an old western town.

"I nearly forgot," Ava said. "I came in looking for a Steve Raichlen cookbook. You know who I mean, the TV host. It's about grilling. I think it came out around 2001." She raised her fingers to snap.

Before she could, I grabbed her hand and guided her toward our celebrity chef section. Luckily Hurricane Jenna hadn't demolished that area. The shelves were tidy and alphabetically arranged.

"Is this it?" I pulled a book from its slot. "Raichlen's *How to Grill: The Complete Illustrated Book of Barbecue Techniques, A Barbecue Bible! Cookbook*." Raichlen offered a lot of show-and-tell and step-by-step instructions.

"That's the one."

"We also have *Bobby Flay's Grill It!* and *Smokin' with Myron Mixon: Recipes Made Simple, from the Winningest Man in Barbecue*." I had stocked up on a few basic books from the Weber grill company, as well, and made sure we had Guy Fieri's *Guy on Fire: 130 Recipes for Adventures in Outdoor Cooking*. Reviewers said his book really appealed to male customers, of which we had many. It wasn't your typically pretty tabletop cookbook; it was filled with humor. I loved the fact that Guy called his outdoor tools his *arsenal*.

I nabbed a few more books from the shelf and handed them to Ava. Snapping waylaid, she continued to browse, so I ventured to the display table and did a quick makeover without standing the books up. Call me foolish once, not twice.

Next, I shifted to the display window to tweak our latest exhibit. Bailey and I had spent all day yesterday putting items in place. We had laid out a crisp checkered tablecloth and built levels beneath it, and then we'd added colorful barbecue tools with a variety of handles, a mini hibachi, some grill lights for late-night grilling, long tubes of matches, and candles. We included a corny-looking chuck wagon cookie jar—I had stumbled across an assortment of kooky cookie jars online and had purchased twenty of them—plus a huge wicker picnic basket, red plastic cups, and a red pitcher. As a finishing touch, we set out mason jars packed with retro cinnamon candy sticks or gumballs.

Staring at the display now, I felt something was missing, but what? A split second later, I snapped like Ava. Books. *Duh!* Yes, we sold lots of unique cooking items in our store, but mostly we sold books, and the display had none.

I roamed the shop and plucked a few titles that would appeal to passersby. Two children's books: *The Gingerbread Cowboy* and *Little Red Cowboy Hat*. As a savvy marketer, I realized that children often pulled their parents into stores. "Mommy, buy me that!" they would cry. Deep in the recesses of my mind, I expected to get paid back in spades when I had children—*if* I had children. They would tug me this way and that, and I would have to comply. *Too-ra-loo*, as my aunt would say.

I added a fun adult book called *The Cowboy Hat Book*, a coffee table–style book that contained the history of the hat, and I placed a used edition of *The All-American Cowboy Cookbook: Over 300 Recipes From the World's Greatest Cowboys* next to that, *used* because it was out of print, which was too bad. Inside there were colorful stories about a few old-time western stars like Gene Autry and Roy Rogers. I had purchased the book for a song at a garage sale. I vowed I would never sell it, but I probably would. For the right price.

"Jenna!" Ava beckoned me with a finger. "Help me with these." She had collected a dozen books.

I hurried to her—see how she gets people to obey?—and I carried her haul to the checkout counter. "What a lot of books. Are you having a party?"

"Between you and me, shh"—she winked twice—"yes, I'm having a private party. *Private* because a certain some-body will not be invited to attend. I've asked a few of my neighbors, including your father, to come for cocktails and heavy hors d'oeuvres tomorrow night. I think your father has invited his beloved. That's entirely all right."

My father, a former FBI man, is a widower and retired

and currently dating Bailey's mother Lola, who is like my second mother. I adore her. Seeing them together always makes me smile. Dad was lost after my mother died.

"Why the secrecy?" I asked as I packed her books into one of our specialty shop bags and tied the handle with rattan ribbon.

"It's a community gathering, if you will, but that certain someone is not, I repeat *not*, to hear of it. Do you understand?"

I nodded, but how could I not tell that *someone* if I didn't know who it was?

Ava peered over her shoulder and back at me with a triumphant—or was it malicious?—gleam in her eye. "See you."

As she left, a chill ran down my spine. At the same time a door slammed. Outside the shop.

I glanced through the window at the parking lot and saw the rear lights of a dark blue Prius flare. Something else flickered, too, inside the car, like sunlight bouncing off a lens of a camera or binoculars. Was someone spying on the store? On Ava? No. Of course not. I was being silly. The driver of the car—I couldn't tell whether it was a man or woman—was probably doing business on a cell phone or using the utility mirror on the visor.

In spite of that logical explanation, another chill cut through me. *Sheesh, Jenna. Lighten up!* I flicked my fingers at the air to rid myself of bad vibes, as my aunt had taught me, but it didn't work. A third shudder jolted me to my core.

Chapter 2

E VER SINCE I returned to Crystal Cove, my aunt, my father, and I had convened at one of our houses for dinner on Sunday night. Sometimes, like tonight, we invited others. Bailey and I had kitchen duty. She was preparing a balsamic barbecue sauce for the steaks my father was grilling. I was fixing a Caesar salad with spicy croutons. I wasn't much of a cook, *yet*—I had graduated to ten-ingredient recipes a few months ago—but I could always manage a salad. I was quite adept at dicing and slicing.

"Feeling any better?" Bailey asked.

Earlier at the shop I had confided how I felt someone had been watching the store . . . or Ava . . . or me. I shrugged. "Not really."

"Are you sure you couldn't identify who was in the car?"

"Do you know how many dark-blue-Prius owners there are in town?" The Crystal Cove community was quite eco-conscious, not to mention that there were plenty of tourists, and any one of them might drive the same kind of car.

"True." She slipped around me and took the ocean-blue peppermill off the counter.

My father's kitchen was streamlined, thanks to my mother's keen eye. She had loved to cook so much that she'd forgotten to teach me. She wasn't a power freak or anything like that; she simply thought cooking good food was a way to show her family how much she cared. She did teach me to paint, and I would always remember our long walks and talks on the beach. My brother and sister hated walks on the beach; that was when I got Mom all to myself.

Bailey said, "Next time you see the Prius—"

"I hope I never do."

"But if you do, take a picture with your cell phone. We'll grab the license plate, and I'll have my mother run it through the DMV." Lola, now the proud owner of The Pelican Brief Diner, was formerly a lawyer and knew how to pull governmental strings. "We'll nail that sucker."

"I'm probably overreacting."

"But you want to err on the safe side." She winked at me.

The safe side. Right. That was why I had reenrolled in self-defense classes at the junior college. I'd been too close to getting clobbered in the past year. Not my fault. I seemed to have a knack for sniffing out bad guys, and the bad guys didn't seem to like that trait very much. Go figure.

Aunt Vera waltzed into the kitchen looking serene in a pale blue caftan, which complemented her creamy skin and bright red hair. No turban tonight. She wasn't telling fortunes; however, her mouth was moving and no words were coming out. Was she divining some kind of good-vibes spell? She stopped abruptly and assessed me while aiming her index finger. "What's bothering you, Jenna?" She wiggled the finger as if it were her magic wand. The silver-and-blue bangles on her wrist clattered with merry abandon. "Come on. Out with it, dear." My aunt could always tell when something was bugging me. She claimed to have ESP, and she probably did, or

I was as easy to read as a Google map, printed directions and all. "Jenna?" she coaxed.

"Nothing."

"Liar," Bailey said and filled my aunt in about my anxiety.

"Traitor," I muttered.

"Concerned friend."

"Trust those feelings, Jenna, dear." Aunt Vera studied my neckline. "Where's the white quartz necklace I gave you?" Quartz, according to my aunt, could dispel negative energy and purify one's mental and physical planes. She expected me to wear it nonstop.

"On the counter in my bathroom. Soaking."

"Soaking?"

"I touched the chain after I'd poured honey into my tea earlier. It was sticky."

Aunt Vera raised an eyebrow. "Why do you even try to fib, dear?"

"I'm not fibbing."

Her eyes sparkled with humor. "Your lower lip gives you away every time. C'mon. The truth shall set you free." She rubbed the phoenix amulet she always wore. I resisted, but the force was strong within her.

"Okay, fine." She was right; I was pretty lousy at lying. "I took it off for my shower and forgot to replace it." I got too involved choosing the right outfit. Red or blue top? Skirt or trousers? I opted for a halter dress with bold blue stripes.

"There, now. Don't you feel better? You should—"
Twang. Crackle.

"What the heck was that?" I tossed the knife onto the cutting board and raced to the patio.

Bailey and my aunt followed.

My silver-haired father with movie-star good looks was standing at the railing, a cordless telephone in one hand, binoculars in the other. The sun was setting along the horizon, its rays highlighting him in a happy golden glow, but my father looked anything but happy. In fact, his square jaw was vibrating with rage. "Answer, dang it!" He was peering down the hill toward the next tier of homes.

"Dad, was that an electric guitar?" I asked.

He didn't answer. He started yelling into the phone: "Lady, you have no right!"

Lola, a shapely woman in her sixties and the same petite size as Bailey with the same short hairstyle although hers was silver, stood beside my father. Despite her size, she could be fearless. She tried to wrest the telephone from my father's hand. "Cary, please. Don't."

"Who is he screaming at?" I asked.

"Sylvia Gump," Lola replied while trying to gain control of the cordless phone.

Sylvia owned Sterling Sylvia, a specialty shop that offered everything from high-end jewelry to silver cookbook holders and bookmark clips. Customers had to make appointments to see Sylvia. I knew a few women who came from as far away as New York to buy her designs. Sylvia had a passion for cooking and was a regular customer at The Cookbook Nook.

"Yeah, you heard me right, Sylvia," my father went on. I had never seen him so openly angry. He was usually an ace at keeping his emotions hidden. "We're building fences to keep you out, do you hear me? That's right, *we*. You've done enough damage. You—" He paused, listening. "Oh yeah? Well, you can burn in hell, too!"

"Cary, no!" Lola finally won the battle and whisked the telephone away. She stabbed the Off button. "Honestly!"

"What's going on?" Aunt Vera demanded.

"Judge for yourself." My father pointed down the hill.

About fifty yards away, at the bottom of my father's property on a stretch of what appeared to be uncultivated land, a group of musicians was setting up amplifiers. They looked about the size of beetles, the bug kind. A musician strummed his electric guitar, and electricity popped again. *Twang. Crackle.*

"Are caterers setting up a barbecue?" I asked.

"Not if I can help it," my father muttered. "That shrew."

Sylvia's house was directly below my father's and was so large it dwarfed the size of all the others in the neighborhood. She had made additions every other year for the past five years, or so I'd heard: an extra room, an expanded kitchen, even an ostentatious patio on top of her roof to take advantage of the ocean view. It was, in a word, a monstrosity.

"Keep your cool, Cary." Lola put a hand on his shoulder.

He shrugged her off. "Don't manage me."

"I'm not, darling. I would never do such a thing." Yes, she would. She winked at Bailey, my aunt, and me.

"How often does Sylvia throw a party?" I asked.

"Weekly." My father spat out the word.

"Please, sweetheart." Lola petted him again. "Don't get upset. Ava will find a solution."

Aha! Now I got it. Sylvia was the certain someone that Ava wasn't inviting to her get-together tomorrow.

"A solution for what?" I borrowed the binoculars from my father and peered down the hill.

"That's my property," Dad said.

"Not simply yours, darling," Lola contended. "It belongs to six of you."

My father faced the group. "A half dozen of the properties in this neighborhood abut each other. When the first settlers came to Crystal Cove, they parceled them out in an irregular pattern. No zoning. Some are pie-shaped, others rectangular. Six properties meet in the middle, at the plateau." Complex math is not my father's forte; he worked as an analyst at the FBI, and possibly, although my siblings and I couldn't prove it, an interrogator, but he is retired and runs a hardware shop and performs odd jobs around town. He knows what's what. "Sylvia has taken it upon herself to use the plateau for her parties."

"In addition to the weekly events," Lola added, "Sylvia has built hedges, fences, and fountains on the property."

"You're kidding," I said over my shoulder. "A fountain?"

"Which is fully plumbed." Lola wiggled a finger. "Look, if you don't believe me."

Through the binoculars, I could see what she was talking about. There was perhaps the ugliest fountain I'd ever seen featuring a nymph and satyr.

"Cheek. That's what Sylvia's got," my father grumbled. "She says the property is hers alone."

"Claiming possession is nine-tenths of the law," Lola said.

"Which is why we've got to challenge her." Dad's jaw was rock hard.

"You did, darling."

"And you know how well that went."

Lola cracked a smile. "Earlier today, your father took Sylvia on at the gas station. She was loading up on lighter fluid and propane tanks, apparently for tonight's bash. Your father called her on it. She ranted at him like there was no tomorrow. She's whip-thin, but she's fierce. He went ape."

I gawped at him. "Dad, you didn't." He rarely lost his composure.

Lola shook a fist. "He warned her—"

"And she spat at my feet," Dad finished.

"Ava Judge is going to challenge her," Lola went on.

"As a Realtor, Ava is quite educated in real estate law," Dad said.

"As am I," Lola countered.

"But I don't want you doing it."

Lola sighed. "Ava advised your father against me leading the charge. Even though she's Sylvia's immediate neighbor, she believes she can remain impartial. I'm not so sure, but what do I know?"

My father grunted.

Lola grinned, obviously sparking the response she had intended. "Ava has invited the other neighbors, including any buyers who are in escrow—"

"To a dinner," I finished. "She mentioned it at the shop earlier. She didn't say why. Dad, I'm so sorry."

"Be sorrier for Ronald," Dad quipped.

Ronald Gump is Sylvia's husband of twenty-five years, older than her by at least fifteen. According to my aunt, Ronald was a confirmed bachelor until he met Sylvia.

"Poor guy," my father went on. "He told me the other day when he was in the shop he's thinking of retiring. Is he nuts?" A bitter snort burst from my father's lips. "At least when he's working, he doesn't have to be around *her* all day."

"Cary, be nice," Lola admonished.

"I'm being more than nice."

Personally, I like Ronald. He's a dapper, feel-good kind of guy who serves as the dean of the junior college. He adores his students and tells them to *dream big*.

"Sylvia must drive him crazy with all this hoopla," my father said. "He's not into this stuff. He's an educator. Sylvia throws the parties to flaunt her wealth."

"Heavens," Aunt Vera gasped. "Is that D'Ann trekking down the hill?" She took the binoculars from me and peered through them. "Oh dear. D'Ann, what are you doing?"

D'Ann Davis, a renowned African-American actress in her forties who usually resides in Los Angeles, owns the stylish home next to my father's. I loved the way she filled her garden with red flowers—red is D'Ann's signature color.

"She's had work done," Aunt Vera said.

"Work?" I echoed.

"To her face. It's so smooth and young."

I retrieved the binoculars and took a peek. "How can you tell that with the mask she's wearing?"

D'Ann, tall and muscular in a tight red tank top and black leggings—*best abs in the business*, one reviewer said—was traipsing down the hill using a walking staff. She wore something over her face that resembled a hockey mask. A silver hair stick that she'd laced through her messy bun glistened in the waning sun.

"The mask is to protect her teeth," my aunt explained. "She took a fall a few months ago and had to have titanium implants. Another fall and her jaw would smash through the back of her head."

"Yipes."

Bailey said, "I love her in *Sinz of the City*."

A couple of years ago, D'Ann played a sorceress from a distant galaxy in a television megahit. Well, not television exactly. Streaming or Netflix or whatever was the hot spot at the time. I am not much of a television watcher, although I had seen D'Ann in a couple of big-screen movies and loved her. She wasn't set dressing; she played smart, sexy women with sassy comebacks. I didn't know what upcoming projects she had planned.

Aunt Vera reclaimed the binoculars. "I fear she's going to confront Sylvia. She is walking like she's on the warpath."

Bailey said, "If she had her magic stiletto from *Sinz of the City*, she could—"

"Honestly." My father seized the binoculars and scowled at all of us. "Lola, call D'Ann. Stop her."

"Oho! Look who's acting reasonable now," Lola taunted. She stabbed a number into the cordless phone and waited.

D'Ann stopped her descent, steadied herself with her walking staff, and pulled a shiny cell phone from a pocket.

"D'Ann, darling, it's me, Lola. Stop. Whatever you're thinking of doing, don't do it. Go home." Lola paused. "Where am I? On Cary's balcony, darling. See me?" She raised an arm.

D'Ann waved.

"Don't take on Sylvia alone," Lola continued. "Please. Tomorrow, at Ava's—" She nodded while listening. "Yes, I know. Sylvia is the devil incarnate and should return to you-know-where."

My father cursed under his breath.

Lola cupped the phone and whispered, "Cary, watch your language." Back into the telephone, she said, "C'mon, D'Ann, there are better ways to deal with the devil. Please. Go home.

We'll attack this as a group, okay? Breakfast on me at the diner at eight A.M., okay?" Lola ended the call.

Bailey *eek*ed with glee. "D'Ann Davis is coming to the diner for breakfast? I'm there!"

"No, she passed on the invitation."

"Dang."

Aunt Vera clapped her hands. "Enough of this nonsense. Dinner, everyone. Let's eat and put this behind us for now."

But we couldn't, because right then Sylvia's band kicked into gear and nearly blasted us off the patio.

My father . . . well, let's just say, he looked like he wanted to blast her to kingdom come.

Chapter 3

BECAUSE I HAD worked long hours and seven days a week for so many years in advertising, I refused to do so or make our employees at The Cookbook Nook do so. However, because we lived in a town that thrived on tourism, we didn't close the shop on weekends, and we dedicated Monday to restocking and taking inventory; therefore, Tuesday was the day we closed. For some reason, this particular Monday seemed to take forever to wrap up. Tons of customers came in searching for just the right grilling cookbook. The shop teemed with children between 3:00 P.M. and 5:00 P.M. At closing, we were bustling to conclude sales. By the time I got home to my cottage, I was too tired to cook dinner. Luckily Katie had sent me home with a to-go box of barbecued chicken thighs. I ate two and stowed the rest in the refrigerator, and then I played with Tigger and attempted to read a chapter of a new foodie mystery. At 9:00 P.M., I tumbled into bed, dead to the world.

On Tuesday morning, refreshed after nearly ten hours of

sleep, I took my morning stroll on the beach, baked a batch of trail ride cookies using a recipe Katie had shared with me—they were packed with healthy fiber and raisins—and painted. Painting is my safe haven. I'm not gifted enough to give up everything and live the artist's life, but I'm not bad. I have been working on a watercolor of the ocean and lighthouse. It's about half done. I intend to hang it above the fireplace in the cottage where I live, which my aunt owns. Her beach house is about thirty yards away. Yes, at some point, I want to purchase my own place, but I'm not quite ready. A one-room cottage is the right size for me—not too much responsibility. And the location is perfect. I treasure being able to roam the beach whenever I want. Unless I win the lottery, I will never be able to afford something of equal value. My aunt had invested well as a young woman. Did I mention that she, being a savvy businesswoman, also owns Fisherman's Village, the shopping center where The Cookbook Nook is located? She has never revealed which cutting-edge stock she purchased in the 1970s, but I figure it had to be some startup in Silicon Valley.

In the early afternoon, I threw on a cute pair of short-shorts and a navy tank top, spritzed myself with sunblock, and took a quickie tour of the city on my bicycle, an old Schwinn that I'd inherited from my mother, complete with basket.

Buena Vista Boulevard was decorated to the max for the Wild West Extravaganza. The Pelican Brief Diner looked like a saloon. Lola had gone all out with the decorating, adding swinging doors, a fake balcony and columns, and even the word *saloon* emblazoned on a placard that hung beneath the restaurant's regular sign. Cowboy boot–shaped flags hung across the upper rim of the window frames. The diner's neighbor, the Play Room Toy Store, had stationed a coin-operated pinto pony next to the front door. Children were clamoring for a ride.

Across the street there seemed to be a sale going on at the Artiste Arcade, a splendid grouping of high-end dress and accessory shops. Women, dressed to the "cowboy" nines, meaning pressed jeans, jewel-studded boots, and fancy silk blouses, were standing in a line. Each was holding a silver ticket. The chatter was vivacious yet competitive. As I pedaled near, I realized the women were hoping to get inside Sterling Sylvia. She was offering twenty percent off on all horse charms for charm bracelets and necklaces. Smart marketing.

Passing B-B-Q, a funky restaurant with a great dance floor, I smelled the most delectable barbecue. Rousing line-dance music was playing through a portable speaker set up on the sidewalk. Customers waiting to get inside were shuffling their feet in time to the music. I recalled a commercial I'd headed up for Taylor & Squibb, Shakey's Steak Sauce. One customer started to dance and then another, until everyone in the crowd was wiggling his or her fanny to the tune of KC and the Sunshine Band's "Shake Your Booty." The rights to the music had cost a pretty penny, but it had been worth it. The commercial was a huge hit and ran for two straight years.

I bicycled to the center of town and noticed a Wells Fargo wagon at the crossroads of Buena Vista and the main road leading up the hill. Cutely, the dancing dolphins that were normally the focus at the junction had been installed inside the wagon and were poking their noses out the windows. Each wore a red bandana around its neck.

Beyond the intersection, in the parking lots that abutted the junior college and the aquarium, stood a slew of white tents and food trucks. None was open to the public yet. I couldn't wait until they were.

Charmed beyond measure, I did a U-turn at the far end of town and rode back to the cottage. I showered, and around 4:00 P.M. I dressed in bright blue capris, slinky white top, sandals, and beach-themed earrings, and then I spruced up my hair and applied a dash of makeup, ready for my date with my boyfriend, Rhett Jackson. Yes, I am officially calling him my boyfriend these days. Rhett, formerly a chef, owns

Bait and Switch Fishing and Sport Supply Store. We have
been seeing each other for about nine months. A few months
ago, I was blessed with the opportunity to meet his family;
they reside in Napa Valley. At first, it was touch and go
whether the trip would take place. Long story short, years
ago, Rhett and his father had a rift because Rhett disobeyed
his father and eloped. That marriage dissolved less than a
year later, but the rift continued until recently, when Rhett
and his father finally mended fences. His parents run a well-
known French restaurant called Intime, a gourmand's delight.
His sisters own a vineyard. I couldn't wait for another visit
to both. I adored his mother and sisters, and I got along well
with his crusty father, who wasn't dissimilar to mine. Rules
are rules.

On tonight's date, Rhett and I were going to catch a cowboy movie—yep, a cowboy movie or what some call an
oater, one of my all-time favorites: *High Noon*, with Gary
Cooper. I loved how the marshal, compelled to face a returning enemy alone, finds the courage. The movie was showing
at The Cameo, the art-house theater located on the second
floor of Fisherman's Village. Afterward, Rhett and I were
going to Bailey and Tito's engagement party. We were closing The Nook Café for the occasion.

At a quarter past four, Rhett rapped on my front door with
his snappy rhythm that never varied. I loved that about him.
He was an upbeat, positive-thinking man, as reliable as the
day is long. I opened the door and drank in all of him: his
brilliant blue eyes that made me feel as if I might be swept
away whole; his hunky frame; the rugged edge of his jaw;
that roguish grin. He gathered me into his arms, and we
shared a warm, sensuous kiss. A moment later, Tigger danced
across our feet. We laughed and broke apart.

"Jealous, buddy?" Rhett picked up Tigger for a cuddle.
"Want your own kisses?"

"Come in for a sec," I said. I wanted to fetch my purse
and make sure Tigger's food dish was filled. As I moved to

close the door, I spotted movement outside. A blur. Was it human? Running away?

"What's wrong?" Rhett placed a hand at the arch of my back.

"Nothing."

"You gasped."

"Did I?"

"What are you staring at?" Rhett set Tigger down and gripped my shoulders. "Jenna."

"I . . . I thought I saw someone dart behind that tree." I pointed at a massive sycamore near my aunt's house.

"I'll go check."

"No, don't." Pinpoints of angst nicked my eyelids. "It must have been a squirrel or something."

"You said *someone*, not something. *Someone* is not a squirrel."

He had a point. There were no yetis or bears in our neck of the woods, either.

"Maybe a large section of newspaper blew off the beach and disappeared behind the tree," I said. "I'm sure my eyes were playing tricks on me. I'm just jittery because . . ." I told Rhett about the edgy feelings I'd awakened with on Sunday morning and about seeing the driver of the Prius later in the day. "Something's got hold of me. You know how it is."

He shook his head. He didn't know how it felt to be afraid. *Ah, men.* They were lucky. Living as a single woman in San Francisco hadn't done me any favors in the trust department. After an incident the first year I was at Taylor & Squibb, I never went into a parking garage alone anymore. I rarely got on an elevator by myself.

"Tigger's not jumpy," I said, "and he's usually my barometer that something is amiss. Maybe it's the weather. It's crisper than normal. Almost electric." I grabbed my things and kissed Tigger good-bye.

As we drove down the driveway, Rhett slowed past the sycamore. No one was hiding behind it. My fear melted away, and I made a mental note to set up an eye doctor appointment . . . and possibly a visit with a therapist.

When we arrived at Fisherman's Village, we jogged upstairs to the second floor. The line for The Cameo was surprisingly long, weaving back and forth along the landing like a snake. Obviously, we weren't the only people who were looking forward to watching an old-fashioned classic movie on the big screen at the bargain deal of two for the price of one.

"Jenna!" a man ahead of us in line called.

"Who's that?" Rhett asked.

"Shane Maverick," I said.

Shane beckoned us to join him and Emily Hawthorne, who was, indeed, *very* pregnant. In her lace blouse and long skirt, she reminded me of a woman who belonged in a Brontë novel: pearly white skin, large innocent eyes, and long curly locks hanging delicately in front of her shoulders.

"Jenna," Shane said, "so great to see you."

"You, too," I replied. He looked even better than he had when I'd run into him at the gym a few months ago, and at that time I had thought he was as fit as an Olympic athlete. Now, he resembled the Marlboro Man. Maybe it was the cowboy hat; maybe it was the jeans and plaid shirt and deep tan. His hair was all one color, too—no gray streak—which made him look younger than his forty-five years.

Shane gave me a hug and then thrust a hand at Rhett while flashing an easy smile. "Shane Maverick."

"Rhett Jackson."

"Nice to meet you, dude."

They shook heartily, but I couldn't help notice that they were sizing each other up.

"Shane and I used to work at the advertising agency together," I said to Rhett. "Now he's managing the Wild West Extravaganza, which has relocated its offices here."

"Congratulations," Rhett said.

Shane grinned. "Life is full of changes. Speaking of

which, Jenna, you know my fiancée, Emily, don't you?" He threw an arm around Emily and squeezed her shoulder.

"Sure do," I said. "How are you feeling?"

"Good." Emily had a dainty, childlike voice.

"What are you having?" I asked. "A boy or a girl, or is it a secret?"

"A boy." She instinctively touched her pregnant belly and blushed.

"Boys can be a handful," Rhett said.

"Tell me about it." Emily chuckled. "I have four brothers."

"Move, Ronald!" a woman shouted.

Out of nowhere, Ronald Gump stumbled toward Emily. The eagle-headed cane he was carrying flipped forward, but he kept his grip. When had he started using that? Shane steadied Ronald and Emily at the same time. Poor Ronald appeared startled. His usually styled salt-and-pepper hair was sticking out in every direction. He pushed his glasses higher on his narrow nose.

Shane stared daggers at Ronald's wife, Sylvia, who was in her midfifties and so thin she reminded me of a fancy candy stick dipped in white icing, her white hair slick to the sides of her head, her mouth swathed with silver lipstick to match her sleek silver clothes and scads of jewelry. Silver was always the color of the day for Sylvia. Even the cell phone in her hand was encased in sparkling silver.

"What's your problem?" she said to Shane.

"What's going on?" he demanded.

"The line was moving." Sylvia entered some urgent message into her phone, or at least it seemed urgent. She was stabbing the buttons. "Ronald wasn't paying attention, like always."

"Well, *we* weren't moving," Shane said.

"Sorry," Ronald mumbled.

"I'm not," Sylvia countered.

Emily tugged Shane's arm and said, "Let's go home."

"No, we're staying."

"How very like you, Shane," Sylvia said, her voice dripping with sarcasm. "You never let the lady choose."

Shane jutted his chin. "What's that supposed to mean?"

Uh-oh. I got the distinct feeling there was a history between Shane and Sylvia. Had he had a liaison with Sylvia on one of his jaunts to town for the extravaganza? She was older than he was, but that didn't mean anything. Was it before he started up with Emily or, um, after?

Emily frowned at Sylvia like she was imagining the same thing I was. "Shane." She pulled on his arm again. "Please."

Shane didn't budge.

"Sylvia, dear"—Ronald nudged his glasses up his nose again—"you're on edge. I get that. It's terribly difficult when the world doesn't go your way, but don't lash out at innocent bystanders."

"Innocent?" Sylvia spun on her heel. "It's all because of you." She lasered me with a wicked stare.

"Me?" I squeaked.

"Your father and that Ava Judge. They're trying to throw me off my game."

"What game?" Rhett whispered.

"Property rights."

"I've hired a lawyer." Sylvia flourished her cell phone. Her lawyer's name gleamed across the top. I knew him. He was a real shark.

"Dear, don't," Ronald mumbled.

"Don't what? Don't tell it like it is? The legal route is the only route."

Ronald leaned on his cane and struggled to pull a twenty-dollar bill out of his wallet. It fluttered into the air. He groped for it, missed, and teetered forward. I reached for him. So did Rhett. Surprisingly, so did Sylvia. Ronald grasped her hand, but his cane skittered and lost its hold on the walkway, and he pitched forward with Sylvia in tow.

"Holy mother of—" Sylvia landed on her rump. She glowered at her husband and, grunting, clambered to her feet. She brushed off her clothes. "See what you've done, you doddering fool?"

He crawled on his knees and gathered the twenty-dollar bill, then used his cane as a prop to support himself as he rose.

"Don't," Sylvia continued to rant. "I repeat, *don't* try to manage me, Ronald. Those two are banding against me. The entire neighborhood is. Including him." She seared Shane with a glance.

"I don't own the house yet," Shane argued.

"Minor detail." Sylvia poked her husband's chest with her forefinger. "Listen to me. It's our property. You don't intend to back down and give it to them because they insist, do you?" Sylvia barked out a laugh. "What am I saying? Of course you do. You always take the easiest road."

"The doors are opening," Emily said.

Sylvia swiveled her head to the right. "Look, there's Tina. I'll get her to secure the two best seats." Abandoning her husband, she charged in the direction of their niece, a long-limbed, dark-haired, twenty-year-old who was an usher at the theater. Tina often stopped into The Nook Café to talk about food with Katie. She hoped to become a chef, but first she needed to graduate from junior college. She didn't seem thrilled to see Sylvia approaching.

"Well, that was fun," Shane gibed.

"Fun? Ha!" Emily said. "She's so evil, I'm surprised no one has done her in yet." She cut a quick look at Ronald. "Sorry, sir, that was rude of me."

"Forget it," Ronald said. "You're not the first to utter the words. You won't be the last."

Chapter 4

AFTER THE MOVIE, Rhett and I headed downstairs to The Nook Café. The sun was setting as we arrived. An orange-pink glow graced the horizon. A number of families with picnic baskets and blankets were filing through the archway between the café and Beaders of Paradise to take the stairs to the public beach below. Their happy chatter mixed with the caws of hungry seagulls made me smile.

Rhett opened the door to the café and allowed me to pass through first. A solo guitarist seated at the far end of the restaurant was singing a lovely rendition of "Cielito Lindo," a song I remembered from my school days, the title roughly translated as *lovely sweet one*. A few of the engagement party guests sang softly along with the chorus, "Ay, ay, ay, ay."

"Hey, you two." Bailey, dressed in a sparkly summer shift with metallic sandal heels and noisy, fun jewelry, dodged a knot of people and met us at the entrance. "I'm so glad you're here! Hello, handsome." She kissed Rhett on the cheek. "And you. Very chic."

She gave me a boa constrictor–worthy hug. *Oof!* This close up, I could feel her heart chugging double time. Was she nervous or excited?

"Follow me," she said. "I'll show you to your table. There are nametags at all the places. I know, because I put them there." *Nervous.* She was talking so fast I could barely make out the words. "How was the movie?" She threw a look over her shoulder. "Tell me all about it. Were there lots of people?"

"Slow down," I said. "Breathe."

"I am breathing."

"Calmly."

Bailey giggled. "Yeah. I guess I'm a little uptight. I want the night to be perfect with a capital *P*. Tell me about the movie."

"It was a blast. Even though everyone knew the ending, we all cheered when Gary Cooper won."

"Let's hear it for men in white hats." Bailey spun around and high-fived me, nearly knocking me off balance. "Oops. Sorry." She steadied me. "Don't know my own strength." She scooted ahead and stopped at a setting for ten. "Here we are. This is the head table. Jenna, you sit there." She pointed. "Rhett, you're next to her."

"Ooh," I cooed, noticing the table decorations. Yes, the tables were covered with white tablecloths, per usual, but the centerpieces—a trio of tall rectangular vases filled with blue orchids and floating candles, each vase tied with blue gingham ribbon—were new and elaborate. On a side bar to our left sat an array of similar floral vases as well as photographs of the happy couple and their families. "Did you put all this together?"

"I did." Bailey buffed her nails on her bodice. "With my mother's help."

"Where is your mom?"

"Over there."

Lola stood with my father near the plate-glass windows.

He was dressed casually in a white linen shirt and beige trousers; she was dressed similarly to Bailey in a shimmery shift and heels. They were staring at the view and chatting out of the sides of their mouths. Or were they arguing? About Bailey marrying Tito? When Bailey first announced they were engaged, Lola worried that they were rushing things. They had only known each other a short time, and at first, they had been antagonists. Well, Bailey mostly, not Tito. In fact, the scrappy journalist had tried to win her over by playing secret admirer. He sent her all sorts of tokens. Neither she nor I realized they were for her. Soon after we put two and two together, and, following his stand-in performance as a magician during one of our events, she fell for him.

"No!" Dad spun toward Lola and stabbed a finger into his palm. Something snagged in my gut. They weren't discussing Bailey and Tito, that was for sure. "It'll be her undoing."

She *who*? Why?

"I swear, that Sylvia—"

"Darling." Lola put a hand on Dad's arm.

"She's a nuisance to everyone in the neighborhood."

Uh-oh.

"Please." Lola rubbed a hand along his back.

My father blew out a long stream of air and seemed to calm down. He was not a hothead by nature. Allowing one's emotions to rule one's actions had been drummed out of him during his stint with the FBI. Sure, there were others who had served with him who weren't in control of their actions, but Dad was cool and calculating. He could see all sides of an argument. That was what he had tried to impart to my siblings and me; I wasn't as good a learner as the other two.

Blowup defused, I said to Bailey, "Where is the groom-to-be?"

"Late. Big story over at The Pier. Lover's quarrel at Boardwalk Hot Dogs." She winked. "I hear it's steamy."

I groaned at the pun.

"I think he also got sidetracked by the stunt show."

"Where is that being held?" I asked.

"Midway down The Pier," Rhett said. His sporting goods store was near the street side of the boardwalk. "They've set up a mock Old West street in front of the playhouse."

"Twice a day, a troupe of players puts on a show," Bailey said. "I hear it's great. Real shoot-'em-up cowboy stuff like you'd see in the movies. The Wild West Extravaganza group hired some guys from Hollywood. You and I"—she motioned between the two of us—"should go see it this week."

"You're on."

A waitress passed near us carrying a tray of hors d'oeuvres.

A delighted smile spread across Rhett's face. "Mmm, Bailey, what smells so good?"

She hooked her thumb toward the kitchen. "Katie has worked up an incredible menu, keeping to this week's Wild West theme."

"Cowboy food for your engagement party?" I said, amazed. "Not French?" Bailey had been telling me for weeks that she'd wanted something upscale with lots of tasty appetizers and elegant cheese platters. My mouth had been watering for days at the thought of onion soup, warm Brie, and *pommes frites*.

"Nope. Barbecue. Tito suggested the idea. Katie is making her famous dry-rub ribs."

"Tonight? Yes!" I cheered. Who needed hard-to-pronounce French food anyway?

"With baked beans, cornbread, and biscuits." Bailey laughed. "I know. It's not your typical engagement party fare, but who cares? If my man wants it, he gets it."

Rhett elbowed me. "I like the way she thinks."

Teasingly I gave him the evil eye. "Don't expect that kind of royal treatment from me." He could cook circles around me.

"By the way," Bailey went on, "you've got to try the

stuffed mushrooms that are being passed around. They have a real kick. Jalapeño peppers are the secret."

"Will do."

She left us to greet other guests.

Rhett slung an arm around my back. "How are you feeling? Any more sightings?"

"Of . . . ?" I searched his face. "Oh, that. Nope. No more mysterious strangers jumping from behind cars or trees. No one is out to get me."

"Care for a glass of wine?"

"You bet."

He went in search, and I joined Lola and my father. Dad eyed me coolly.

I raised both hands in defense. "Am I intruding? Got a big secret you can't share?"

My father's nostrils flared.

"Hey," I said, "no matter what it is, I'm not the enemy. Seriously, what are you two discussing? You certainly don't look like you're at a celebration party. You're all frowns."

Dad forced a smile. "It's nothing." He extended an arm. I curled into it for a hug.

"Is this your way of saying *don't worry my pretty little head*?" I chided.

"Something like that."

I broke apart and leveled him with my gaze. "Dad."

"Jenna."

"Are you two arguing about Sylvia Gump?"

Lola swatted my father's arm. "I told you people would hear us."

"Only Miss Big Ears," my father teased.

Yes, I had big ears. Not in the Dumbo way. I could hear well around corners and down halls. Back at Taylor & Squibb, I was always on the alert for office gossip to avert getting ambushed at a meeting. If my boss was unhappy, I wanted to know as soon as possible.

"What's going on with Sylvia?" I asked.

"Nothing."

I tilted my head. "Saying *nothing* is not going to make me go away. Did you and the other neighbors reach an agreement at your meeting last night? Did Ava come up with a brilliant idea how to stop Sylvia from what she's doing?"

"Poor Ava," Lola said.

"Why *poor Ava*?"

"Sweetheart." My father rubbed Lola's arm. "Let's keep it between us."

She sneered. "This from the man who was talking so loudly his daughter heard him halfway across the room."

"Don't start."

"Cary, Jenna can keep a secret."

A frisson of worry zipped through me. "What secret?"

Lola lowered her voice. "Sylvia has been doing nasty things to Ava, targeting her, trying to get a reaction. She told her gardener to move Ava's trash cans yesterday so the trash pickup wouldn't empty them."

"How silly."

My father said, "She also had her housekeeper park in front of Ava's driveway so Ava couldn't move her car. I went for a stroll and caught the two of them shouting."

"Ava and the housekeeper?" I asked.

"Ava and Sylvia. Ava was so mad, I worried she might pop Sylvia in the nose."

"She wouldn't." I gasped.

"There were threats exchanged. Ava raised a hand. Sylvia put up her dukes."

Lola *tsk*ed. "It was outright cruel what Sylvia did. Ava needs her car for business. She had to call a tow truck to move the obstruction."

"Why is Sylvia acting like this?" I asked. "Does she need to be on sedatives? Is she going through a midlife crisis? I saw her upstairs with Ronald a bit ago. She pushed him straight into Shane Maverick."

My father said, "I know Shane."

"How?"

"He purchased the house next to Sylvia, on Azalea Place. It's in escrow. Sylvia is up in arms about it. She said she put a bid on the house, but Ava blocked her from getting it."

"Blocked her how?"

"Ava asked for city council intervention claiming Sylvia, by owning too many houses, would create a monopoly of some sort."

"What would Sylvia want with two houses?" I asked.

"She doesn't want two," Lola said. "She wants to buy all the houses that go on the market."

"That's nuts." I glanced between Lola and my father. "She doesn't have that kind of money, does she?"

Lola rolled her eyes. "I guess she does very well with her jewelry business."

"Ronald has a penny or two," Dad grumbled.

Lola added, "I think she wants to throw up roadblocks to Ava, in particular."

"Because she thinks Ava is the rabble-rouser?" I asked.

"Exactly." Dad sucked in a sharp breath and exhaled through his teeth. "Last night, at the end of the meeting— nearly the whole neighborhood attended—Ava asked those of us with property lines on the plateau to convene there. She talked each of us into building fences on our respective properties so we can delineate the area. When we do, Sylvia won't be able to do what she's doing. She'll have a swatch about five feet by five feet."

"I told Ava if she isn't careful—" Lola clapped a hand over her mouth; her eyes welled up. "Well, I can't imagine what might happen. Right there, in front of all of us, she destroyed the brick wall Sylvia built."

"What brick wall?"

"Didn't you see it?" my father asked. "Through the binoculars. About yay high"—he raised a flat hand to his midchest—"beyond that hideous fountain."

My mouth dropped open. "Wow."

"Darling, talking about this is upsetting all of us," Lola cooed. "Let's not discuss Sylvia any more tonight. Make me a promise." She pecked my father's cheek.

"Yeah, okay."

"You, too, Jenna," Lola pleaded. "No more worrying about what can't be fixed this very minute. It's Bailey and Tito's night. Speaking of which, where is he?"

As I started to explain, Tito Martinez entered the café. When I first met him, he had rubbed me the wrong way. He was super eager and in your face, like a dog itching for a fight. Now, in his yellow tweed jacket, open-neck white shirt, black trousers, and black loafers, he looked suave and calm. Working out at the gym was doing wonders for his carriage. He walked with a swagger packed with confidence, not ego.

He swooped Bailey into a hug and planted a kiss on her lips. "*Mi amor*, let's get this party started."

Bailey grabbed a cowbell from one of the tables and clanged it. "Eats!"

I downed more than my fair share of ribs. I even ate a portion of apple pie à la mode. Heaven.

When Rhett and I got home, he scanned the perimeter of my house, after which he came inside and peered into each closet and behind every door. Tigger accompanied him. Finding nothing and convinced I was safe, Rhett kissed me good night and left.

I, of course, went to bed feeling like a weakling. I mean, *c'mon*. I needed my boyfriend to check out my place? No one was hounding me. I was imagining things, right?

WEDNESDAY MORNING, I dressed in leggings, tennis shoes, and a fashionably torn Cal Poly sweatshirt—fashionably torn because that was what was in vogue when I went to college at Cal Poly. At a quarter to seven, knowing a fast walk would do me wonders, I hustled to the beach to clear the cobwebs. The air was crisp. A light mist hovered over the ocean. The strand was empty of people.

Near a smoldering fire pit—apparently someone had enjoyed a party late last night and into the wee hours—a seagull dive-bombed me. Had I drawn near to its breakfast, possibly a dead fish that it had dropped?

"Sorry, buddy," I yelled and darted away to escape its cawing craziness.

In the mad dash, I caught sight of a string of horseback riders moving along the road parallel to me. In about a mile, they would ascend the hills. There were tons of fabulous trails to explore. What a fun day ahead for them.

As I neared The Pier, I noticed a figure hovering in the shadows by one of the pylons. My pulse started to chug double time. Not only wasn't I a fan of strangers in parking lots or elevators, I wasn't eager to run into one on a deserted beach. I did a U-turn but stopped when someone—a woman— screamed. I whipped around.

The woman was standing on The Pier and pointing. People gathered near her. All started jutting arms in the same direction as she, toward the hills behind me.

One yelled: "Fire!"

I pivoted and gaped. On the hill, near my father's neighborhood, an orange-red fire lit up the sky.

Chapter 5

I DARTED INTO THE cottage, fetched my cell phone and purse, told Tigger to stay put, and hightailed it to my father's house in my VW Beetle. On my way, I telephoned Dad at home. He didn't answer. I reached his voice mail. "Are you okay?" I yelled, then ended the call and tried his cell phone. He didn't answer that, either.

By the time I arrived at Pine Lane, my father's street, my adrenaline was pumping double time, and my mind was fraught with worry. People in various stages of dress—some in robes, some set for work—were milling near a curb with a public outlook. No houses blocked the ocean view. Two police cars and two fire trucks had parked on the road. Firemen aimed water through hoses at the now-nonexistent blaze, which was not my father's house, thank heaven, or any house. The fire seemed to have erupted in the open area down the hill where Sylvia had held her party the other night.

What had started the blaze? A spark, an ember, an arsonist?

I searched for my father among the curious people. I didn't find him. "Have you seen Cary Hart?" I asked an elderly woman. She shook her head. I ran to my father's house and pounded on the door. No one answered. "Dad!" I bellowed.

Silence.

Call me crazy, but I was worried. Where was he? I charged toward one of the police cars. They were empty. I saw Chief Pritchett—Cinnamon—and a couple of her deputies on the plateau below. Though Cinnamon was a well-built, athletic woman, she appeared puny standing next to her subordinates. They seemed to be entrenched in a conversation. I hailed her, but she didn't acknowledge me. I headed toward the path that ran alongside my father's house.

"Miss, halt!" A skinny deputy, hanging back and managing the onlookers, aimed a finger at me. "No civilians allowed." He put a hand on his holstered gun.

I saluted and made a U-turn. I raced to my VW thinking if he wouldn't allow me to go *down* to the crime scene, I would go *up*. I drove to Sylvia Gump's sprawling house on Azalea Place. At least in one regard, the Gumps had conformed to city standards—the roof, what you could see of it, was red—and to Sylvia's credit, she, like Ava Judge next door, had a gorgeous, well-tended garden.

There were no fire trucks on the street, but there was a parked patrol car. Its driver was not inside; I didn't see an officer anywhere. Taking my lead from Sylvia—if she could trespass, I could, too—I jogged to the side of the Gumps' house and up a set of stairs.

As I neared the rear of the house, the hideous-looking fence on the side of the porch snagged my attention and made me almost ram into a rear set of stairs. In the nick of time, I veered right and avoided catching my calf on a stair corner; however, I caught a heel on wet grass and skidded about ten feet, like when I was a girl doing Slip'N Slide. I remained on my feet, barely. I spun around and glared at that fence and then the stairs, which from this angle were quite visible. They were loaded with shoes and a collection of female-sized garden boots that would make Martha Stewart envious, if she could stand the mud and mess on them.

Move on, Jenna!

Past the house was yet another set of stairs heading upward toward the plateau. They seemed makeshift, like someone had stacked stones with no solid base. A gentle tremor beneath the earth might make them skid into the Gumps' backyard. *Trespasser, beware.*

Gingerly I scaled those and sprinted to the scene. When I arrived, I made a beeline for Cinnamon. Though she was wearing her standard broad-brimmed hat, she held a hand overhead to shield the morning sun from her eyes. I gazed in the direction she was peering, at the wreckage: charred bushes, ash-streaked nymph-and-satyr fountain, scorched ground. Beyond the mess stood the semidemolished brick wall. A pile of brick pieces, some broken and some intact, lay beside it, all untouched by the fire. Lola said Ava had caused that mess. Yipes. Talk about angry.

"Cinnamon." I hurried to her. "Chief!"

She pivoted. Her blunt hair swung with the motion. Her expression was not welcoming. "Jenna, you shouldn't be here."

"Careful, guys!" Bucky Winston, a handsome firefighter with the brawn of a male weightlifter and the easy smile of a jokester, was in command of the crew. A couple of men were using rakes to move the charred bramble to one side. "Don't tamper with the body."

"Body?" I yelped. I strained to look where Bucky was standing.

Cinnamon nudged me away. "Jenna, go home," she ordered, then revised that. "No, wait. Stay." She squinted. "Where's your father?"

"I don't know. I'm looking for him."

"Why?"

"Because he's not at home, and he's not answering his cell phone, and I saw the fire on my morning walk, and"—I slurped in air—"who's the victim?" I choked on the last word.

"Sylvia Gump."

A man moaned. To my right. Ronald Gump, as pasty as wet clay and looking every one of his seventy-plus years, was standing near the cluster of firemen. He was dressed in flannel pajamas and leather slippers and leaning heavily on his cane. He removed the sunglasses he was wearing, rubbed a palm against one eye, and replaced the sunglasses. Poor guy.

"What happened?" I asked Cinnamon.

"Fire."

"I can see that. What was Sylvia doing there?" Was she trespassing again and putting in a fire pit or something else that required natural gas? Had her misguided efforts gone kablooey? "Did she set the blaze?"

"She couldn't have."

"Why not?"

"Because—" Cinnamon hesitated. Her chest rose and fell. "Because she was murdered."

"Murdered? How?"

"Jenna, it's not your business."

"What started the fire?"

"Lighter fluid."

"It doesn't look like it was ablaze for long."

"That's because someone called 911 minutes after it ignited."

"Who?"

Cinnamon said, "The dispatcher said she wasn't sure. The call was untraceable."

"Do you think whoever killed Sylvia set the fire?" I asked. "Possibly a neighbor who didn't want the area to go up in smoke?"

Cinnamon seared me with a glare. "Don't theorize."

Ronald moaned again. He was shaking his head; his free hand was weathering the collar of his pajamas between his

thumb and forefinger. He seemed to be in total distress. He
mumbled something, and I flinched. Had I heard him right?
Did he utter my father's name?

"Cary," Ronald said, louder this time. No mistaking the
word. "Cary did this."

"What?" I yelped again. I was getting good at it. "Cinnamon . . . Chief," I quickly revised. She might be my friend,
but I had to show her the respect she deserved. "No way
would my father—"

"Cary killed my Sylvia."

I stared daggers at Ronald. "He. Did. Not. Do. This."

Cinnamon touched my shoulder. "Jenna, calm down."

"I will not calm down." I wriggled away. "You know my
father."

"Ronald saw him."

"Where?" I flailed a hand. "When?"

"Running away from the blaze."

"Not possible. No way." My heart was chugging so fast
I could barely breathe.

"You said you called your father."

"Yes. I didn't reach him."

"Text him."

"If you're so eager to find him, why don't you text him?"

"Jenna."

"Fine," I snapped like a disgruntled teenager. Raw emotions were hard to curb, even at the ripe age of thirty. I pulled
out my cell phone and typed a text to Dad: Where R U? He
didn't respond. I showed the screen of my cell phone to Cinnamon and said, "While we wait, tell me everything, from
the beginning."

She blinked back tears, and suddenly I realized how hard
she was taking this. She adored my father. He had been her
mentor. At my mother's insistence, he had rescued Cinnamon when she, speaking of bad teenage habits, was heading
down a path toward juvie. "Around six A.M., Mr. Gump—"

"Ronald—"

"Wakened to the smell of smoke. He hobbled to the window and saw the blaze. He called the fire department, too."

"Too?"

"A team had already been dispatched."

"Who called it in first?"

"I told you. An anonymous caller."

"Let's hear it for good citizens."

Cinnamon's mouth quirked up, but there was no humor in the smile. "Mr. Gump . . . Ronald . . . saw your father fleeing in a red plaid jacket."

"Did he actually see Dad? Did he make out his features at that hour of the morning? Lots of people own red plaid jackets."

Cinnamon's nose narrowed as she drew in a breath and let it out. "Jenna, I'm on your side. I'm on your father's side, too."

"Good to know." I worked my jaw back and forth.

"Whoever was in the jacket fled over the crest, right near your father's house."

My insides drew into a knot.

"The crew arrived," Cinnamon continued, "and they went to work to put out the blaze. By that time, my team and I had arrived. Once the fire was out, we saw the charred remains of Sylvia." She sighed. "Ronald told the crew your father and Sylvia argued on the telephone Sunday night. Ronald said Cary—your father—told Sylvia to *burn in hell*."

I flapped a hand. "Sylvia said it first."

"So you heard this exchange?"

I blanched. Open mouth, insert foot. Dang.

"Jenna?"

"It was during our regular Sunday night dinner," I said. Cinnamon had joined us a few times for our weekly meal. She was considered family. "Sylvia was throwing a loud party. Dad phoned her. She screamed at him. He was simply echoing what she said."

"Ronald mentioned that."

"Sylvia is . . . *was* trying to usurp this property." I pointed at the charred area. "Lots of people in the neighborhood had a beef with her about it. In fact, all of them got together to discuss what to do about it."

"Like who?"

"I don't know. Ask Ava." I gulped. The musty smell of damp smoldering hillside made me want to heave. I pressed down the impulse.

"I heard your father took Sylvia on at the gas station, too."

"Says who?"

"Bucky." Cinnamon's boyfriend, the hunky fireman. "I believe Sylvia retorted: 'Over my dead body.'"

I moaned. "She was buying fuel, like for a barbecue. Dad warned her not to put on another party, and she—" I glanced at the scorched area and wild, alternative scenarios scudded through my head. The lighter fluid. The propane tanks. "Maybe this isn't what it looks like. What if Sylvia lured my father up here to goad him into doing something rash? What if she set the blaze, hoping to trap him and kill him? What if she died of smoke inhalation before he got here?"

"She didn't."

"How do you know?"

"I can't tell you."

"What if—" I bit my lip. In every one of the scenarios running roughshod through my brain, my father appeared guilty, because if he had come to the site and didn't try to save Sylvia . . . *argh!* "It wasn't Dad. You know he didn't do this. He couldn't. He's a pacifist. He—"

"Chief!" Bucky called. He hailed her over. "You've got to see this."

Cinnamon said to me, "Hang tight," and traipsed through the muck to where Bucky was standing. "What?"

He pointed.

I stood on tiptoe, trying to catch a glimpse over one of the firemen's shoulders, to see what they were discussing.

Marlon Appleby, Cinnamon's second-in-command, a man

with big ears and square jaw, strode to my side. "Hey, Jenna," he said, concern in his tone. Usually he was stern with me, but he seemed more tolerant this time. Why? Because he was dating my aunt, or because I looked like one vulnerable mess of a woman? "Sorry, but you'll have to move back."

"Can you tell me anything about what happened? What evidence do you have against my father other than Ronald's statement? How did Sylvia die? Are there footprints? Please, detective, give me something." I tried to hold back the tears that were filling my eyes but couldn't. Moisture dripped down my cheeks. Swell. I wasn't merely a vulnerable mess; I was a bleary-eyed, ridiculous mess. "My father . . . he didn't—"

My cell phone buzzed in my pocket. I wriggled it out and read the text: Hi, Tootsie Pop—my father's nickname for me since I was a tween; I hated it, I had outgrown it, but what could I do, demand he stop? I continued reading: Fishing. Will call soon. Hope it's nothing important. That was a longer message than I'd ever received from my father. He was old school and preferred analog or even the written word to digital, but Lola would have none of that. She made him promise never to leave home without his cell phone.

I texted back: Yes, it's important. Sylvia Gump is dead. The police think she's been murdered. By you. Call me.

My cell phone rang in an instant. I stabbed Accept. "Dad?"

"What happened?" He sounded out of breath. The connection wasn't good. It was crackly with static.

I quickly explained.

"How did she die?" he asked.

"I can't get the police to cough up any information." I glared at Detective Appleby, who was standing stoically by my side.

"Tell Cinnamon I was nowhere in the vicinity," my father said. "I left for the lake well before dawn, and sunrise was at five forty-seven A.M. Fish don't bite once the sun is up."

"Where are you now?"

"Hiking back to my car."

"Is anybody there?"

"I went alone."

I huffed. "I mean, are there other fishermen?" I splayed a hand in frustration.

"I don't see anyone else. It's midweek."

I sighed. "Dad, this doesn't look good."

"It's my word against Ronald's."

"Does he have any reason to lie?"

"Maybe he killed her."

I shook my head. "C'mon, have you seen Ronald Gump? He's not a big man in the first place, and now he's walking with a cane."

"I didn't do this!" Dad barked. Stern, authoritative. Good. That meant his FBI persona was kicking into gear. "What do they have on me?"

"As far as I know, they only have Ronald's word that you were in the area. He saw you running away in your red plaid jacket." The one my mother had given him on their twentieth anniversary. She had laughed and said it was so brash that it would scare off any old bear in the woods.

Dad snorted. "Ha! That lets me off the hook. I don't own that jacket anymore."

"You don't?"

"Lola hated it so much, she made me donate it to Goodwill."

"Dad, that's great. That's wonderful. I'm going to tell Cinnamon now."

"Don't. I'll be there soon. I'll tell her myself."

Chapter 6

A HALF HOUR LATER, my father pulled up in his Jeep. In my presence, he and Cinnamon discussed his whereabouts and Ronald's account. My father reiterated what he'd told me about the plaid jacket. Cinnamon asked whether he had a Goodwill donation receipt. He was pretty sure Lola would; she didn't throw any paper away. *Once an attorney, always an attorney*, he joked. Cinnamon released him on his own recognizance to fetch said receipt. Then she dismissed me.

Needless to say, I was ticked. How could she not accept Dad's word? She wanted proof? The nerve. I did not obey the speed limit as I drove home. Okay, I did, but I didn't want to. I flew into the cottage and slammed the door. Poor Tigger squealed. I apologized profusely and scooped him into my arms. Once I felt his purr against my chest, my pique lessened, and I regained my composure, and I forgave Cinnamon. She was only doing her job and doing it well, like always.

I showered to rid my body of the stink of the fire, and then

I dealt with choosing an outfit. I wanted to dress in clothing that would raise my spirits. Pink or purple? Per Aunt Vera, purple-aura people are highly psychic. I could use some of that about now. On the other hand, people who have a predominant amount of purple in their aura are seen as mysterious and secretive. A pink-aura person, however, is a natural healer and sensitive to the needs of others. That kind of person hates injustice and strives to make the world a better place. I chose a hot-pink blouse, white capris, and floral sandals and appraised myself in the mirror. Not bad for a woman whose father might be going to prison.

I fed Tigger and ate a bite myself—toast with honey and tea; not much else sounded good. At 8:30 A.M., when I was convinced that all would be right with the world, I exited the cottage, and wouldn't you know, a seagull screeched and nearly knocked me for a loop. In a snap, worry snaked its way back into my psyche. What if Lola didn't have the receipt? What if Dad was slapped in prison for a crime he didn't commit? What would it take to prove him innocent? Dang!

By the time I arrived at The Cookbook Nook, I was worked up again. It didn't help that word about the blaze and Sylvia Gump's death had spread. Customers waiting for the shop to open lowered their voices to a whisper when I drew near, but I could hear what they were saying: my father might be guilty of murder.

I pressed through the group to unlock the door and caught a glimpse of the old-fashioned jail décor rimming the doorway. Shoot! So much for whimsy. Down it would have to come.

"We'll be open in a few minutes," I muttered and entered. As I shut the door, I locked eyes with my aunt Vera, who was sitting at the vintage kitchen table where we always had a culinary jigsaw puzzle going.

She bolted to her feet but couldn't rush to me because her heel caught in the hem of her rose-pink caftan. "Drat!" she muttered.

I moved to help her.

After we freed the heel, she gazed at me. Fear flickered in her eyes. "Is it true? Is your father a suspect?"

"Oh, Jenna, you're here!" Bailey abandoned her project of setting out wagon train–style glazed cookie jars and rushed to the two of us. She, too, was dressed in pink and white: pink skirt, white peasant blouse. "Is it true? Please say it isn't."

I set Tigger on the floor and gave his rump a pat. "Go. Play."

"Pepper Pritchett poked her nose in a few minutes ago." Bailey pointed out the front door. Pepper owns the beading boutique called Beaders of Paradise across the way. Her daughter is Cinnamon.

"She is such a gossip," Aunt Vera snipped.

Bailey agreed. "She said your father—"

"Pepper is telling the truth," I cut in. "Dad is a suspect, but he has an alibi."

"Verifiable?" Bailey asked.

I threw her an acid look. "He. Did. Not. Do. This."

"No, of course not, but, you know, Ronald Gump said he saw—"

"Someone running, not *doing* the deed. Besides, he's getting on in years."

"I resent that," my aunt said. "We're the same age."

"He's a number of years older than you and looks it," I countered. My shoulders slumped as the shock of the morning sapped me of energy. "He says he awoke from the smell of smoke, but for all we know, he could've been half asleep and dreaming about someone in a red plaid jacket."

"Red plaid jacket?" Aunt Vera said. "Your father has—"

I held up a hand. "Yes, he used to own a red plaid jacket, but Lola donated it to Goodwill." I added that Cinnamon had asked Dad to provide the receipt for the donation.

"That won't prove anything," Bailey said. "I give to Goodwill all the time. I never write down exactly what I donate."

"Cinnamon seemed to think it would help his case."

"C-case!" my aunt sputtered. "Oh my." She withdrew a

tarot deck from the pocket of her caftan and returned to the vintage table. She flipped up three cards.

"Not now, Aunt Vera," I said, but she wouldn't listen. Her gaze moved back and forth as she silently reviewed the reading. I didn't want to know what the cards revealed and told her so. "Don't go to the dark side," I warned her. "Dad is innocent. I reminded Cinnamon that there are more people who might have wanted Sylvia dead." Though I liked Ava Judge and others in the neighborhood, I wasn't willing to write them off as suspects.

"Don't forget that Shane person," my aunt said. "He bought a house on Sylvia's street. He's probably as upset about the noise and hoo-ha as your father. And then there's—"

"Enough speculating. We need to let in customers. Remember, we're here to help folks have happy days. Sunny days. Turn that frown upside down," I commanded like a camp counselor. "We'll discuss this later."

"But—"

"No!" I couldn't help glancing at the cards my aunt had turned up, none of them good. Like Scarlett O'Hara, I would think about that *tomorrow*. Or certainly later in the day. Business as usual, for now. No hoodoo-voodoo, mind-blowing downer thoughts. I hurried to the front door and whipped it open. A cool breeze rushed in, as did a flurry of new customers. "Good morning," I chimed.

A few echoed my greeting.

"Jenna!" Katie bustled down the breezeway that connected the shop to The Nook Café, her toque atilt, her chef's coat unbuttoned. The yellow gingham dress she wore beneath the coat looked rumpled, as if she'd grabbed it from a laundry pile. "There you are."

I am fairly tall; Katie is taller and bigger all over. She swooped me into a hug. Her wild curls batted my face. Usually Katie is a laugher, but no whooping chortles were popping out of her right now. In fact, she sounded close to tears when she said, "I heard the news."

"We're not discussing it."

"Okay. Got it. You bet." She held me at arm's length and forced a smile. "'Bravery is the capacity to perform properly even when scared half to death.' Who said it?"

"Omar Bradley." I cocked a hip. "Has my father been coaching you?"

Katie offered a silly smirk. "Yep."

Throughout my life, my father had made me memorize famous quotations. Apparently, he was challenging my pal to do the same thing. Per Dad, you never knew when you needed a mental pick-me-up. Today, he was right.

"Tell him he's in my prayers," Katie said.

"I will."

"That Sylvia Gump." She clucked. "I'm not surprised she's dead. She fought with everyone."

"What do you mean?"

"I saw her the other day at the café, arguing with that pretty actress."

"D'Ann Davis?"

"That's the one."

The telephone near the register jangled. Bailey answered, then waggled the receiver. "Jenna, for you. It's Rhett."

I told Katie to hold that thought and took the telephone from Bailey. "Hi."

"I just heard," he said. "How are you? How is your dad?"

The concern in his voice made me well up. I dabbed the tears with my fingertips before they could fall. "I'm fine. He's fine." I recapped the situation. "I'm telling you what I told everyone else: sunny side up for now. Dad will tell me when he needs my help."

"*Our* help," Rhett said.

"Thanks. You have no idea how much that means to me. What's the rest of your day like?"

"Busy. We have a lot of Wild West events on The Pier today. Want to stop by later?"

"I might."

"Great. I look forward to seeing you. Love you," he added, as if he said it every day of the week. He never had. *We* never had. Did he realize? There was a slight hesitation before he hung up. I cradled the telephone and tried not to make too much of his parting words. People say things all the time they don't mean. Did he love me? Did I love him?

Katie inched closer and leaned her elbows on the sales counter. "You've got that"—she twirled a finger—"dreamy look in your eyes."

"Do not."

"Do."

We have been friends for so long, we can return shorthand taunts like badminton birdies.

"About Sylvia—" I stopped as a blur of black whizzing by the front window caught my attention.

Katie followed my gaze. "What are you gawking at?"

I wasn't sure. A person, definitely—I couldn't make out whether it had been male or female—but a quiver of uneasiness swizzled up my spine.

"Nothing," I muttered, hating that I was so jumpy. I shook my shoulders and then shimmied my whole body in an effort to shed whatever was going on with me. My father was innocent. No one was spying on me. Whoever had slipped past the door must have been a beachgoer and disappeared down the steps leading to the ocean. Totally innocent.

"Jenna? Are you okay?" Katie asked.

"Yep. Back to Sylvia." I tucked my hair behind my ears. "Did you hear what she and D'Ann were arguing about?"

"Not really, but D'Ann was looking plenty feisty if you ask me. She was bouncing around on the balls of her feet like a boxer and throwing air punches."

"Maybe they weren't arguing at all. Maybe D'Ann was telling Sylvia about a new role she got in a movie."

"Gee, I hadn't thought of that," Katie said. "Bad me. Always thinking the worst."

"Stop it," I chided. Katie rarely thought the worst of

anyone. I, on occasion, did, and right now I couldn't help wondering whether D'Ann, like the others in my father's neighborhood, had some sort of beef with Sylvia that might have made her lash out.

"Are you ready for me to bring in the goodies for the gingerbread town demonstration?" Katie asked. "I'll need space." She signaled that bookshelves would need to be moved. Luckily, all our bookshelves were on coasters and glided easily whenever we wanted to rearrange. "We'll need to set up chairs, too. Our guests are due in an hour." We offered reserved seats for these events.

"Will do! In the meantime, bring out some of those cookies you baked." The other day in the café's kitchen, I had spied a few test cookies that Katie had fashioned to look like cowboy boots and horses; she had iced them in scrumptious sunset colors. "I'm starved and I need sugar!"

"I'm on it."

While Bailey and I rearranged the store and set out folding chairs, a pair of female customers strolled in. Tourists, I figured. I didn't recognize either of them.

"Hello," I chirped merrily, getting the all-knowing look from Bailey. Perhaps I was overplaying my happy-go-luckiness, if there was such a word. "Don't mind us," I added and told the women about the gingerbread demonstration in an hour. "It will be standing room only, if you don't have tickets."

"Oh, but we do," the shorter of the two said. "I picked them up the other day when I had my fortune told. Hello, Vera!" She wiggled her fingers at my aunt, who was still studying the tarot cards. "Your prediction came true." Giggling, the two women sauntered to the dessert section.

"So how are the wedding plans going?" I asked Bailey.

She frowned. "Exactly what do you think I've accomplished since last night's reception?"

"Don't get snippy with me. Do you have a date?"

"A couple. It depends on the venue."

"What are your choices?"

"We're going back and forth between a church and a vineyard and Nature's Retreat with its spectacular view."

"I pick the latter." Nature's Retreat is a lovely inn tucked into the hills. "You know what could be fun? Have a bunch of artists around that day painting portraits of the guests in the garden. Wouldn't that be cool?" Crystal Cove draws artists to its shores all the time. There is an artist camp in the hills that offers four- and six-week sessions.

"That sounds like something you'd like for *your* wedding."

"I'm not getting married."

"Right now. But you might in the future."

My cheeks flushed. Had she overheard Rhett say he loved me? I brushed the thought aside. Marriage. No. I wasn't ready. I wasn't sure I would ever be ready again.

"Do you have a wedding dress and a florist?" I asked.

"All in good time. Don't rush me."

"Ahem." I purposefully cleared my throat. "I know how much you like to be prepared. Speaking of which, have Tito and you decided where you're going to reside?" Tito lives in a house that is too square, in the geometric sense: square bedroom, square living room, square kitchen, square patio. There isn't a rectangle to be had. At first glance, it had driven Bailey crazy. On the other hand, her apartment is too small for the two of them, plus they want a place with a yard so their American shorthair cat, Hershey, who has finally warmed to Bailey after she stopped being nervous around him, can roam.

"Not yet. I think Tito is finally on board to work with a Realtor."

"Ava Judge?"

"Tito's leaning toward the other one, the *guy* Realtor." She rolled her eyes.

"You have a say."

"And I've said that I want Ava."

"Aren't relationships fun? There's always something to negotiate." I was speaking from experience. When my husband,

David, and I first rented a place together, we went round and round about clutter. He hated it; I liked to have my *things* nearby. Never good at arguing, I caved and wound up storing my lifetime assortment of books. They were now resting comfortably on shelves in my cottage.

"Oh, there's no negotiation on this," Bailey said. "I'll get Ava."

Unless she's guilty of murder sailed through my mind.

Chapter 7

AN HOUR LATER as the crowd in the shop was settling into chairs, a vivacious, silver-haired elderly woman with expressive eyes, one of the biggest cookbook collectors I know, strolled in. Everyone in town called her Gran; her real name was Gracie, which she hated. She had relocated to Crystal Cove a year ago to help her daughter-in-law with the children. At least, that was her story. The daughter-in-law told it differently. She hadn't wanted Gran to spend the rest of her years alone in the bitterly cold Northeast.

"Hello, girls!" she crooned.

"Hi, Gran," I said.

Bailey beckoned her to the sales counter. "I've got those books for you, Gran." She pulled a stack of four books from beneath the counter. A rubber band secured the stack.

Gran joined Bailey. "How are the wedding plans going, dear?"

"They're going."

Gran brushed Bailey's hand. "Don't rush anything. A

wedding is a memory for a lifetime." Her husband of fifty years passed away two years ago. On many a rainy day, Gran came into the shop, sat at the vintage table, and told us stories about him. He loved to fish. He loved to read. He knew everything there was to know about international politics. And what a handsome devil he was. "Did I tell you that my daughter-in-law is going to get married again? I'm so thrilled. My son would want that for her and the girls." Gran pressed a hand to her chest. "May he rest in peace." Her son had died about two years ago, as well. Way too young.

"Oh, by the way"—Gran pulled out a wad of cash to pay—"we're starting a family cookbook club. The girls want to learn to cook. Each week, we'll buy a new cookbook and plan three recipes, one recipe for each girl. It's going to be so much fun. We'll start with simple things." Gran gestured toward me. "Like you started out, Jenna. And of course, we'll make cookies. Lots of cookies. That's how I won over my husband." She winked. "He loved my snickerdoodles."

"I'll bet he did," Bailey cracked.

Gran swatted her fondly. "Don't be impertinent, Miss Sassy."

"You love when I am."

Gran stammered and then flushed pink. "My, my. Listen to us, joking as if everything in the world is hunky-dory." She faced me. "Jenna, I'm so sorry to hear about your father."

"He didn't kill Sylvia Gump."

"Of course he didn't. Never in a million years."

Bailey slipped Gran's books into a bag and tied the handles with rattan. "Here you go."

A gaggle of women strolled into the shop, each talking loudly enough for me to know they were discussing the murder. When they saw me, they stopped short. One gasped. My shoulders tightened; my jaw ticked with tension. Would I . . . *dare* I . . . tell them to stop gossiping? *Breathe, Jenna.*

Luckily Katie breezed into the shop pushing a cart filled with gingerbread goodies including premade gingerbread ghost town cutouts as well as cutouts of gunslingers, horses, and train tracks. In addition, she had stocked the cart with a variety of colored icings and assorted candies plus tools and the cookies I'd requested, nicely displayed on a child-proof tray.

"Everyone, grab a seat!" Katie shouted. "Jenna, pass the treats. Let's get started."

With her arrival, the discussion about my father was officially tabled.

As I doled out cookies, taking one for myself, Katie introduced herself and waved a hand above her display. "Here are a few tips for making the best gingerbread town. First, don't try to do it all in one day. I like to make my dough ahead, chill it, and then bake it. I bake in small batches, and as each comes out, I trim the edges so they're even. As you know, cookies don't always bake evenly, and a gingerbread house is essentially a set of big cookies." Katie exhibited a one-inch thick piece of Styrofoam board. "Use something like this as your base so you can stick toothpicks into it to keep things propped up if necessary."

Gran raised her hand. "Katie, I like to put my houses together with real sugar instead of royal icing. Do you do that?"

"I do, Gran. Good point." Katie set the Styrofoam aside. "I keep a pot of liquefied sugar on the side and use it as the glue. It's messy, but it sets so much faster. You can do all the little details with the royal icing. I like to put my icing in a disposable piping bag"—she held up a piping bag—"but I don't use a tip. I simply cut a little bit off the end. That keeps the icing from drying out while I'm working." Katie jutted a finger. "Important to remember: plan on the project taking much longer than you think, and be ready to clean up a huge mess."

The crowd laughed.

And so it went for a good hour. While Katie talked, she pieced together a town. When she finished, there were tons of *oohs* and *aahs*. She had used items like Shredded Wheat to create bales of hay, pretzel sticks to make fences, and black licorice for hitching posts. At the conclusion, Katie gave each participant a bag of goodies to use as decoration as well as a recipe for gingerbread and a detailed set of instructions.

While many customers moved closer to admire Katie's handiwork, others lined up to purchase any one of a number of gingerbread house cookbooks, including the darling *A Year of Gingerbread Houses: Making & Decorating Gingerbread Houses for All Seasons*. Granted, the book didn't have a Wild West theme anywhere between its covers, but there were designs for Valentine's, Halloween, Christmas, and more, a perfect all-occasion delight that thrilled our customers.

As the shop cleared and Bailey started putting the place back in order, Gran sidled up to me and crooked a finger for me to follow her to a spot near the stockroom. I did.

"Jenna, dear, I didn't want to say anything earlier, but—"

"Gran, please. Let's not discuss the murder."

"Dear, I think you'll want to know what I have to say."

I motioned for her to proceed.

"I was in Sterling Sylvia the other day, buying a charm for my bracelet, a sweet threesome of my granddaughters. Sylvia made it especially for me. She was quite clever that way, rest her soul. Anyway, I'm not normally a gossip, but D'Ann Davis was there. Mind you, D'Ann and I aren't close."

I wasn't sure D'Ann was close with anyone. While browsing the store a month ago, she'd said that a celebrity had to keep her distance. People always wanted things from her, whether it was an introduction into the movie business for themselves, their children, or extended family, or a simple brush with fame. The reason she had purchased a second home in our sweet town was so she could enjoy some privacy.

"D'Ann was arguing with Sylvia," Gran went on.

I flashed on the account Katie had told me about D'Ann arguing with Sylvia and bouncing around like a prizefighter.

"Although they were standing at the rear of the store," Gran went on, "I could hear what they were saying. I have excellent hearing for a woman my age." She gestured for me to check out her ears. "No hearing aids."

"And?"

"D'Ann was warning Sylvia that her reputation would be ruined if word got out, and Sylvia had better fix it, sooner rather than later."

"Fix what?"

"*That* I can't be sure about, but"—Gran lowered her voice—"if you ask me, I think D'Ann believed one of those expensive pieces she bought from Sylvia was paste. She said Sylvia was swindling her, and believe you me, no one likes to be scammed."

AROUND LUNCHTIME, I retreated to the teensy office tucked into the stockroom, and, figuring Dad had been too preoccupied to contact my siblings, first called my sister, Whitney, a mom of three and living in Los Angeles, and then contacted my brother Mitchell, an architect who lived in Napa. Whitney shrieked when I told her our father's situation and said she would drive up that instant. I calmed her—no easy task—and told her to stay put; I would keep her in the loop. Mitchell, as laid-back as ever, said he knew Dad was innocent and justice would prevail. In the meantime, he would go to an ashram and meditate. His soothing tone did wonders for my own peace of mind.

Following those two calls, I dialed my father's cell phone number. I wanted to know where things stood between the police and him. He didn't answer. After three attempts, I called Lola, who sounded frantic. They hadn't found the Goodwill receipt yet, so she had sent him to pick up some sandwiches at Mum's the Word Diner while she turned her house upside down looking for the blasted thing.

"What a nightmare," was the last thing Lola said before ending the call.

A nightmare, indeed. I clasped my purse and told my aunt I would be back shortly.

Bailey caught me at the door. "Where are you headed?"

"To The Pier to find my father."

"I'm coming with you. I've heard parking is a zoo. The Wild West Extravaganza events down there are hopping. You might need my help."

Minutes later we arrived at The Pier. Similar to the Santa Monica Pier in Southern California, which was recognizable because movie companies regularly used it as a set piece, The Pier in Crystal Cove was a long boardwalk featuring a carousel, carny games, shops, and eateries. In addition, there was a small, rustic theater that offered a variety of entertainment and a huge sport shop, owned by Rhett.

At the parking lot entrance, Bailey said, "As I predicted. This place is jammed. Out you go! I'll look for a spot."

On the boardwalk, hordes of people strolled along enjoying the fabulous spring weather—singles, couples, and families, many dressed in western garb. Aside from the movie *Footloose*, I had never seen so many women wearing shirts tied at the midriff, cutoff jeans, and western boots.

Hawkers with tickets met me at every turn offering rope-jumping lessons, mechanical bull rides, and more. I ignored them, my gaze keen for my father.

Bailey swooped in beside me and knuckled my shoulder. "Hey, look, the stunt show is under way!"

Halfway down the boardwalk, beyond Mum's the Word Diner, a crowd had gathered in front of The Theater on The Pier. The group burst into laughter.

Pop, crack! A fake gun fired. Then another.

Bailey dragged me closer.

Two men—outlaws—stood atop the roof of the theater.

Another man—the sheriff—posed below, gun aimed. He was trying to take out the goofy outlaws—*goofy* because one was doing a ridiculous dance on the roof and the other was flapping his hat and yelling, "Catch me if you can!"

The crowd laughed uproariously.

As we neared the diner, I said to Bailey, "You watch the show. I'm going inside." I veered left and entered. I didn't see my father and asked Rosie, a waitress who loves the color purple right down to the highlights in her crimped black hair, whether she had seen him.

"He left with a to-go bag, Jenna-juices-juggernauts." Rosie is a huge fan of mnemonics, a memory device that helps her recall larger pieces of information, like names and faces and long lists of food orders. Every time I come in the diner, she has a new grouping for my name. "I think he headed toward the far end of the pier. You know how he loves to watch the other fishermen."

I exited and searched for Bailey. She wasn't watching the stunt show; she had moved to where a woman with braided pigtails was teaching folks how to do the Texas skip, a rope trick where the person holding a long rope with a vertical loop starts twirling. As the loop widens to human size, the trickster leaps through. Back and forth. A pile of ropes and multiple pairs of boot spurs hung on a nearby rack.

"Yeehaw!" the pigtailed woman yelled, making the trick look easy. After a demonstration, she stopped, let the rope fall to the ground, and said, "Who's up first?"

Bailey thrust her hand into the air. She was holding a ticket. "Me!" She bolted toward the woman but paused when she spotted me. "Oh, hey, Jenna, I was—"

"My father is that way."

"Right." She peeked at the roping woman and back at me. I could tell how much she wanted to do it. "Go ahead. I'll deal with Dad."

"Are you sure?"

"Positive. It'll be better that way. One on one."

"I'll teach you how to do this later."

I aimed a finger at her. "I'll hold you to that promise."

As I weaved through the sea of people, I heard Bailey whoop with glee, and sorrow snared my heart. Oh, to feel so carefree right now.

I found my father exactly where Rosie thought he would be, at the end of the boardwalk admiring another fisherman's catch.

"Dad!" I yelled and rushed to him.

"Jenna." He slung an arm around me and kissed the side of my forehead. "What's up?"

I scowled at him. *What's up?* Mr. Casual, as if I were there to pay him a social visit? "Why aren't you answering my phone calls?"

He withdrew his cell phone from his pocket and muttered, "Well, I'll be. I never heard it ring."

"That's because it's set on vibrate." I snatched it and switched the sound button to On. I stuffed it back in his hand.

"I didn't feel it vibrate, either." He arched an eyebrow. "I repeat, 'What's up?'"

"You. Cinnamon. Sylvia." My voice spiraled upward. "I've been worried sick, and—"

My father put a finger to my lips. "Shh."

"I spoke to Lola. She hasn't found the receipt for Goodwill."

"She won't need to."

"Why not? Because a witness who saw you at the lake came forward?"

"No."

"Then you need that receipt!"

"Let's walk." He bid good-bye to the fisherman and, while escorting me along the pier, opened his to-go bag from the diner. "Want a French fry?"

"No. Look, Dad—"

"Jenna, relax."

"How can I?" I wriggled out of his grasp. "What time did you leave this morning?"

"Like I said, well before dawn, which was—"

"Five forty-seven. Got it." I licked my lips. "It's an indelicate question, but can Lola corroborate that?"

"No. We don't cohabitate, but we will soon."

"What?" I squeaked. "You're moving in together?"

"We're talking about getting married."

"What? You can't."

"Of course we can. We're both adults. We don't need your—"

"No, I mean, you can't get married before Bailey says 'I do.' Please. Don't steal her thunder. She's so . . ." I twirled a hand. "It's taken her a long time to say yes to a man."

Dad slipped a hand around my elbow and squeezed. "I love how you watch out for your friends."

"I'm not kidding. Don't mess this up for her."

"Lola said the same thing. We're all on the same page."

I breathed easier. "Okay, back to you. You went fishing early. Then what?"

"I got your call, so I came back to meet with Cinnamon."

Out of nowhere, I felt a presence. Moving along with us. At our pace. I searched for Rhett, thinking maybe he had seen me pass his shop and came to find me, but I didn't see him. Farther ahead, a man in a baseball cap peeked over his shoulder. The visor cast a shadow, obscuring his face. Was he looking at me? He whipped his head to the front and picked up his pace. To avoid me? No, of course not. How ridiculous. Being upset about my father was making me suffer paranoid delusions, yet again.

I refocused on my father. "Did you catch anything this morning?"

"Sure, but I threw it back in, as I usually do." He halted and swung me to face him. "Jenna, I did not kill Sylvia Gump."

"I know that, but why would Ronald lie about seeing you there?"

"Maybe he saw someone who looked similar to me. A man or even a woman my size. Maybe he didn't see anyone and the rumors are true."

"What rumors?"

"He's losing it. He's addled. There's been talk. Supposedly, he's retiring. No one is going out on a limb and calling it early-onset Alzheimer's, but let's say he's not completely attentive to detail."

"Ronald said he saw a man in a red plaid coat."

My father's eyes grew steely. "Whose side are you taking?"

"I'm not taking sides."

"Sure sounds like you are." My father marched ahead.

"Dad!" I chased after him and grabbed him by the shoulder. "Who else could have killed her?"

"I hate to think negatively about anyone, and I hate to speculate."

"Speculate! Please!"

"Jenna, I can defend myself. Stay out of it." He quickened his pace and made a beeline into Bait and Switch Fishing and Sport Supply Store.

Chapter 8

BAILEY NABBED MY arm at the threshold of the sporting goods store. "Hey!"

"Let go. I've got to catch up with my father. He—" I paused. A cord of rope hung over her shoulder; she carried a pair of spurs in her left hand. "Did you buy those?"

"Yep! They're nickel silver spurs with seven-pointed rowels that will jangle until the cows come home."

I arched an eyebrow. "Boy, are you easy."

"I'm hooked. Wait till you see me go. It's like jumping rope. Remember how we used to love to jump rope? I even remember your favorite song: 'Not Last Night but the Night Before.' Remember the lyrics? 'Twenty-four robbers came knocking at my door.' Ooh, I loved that one! Especially the speed counting. 'One, two, three'—" She stopped abruptly. "Hey, what's going on? You look like you're about to blow a fuse."

I hitched my head toward my father, who was retreating to the section with fishing rods. "He's trying to ditch me."

"Why?"

"We exchanged words. He wants me to butt out, except I won't. I'll win him over. I'm sure of it. Go back to the shop. I'll fill you in when I return."

"Ahem." She pinched my arm. "Did you forget I'm your ride?"

"I'll get a lift or I'll hoof it. Don't worry."

I plowed after my father, intent on finishing our discussion. I found him chatting with Rhett by a wide selection of rods. Dad owned quite a collection.

Rhett, who was also a dedicated fisherman, handed my father an aqua-and-black rod. "This is the newest Scott fly rod, a Tidal."

"Dad!"

He spun toward me, his eyes steely. "You followed me?"

"Yep." I grinned broadly. "I'm hot on your trail."

My father blew a stream of frustrated air through his nose. "This discussion is over."

"Not by a long shot." I moseyed up to Rhett and kissed him on the cheek. "I said we'd meet up. I didn't expect it to be under these circumstances. Sorry, but I can't hang out for long."

"I'll take every minute I can get." Rhett ran his fingers down my arm and took hold of my hand.

I shivered with delight. The man was definitely going to win my heart and soul at this rate. But not right now. I squeezed his hand, then released it and refocused on my father. "Dad, we need to discuss your defense."

My father's mouth quirked up on one side. "Oho! Now you're an attorney? When did you pass the bar?"

"C'mon. I just want to make sure that—"

"Cary!" a man bellowed loudly enough to rouse Rip Van Winkle.

We all turned. Shane Maverick, wearing jeans and a short-sleeved shirt with the Wild West Extravaganza logo on it, was standing in the shoe area examining a hiking boot.

"I thought I heard your voice," he said.

"Shane!" my father shouted, as if calling to a long-lost friend. "Join us." He beckoned him, obviously hoping that if he added another person to our group I would end my interrogation. I wouldn't.

"Dad."

"Not now, Jenna."

Shane sauntered to us, a sample boot in hand. As he walked, the muscles in his arms flexed. I heard a couple of female customers audibly swoon; yes, he was that good looking. Shane came to a stop and acknowledged me with a quick appraisal. "Jenna, you look beautiful, as always."

"Get out of here," I joked. Beautiful? I'd dashed down the boardwalk. My hair had to be a wreck, and my cheeks were probably flushed—not my best look.

"You do. Fresh and sun-kissed." Shane made eye contact with Rhett. "How're you doing?"

"I'm well, thanks," Rhett said, his tone measured.

"Say, Cary." Shane met my father's gaze. "I heard what happened to Sylvia. What a shame. Someone told me the police are looking into you as a suspect. Supposedly Ronald Gump saw you. Tell me it's not so."

"Ronald thinks he saw me, but he didn't. I'm innocent. I was fishing, but that doesn't seem to matter." He leveled me with a gaze.

I mouthed, *I do believe you.*

He heaved a sigh, and for the first time, I noticed his shoulders were sagging and his voice sounded hoarse. How I wished I could cart him back to my place and fix him a comfort-food meal, using one of my mother's recipes. I had perfected a few of his favorites, including her turkey meat loaf.

"My condolences, man," Shane said.

"Thanks."

"How do you two know each other?" Rhett asked, looking between Shane and my father.

"I've bought a home in the neighborhood," Shane said.

"He hasn't closed escrow on the house yet," my father added.

"We're days away," Shane said. "None too soon for Emily. She's about ready to pop."

"When are you two getting married?" Rhett asked.

Shane stiffened. "That's a sort of private question, don't you think?"

"I don't know, is it? You're engaged. Most people who are engaged set a date." There was a bite to Rhett's tone.

Shane grinned, but the smile didn't reach his eyes. "Don't worry, dude. I'll make an honest woman of her. By the way, I want a pair of these boots. Size twelve." He shoved the boots in Rhett's direction.

Rhett didn't accept them. Instead, he called over a sporty saleswoman and asked her to find the boots for Shane. She hurried off. Something curious passed across Shane's face, like he was miffed Rhett hadn't done his bidding. Then Shane swiveled, turning his back on Rhett, and Rhett flinched. He rotated his head to loosen the tension in his neck.

"Are you okay?" I whispered.

"Yep." He wasn't; he was lying.

Men.

"Cary, listen, heads up," Shane said. "Bad news on the horizon. I was hanging around outside the Gumps' house— you know, my house is on the other side—and I was trying to get a feel for what was going on. That's when I saw Mrs. McCartney. She said she spied you in the vicinity around six this morning. Isn't that about the time Sylvia was murdered?"

"I wasn't anywhere near there. That old sourpuss." My father ground his teeth together. "She's had it in for me for years. Her husband wanted to buy Nuts and Bolts. I offered a better price."

The way my aunt told the story, Mrs. McCartney wasn't always mean-spirited. She fell to pieces when her husband passed on, which happened a week after he lost the hardware store deal. Needless to say, Mrs. McCartney believed that my father, by buying the shop, took away her husband's will to live.

Shane folded his arms across his chest. His muscles pressed at the seams of his T-shirt. "Wasn't she the holdout in the neighborhood, Cary?"

"Holdout?" I asked.

"She didn't want to go along with Ava's plan," my father said.

"What plan?"

Shane guffawed. "Jenna, didn't you hear about the pow-wow?"

"Are you talking about the meeting Ava orchestrated?"

"Bingo!" Shane aimed a finger at me. "Boy, was it rousing."

I squinted at my father, hoping he would explain.

"Like I told you last night at the engagement party, sweet-heart," Dad said, "Ava asked us to erect fences to delineate the properties. She arrived with plat maps of the various properties, once again proving Sylvia owned only a small swatch of the plateau. Lots of people said something had to be done. Mrs. McCartney was one of them, but when she saw me, she did a U-turn. She wouldn't take part, claiming it was too costly, and what did she care about an old useless piece of land—useless to everyone except Sylvia, of course." My father's nostrils flared.

Shane whirled a hand as he continued the story. "Ava planned to give a reporter the story. She wanted it plastered across the front page: *Sylvia Gump is a horse thief.*" Shane swiped the air to paint the headline. "By the way, Ava made sure we all knew that years ago, horse theft was extremely common, before cars came on the scene. Punishments were often severe, with several cultures—I'm not sure about ours—pronouncing the sentence of death upon thieves."

"We all voted no to that idea," my father said. "No calling her a horse thief."

"Yeah, but we said yes to a *story*," Shane said. "We would

declare Sylvia a nuisance and a bully. I can just imagine how she would've reacted to something like that in the paper." He slapped his thigh. "That Ava, she's a real go-getter. By the end, she had us all swearing we would do whatever it took to get Sylvia to back down and stop encroaching on our land."

"*Whatever it took?*" I screeched. "Dad?"

My father flapped his hand. "Don't worry. We all knew what that meant. Whatever it took through proper channels, not murder."

"Even so, that kind of testimony could be damaging."

Shane said, "For all of us, if you think about it. Ava especially. Say, what's her alibi? Do any of you happen to know? She loves the neighborhood. She might—"

"She's devoted to Crystal Cove," my father said, cutting him off.

"Yeah." Shane snorted. "She's so dedicated that I wouldn't put it past her to get rid of Sylvia so property values wouldn't plummet."

We all grew quiet.

Dad broke the silence. "Ava's a good person."

"And a good Realtor," Shane added. "She helped me get my house for a song."

Dad brandished a finger. "That's because your seller had to move quickly in order to take care of his mother in Florida. He was willing to take the first offer that came his way."

I said, "I heard Sylvia hoped to buy your house, Shane, but Ava thwarted her."

"Who knows what the real story is?" Shane said. "For all I know, Ava rushed us into the deal because there's a body buried beneath the—" He balked. "Sorry. That was insensitive of me, considering the circumstances."

Dad addressed Rhett. "What do you think?" My father adored my boyfriend. They were buddies. They talked reels and rods and lures and life. They often went fishing together. If only they had teamed up this morning.

I glanced at Rhett; he shrugged, signifying he had no opinion about real estate disputes. He lived in a small cabin in the woods. Private and serene. No neighbors.

"Sylvia," my father muttered. "She had no taste, but she didn't deserve to die."

"No taste?" Shane carped. "That's putting it mildly. Her place is a patchwork quilt. A real eyesore."

"Except for the garden," I noted, "which is pristine."

"That's Ronald's doing," my father said. "He has a green thumb. He tweaks it at night when he gets home from work and nonstop on the weekends. Have you seen his roses? They're not that easy to grow in our climate, but he makes it happen."

"Ronald," Shane grunted. "He's fairly worthless otherwise."

"Don't say that," I said, surprised to find myself defending the man who had accused my father of murder. "He's beloved at the junior college."

"Perhaps he is," Shane agreed, "but he wasn't beloved by Sylvia. I overheard them, after the powwow. They were arguing on their patio."

"Where were you?" my father asked.

"Checking out my new digs." Shane's future house was directly east of the Gumps' house on Azalea Place. "It was a gorgeous night. The place is unoccupied. The view is spectacular. I stole onto the porch. Anyway, there they were, the two of them, going at it. Ronald was telling Sylvia she was wrong. He said, 'Love makes the world go round.' She screamed that he didn't know what he was talking about and told him to shut up. Then he ordered her to put down the canister."

"What canister?" I asked.

"I don't know. Ronald said, 'Do you want to blow up the entire neighborhood?' so I imagine he was talking about a propane canister, but I couldn't see them. They've put up a six-foot-tall fence on either side of the patio." He was referring to the same hideous fence that I'd noticed when charging to the plateau. "Ava told me they built the fences to block the wind, but I'd bet it's so neighbors can't get a gander." Shane frowned. "Talk about a blot on the landscape."

"You can plant bushes to camouflage it," my father suggested.

"That's exactly what I intend to do." Shane linked his hands behind his back and stretched his pectoral muscles. "Say, do you think Sylvia could have set the blaze herself using that gas?"

I was pleased that I wasn't the only person who had come up with that theory, but I shook my head. "She couldn't have. She was already dead."

"How do you know that?" Rhett asked.

"Cinnamon told me."

"How did she die?" Dad said.

"Cinnamon wouldn't reveal that." I glanced at Shane. "Do you have any idea?"

"Nope. There's been a lot of speculation from those in my employ. A gun, a knife. Maybe she and Ronald came to blows. Sylvia can pack a mean wallop. Ronald could have countered with one of his own. Bam! Right to the kisser."

Or plowed into her with that cane of his, I mused.

"Sir." The sporty saleswoman returned with a box of shoes for Shane.

"I'll be right there." Shane glanced at his watch. "Hey, sorry, folks. I've got to get a move on. Good to see y'all." He patted my arm as a good-bye and followed the saleswoman to the register.

Rhett watched him leave. His nose flinched, showing his displeasure.

"Why don't you like him?" I asked.

"He's got a reputation as a player. Did you know he was asked to leave his last job?"

"Really?"

"How do you know him again?"

"Shane was one of the premier salesmen at Taylor & Squibb. He could tell stories that made people hang on his every word."

"Stories," Rhett mumbled, "as in lies. Did your firm fire him, too?"

"I honestly don't know. Shane and I lost track after David died, and after—" I swallowed hard. After I took a leave of absence. Three months of therapy. Three months of tears. The memory of his death was still fresh. Would it ever diminish? "Do you think he's lying about hearing Ronald and Sylvia argue?"

"No, but I get the feeling he has a history with Sylvia."

"Ha!" I flicked Rhett's arm. "I picked up the same thing."

My father said, "Me, too, when Shane said Sylvia could *pack a wallop.*"

I peered at Shane, standing beside the register—big grin. The saleswoman was smiling, too. Were they flirting? Was Rhett right that Shane was a player? I contemplated again about the timing of things. How often had Shane come to town since the Wild West Extravaganza group hired him? Did he have an affair with Sylvia? Did Sylvia approach Shane recently and say she would tell Emily about their affair? Did Shane kill Sylvia to protect his chance for future happiness? No way. I had worked with Shane. He was a wag, a card. I couldn't imagine him capable of murder, but then I'd been wrong before.

Chapter 9

I ASKED MY FATHER for a lift back to The Cookbook Nook. He agreed to do so, but he made me swear I wouldn't ask him anything more about the murder. Grudgingly I acquiesced. I have to admit that I believed my mere presence in his Jeep would get his lips flapping, but he didn't talk. Not a word. He didn't even comment on the density of people in the parking lot or the sluggishness of the traffic on the main road. When we arrived at Fisherman's Village, he did say he was looking forward to eating the sandwich he had picked up at Mum's the Word, and before I closed the car door, he mumbled, "Don't worry about me."

Inside the shop, I pushed aside thoughts of the murder and Dad's predicament, and I concentrated on work. I straightened shelves, smoothed wrinkles in aprons, polished the salt shakers and pepper mills, and rearranged cookbooks—it is amazing how shifting a book to a new location can attract a customer's eye. An hour into my chores, I took a breather and breezed through a new acquisition: *A Taste of Cowboy: Ranch*

Recipes and Tales from the Trails, which made me smile. There was an entire section of cowboy lingo—*cookie,* for example, meant the chuck wagon cook—and there were some of the most fascinating photos of cowboys, on the range and elsewhere. Also, I discovered a recipe that I had to try soon: blueberry lemon morning cake. Yum! But then I flipped the page and saw a cowboy who reminded me of my father, and my heart wrenched.

"Back to work," I muttered. I didn't want to dwell on the *what ifs.*

Midafternoon, a frazzled mother with six children in tow, all of them under the age of ten—the three girls were hers; the three boys, her ill sister's—shuffled into the store. She needed an activity for the little scoundrels, as she called them—pronto. She was a regular customer. How could I deny her? I directed her to the children's corner while I fetched fresh art materials. I placed a sheet of ecru construction paper in front of each child and suggested he or she paint a Wild West scene with horses or mountains or something they had seen in town for the extravaganza.

One child yelled, "Stagecoach!"

Another chimed, "Horsey!"

"How about some snacks?" I said to the mother, who had sunk into a nearby beanbag chair. Tigger sneaked into her lap.

She began to stroke his back rhythmically. "Sounds divine."

I put in a call to Chef Katie and asked what she had on hand. She told me she would be out in a jiffy with a surprise.

Minutes later, she swooped into the shop carrying a tray of plain sugar cookies shaped like horseshoes and a bucket filled with colored icing. She set the tray in the center of the children's table. Instantly one of the boys picked up a cookie and started twirling it on his finger. His beleaguered aunt gave him the evil eye. He stopped.

Katie said, "When you're done with your artwork, kids, decorate these."

"Can we eat them?" one of the girls asked.

Her mother nodded. The kids cheered.

I mouthed *thank you* to Katie.

"Don't thank me yet. I need help."

"With . . ."

Katie beckoned me to the sales counter and withdrew a wrapped sandwich from the pocket of her chef's jacket. "Here." She handed it to me. "You skipped lunch."

"Are you a mind—" I stopped. "What in the world have you been cooking?" Her jacket was splattered with red.

"Barbecue sauce."

"Which kind? St. Louis? Carolina?" Back in my early days at Taylor & Squibb, my boss sent me around the country to taste-test barbecue sauces. We had a client who wanted us to market a zesty sauce that featured chipotle. The boss told me to be prepared to talk *flavor.*

"My own secret recipe," Katie said. "It's a mix between a Memphis- and Texas-style, and boy, does it spit." She winked. "But, remember, a clean cook is not always a good cook."

"Who said that? Julia Child?"

"Me. It's my excuse, and I'm sticking to it." She guffawed. "Anyway, here's where I need your help. I have to create a menu for tonight. The mayor is bringing the city planners into the café. She wants an authentic Wild West–themed dinner."

"And you're asking me for suggestions?"

"You might not be a seasoned cook yet, but you are a foodie. It's got to be something different than the dinner I served at Bailey's engagement party."

"I've got an idea." I envisioned a dinner I'd had with David on our first vacation together. "How about buffalo carpaccio with a cumin dry rub dressed in a sweet oil and accompanied by a spicy aioli sauce."

Katie's eyes lit up. "Where on earth did you eat that?"

"In Las Vegas." The meal consisted of seven appetizer-sized courses. We had dined for three delicious hours.

"Continue." She started scribbling down my suggestions.

"Serve a porterhouse or rib-eye steak with blackberry compote and pan-roasted carrots."

"Yum."

"Or you could try an espresso-rubbed elk or venison steak."

"Love it."

"And for dessert, hmm . . ." I paused, remembering one of the most delightful desserts I'd ever tasted, when David and I drove north of San Francisco. "Chocolate *budino*." I described the pudding that was also a cake. The chef had served it with vanilla ice cream drizzled with olive oil, of all things. "It's not cowboyish, but you can tweak it however you'd like. Maybe add some smoky chopped nuts."

"Perfect." Katie wrote an exclamation point next to that and grinned. "I'm inspired, as I'd hoped. Thanks. Would you like a specialty coffee to go with the sandwich?"

"No, thanks."

"Okay, then, catch you on the trail," Katie said and scurried away.

The moment she disappeared, thoughts of my father's predicament started to worm their way back into my psyche. I tried to block them, but I couldn't. I eyed Bailey, on her break, outside in the parking lot. She was working on a rope trick. A crowd had gathered to watch. Recalling her promise to teach me and certain that was exactly what I needed, I scanned the shop.

The frazzled mother was still nestled in the beanbag chair, stroking Tigger; her brood was merrily occupied. Only two other regular customers roamed the aisles. I knew them; they were browsers. They wouldn't approach the sales counter for at least an hour. My aunt, who was sitting at the vintage table with her eyes closed and holding the hand of a young willowy redhead who had elaborately beaded and braided hair, could easily handle any customer requests as long as she didn't mind pausing whatever she was doing—an aura reading, perhaps?

"Aunt Vera, I'll be outside for a few minutes if you need me." I set aside the sandwich and hurried out.

It took me a few moments to press through the crowd. Once I neared the front, I could see Bailey's fancy footwork.

"Woot! Woot!" she yelped as she jumped back and forth through the loop, her pink skirt swishing around her thighs. The spurs that she had fitted over boots—where had she found the boots between the time she had left me at The Pier and now?—jangled like crazy.

The crowd applauded.

Bailey caught sight of me and let the rope swing to a standstill. "Hey, girlfriend, are you here to learn?"

"I need to do something to . . . you know." I twirled a hand: *clear my head.*

She eyed my feet. "In flip-flops? I don't think so."

"Right. Back in a sec." I tore through the shop, into the stockroom, and fetched a pair of white Keds I kept on hand for emergencies, like climbing ladders to collect books off the top shelves. I kicked off my sandals, slipped on the tennis shoes, and returned to Bailey.

She offered me a coil of rope. "Grab hold." She showed me where to place my other hand.

The crowd didn't hang around while I made pathetic attempts at twirling the rope into a vertical human-sized loop. I couldn't blame them. Drivers in search of a parking spot, however, were more forgiving. They veered around me, giving me plenty of room.

Bailey coached me with patience. "Don't worry. You'll get the hang of it. Try again."

After twenty minutes of twirling and my loop never holding fast, my forearm was exhausted and I was perspiring like I had taken an hour-long run.

"Good exercise, isn't it?" Bailey said.

"I'm beat and deflated." I started to hand the rope back.

Bailey shook her head. "Uh-uh, c'mon. Your mama didn't

raise no quitters. One last time. I know you'll get the hang of it. It's all in the wrist." She demonstrated with a flick.

I tried again, and this time the rope whirled into a vertical loop and held its shape. Cool.

"Leap through."

I did.

"Again."

I obeyed.

Bailey said, "That's it. Now, think in counts of four." She started to clap and chant: "'Not last night but the night before . . .'"

I felt the rhythm dancing through my entire body; it was exhilarating.

When Bailey ended the jumping rhyme, I let the rope settle on the ground, and she patted me on the back. "Next time, you'll do it wearing spurs."

"As *if*." I snorted. "That'll be the day."

"You will, and you'll like it." She coiled up the rope, removed the spurs, and handed them to me.

"But you bought them."

"And I can lend them. Besides, there are plenty more where those came from."

I hurried to the stockroom, set my rope and spurs by my purse, and washed up. I really was a sticky mess, but at least I was thinking clearly. I knew, given time, I could figure out how to help my father without ticking him off.

Bailey washed up after me and joined me at the sales counter. She tilted her head toward the front of the shop. "Your aunt looks super worried."

Aunt Vera was still seated at the vintage kitchen table. Her redheaded client was nowhere in sight. Two tarot cards sat on the table, face up. My aunt's forehead was seriously creased. Uh-oh.

I edged around the counter and moved to the table. "Why the frown?"

My aunt let out a whoop. "Jenna! You startled me." She scooped the cards toward her.

I gripped her wrist. "No, ma'am. Stop. Do not replace the cards in your pack. What are you trying to hide?"

"Hide? Me?" She resisted. "Nothing."

"Is it about Dad?"

"Heavens, no." She wagged her head. "This is not about your father."

"Aunt Vera, spill." I overarched an eyebrow and screwed up my mouth. Usually that made her laugh; not this time.

"Dear, it's simply . . ." She sighed. "I was watching you out there in the parking lot jumping rope. You seemed so carefree that I wanted to see what your future might hold, and . . ."

My stomach did a nervous cha-cha. *My* future. She was trying to read me? Why? All those pesky paranoid feelings I'd been feeling over the past few days blossomed into one huge ball of fear. "Show me."

Reluctantly she placed the first of the two cards on the table. I recognized the card. The Death card, with Death sitting on a white horse and all those around him paying homage. The picture signifies that Death is not finicky. Death will take all.

"Aunt Vera," I said sharply, "you know that card is the most misunderstood card in the deck."

"Many people would shake in their boots if they saw it," she countered.

"Yes, but not me." It was the truth; suddenly I felt as calm as a pond. Paranoia gone. *Poof!* "You've opened my eyes to tarot. The Death card doesn't mean I or anyone I love is going to die. In fact, you've taught me to interpret it productively. For example, it might symbolize the closing of one door to open another."

"Open a new window," she crooned, like the vivacious aunt in the musical *Mame*.

"Or it simply means I have to put the past behind me." I

thought of David and believed I had let go of my memories of him, and yet I had been thinking about him a lot lately. Probably because the anniversary of his death had passed so recently. Apparently I needed to let go *more*. "What's the other card?"

She held out the Two of Cups. Most consider it a marriage card. The picture is of a man and a woman facing each other, exchanging gold cups. The image hints at new partnerships.

"Why are you worried about that?" I asked.

"Because I rarely see this pairing: Death and the Two of Cups. Death and marriage. Is everything all right with Rhett?"

Her question sent a chill through me. "Why would you ask?"

"David is gone. Rhett is in the picture. How is he? How are the two of you?"

I shifted weight while sizing her up. Had she overheard Rhett tell me on the telephone that he loved me? Did she imagine wedding bells? "You're toying with me," I said.

"I am not." Her gaze was earnest. "How is his health?"

"Superb."

"Has he asked you to marry him?"

"Of course not. We're dating, that's all."

"Did you fight about something?"

Worry skittled down my back. Was she sensing the friction that had occurred between Rhett and me after the chat with Shane at Bait and Switch? Rhett had called Shane a player and had questioned me about my connection to him. "Aunt Vera"—I touched her shoulder—"everything is fine. I'm handling things. Rhett is healthy. Put those cards away, please, and don't do my readings unless I'm here to initiate, okay?"

Reluctantly she agreed but then rose to her feet and did a little two-step dance to the stockroom while intoning a chant welcoming positivity.

After work I grabbed Tigger, my purse, and the rope and

spurs Bailey had given me. I set the latter two items in the trunk of my VW and headed home. Even though I'd skipped eating the sandwich Katie made me, dinner didn't sound appetizing; worry makes anything healthful sound unappealing. But dessert sounded good. Specifically, a chocolate *budino*. Too bad I couldn't cook one. It required way too many steps, including baking the little pots of goodness in a pan filled with water. However, I figured I could whip up a basic chocolate pudding using my mother's recipe. Cook, plate, and refrigerate. Easy.

I set Tigger on the floor and nudged his rump. "Play until I put out your food," I said.

He romped to the Ching cabinet and searched for something beneath, probably a ball of yarn. He had at least three balls hiding somewhere in the cottage.

As I gathered the items I needed from the refrigerator, I heard an unsettling sound outside—a *crack*. I ran to the window and peered through it. The sun had set, and with no moon, the light was too dim to make out the features of the lone person running. Had he—I decided the runner was a *he* by his long torso and length of stride—been looking into the cottage? The figure ran toward a trio sitting beside a bonfire on the beach. Seeing the bonfire made me think of Sylvia, but I shoved the thought aside. I didn't want to think about her or my father's plight tonight.

The runner patted the arm of one of the people at the bonfire and shook hands with another. Friends. Nothing to worry about. I was a whack-job, seeing strangers everywhere. What in the heck was wrong with me? The guy had probably missed the public path to the beach and had cut past my cottage. Harmless.

I switched on my iPod and tuned it to an album by Linda Ronstadt. While measuring the sugar and cocoa for the pudding, I found myself humming "I've Got a Crush on You."

The song yanked me back to a moment with David, on one of our first dates, sitting on the porch outside my aunt's house. The sun was setting over the horizon. This song was playing through a speaker on the porch. I brushed David's bangs off his forehead with my forefinger. He had the kind of hair that naturally fell down in a hank.

"You're staring," David said.

"No, I'm not."

"Yes, you are. You're staring at it."

"It *what*?" I fibbed.

"The hole in my forehead." David clasped my hand and rubbed his thumb in the hollow of my palm. "Truth."

"It's not a hole," I whispered.

"Sure it is. A dime can fit in it. Want to know how I got it?"

I did. Desperately. I wanted to know everything about him. Teasingly, I said, "A drill? A ski pole? An arrow?"

"A candlestick, in the dining room."

I gaped. "You're kidding."

David smiled the winning smile that had melted my heart the moment I met him. "My sister and I were playing *Clue*," he went on. "She was losing, and being the sore loser she is, she chased me around the house and nailed me in the dining room."

I started to giggle. "Were you Professor Plum?"

"Who else? The oldest gets to choose his identity first. My sister, as usual, picked Miss Scarlet. Was she ever red-faced when my mother lit into her."

"Did it hurt?"

"When Mom lit into her?"

"When she hit you."

"Let's just say the blood, pain, and suffering have been worth the good conversation opener. My father says the scar gives me character. What do you think?" He twisted his face one way and then the other, allowing me to view both profiles.

"Very distinguished."

Something *cracked* outside again, making the memory of David go *pfft*.

I switched off the music. Tigger yowled.

"Shh!" I hissed and, with measuring cup in hand, bolted to the front door. I listened. Nothing. I peeked through the peephole. Not an iota of movement. No shadow. Not even a whisper of wind. I willed my breathing to calm down. *A squirrel must be the culprit,* I told myself. The critter probably jumped from the rooftop to a branch, and the branch gave under its weight.

Not convinced, I raced to the window that faced the beach. I peeked through the break in the curtains. Three people were sitting by the bonfire, not four.

Chapter 10

OU'RE IMAGINING THINGS, I told myself. *You're fine.*
Nothing to worry about. Even so, I double-checked all
the bolts on my windows and doors, and I slept fitfully with
a fire poker in my bed and Tigger, snoozing like a champ,
nuzzled close to my neck.

Thursday morning, in the light of day, I convinced myself
again that squirrels had, indeed, made the sounds and that
the figure fleeing from the cottage was simply someone
running. We had a lot of exercise buffs in Crystal Cove.
However, when I went out for my morning jog and spotted
footprints heading to and from the bonfire directly to the
cottage window, my gut clenched. Someone had been peeping in my window. Gack!

At the shop, Bailey nearly accosted me the moment I
walked in the door. She gripped the sleeve of my blouse.
"It's food truck day!" she exclaimed, more pumped up than
I had ever seen her. "Your aunt said that midday she'll man
the shop. We can go support Katie."

In the parking lot shared by the junior college and the Aquarium by the Sea, dozens of food trucks from as far south as Monterey and as far north as Redwood City planned to convene and offer their wares. All were required to feature a Wild West theme. A number of local restaurants were getting into the act. Each had rented trucks and obtained the proper permits. For The Nook Café, Katie planned to serve sliders with her secret barbecue sauce.

Business hummed throughout the morning. A pair of sisters came in looking for a copy of *The Texas Cowboy Cookbook*. We had it in stock. It was a generously illustrated book with terrific historical photos and amusing illustrations. The women raved that they had seen it at a friend's house. She had served the most amazing flank steak with a dry-rub seasoning using a recipe straight out of the cookbook.

With each customer I did my best to be ultra charming because, at my core, I was edgier than a razor blade. I silently questioned how Cinnamon was doing with her investigation, and I couldn't shake the notion that someone was spying on me. Of course, feeling that I might be truly paranoid, I didn't mention a word to Aunt Vera. I didn't want her to do another tarot card reading. *Keep your head in the sand, Jenna*, a therapist once said to me. *That's the smart way to avoid reality*. Being the grown-up that I am, I mentally thumbed my nose at her.

At noon, while I was wrapping up a sale for a zaftig customer who had purchased three copies of the same cookbook: *Jalapeño Poppers: and Other Stuffed Chili Peppers*, by Michael J. Hultquist, a delightful book with no pictures but great recipe titles, Bailey zipped toward the counter waving her arms. "It's time, Jenna! Food trucks, here we come!"

I apologized to my customer for the rather abrupt interruption.

"Darling," the woman said, "it's not a problem. I'm headed to the food truck event, too. I've heard there's going to be a hot-and-spicy truck. Can't miss that!" She leaned in and whispered, "That's how I like my food *and* my men." She sashayed out of the shop, chuckling.

Aunt Vera told Bailey and me to scoot, and minutes later, we were weaving among the throng of people who had come to enjoy the event. The din was astonishing; the aromas emanating from the horde of food trucks, appetizing. There were old and young visitors, locals and tourists. No one theme dominated the choice of clothing. Some wore western garb; many wore what a typical person in Crystal Cove would wear: shorts and a T-shirt. I was glad I'd thought to bring a visor. The sun was blazing hot for May.

In the middle of the activities, a live band was playing a zesty tune by Florida Georgia Line called "Sippin' on Fire." How appropriate for the occasion, I thought. Across the way, I saw a food truck for Save the Wild Ones. I was familiar with the group; volunteers helped mend injured wild animals like deer, coyotes, and even skunks. Our local veterinarian, whom Tigger adored, headed up the organization. I was surprised to see Shane Maverick inside the truck handing out shish kebabs to customers.

"What's he doing?" I asked Bailey.

"He's a volunteer, I presume. Don't you remember?" She elbowed me. "Ava said he's an animal safety buff. No Wild West Extravaganza animals will be hurt on his watch."

"Okay, but why is he the chef?"

"Because he has created his own steak sauce."

"And you know this how?"

"Because I can read."

"Huh?"

"See the sign Shane's assistant is putting up?" Bailey pointed. "You know her. She came in to see your aunt the other day."

To the right of the food truck, the willowy redhead who had come in for an aura reading, her elaborately beaded braids now looped into an Oscar-worthy updo, was setting a sign behind an arrangement of dozens of bottles of sauce on a display table. I knew her name but couldn't come up with it. A big *U* was embroidered on her knit purse. Uma, Ulla, Una? Whatever. The sign read: *Shane's Super Duper Steak Sauce, $2/bottle.* All proceeds would benefit Save the Wild Ones.

I mumbled, "What doesn't Shane do?" He was a man of many talents.

Nearby, Ava Judge was waiting in line for a shish kebab. She didn't seem interested in the food. Perhaps she was hoping that Shane, despite the fact that he was engaged, would take an interest in her.

Seeing them in proximity made me wonder again about Sylvia and her relationship with Shane. Had she been aware of Ava's interest in him? Even though she was married, did she confront Ava, her archrival, and tell her *hands off*? Did Ava strike the killing blow? I liked Ava, but, honestly, I wanted someone other than my father to be the police's main suspect. Ava had incited the neighborhood to turn against Sylvia. She lived next door to the Gumps. She could have met Sylvia at the scene of the crime, attacked her, lit the fire, and returned home in a flash. What was her alibi?

Bailey cut into my musings. "Did I tell you that we got CC Vineyard as the venue for our wedding?"

"Wonderful. When's the date?"

"Late September. Right before the harvest so the vines will be loaded with fruit." She elbowed me. "Hey, isn't that Ronald Gump?"

The crowd parted near the Save the Wild Ones truck, and Ronald and his niece Tina came into view. Both were nibbling on shish kebabs. The short-shorts Tina was wearing made her long legs look even longer. She had drawn her dark hair into a knot, with strands sticking out of the knot every which way—very hip. In between bites, she seemed to be consoling her uncle, who was leaning against his cane as if it were the last thing that could prop him up. Occasionally

Shane, from his post inside the truck, would say something and Tina would laugh.

A couple of coeds passed by and shouted, "Hey, Dean Gump! Looking good."

Ronald acknowledged them bravely, doing his best to mask his pain, and then tossed his kebab into the garbage.

"Why in heavens is he out and about when Sylvia isn't laid to rest?" Bailey exclaimed.

"He probably needs something to distract him." The day after I learned David was missing at sea, I had gone to work. To keep mobile. To keep my brain active. To keep me from dwelling on the horribleness of it all. It wasn't until a week later that I fell apart and took the three-month leave of absence. "Fresh air and sunshine might do him good."

"When's the funeral?"

"I don't have a clue."

"Bailey!" Tito cut through the crowd, shirttail flapping against his trousers, baseball cap backward, not helping a whit to block the sun. He caught up to us, slipped his arm around Bailey's waist, and planted a big kiss on her cheek.

Bailey, who used to shun public displays of affection, enjoyed it. She hooked her arm through his.

Tito gave her a little squeeze. "Let's get a bite at the Nook Café truck. I heard Katie's sliders are out of this world."

Bailey said, "Jenna, c'mon."

I started in that direction but stopped when I heard someone call my name. I turned. Cinnamon, in uniform, and her boyfriend, Bucky, were strolling toward me. Apparently it was couples' lunch hour, and I was not a couple. Hmm. I had to rectify that. I would touch base with Rhett after the food truck event and make sure he and I were okay. We had a date tonight, if I wasn't mistaken.

I said to Bailey and Tito, "Go on. I'll catch up."

They hurried away, and I waved to Cinnamon. Even though she and Bucky were walking at an easy gait, she appeared tense. She was wearing sunglasses, so I couldn't see what she was actually feeling. Why single me out? Did she want to grill me about my father's alibi?

"What's going on with Dad?" I said as she drew near. "Are you going to arrest him?"

"Whoa!" She held up both hands. "Nice day, isn't it? Have you tried the chili dogs down the way?"

"I haven't. My appetite is nil because of my dad's status. Fill me in. Please."

Cinnamon sighed. "We have not arrested him, but some people in the department are pressing for me to act, and it doesn't look good. Mrs. McCartney—"

"I heard what she said. She despises my father. She thinks—"

"I know she believes your father is responsible for her husband's death. She's wrong, and I told her so."

"She says she saw Dad in the area at six A.M., but she couldn't have. He'd gone fishing by then." I couldn't curb the tension in my voice. "If she really saw someone, and that's a big *if*, then it had to be someone else. Another enemy of Sylvia's." The moment the word *enemy* flew out of my mouth I regretted it.

Cinnamon let it slide. "Are you saying Mrs. McCartney is lying? To what end?"

"'The croaking raven doth bellow for revenge,'" I quoted.

"That's from *Hamlet*," Bucky said.

"Show-off." Cinnamon elbowed him. "I never studied Shakespeare. Look, Jenna"—she reached out and took my hand—"I believe your father is innocent. I do. Trust me. I will handle Mrs. McCartney and all the naysayers. You know how much I care about him."

I did.

"So please," Cinnamon went on, "no questioning suspects."

"I haven't questioned—"

"Yes, you have. Your father."

A flush of embarrassment warmed my cheeks. Shoot.

Cinnamon squeezed my hand. "I know you mean well, but there is a killer at large. Back off. Let me do my job."

She tugged on Bucky's arm and led him away, leaving me standing there, seething. Not at her. I was mad at the Mrs. McCartneys of the world who would doubt my father's integrity. And, yes, I was mad at Dad for blabbing to Cinnamon.

"Hey, pretty lady." Shane hailed me from inside his food truck. "Come get a sample."

The crowd had thinned by the truck. Ronald and his niece had moved away. Ava, who was standing at the condiment table, spun around. She glowered at me. The look vanished in a nanosecond. Had she thought I was Emily and that was why Shane had called out *pretty lady*?

"I've got a special sauce you have to try out," Shane went on. "It's hot, hot, hot. Like you."

"Ha-ha, Shane," I said. "I'm taken."

"Don't see a ring."

"Okay, then *you're* taken."

"Spoilsport."

Ava glided toward us and stood right below the counter. She fluttered her eyelashes at Shane, confirming my suspicion. She was interested in him, engaged or not.

"Where's Emily?" I asked Shane.

"Teaching a piano lesson. She'll do so until she delivers. She's that dedicated." He scratched his chin. "At least I think that's where she is. I don't keep tabs on her; she doesn't keep tabs on me. We have a trusting relationship."

I wondered if Emily would say the same thing.

"So what'll it be?" he asked. "One or two kebabs?"

"Fire!" a woman yelled. Then another person joined in the shout. All were pointing, at Shane's food truck.

Suddenly I saw flames licking up behind him. "Shane!" I pointed.

He whirled around. "Holy heck!" He grabbed a towel to douse the fire; it lit like a torch.

"Shane, drop the towel and get out!" I searched the crowd for Cinnamon and Bucky. They hadn't strolled far. "Bucky!" I screamed. "Fire! Help!"

With big long strides, Bucky hurtled toward the truck. "Out! Now!"

"There's a fire extinguisher over there," Shane said as he exited.

Bucky leaped inside and fetched the extinguisher. Lightning quick, he doused the flames. White foam went everywhere.

Shane looked pale. He bent forward and braced his hands on his knees. "How did that happen?"

Bucky bounded from the truck and brushed foam off his clothes. "I think your specialty sauce boiled over. When it connected with the gas flames, whoosh! Guess you didn't have a fire-suspension system installed."

"I wouldn't have a clue what the truck has," Shane said. "We rented it."

"Yeah. That's always the way." Bucky laid a firm hand on Shane's shoulder. "Are you okay, pal?"

"Yup, thanks to you."

"Good thing Jenna has a set of lungs!" Bucky quipped.

"Good thing," Shane echoed and winked.

I reddened.

Ava rushed to Shane and clutched his arms. She cooed her concern. Shane tried to wriggle free.

Bucky said to me, "Are you all right?"

"Yes. I wasn't even close."

"Shane's steak sauce seems to be a hot ticket right about now. It's everywhere."

"People buy things to support a good cause."

"No, that's not what I mean. We found a metal bottle cap exactly like the ones on his bottles at the site where Sylvia Gump—"

"Bucky!" Cinnamon drew near and held up her hand. "Uh-uh. Do not leak that information."

He cocked his head. "At least I didn't mention about the hair thingie."

"What hair thingie?" I asked, eager to learn something. Anything.

"That Sylvia was stabbed with. You know, like Japanese girls wear. Right through the heart. They're real pointy."

"Bucky. Stop. Talking. Now." Cinnamon didn't need a bullhorn. She could have been heard across a football field.

Bucky splayed his hands. "It's not like it matters, babe. There weren't any fingerprints on it. You don't have a clue who it belongs to."

"That's it." Cinnamon nabbed her boyfriend by the arm and lugged him beyond the growing crowd. He shimmied free of her and threw his arms wide, clearly wondering what he had done wrong. She said something that visibly ticked him off; he marched away.

Cinnamon glanced at me over her shoulder, like it was my fault.

What? I mouthed.

She shook her head like I was too trivial to deal with and hurried after Bucky.

I considered what Bucky had said . . . had *leaked*. Sylvia was stabbed with a hair stick. She sold those in her store. With her ultra short hair, I doubted she'd owned any herself, but she might have. On the other hand, D'Ann Davis owned one or two. The other night, when she had stalked down the hill to confront Sylvia at her soiree, she'd secured one in her hair. Did that make her guilty? Not necessarily.

Bucky's other revelation tickled the edges of my mind, too. A metal bottle cap had been found at the scene, a bottle cap that he believed came from a bottle of Shane's specialty steak sauce. What other clues might the crime scene reveal?

Chapter 11

CURIOUS AS ALL get-out and eager to visit the crime scene to see if I could find something that might exonerate my father, I raced back to the shop. After making sure my aunt could hold down the fort—she could, but she begged me to take Tigger; he was acting stir-crazy—I snatched my spare pair of Keds tennis shoes and drove to my father's neighborhood.

A moving truck blocked the area in front of his house on Pine Lane. Movers were loading furniture from the house across the street. I didn't know the couple that lived there at all, but I had always found their place interesting. The plants were uniformly green and planted in identical rows, as if the husband or the wife had obsessive-compulsive disorder. The only spot of color on their home was the red roof.

The wife peeked out the front door and shouted something to the driver of the moving truck. She spotted me and offered a big smile, as if everything in the world were normal. But it wasn't. A fire had lit up the sky yesterday, a woman had died, and my father was suspected of murder.

I parked farther down the street, switched into my tennis shoes, and, with Tigger tucked in my arms, hurried back to my father's house. There was no crime scene tape, nothing to impede my progress. I stole to the rear and paused beneath the overhanging patio. The view of the ocean was incredible from every position on the hill. The blue sky filled me with awe; the wafting breeze invigorated me. I set Tigger on the ground and whispered, "Keep up."

The hillside beneath my father's house was a tangle of plants with no strict plan. Dad had designed it himself, preferring a natural look to something constrained like the neighbors' front yard. Some of the terrain was terraced to hold the hill. Other parts were steep and fitted with huge boulders, willy-nilly. Over the years, Dad had tested out a number of plant choices. The ones that had thrived were yellow-flowering gorse, sturdy azaleas, hearty lavender, and wild poppies.

Tigger sniffed as we weaved between plants. I did my best not to catch my capris on the gorse or scratch my bare calves.

Minutes later we arrived at the area where the fire had been set. It was no longer roped off by police tape. Footprints were everywhere: large and small. If the police had found a set for the murderer, I wouldn't be able to tell. I eyed the charred bushes and the dreadful nymph-and-satyr fountain. I thought of Sylvia lying nearby, a hair stick lodged in her heart, and my stomach soured. She had been a mean, vindictive woman, but I didn't wish a violent death—or any death—on anyone.

On any given day, Tigger, the daredevil, loves to climb to the top of everything and leap from high spot to high spot with abandon. Today was no exception. He romped ahead of me and charged to the loftiest point of the fountain, the raised fist of the satyr. The scamp steadied himself and peered down the other side. I could only imagine his viewpoint. It would be like me standing at the Top of the Mark in San Francisco and looking at California Street. Tigger meowed loudly—so much for our adventure remaining clandestine—and dove off. The instant he hit the ground he started scratching beneath the ash and wet leaves. I scuttled around the fountain to see what he had found. The water from the fire hoses used Wednesday had left a mushy mess. My shoes squished in the muck. Tigger meowed a second time and sneaked a peek at me.

"What are you after, cat?" I muttered. A dead bird? A dead mouse. *Oh, joy!* "Let me see." I crouched to examine his treasure. It was something shiny. Was it a second steak sauce bottle top?

Gingerly I plucked the object out of the mess; it turned out to be a square, somewhat scuffed cuff link. The initials *SM* were etched into it. My heart skipped a beat. Did it belong to Shane Maverick? How could it have gotten here? The same way a bottle cap would have gotten there, I determined. Shane must have been at the crime scene. Did he and Sylvia argue? Did they come to blows? Did she yank the cuff link off his shirt? Why would he have been wearing cuff links? Citizens of Crystal Cove were a pretty loose and casual group. Few people dressed to the nines. Even the shop's attorney wore short-sleeved Hawaiian shirts.

Forget it, I told myself. A cuff link proved nothing. Neither did a bottle cap for steak sauce, which was why Bucky thought he could share that tidbit with me. Maybe Sylvia had the cuff link on her, I reasoned. She was a jeweler, after all. Perhaps Shane had given her a set to polish. As for the steak sauce bottle cap, Sylvia could have brought the bottle to the plateau to enjoy a picnic. She opened the bottle, and the cap popped off and flew into a pile of leaves. She abandoned it and took the capless bottle back to the house.

And, hey, Sylvia hadn't been the only person in the area in recent days. Her partygoers had gathered here.

Also, during the powwow Ava threw Monday night, a

group of neighbors went to the plateau to talk about putting up fencing.

I kicked leaves with the toe of my shoe in frustration. Tigger, thinking I was toying with him, jumped at my feet.

"No!"

He ignored me and leaped again.

"Tig-Tig, I mean it." I nudged him.

He sprang to the right and started pawing more leaves.

"Hey," I whispered. "What've you discovered?"

Something red. Fabric, tucked beneath the brick rubble. I recalled the morning of the murder when I had glimpsed Sylvia's body at the crime scene, right before Cinnamon spun me away. Sylvia had been dressed in a red outfit. Was the fabric part of her dress?

I bent down to inspect it.

At the same time, something went *crackle-snap*. Behind me. To the east.

Tigger froze.

I jolted to a stand, my heart drumming my rib cage. "Who's there?" I didn't see anyone. "Dad?" I yelled, thinking— *hoping*—he had come home, seen me surveying the grounds, and decided to join me.

No response. Was someone hiding behind one of the oversized boulders?

A motorcycle roared to life on Azalea Place. Whoever was on the motorcycle kept revving the engine. The rumble freaked out Tigger. He bounced and pounced and ducked behind my legs. Trying to avoid squishing him, I tumbled to the ground. He squirted to the left.

"Of all the—" I tried to grab him while scrambling to a stand. He eluded me. I tripped and caught myself with my palms. "Tigger, shh. Settle down." If someone was on the hill and intent on catching me, now was a good, vulnerable time.

I heard *clickety-clack*—footsteps on wood. Overhead. At D'Ann Davis's house. "Hey!" I bellowed in the direction of her porch.

D'Ann's gal Friday—was that an appropriate term nowa-days?—her *assistant*, a bubbly, twenty-something woman with mocha-toned skin, came into view and tilted forward over the railing. She was carrying an armful of clothes. Red clothes.

I glanced from her to the fabric beneath the rubble and leaves. D'Ann's signature color was red. What if D'Ann met Sylvia that morning? What if they struggled? What if Sylvia pushed D'Ann, and D'Ann reeled backward, snagging what she was wearing? No way. The police wouldn't have missed the clue, unless they didn't consider the area near the brick wall part of the crime scene, plus leaves had covered it. By the time the firemen's hoses had doused the place—

"What are you doing down there?" the assistant called.

What answer should I give her? Certainly not the truth: *snooping.* Day hiking sounded absurd, seeing as I was in a pretty blouse and capris. "I came looking for my father," I lied, "and my cat ran away from me." I scooped Tigger into my arms to prove my point. "Do you see anyone around?" I asked while mentally berating myself. I should have said, *Do you see my father around?* but I really wanted the young woman to scan the area and tell me if she saw someone else— a lurker—who might wish to do me harm. Granted, any num-ber of critters living in the hills could have made the *crackle-snap* noise, but Tigger's heart was chugging as fast as mine. He wasn't a scaredy-cat by nature. "How about a predator like a bobcat or coyote?"

"Nope."

She sounded sort of edgy, like she was vamping. Did she spy D'Ann nearby? Was she covering for her boss? Had D'Ann ventured down the hill to remove the suspicious fab-ric only to find me nosing around?

"Care for iced tea?" the assistant asked.

"Sorry. I have to pass. I have a special event at the shop." Benjamin Franklin said: *Half a truth is often a great lie.* I did have an event: tallying the last two week's receipts. "See you!" I said breezily and, with Tigger in tow, hurried up the hill and past my father's house to my car.

Moments later, as I was heading toward town and passing Azalea Place, I saw something that made me slam on the brakes. Shane Maverick was climbing into a black truck parked in front of his future house. Had he followed me from the food truck event? Had he stalked me on the hill? Did he skedaddle while the motorcyclist was revving the engine?

Shane spotted me and bellowed, "Hey, Jenna!" He gestured for me to turn onto the street.

Criminy, as my mother would say. Caught like a fly on flypaper. If I pretended not to notice him, it would seem suspicious. On the other hand, as paranoid as I'd been acting lately, I could have imagined the *crackle-snap* on the hill. Shane could be innocent. D'Ann and her assistant, too. Except Tigger had reacted.

I counted two women on Shane's side of the street; one was hand-watering her garden and the other was watching her toddler play on the grass. I would not be at risk as long as I remained in plain view.

Cranking up my nerve, I veered onto the lane.

Shane shut the door of his truck and approached me as I parked and exited my VW. "You look nice."

Yet again I questioned his eyesight. I was a perspiring mess. My capris were dusty and in dire need of dry cleaning. My Keds were yucky. Heaven knows what my hair looked like.

Even so, I said, "Thanks."

"How do you like my place?" He gestured toward the English cottage next door to the Gumps' house. I hadn't noticed how adorable it was when I had gone hunting for my father Wednesday. Dormer windows were tucked into the undulating red roof, and at the entry to the pathway stood a quaint stone arch cloaked with ivy. The garden, which was overgrown and needed tending, was packed with lavender, wildflowers, and vines of roses.

"Nice," I said.

He grinned. "Emily's going to love it, don't you think?"

"You bought it without asking her approval?"

"She said, 'Surprise me!'"

"Wow. Do you even know if she likes this style house?"

"What does it matter? She'll be so busy with the kid." The *kid*, not the *baby*. "Were you visiting your dad?"

"What? No." Another lie. Would my nose start growing like Pinocchio's? "I've lived here for nearly a year, and I haven't toured every street. I wanted to take a break from work and get an eyeful."

My answer seemed to satisfy him. He said, "Beautiful day for a drive."

"Why aren't you serving up your barbecue at the food truck event? It seemed like you were the hottest ticket there."

"Hot! Ha-ha. Funny. Three-alarm hot!"

"I didn't mean—" I faltered. "I'm glad no one got hurt."

"I'm thrilled you were there to warn me," he said. "We wrapped up after that. Lunchtime was over, and the crowd thinned. We sold nearly all the steak sauce, so we made a profit."

"Speaking of which, since when have you been making steak sauce?"

"Since the dawn of time. It's my dad's recipe with a real Irish whiskey kick to it."

"No, I mean, now . . . here . . . in town."

"A couple of days or so. Save the Wild Ones asked, and they provided the supplies. I obeyed." He shrugged. "No big deal."

"How long have you been associated with that organization?"

"A month or so. I've always been into rescuing something. In San Francisco, I rallied to save the sea lions. In Santa Cruz, I preserved the Mount Hermon June beetle."

"A beetle, really?"

"Yup. *Polyphylla barbata*. Shiny little guys." He nabbed

my elbow and pushed open the swinging gate. "Come inside. Let me show you around."

Even though he seemed like good old likable Shane, I wasn't ready to give him the benefit of the doubt. "I can't." I jerked a thumb at my car. "I've got to be getting back. We have an event at the shop." *Now it was* we? *Liar, liar.*

"No worries." He let the gate swing shut with a bang. "I probably couldn't get in anyway. I asked Ava to meet me here, but she's late."

Ava. Was she the one I had heard on the hill? Was she even coming to meet Shane, or was he fibbing to cover why he was there?

"Did you ever check with Ava and learn what her alibi was the morning Sylvia was killed?" I asked.

"Nope. Not my business, though the more I think about it, the more I doubt she could have killed Sylvia."

"Why not? Maybe she was jealous of your relationship with Sylvia."

"My relationship with Sylvia?" he sputtered. "Where'd you get that idea?"

"Am I off base?"

He screwed up his mouth and didn't respond.

"Ava is into you," I said, remembering the wicked look she'd given me at the foodie truck event. "If she knew that you and Sylvia had an affair—"

"Hold the phone. We did not."

"No?" I tilted my head. "When we were chatting at Bait and Switch, you said Sylvia could *pack a wallop*. Why would you say something like that unless you'd had personal experience? Did you make a pass? Did she slap you?"

"No, she—" Shane drew in a deep breath. "I never could keep anything from you, Jenna." He rubbed the back of his neck. "Yeah, okay, so we had a thing. It was brief. No big deal."

"I'll bet it would be a big deal to Emily, and I think it *is* a big deal to Ava."

"Ava." He grumbled.

"You had a fling with her, too, didn't you?"

He raised an eyebrow. "Who are you, my therapist?"

"Did you give her hope?" I asked. "Did you tell her you were done with Sylvia and that you were going to end it with Emily, baby on its way or not?"

Shane flushed bright red. After a long moment, he said, "All right, yes. I encouraged Ava, and she and I hooked up, but it was pre-Emily, and we ended it." He hesitated. "Look, Emily doesn't know a thing. You can't tell her. It'll drive her nuts. See, she's crazy about me, and . . . she's only been with one guy ever"—he smacked his palm against his chest—"me. It would crush her to know I've been around the block a time or two."

"Shane," I *tsk*ed, "she's well into her thirties."

"But she's an innocent, I'm telling you. A little filly fitted with blinders."

A little filly? C'mon. Was he putting on an act? Was Emily? What if she had confronted Sylvia? No, I couldn't see it. Emily was teeny and in her pregnant condition probably weaker than a flea. However, I recalled a Girl Scout leader I'd had, nick-named Bambi, who was no bigger than Emily, yet she could build a fire in twenty seconds flat and take out a snake using her hiking stick with one firm thwack. Plus, Emily did say she had four brothers. I would imagine she knew how to wrestle.

Shane gripped my arm. "Promise you won't say anything to Emily. Please."

"You should tell the police about your relationships with Ava and Sylvia."

"Why? You don't think . . ." He splayed his arms. "Hey, I didn't have any reason to kill Sylvia."

"I didn't say you did, but you should be forthcoming."

Chapter 12

WHEN I RETURNED to the shop, the door was locked, the sign flipped to reveal my aunt's favorite response: *Back in a bit*. Where had she gone? One customer, a shapely tourist who had heard about us through the grapevine, was waiting patiently outside. She traipsed in after Tigger and me and quipped that everyone in town must be taking a siesta after the food truck event. She herself was feeling quite full and satisfied.

Once she paid for a copy of *Barbecue! Bible* by Steve Raichlen, the most recent version of his popular series, which she said was the perfect gift for her mother-in-law-to-be, she exited, and I set to work on the receipts. Until everyone in the world decided to go digital, paper would be an issue for shops like ours. Using an adding machine, I calculated the receipts and then paid attention to the cash in the till. I stored all of our income in the safe in the stockroom and returned to the sales counter.

A short while later, Katie rushed in with a picnic basket

slung over her arm. "Hoo-boy! What fun!" She smacked the counter with her palm.

"You look a wreck," I said.

"Yep, I do." Her chef's coat was splattered with a variety of red- and yellow-based sauces. Her hair peeked out every which way from beneath her toque. She whipped it off and fluffed her curls. "But I don't care. How I love the immediacy of a food truck. No time for prep." She twirled a hand as if she were still in the truck and commanding her sous chef. "Another slider. Turn it over. Next! Love it!"

"Are you saying you want that as your regular job?"

"No way, but it was a real kick in the you-know-what. Now it's back to reality. I have to focus on the menu for yet another party we're dishing up at the café." She spun to her right and whirled back. "Oh, I almost forgot. Rhett was looking for you at the event."

"I didn't see him."

"I know. You disappeared. You should call him. He seemed like a lost puppy."

"Rhett will never look like a lost puppy." He was the most self-reliant man I'd ever met.

"Where did you go, by the way?"

"Me? Nowhere. Nope. I was here." Man, the lying thing was becoming an issue. I had to curb it and fast.

Katie raised an eyebrow, clearly not believing me. "Jenna-a-a."

"I went on an errand." A half-truth. Better.

"Speaking of wrecks, what's with your shoes?"

I glanced at the muddy Keds. "I stepped in a puddle." I had. A puddle of muck. It wasn't a lie. "But I'm back. Here." I aimed a finger at my feet. "Rarin' for a good time. Now, leave." I nudged her. "Go. Cook for the masses. But bring me something to eat when you get the chance."

"Silly me, I almost forgot." She opened the lid of the basket she was carrying and withdrew a mini burger wrapped in parchment paper. "For you. It's a turkey and cheddar cheese slider with my special sauce, a mustard-honey concoction. Enjoy." She hurried down the breezeway and disappeared.

I peeled back the parchment paper; the aroma made my mouth water. I took a bite of the slider and hummed my appreciation. Salty and sweet and sloppy. Heaven.

After I polished off the last morsel, I tossed the parchment, washed my hands, and hurried to the telephone. I called Rhett, but he didn't answer. I apologized that I had missed him at the food truck event. I didn't tell him where I'd gone. He would understand, of course, that I was trying to protect my father, but I didn't want him to worry. I said I hoped to see him around the campfire tonight—the Wild West Extravaganza was hosting a cowboy sing-along on the beach; a week ago, Rhett and I had made plans to attend together—and I ended the call.

Then I dialed the precinct. I wanted to tell Cinnamon about the fabric I had seen beneath the rubble. If only I'd had the wherewithal to tug it free. On the other hand, the fabric was outside the realm of the crime scene and might have had nothing to do with the murder. Maybe it was Ava's, from when she had demolished the wall.

A clerk answered. Cinnamon was in the field and unreachable. The clerk would relay my message. I thanked her and ended the call.

Two customers dropped into the store in the late afternoon. One wanted a copy of each culinary mystery we carried. I collected over a dozen for her, including the delicious *The Diva Steals a Chocolate Kiss*. The other asked for *The Pioneer Woman Cooks: Food from My Frontier* plus *The Homesick Texan Cookbook* by Lisa Fain, a chef in New York who had re-created the wonderful tastes of home that she had savored at church suppers and backyard barbecues, like warm bowls of chili con queso and chicken-fried steak served with cream gravy.

As those two departed, a button of a woman who owned

a china shop down the street scurried in giggling. "You won't believe what happened. This morning, I stepped away from the hot stove for five seconds. Five." She splayed her fingers. "And, oops, my pot holders went up in a blaze. I have to buy another pair. My stepmother is coming to dinner, and you know her." I didn't, but she had mentioned her taskmaster stepmother on a previous occasion. "Perfect is as perfect does." She made a beeline for the pot holders. "I'd make a pair if I had the time, but I must get the soufflé in. Aha, I see them." She nabbed two red mitts and dashed back to the counter to pay, then hurried out. A whirlwind.

Around 5:00 P.M., Aunt Vera called and apologized for leaving the shop unattended. She hoped I didn't mind. Deputy Appleby had dropped by and asked her to coffee. The shop was devoid of customers. She thought she would be gone only a few minutes. Before she knew it, time had sped by. I assured her it was fine; she didn't need to spend every waking second at the shop. She thanked me profusely.

Soon after, Bailey checked in by telephone. She was tittering like a schoolgirl, blathering that she . . . *she* . . . had played *hooky*; she called herself a dilettante and a ne'er-do-well, and claimed it was all Tito's fault. He had dragged her to a wedding shop to pick out her dress. How could she say no? What man wanted to do such a thing, other than Richard Gere in *Runaway Bride*, but that was definitely not Tito, and, well, champagne was involved, and she couldn't wait for me to see the dress, it was so-o-o beautiful and—

I cut her off by absolving her of her sins. She laughed some more and said she would see me tomorrow.

At six on the dot, I gathered Tigger, closed shop, and drove home.

When I parked at the cottage, I didn't see anyone in the vicinity and convinced myself that over the past few days I had been hearing noises and making up phantoms that weren't really there. I was ready to set a therapist appointment until I remembered the rope and spurs that Bailey had given me, and I decided one round of rope jumping to boost my endorphins would do me more good than any time spent in a therapist's chair. Luckily, I was still wearing the Keds and not my sandals.

I popped Tigger into the cottage and closed the door, pulled the rope from the trunk of my VW, and, in the driveway, attempted a few jumps of the Texas skip. Sadly, I wasn't nearly as good this time as I had been in the parking lot by the store. Apparently I needed Bailey as a coach.

Vowing to get better, I coiled up the rope and replaced it in the trunk of my car. Then I hurried inside, fed Tigger, and went to take a shower to get ready for my date. As water cascaded over my face, visions of the creep in *Psycho* attacking Janet Leigh played in my mind. Faster than you could spell Y-I-P-E-S, I popped out of the shower, toweled off, and dressed in a white scoop-necked T-shirt, jeans, denim jacket, and boots. I tied a turquoise scarf around my neck—I didn't own a kerchief—and then I assured Tigger I wouldn't be home late. A kiss to his nose sealed the deal.

Walking down the beach, paying attention to my environment as well as to everyone who was out for a good time, I headed south toward The Pier. The sky was a deep, dusky gray and cloudless. A full moon was rising over the mountains to the east. The bonfire, which was set far away from The Pier, blazed orange and gold. Tons of people, all silhouettes backed by the glow, roamed nearby.

As I drew closer, I could hear members of the throng singing "By the Light of the Silvery Moon." When that song ended, a group struck up "Back in the Saddle Again." Not everyone knew the words; there was a lot of laughter about that.

I weaved through the crowd wondering how I would find Rhett, and then I heard him. He had a rich, powerful laugh. He was standing near a hot dog vendor with Tito, who was regaling him with a story.

"Kid you not," Tito said, hands wide, painting the account,

"a little boy on a trike at five in the morning. *Whoosh!* Straight across my path. The mother comes running out"— Tito snapped his fingers—"and nabs him in two seconds flat!"

"What happened?" I pecked Rhett on the cheek.

"Accident averted. How are you?" He nuzzled my neck. "When you called, you sounded stressed."

"Did I?"

He gave me a knowing look. "Want a beer?"

"Do I! And a spicy hot dog."

"I'll be right back."

I said to Tito, "Where's Bailey? I heard you went dress shopping."

"She's a little, how do you say, under the weather?"

"Too much of the bubbly?"

"My fault. I should know her limits."

"So should she." *Listen to you, Jenna Hart. Do not judge, lest ye be judged.* "Is she in bed? Does she need me to drop in?"

"No. Don't worry. I'm going to check in on her. She wanted me to come here first. 'Do your thing,' she said. 'Get a story.'" He tapped the pad and pen that were invariably tucked in his shirt pocket.

"And did you?"

"Not yet. It's the life of a reporter. Some days yes, some days no. So far, everyone is behaving. Aha! There's the mayor. She always has something fit to print. *Adios.*" Tito charged toward her.

As I stood by myself, a chilly breeze tickled my ankles. At the same time, I felt eyes on me. I shivered and scanned the horde of people. No one was staring at me. I spun to my left and gazed at The Pier. A lone man, unrecognizable even in the full moonlight, stood at the end. His arms were raised. A glint of light flickered near his face. Was he holding a camera? Binoculars? Was it the same person I'd believed was spying on me in the parking lot the other day? The same one who had sneaked around my cottage?

Fear cut through me, but I forced myself to calm down. No one was going to attack me in this throng.

Even so, I continued to observe the stranger. After a long moment, whoever it was pivoted and peered off in a more southerly direction, and I felt like a ninny. It was probably a tourist having a look-see. So why was I spooked? There were others on The Pier. It wasn't like he had posted himself in some remote location. Again, I considered touching base with a therapist. I was only thirty and way too young to fall apart.

Tamping down my anxiety, I searched for someone to latch on to until Rhett returned. Near the most boisterous singers, I caught sight of Mrs. McCartney, who reminded me of a scarecrow with her stick-straight red hair and floral top and trousers. I was surprised to see her. She wasn't known to be very social. She was standing with a plump, gray-haired lady in a furry sweater. Both were holding plastic cups fitted with straws. Both were smiling.

Hmm. Was Mrs. McCartney open to a few questions? Would extracting information be harder than trying to squeeze juice out of an unripe lemon?

Slapping on a big smile, I sidled up to them and introduced myself. Mrs. McCartney's nose scrunched up, not in a nice way. Did I smell bad? Maybe she didn't like the fragrance I'd sprayed on. Well, I didn't like the red lipstick she had swathed on her thin lips; it didn't match her freckly skin; and her eyes were beady and hawklike, but would I make a face? No, I would not.

Up close, her friend reminded me of a huggable cat, especially given her little pink nose, bright alert eyes, and multicolored short hair. She gazed between us. "Do you two know each other?"

"I am acquainted with Jenna's father," Mrs. McCartney said, her tone dismissive.

"And you know me, too." I smiled with gusto. "You've come into The Cookbook Nook."

"Once."

"For a cupcake cookbook. You bought *Your Cup of Cake* by Lizzy Early."

"You remember that?" the friend asked.

"I try to remember what all my customers buy." I addressed Mrs. McCartney. "I told you about the author, who is a darling woman from Portland, Oregon, remember? You said the cupcake photos in the book were some of the most gorgeous you had ever seen. You also said that your two granddaughters were coming to visit you. You wanted to make them a special treat when they arrived."

Mrs. McCartney's eyebrows arched up. "You have a steel-trap memory."

I didn't. Not really. I had to work hard to drum up details, but boy, was I glad I had. Mrs. McCartney's shoulders relaxed. Her friend beamed at me.

"Shame about Sylvia Gump," I said.

"Shame, indeed," Mrs. McCartney said. "Nasty personality, but no one deserves to burn to death."

"You live in the area, don't you?" I asked.

"Yes. Why?"

"I heard you saw my father that morning. What were you doing out so early?"

"Silly Mellie"—she jutted a thumb at her friend—"lost her cat. She called me in a panic. There we were, rambling through the neighborhood, hunting with flashlights." She glanced at Mellie. "I don't go out of my way for humans, but I will always help search for a cat. I have five of my own. I know what curious creatures they can be."

"My poor kitty." Mellie smiled as though the whole affair had been fun. "She was having a litter beneath the house. I didn't even know she was pregnant. She sure gets around."

Mrs. McCartney said, "Neither of us believes in spaying, but we always find homes for our four-legged friends."

"Yes, we do." Mellie clawed the air and Mrs. McCartney mirrored her, like they were performing a sorority pledge.

Together they chimed, "The best things in life are furry."

In spite of myself, I was starting to like both of them.

"I was gathering up the last one," Mrs. McCartney went on, "when I saw your father leaving the house with a fishing pole."

To confirm, I said, "You said it was dark."

"No, I said we were using flashlights."

"Was it dark?"

"It might have been."

"If it was, that means it was before sunrise, which occurred at quarter to six."

"So?" She sniffed.

"The fire started around six A.M."

"What are you now, a forensics expert?"

Mellie nicked her friend with a knuckle. "Be nice."

I said, "Mrs. McCartney, did you tell the police that it was dark when you saw my father?"

"They didn't ask. I merely said I saw him. That established his whereabouts."

"Way before the fire," I said. "He went fishing."

"I can't confirm that." She pursed her lips.

"Did you see him near Sylvia Gump's house?"

"I can't attest to that, either, but that's the rumor."

"Because of you. You implicated him!"

"Don't raise your voice at me, young lady." She wagged a finger. "I can't help it if people take what I say the wrong way."

"But—" I was dumbfounded. Didn't she realize what she had done?

"Oh, listen, Mellie," Mrs. McCartney said. "They're singing 'You Are My Sunshine.' That's my favorite song. I don't want to miss it!" She nabbed her friend's arm. "By the way, Jenna, that ginger cat of yours is the most adorable thing. If you ever find he's too much for you, I'll be glad to take him in."

They departed in a hurry, leaving me speechless.

"Who are you staring at?" a woman said from behind.

I spun around. Cinnamon was staring at me. She was dressed in uniform and standing with her hands on her hips, looking very official.

"Wh-what?" I stammered, knowing exactly *what*. She had caught me chatting with a witness. "I can talk to the locals."

Cinnamon tipped her head but didn't utter a word.

"Fine," I blurted. "Yes, I was questioning Mrs. McCartney about seeing my father on the morning Sylvia was killed." So much for my ability to lie. I would be terrible under interrogation. Who needed truth serum? I was ready to blab everything. My mother had been as skilled at intimidation as Cinnamon.

She: *Did you take the last cookie, Jenna?*

I: *Who me? Why, yes, I did, Mom.* No hesitation.

"My father is under suspicion, Chief," I said. "What do you expect me to do, sit on my hands? Is that what you're doing?" My cheeks stung with anger. Why, oh, why did she bring out the worst in me? We were friends. When she wasn't investigating a murder, we went out for coffee. She liked a latte with a double hit of espresso. If I know something like that, shouldn't we be able to trust one another? And, honestly, a few months ago, she had asked me to keep my eyes and ears open on another case. Granted, she had rescinded that request a day later, and at the foodie truck event earlier she had warned me to butt out.

"Jenna, I—"

"Look, I know you adore my father and want him to be as innocent as I do. And I know you're doing all you can." I chopped a hand against a palm to make my point. "However, please listen. Mrs. McCartney told you she saw Dad in the vicinity, but she didn't say when, and it was way earlier than you think."

"Are you sure?"

"She told me it was dark. That means it was before

sunrise. She said she never gave the police a specific time because no one asked. Don't you see? She meant to get Dad in trouble." I sighed. "Her new statement, seeing him pre-dawn, should be enough to exonerate him."

Cinnamon shook her head. "I'm sorry, but Sylvia Gump could have died closer to that time. The coroner is working on the time frame."

"But the fire! Dad was long gone by the time it lit up. And Ronald Gump smelled smoke at six, right?"

"We don't know that your father was *long gone*."

"Sure we do. He said so."

"Jenna, we need someone"—Cinnamon spoke slowly, like she was tutoring a challenged child, namely *me*—"who saw your father away from the crime scene. Far away. Say at the lake."

I regarded her for a long moment, and then, heedless of the flak I would take for visiting the site, said, "I found a cuff link at the crime scene."

Cinnamon exhaled through her nose.

"There was no police tape," I added. "It's my father's property."

"It's communal property." She offered one of her infa-mous glares. Where had she learned that? In cop school? My boss at Taylor & Squibb had her beat. Whenever he was unhappy, he glowered like a feral saber-toothed tiger. The look had sent shivers to my toes. Cinnamon's didn't.

I met her stare. "I went there to see if I could find some-thing that might point the finger at somebody other than my father. Bucky said—" I balked. Bad me. I didn't need to bring her boyfriend into it.

"I heard him. He said we found a steak sauce cap."

How much had he suffered for that blooper?

"That could have been there for weeks," Cinnamon added, "because of Sylvia's infamous parties."

I shifted my feet. "Initials were etched on the cuff link that I found: *SM*. Did you ask Shane Maverick his alibi?"

"Jenna, stop." Cinnamon held up a hand. "Did it occur to you that the initials on the cuff link might belong to Sylvia? Her maiden name is May. Sylvia May. *SM*."

I didn't back down. "Why would she wear cuff links?"

"She sells them in her store," she stated. "Why would Shane wear them?"

Exactly the question I'd asked myself while nosing around. "Maybe he took them to Sylvia to polish for his impending nuptials. Did you know Sylvia tried to purchase the house Shane bought, but Ava blocked her? What if Sylvia threatened to bar the sale? What if that made Shane so angry he lashed out? Also, I found a piece of red fabric in the rubble of the brick wall."

"The wall beyond the crime scene?"

"Yes. D'Ann Davis's signature color is red. What if she—"

"Don't you like D'Ann?"

"Of course I do, but somebody killed Sylvia, and it wasn't my father. Did you see the fabric? What if D'Ann and Sylvia fought? D'Ann wears those hair thingies, and—"

"Jenna, time out." Cinnamon formed a T with her hands, then softened her voice. "I love your Dad. You know that." I had never seen her cry, but she seemed near tears.

"He didn't do it."

"But I've got to *prove* it. Do you understand? I'm scouring the area for witnesses. I've talked to some men who are working a landslide project down the road. None were in the neighborhood at that hour. I questioned a few construction workers, too. Same thing: too early. By the way, in my next life, I want to be Mrs. Tyvek." She offered a quirky smile, obviously trying to ease the tension between us. Tyvek isn't a person. It's the name of a product used to paper frames of new house construction. Just look around, and you'll see it. The DuPont company owns the trademark. I know because I did an ad for a competitor.

"I didn't think you were into money," I quipped.

"I'm not. Neither is Bucky. But we want to own a house

bigger than his one-room flat or the fiasco I call home. Public servants don't get paid enough."

"My father will give you a loan when you're ready."

Cinnamon barked out a bitter laugh. "Oh yeah, that would be just what I need, someone in town thinking I'm letting your father off the hook because he loaned me cash."

"I see your point. Hey," I said, my mind in overdrive, "were there any kids waiting for the bus at six A.M. Wednesday morning?"

"No. Too early."

"What about gardeners?"

"None are allowed to start until after seven A.M.; it's a city ordinance."

"But maybe there were a few in their trucks, raring to go."

"Please, Jenna, I will clear your father. I promise. Stay away from this investigation."

I didn't nod. I was done with lying.

Chapter 13

I JOINED RHETT IN line, and, after we nabbed two beers and two hot dogs, we returned to the sing-along and stood at the outer rim of the crowd, which was crooning "The Streets of Laredo." A young cowboy had done wrong. We joined in the last verse, and a pall settled over the crowd. There was nothing happy about hearing that a young man was shot down, especially when you didn't know the crime he had committed. I thought of Sylvia. What had she done to make someone want to impale her and burn her?

"What's wrong?" Rhett asked, then shook his head. "Dumb question. Your dad. Sylvia. Got it. Are you okay?"

I snuggled into him. "I'll be fine," I said. *Bullpuckey*, as Bailey would say.

A couple of hours later, with our throats raw from singing, Rhett walked me home. We held hands. I loved the closeness. By the time we reached my cottage, Rhett had wrapped his arm around my back, and I was feeling tingly to my toes.

He kissed me on the porch, gently and tenderly, occasionally swatting an errant moth that wanted to spoil the mood.

After the fifth moth swatting, I giggled and said, "Would you like to come inside?"

"If I do, I won't leave, and I have to be up early. I've got a date with Old Jake and some of his buddies."

Old Jake was a gnarled and weathered man in his mid-seventies who had drifted into town when my father was a teen. Though he and my father were a good decade apart, thanks to a rich history between them, they had become good friends. I sighed. If only Jake had gone fishing with Dad Wednesday morning.

Rhett added, "I promised the guys that I'd take them cowboy fishing."

"You're making that up."

"I'm not."

"What the heck is cowboy fishing?"

"Fishing for something that you can tell a tall tale about."

"Ha-ha!" I smacked his arm.

He drew me in for another long, luscious kiss, and whispered, "How about going to see the pole-bending event with me tomorrow afternoon?"

"I've got things to do at the shop," I murmured.

"Ask your aunt to cover for you."

How many times could I beg off from work? We needed another assistant. Could we afford one? Yes. Sales had been booming.

"C'mon," Rhett said.

I grinned. "Okay. Why don't I meet you there around four?"

"Sounds great. Until then."

He kissed me again, and I felt like I'd been drugged with a love potion. I pressed open the door to my cottage. My knees were weak, but not too weak to walk in without stumbling. I wouldn't want the guy to think I was head over heels in love with him.

As he drove off, I switched on a light and bolted the door. Tigger didn't pounce at my feet, however. That was when I detected a scent, a very familiar scent, heavy with lime and mandarin oranges and a hint of cedarwood and spice—Clive Christian cologne.

My breath caught in my chest. And suddenly he was on me. His hand on my mouth. His arm cupping my back. I couldn't scream. I didn't want to. Slowly he released his hold.

"David! How . . . why . . . you're alive!" I felt the floor rushing up, the ceiling caving in. "Is it really you? I only drank one beer. I'm not tipsy."

"Yeah, it's me, hon," my nondeceased husband said. He had never called me sweetheart or babe, always hon, short for *honey*.

"Let me go."

He did. I whacked his chest.

"Ow!"

I smacked it again. "You. Were. Declared. Dead!"

Tigger darted to us, mewling his concern. Apparently the little traitor, who I had believed until now was a good alarm cat, liked my dearly nondeparted. He weaved in and out between our legs, tail brushing, questioning.

I thumped David's chest again.

Tigger yowled.

"Hush, cat." I pushed away from my husband—Was he my husband if he wasn't deceased? What was the statute of limitations on marriage vows?—and roamed in a circle, balling and releasing my fists. "The police thought I might have killed you. I mourned. We all mourned. And then I found your note—" I halted. "How did you get inside?"

"You left the door unlocked."

"I don't do that."

"You did this time."

In my haste to get to the sing-along, maybe I had. How *unlike* me. Especially given the fact that I had been so edgy lately.

"Was it you spying on me outside my shop?" I folded my

arms across my chest, shielding myself with imaginary armor, and took in David. His eyes were hangdog; his face, sort of slack. "Well? Was it?"

He didn't deny it.

"And on the beach the other day? And outside the cabin? And again tonight?"

"I couldn't find the courage to approach you. You seemed so content. So easy with your life. I even followed you to where that woman was killed."

"That was you trailing me down my father's hillside? You made a noise."

"And hid behind a boulder."

All that time, I believed I was going nuts. I mentally crossed the therapist appointment off my list, but then added it right back. My husband was alive!

"I've been living like a bum in the Prius," David went on, "waiting for the right moment."

"Your note said you were going to kill yourself." I stumbled toward the couch.

"Jenna, I . . ." His mouth was thin, quivering. Where had he been? What had he been going through? What could have driven him to break my heart? He moved toward me.

I held up my hand, warning him to stay back. "David." I had often said his name in a prayer; now it sounded dirty and mean.

He was dressed exactly the way I'd seen him last, in a white shirt and jeans, his hair tousled. He extended his arms. "I'm sorry, hon. There's no excuse."

"No excuse?" I eyed a stack of cooking magazines on the coffee table and considered using them as ammunition. One by one. Mini missiles to take him down. "You let me believe—" I jammed my fist into my mouth and bit back a scream.

He drew nearer. "Jenna, I'm sorry."

I raised a warning hand. He froze. "You bilked your clients," I said. "I found the evidence."

"I regret that, every day of my life."

"I didn't find your note for two years. Two!"

"About that. I don't understand why it took you so long."

I did. The weight of it dragged on me. "Because your mother asked to be useful. She was supposed to clean out your gym locker. She couldn't bring herself to do it."

"Does she—"

"Know what you did?" I wagged my head. "No, I never told her. I made as many reparations as I could with the gold coins you hid in the lucky cat statue."

"You didn't have to. The debt was mine and mine alone."

"I couldn't have lived with myself otherwise." I growled. "Those dratted gold coins." I started to shiver; my mouth was dry. "Why are you here?"

"I need to make peace with you before I die."

I scoffed. "Now you're dying? Like, for real?" I couldn't believe how flip I sounded, but after what he had put his family and me through . . . "What are you dying from, David? Tell me."

"Renal failure. CKD or chronic kidney disease."

"People don't die from that."

"Yes, they do, if they only have one kidney left."

"One?"

"I lost one as a kid. I never told you." His face twisted with so much pain, he had to be telling the truth. This time.

I sagged against the couch and braced myself with my hands. "I'm sorry."

"Don't be."

"Why did you fake your death?"

"Because I was wicked. Corrupt. I deserved to die."

"But in the end, you couldn't do it."

He nodded.

"Where did you disappear to?"

"Nevada and Arizona and Colorado. I went to New Mexico, too. You always wanted to go there. It's pretty."

"Stop!" I bounded to my feet, anger rearing its lovely head again. "Why grace me with your presence?"

"I need to make restitution. I need your forgiveness. I have less than a month to live."

"A month?"

"Just so you know, I've surrendered to the San Francisco police for my crimes, but they were surprisingly understanding, given the circumstances. They've allowed me a week to put my affairs in order. I'll serve out the rest of my time in jail."

"You're lying."

"Remember Detective Dyerson, who handled the case?"

Did I ever. She and I had talked ad infinitum about my possible guilt. *Where is your husband? How good a sailor is he? There's no body.*

David pulled a cell phone from his jeans pocket and stabbed in a number. "Detective Dyerson? My wife . . . Jenna Hart . . . would like to speak with you." He pressed the speakerphone option and offered me the cell phone.

I grabbed it, but I didn't know what to say. How did I know this wasn't a scam? How could I be certain the woman on the other end of the line wasn't someone David had paid to snow me?

"I never thanked you for the note you wrote me last year," Dyerson said, cluing me in immediately that she was legitimate. I had written after finding David's suicide letter. "Thank you"—she hesitated—"although now it feels a little anticlimactic, doesn't it?" She let out a low, throaty laugh. "How are you?"

"I'm with a man I believed was dead. How would you be?"

"Not as shocked as you, I imagine. How is your father?"

"Do you know about—" I hesitated. I didn't need to share Dad's predicament. "He's okay."

"Still a do-gooder?" she went on. "I remember the two of us talking about all the houses he built for Habitat for Humanity." The woman had taken pains to pull that information from my father; he never bragged about it.

"Yes. He's a very good do-gooder." And *not guilty*. But

back to the current situation. "David tells me you've given him time to sort out his affairs."

"That's true."

"And he's not lying about his health?"

"No, ma'am. I've seen the doctor's report. He's end-stage, if he didn't tell you."

End-stage, I thought. *Terminal.*

"He has given your address as his current location, is that correct?" Dyerson asked.

I glanced at David. He smirked. Not in a bad way. In the impish way he used to, whenever he made plans and didn't consult me.

"Ma'am?" the detective said.

Please, David mouthed.

I remembered the moment I met David. We were at a fraternity party. I'd broken up with a full-of-himself jock. David was standing alone by a window holding a glass of wine. He offered me a sip and told me he was thinking about becoming an investment banker. He was smart. Funny. And not at all full of himself. In fact, he was self-deprecating. We talked for hours. The connection was intense. Yes, he hurt me to the core when he ran from his life . . . *our* life . . . but I had to help him this one last time.

"Yes, that's right, Detective."

"Good," she said. "What is your personal contact number?"

I gave it to her.

She thanked me and wished me well.

I ended the call and faced David. What a trusting soul the detective was to let him walk, but then how many of her suspects, or in this case dead bodies, waltzed back into her life and reopened a case with the promise to close the case for good in four weeks?

Putting worry about my father on the back burner, I said, "You're here. Talk."

Chapter 14

I FIXED TEA AND arranged crackers and cheese on a plate, and David and I settled onto the sofa. Tigger nestled into David's lap, and David stroked him constantly while he told me about his downward spiral into debt; his fear about telling me what he had done; the weight of his decision to end his life, and then the duplicity—to figure out a way to escape. Though it was no excuse, he said as a kid his parents had bailed him out so many times, it had made him weak. I asked why he hadn't consulted his mother and asked her for money to pay back his debt. He said he couldn't. His father had died the year before. She was so fragile. Learning what he had done would have crushed her. Leaving her out of his problem was the one valiant thing he could do.

Around 2:00 A.M. David said, "Remember those early times for us"—he yawned—"when we were scratching for success, dining solely on pretzels and beer?" He smiled wistfully. "I wish I could go back to that time."

I didn't. I had worked hard to get ahead, to build a future, to be able to afford filet mignon if I so desired. "The renal failure," I said, switching the subject. "When did you learn about it?"

"A month after I disappeared."

"Are you on medication?"

"No. I'm not a good candidate for a donor, either. No insurance. It's my fault. I didn't take care of myself. When I ran, I started drinking"—he yawned again—"too much." He glanced at his watch. "Wow. It's late." He touched my hand. I flinched. "Sorry. I didn't mean . . . You know I wouldn't . . ." He ran his hand through his hair, pushing bangs off his face. "I screwed up, Jenna. I'm sorry."

We sat in horrible silence for a few minutes, and then he set Tigger on the ground and said, "You'd better get some sleep."

"And you."

He crackled out a sad, tormented laugh. "Yeah. I don't sleep much nowadays."

I cleaned up our dishes, gave him a pillow and blanket, and laid out a towel and fresh toothbrush in the bathroom. I washed first and snuggled into bed. I listened for a long time as he cleaned up, and then I heard him settle onto the couch and try to stifle sobs. It took all my reserve not to console him.

On Friday morning, clad in yellow pajamas decorated with multicolored kittens, I made David a quick breakfast. Afterward, I dressed in a summery, upbeat lemon-yellow dress and sandals, cloaked myself yet again in imaginary armor, and advised David to do what he had promised to do—get his affairs in order: call his mother, contact his sister, and meet with a pastor if he needed one. We had a few terrific pastors in Crystal Cove. Then I departed, leaving Tigger in David's care. The little guy was a natural Florence Nightingale with his pawing, licking, and nurturing.

By the time I arrived at The Cookbook Nook, Bailey was already there, rearranging cookbooks on a display table.

Like me, she knew the value of getting covers of books in front of customers. Simply seeing spines and titles didn't entice someone to purchase. At the front of the grouping, she set *Chili Cookbook*, a deliciously short-titled cookbook by Gooseberry Patch, written by a couple of stay-at-home moms who wanted to share easy and long-treasured family recipes. The book was good for children, beginning cooks, and chili lovers.

I was glad to see that Bailey had revived from her over-indulgence while buying her wedding dress.

When I asked her the cure, she said, "Water—gobs of it. It's a miracle drug."

"Did you bring a picture of the dress?"

"Are you kidding? No! It's a surprise." Apparently she had forgotten how she said she couldn't wait for me to see it. "Hey, you look bleary-eyed." She stopped rearranging and followed me to the counter. "What's going on?"

I stowed my purse and popped open the register. Cash looked freshly restocked. I banged the drawer shut.

"Where's Tigger?" Bailey asked.

"At the house."

"You never leave him home. Talk to me. Are you stressing out? Look"—she reached across the counter and clasped my wrist—"your father is going to be fine."

"Is he?"

"My mother is scouring the town for a witness who can place him at the lake. She's going door to door, shop to shop."

"Dad said he didn't see anyone at the lake. He didn't mention seeing anyone on the road driving back to town, either."

"That doesn't mean anything." Bailey released me. "I've driven places and often never had a clue how I got there. I'm not saying those are good road skills, but sometimes I go on autopilot and, whoosh, with my mind awash in other thoughts, I move from point A to point B in a fog."

"My father isn't like that. He's—"

"Why are you being so contrary?" she snapped. "What's

bugging you? I'm trying to stir up positive vibes, and you're shooting me down. Did you forget to eat? Is that what this is about? Katie is making a batch of chili and some barbecue fudge. I think she's—"

"David is alive."

"What?" She slapped a hand over her mouth.

"He's at the cottage." I filled her in on the events of the past few days, my feeling that I was being watched, and then David showing up after the sing-along.

"Omigosh," she yelped. "What are you thinking, allowing him into your home?"

"He broke in, or rather, I left the door unlocked."

"You've got to kick him out. You're in danger."

"No, I'm not. He's dying, Bailey."

She rolled her eyes. "Yeah, right."

"He has kidney failure and only one kidney. He has a month, maybe less."

"He's lying."

"He's not. You should see him. He's as pasty as dough. He surrendered to the San Francisco police and begged to have a week to set his life in order."

"And they agreed?" Bailey smacked the counter. "I don't believe it."

"I talked to the detective in charge."

"Wow, wow, wow." Bailey regarded me, her eyes filled with concern. "How do you feel?"

"Shell-shocked. Confused. I'm still married, I think."

"No way." She chopped one hand on the other. "No court in the land would hold you to that."

"I think some court would." I settled onto the stool by the register and rested my elbow on the counter, my chin in my hand. "Dad—"

"Is going to be fine."

"I was going to say my father is going to be furious when he finds out about David."

Bailey frowned. "Don't tell him."

"Ha! He's as psychic as my aunt, though he won't admit it. He knows everything I'm going to say before I tell him."

The door to the shop pushed open, and my aunt entered, looking quite stylish. She wore a turquoise caftan with strands of colorful beads and bangles, and carried a matching turban under her arm. She had even done her hair and applied makeup. "Good morning, ladies," she said.

"Good morning," I responded. "Why are you so dressed up?"

"I have a date at lunch."

"With the detective?" I asked, excited for her.

"Yes." She blushed. "Will you cover for me?"

"Of course." Not until after I moved home to Crystal Cove did I learn about the man who left my aunt at the altar over thirty years ago. He had been the love of her life. He never explained why he left her and married another woman, and he never would. He died less than a year later. She deserved every happiness, and she looked tickled pink about seeing Deputy Appleby. I added, "If you'll cover for me at four."

"Done." Aunt Vera stowed her tote in the stockroom and returned to the counter. She gazed at me and tilted her head. "Something's different." She twirled a finger in my direction.

"New lipstick," I quipped.

Bailey thwacked my arm with a finger. "Tell her."

But I couldn't because the door flew open again and D'Ann Davis rushed inside in a red sheath and high heels. Her red cape flew behind her, making her look like she was ready to take flight.

"Vera!" she cried. "I need a tarot reading."

"Now?" Aunt Vera said. "The shop isn't even open." She whispered to me, "Don't mention the face or dental work that I told you about."

"My lips are sealed." If not for the pained expression in the famous actress's eyes, I would swear she wasn't a day over forty. Her café au lait skin was perfection, her kohl-rimmed eyes shimmering with energy.

"Please. It's a dire emergency." D'Ann clasped my aunt's

hand and pulled her to the vintage table. She plopped into
the chair opposite and fidgeted with the hair clasp holding
her iron-straightened hair in place.

"What do you want to know?" my aunt asked with a
patient tone. "About a job? A man? Family?"

"Turn the cards," D'Ann ordered.

Bailey moved behind the counter and whispered to me,
"I had no idea she was so bossy."

I replied sotto voce, "I'm sure she gets her way all the
time. She's a star."

Aunt Vera pulled a pack from the pocket of her caftan
and obliged. She would never refuse a customer in need.
She flipped over the first tarot card: The Empress.

D'Ann grunted. "That's Sylvia Gump, I assume."

"Why Sylvia?" Aunt Vera asked.

"She was deceitful."

The Empress card depicted nothing about someone being
devious. It was a beautiful card featuring a queen wearing a
starry crown and holding a brilliant scepter. She sits on a
throne, showing she has dominion over all. I recalled the
quickie conversation with Gran, who mentioned seeing D'Ann
argue with Sylvia at Sterling Sylvia, claiming Sylvia had
swindled her, and Sylvia had better *fix it*.

I edged around the counter and drew near to my aunt.
"D'Ann, did you have a gripe with Sylvia?"

Aunt Vera threw me a look. She didn't like it when someone, even I, interrupted a reading.

"A friend saw you at the shop," I went on, "exchanging
words with Sylvia."

D'Ann sniffed. "Sylvia couldn't be trusted. Oh sure,
people came from all over the world to buy her stuff, but
she was as sly as the devil."

"Why would you say that? Did she sell you something
under par?"

"How about a pair of earrings that weren't sterling silver?
She was nefarious."

One pair of earrings? That was why D'Ann was up in arms? She had to be worth millions. *Don't sweat the small stuff*, as my mother used to say. I glanced at Bailey, who was talking on the telephone. She didn't return eye contact.

My aunt turned up the second tarot card: The Lovers.

D'Ann tapped the card. "There! That represents Sylvia, too."

"Why?" my aunt asked, as calm as the azure sea.

"Because she was a man-stealer. She had designs to take Shane Maverick away from sweet Emily."

"But Sylvia was married," Aunt Vera chirped.

"That wouldn't have stopped her."

After talking with Shane, I feared that was true. "Did Ronald know about the affair?" I asked.

"Ronald? Not a chance, the poor fool." D'Ann tapped her temple. "I don't think that man would know the meaning of the word *jealous*. He idolized Sylvia."

My aunt flipped over the third tarot card: Justice.

D'Ann beamed. "Ha! I knew it."

What did she know? The card features a woman in a red robe. Typically, the card signifies that events have worked out as they were designed to and decisions made in the past were the right decisions, or something to that effect. Did the card signify that today? The judge was, after all, clad in D'Ann's signature color. I didn't believe in all this hoodoo stuff, but perhaps the card was pointing a finger at D'Ann as the murderer.

Offering no clarification about why she had demanded a reading—was she feeling vindicated because she believed Sylvia's death was preordained?—D'Ann bolted from her seat and sailed toward the door. My aunt called after her, but D'Ann didn't break stride.

My father, who was entering, held the door open for D'Ann as she exited, and then he charged in with the same intensity D'Ann had minutes before. "Jenna, is it true? He's alive?"

I cut a look at Bailey, standing behind the counter, straightening bookmarks. She eyed the telephone and peeked at me. Had she called her mother? Did Lola alert my father? Swell!

"Dad." I approached him, arms extended, palms to the floor. "Keep calm. It's okay."

"No, it's not. I'm going to call Cinnamon. We'll sic the police on him."

"Dad, don't!"

"Him, who?" my aunt asked.

Quickly I explained the situation to my aunt and defended David's choices.

"Oh my." She raised her arms overhead, her mouth moving silently. Another chant. Double swell.

"Everyone, chill," I ordered. "Try to understand. He needs me."

"He's using you," my father exclaimed.

"I'm a big girl. I can handle it. Trust me. Please. Please. Please." Tears threatened to fall. *No*, I warned them. *Don't you dare.*

My father held his breath, and finally his anger melted. He sighed and dragged me into a hug. "It's tit for tat, sweetheart. You worry about me; I worry about you."

We remained in the hug for a long moment, and then I pressed apart and said, "About that . . . has Lola found any witnesses? Anyone at all who might have seen you?"

"Not yet. But she's as stubborn as you. What will you tell Rhett about David?"

I gulped. From the moment I'd set eyes on David, I had been consumed with thoughts of him, us . . . *me*. I hadn't thought a whit about Rhett.

Chapter 15

SEEING AS I'D agreed to meet Rhett at the pole-bending competition in the late afternoon, I decided not to call him. Okay, maybe I was chicken, but honestly, anything I needed—*wanted*—to say had to be said in person. I texted him on my cell phone to confirm our date; he texted back: Can't wait. Meet you by the stadium seat entrance.

Feeling guilty for not spilling the beans, I suddenly had a craving for chocolate. I hurried to the Nook Café kitchen and begged Katie for a bite of the barbecue fudge Bailey had mentioned. She was more than happy to oblige. She wasn't sure if her taste buds were failing her. She needed another lab rat. I loved it. It was zesty and extremely satisfying. She had used crisp, crumbled bacon in the recipe and had sprinkled the top with a mixture of peppery spices. The combination of sweet and salty was amazing.

"Katie, you've done it again. This is downright sinful!"

She beamed.

"I think it's about time you write a cookbook." A few

months ago she had mentioned wanting to do so. "No more stalling. No more delays."

"Do you really think so?"

"Even if you self-publish it, think of all the customers who will want to purchase it at the shop. We can set some by the register in the café, too."

She bubbled with enthusiasm.

"On the other hand," I kidded, "don't do it, because then I'll have to worry about whether some big muckety-muck will steal you away."

"I'll never leave Crystal Cove."

"Never?"

"Not if Keller has anything to say about it." Her grin spread ear to ear. Keller was her boyfriend of a few months, a novel guy who rode around town on his bicycle churning homemade ice cream. He was Katie's first serious relationship; she hadn't dated in high school or college.

"You'd kowtow to his wishes?"

"Jenna, sometimes you only get one love of your life. He's it."

Her words hit me hard. One love. Way back when, I had thought David was my one love. Losing him and then suffering the jolt of his betrayal and the double jolt of his surprising rebirth was sending me reeling.

I nabbed another chunk of fudge—chocolate fixes lots of problems—and then offered to set out a plateful in the breezeway. Katie gushed with thanks and reminded me that tonight was the dance hall theme at the café. I should stop by with Rhett. I told her I would try.

Throughout the morning, I anxiously reviewed what I would say to Rhett about David. In between, I paid strict attention to customers.

At one point, a trio of Chocolate Cookbook Club members arrived. I steered them to the fudge in the breezeway, and you would have thought I had saved the world. Or rather, Katie had. Many were demanding that she sell the chocolate by the pound.

Around 2:00 P.M., as I was explaining to a customer and her husband how to organize the cookbooks in their house—she owned over one hundred; her husband said they were scattered, slapdash on the shelves in the kitchen and in cubbies throughout her house—a thirty-something single mother glommed onto my arm.

"Wait, Jenna!" She beckoned a girlfriend who had entered with her. "We'll want to hear this."

They gathered and grew attentive.

"My suggestion would be to figure out how you access your cookbooks," I said. "Not everyone does the same thing. For example, when you want to find a cookbook, do you think of the cuisine, the technique, the author's name, or the title?"

"Title," the single mother answered.

"Do you think of the course: soups and salads, appetizers, entrees, et cetera?" I asked. "Depending on your answer, I'd organize them along those lines."

"I use a card catalog," her friend said.

The woman laughed. "That's because you're a librarian."

"I organize them by size," the customer I'd been addressing said.

Her reed-thin husband laughed. "That's because you bought them for their beauty. You don't cook."

She batted his arm. "Do so."

He rolled his eyes.

The discussion continued for almost an hour, and I made another mental note. Perhaps a page on the shop's website showing how to organize cookbooks might be a good sales tool for the shop. Maybe we could share it visually on one of those picture-lover forums. I jotted the idea down on a list I kept running on the computer; I never left an idea to roam inside my head. Idle ideas had a tendency to go *poof*.

At half past three, after wrapping a customer's purchase that included a couple of specialty books I'd ordered to celebrate the Wild West Extravaganza—the first, *Every Cowgirl Loves a Rodeo*, a cute children's book that featured fabulous drawings and a sweet story, and the second, *Cowgirls: Commemorating the Women of the West*, a beautiful coffee table–style book that had earned lovely reviews about how the author had captured the glamour as well as the grubbiness of being a strong, hard-working female—I set off to meet Rhett. My stomach churned with anxiety. What would I say? How would he react?

FOR THE POLE-BENDING event, the Wild West Extravaganza group had rented Midway Motocross, the dirt bike track located north of town, a half-mile beyond the junior college. The track was a large dusty oval set at the foot of a grassy knoll. The extravaganza committee had done a bang-up job of gussying up the area, setting up red-and-white-striped tents for food vendors as well as occasional shade, tying bundles of red balloons onto every available pole or staff, and stringing red triangular flags around the entire facility. Spectators were dressed similarly to what the attendees had worn at the foodie truck event. I was overdressed in my summery dress and sandals.

Over a loudspeaker, an announcer introduced the participants in the first pole-bending contest. There would be eight in all. A teenage couple walked in stride with me. She was explaining the nuances of pole-bending to her boyfriend.

"It involves one rider on a horse, running a weaving path around six poles arranged in a line. Sort of like skiing the slalom course. Each pole stands twenty-one feet from the other, and the first pole is twenty-one feet from the starting line." Her companion nodded his understanding. "A horse can take its position either to the right or the left of the starting pole, but then they have to run the remainder of their pattern accordingly. If they knock over a pole, they get a five-second penalty. Got it?"

"Jenna!" Rhett called to me from the entrance to the stadium seats. He looked as handsome as ever, clad in jeans and a simple white-and-blue plaid shirt and, unlike everyone else, tennis shoes.

My stomach did a flip-flop at the sight of him. Unfortunately, not the good kind. Oh sure, I had the fleeting notion of sweeping him beneath the rustic bleachers and smothering him with kisses before I told him anything, but I squashed the idea. There was no privacy. Everyone would see us. I hurried to him, rehashing what I would say. When I drew near, my mind went blank.

"Hey," I said. Real smooth. I slipped into his outstretched arms and we kissed pristinely.

He nudged me away. "What's up?"

"What do you mean?"

"Don't kid a kidder. You look dazed, as if you've seen a ghost."

"Nice thing to say to a girl." I forced a smile. "How about, 'You look radiant, glowing, ethereal'?"

"Je-e-enna." He dragged out my name.

"Not here."

I slipped my hand into his and led him to a knoll, far from the swelling crowd. A cheer cut through the air. The first race had started. Dang. I had really wanted to catch a glimpse.

A warm breeze brushed my cheeks, but a chill skittered through my core. *Dive in anytime.* I licked my lips and began. "I've had a bit of a shock."

"Is it your father?"

"No, Dad's rallying. He hasn't been arrested. I honestly don't know what's going on with that. I've got suspects rotating in my mind—" I wiggled my free hand beside my head. "That's not what's bothering me." I drew in a deep, calming breath and let it out. "Wow, how do I say this?"

"Spit it out."

"My husband. David. It's complicated."

Rhett gripped both my hands. "Does this have something to do with how I ended our telephone call the other day, saying, 'I love you?' Because if it does—"

"No. I mean, yes. I love you, too." There. I said it. I meant it.

Rhett shook his head, not grasping the problem. "Then what about your husband?"

"He's alive."

Rhett released my hands and staggered backward. He spun on his heel while running a hand through his hair. When he made a full three-sixty and faced me again, he looked as if he were the one who had seen a ghost. "He's alive?"

I told him everything in one quick stream: David observing me; entering my cottage; spilling his life story; and the SFPD allowing him a week to finalize things. "He has one month to live."

"How can you be sure?"

"Because he told me so."

"He's scammed you before."

"The detective confirmed it."

Rhett moaned. "And he's staying with you? You're letting him?"

"What else could I do?"

"Boot him home to his mother, and then"—Rhett clasped my arms—"divorce him."

"Divorce?"

"You're married, Jenna."

"No court—"

"The law is the law. He didn't die. You're married. And . . ." He released me. "I don't date married women."

"You're being unreasonable."

"Am I?" Rhett's nostrils flared. "I don't think so. Your husband, a known criminal, is in your house. By his very presence, you could be implicated in any future misdeeds."

"He's dying!"

"When he does, give me a call." Rhett heaved a sigh filled with a thousand unspoken words and stomped away.

Tears flooded my eyes, and a string of angry terms cycled through my mind: *jerk, idiot, miscreant.* But when I regrouped, I knew Rhett wasn't any of those. He was hurt. I hadn't explained the situation well. It was my fault. I had let my dying husband back into my life and had allowed the new love of my life to walk out. Fantastic. Now what?

"Jenna?" Bailey rushed to me, tissues extended. "I saw Rhett heading the opposite way. He looked peeved."

"I told him about David." I took the tissues and dabbed my eyes. "We fought. He's upset." I gazed in the direction that Rhett had gone, and a horrible notion struck me. What if he finds someone else, and *bam*, just like that, he and I are history?

Tito, dressed like many at the pole-bending event with a cowboy hat resting jauntily on his head, joined us. "Don't worry, little lady." He tipped his hat backward with one fingertip and jutted a hip, a pose he must have seen in an oater movie. "Men need time to cool down."

Bailey shot him a look. His face warmed red.

"How much time?" I asked. "My husband"—the word stuck in my throat—"could be in town for a while."

Bailey said, "You said he's sick. Dying."

"He is. He has a month or less. He—" I gulped. "What if Rhett's right? What if David scammed the detective?"

"Even I don't believe that." Bailey pulled a bottle of water from her tote and thrust it at me. "Drink. You look like you're going to be sick. Speaking of sick, Tito"—she nudged her boyfriend—"tell her."

"*Sí.* Of course." Tito settled into his regular personality, no gimmicks, no cowboy-isms. "I had to do a delivery the other day."

Bailey continued for him. "Pitching out *The Crier* because his cousin got sick."

"I'm sorry," I murmured.

"It's *nada*," Tito said. "Sinus infection. He's on meds."

"Go on," Bailey urged.

"I was delivering the paper in the hills the morning Mrs. Gump was killed."

"In your father's neighborhood," Bailey added.

My worries about Rhett and David vanished. "Tito, did you see my father?"

Bailey said, "No, he saw Mrs. McCartney and her friend."

"*Sí*. They were yelling, 'Here, kitty, kitty.' It was around five A.M."

"Are you sure?" I shook my head.

Tito tapped his watch. "I am certain. I know because I was busting my chops to finish up by six fifteen so I could get to work. I was only halfway done with the route, but I was making good time."

"I have to contact Cinnamon."

"I also saw that actress," Tito said.

"D'Ann Davis?"

"*Sí*. She was doing something outside her house."

I shook my head, not understanding.

"She was performing a ritual," Bailey inserted. "That's what you called it, *mi amor*."

"*Sí*, a ritual. She was scattering things." He plucked imaginary items from his hands. "And she jumped on them." Tito hopped in place.

"What things?" I asked.

"White things."

Bailey tapped Tito's arm. "You thought they might be flower petals. They fluttered as they fell to the ground."

"White?" I shook my head. "D'Ann only grows red roses and red azaleas."

Tito winked. "Perhaps she had a special admirer who sent her white roses."

"Or you suggested that Sylvia might have sent the flowers to taunt her," Bailey offered.

I looked between them. "Why would Sylvia taunt D'Ann?"

Bailey winked. "Remember how Gran said D'Ann and Sylvia argued?"

"Right."

"Well, maybe Sylvia, knowing D'Ann only likes things that are red, thought that would be a funny gesture. She sent them, and D'Ann lost it. She scattered them on the ground and jumped up and down on them."

GRILLING THE SUBJECT 141

If Sylvia did send the flowers, or whatever the white things were, did D'Ann, in a snit, storm to Sylvia's house and demand an explanation? Did things get out of hand? Why had D'Ann burst into the shop earlier and asked for a tarot card reading? I couldn't believe one pair of fake silver earrings would push her over the edge.

"Tell Jenna the other thing"—Bailey rubbed Tito's forearm—"about seeing Ava Judge in the neighborhood, too. You said Ava seemed sneaky."

"*Sí*. She was walking the perimeter of the house that Shane Maverick bought."

I gaped. "At five in the morning?"

"By then, it was closer to six," Tito said. "I was doing the reverse route by then."

I assumed he meant he had delivered papers on one side of the street, hit the end of the cul-de-sac, and made a U-turn.

"She was dressed in a black overcoat," Tito said.

"Are you sure? Could it have been a red plaid jacket?" Maybe Ronald saw Ava running from the scene of the crime and assumed she was a man, namely, my father. She is tall, and if she had been wearing heels, per usual, she would have appeared even taller. I said, "It was somewhat dark and hard to make out colors."

"It was a black coat. My eyesight is one hundred percent. *Perfecto*."

Bailey aimed a finger at me. "What if Ava wore a jacket underneath the overcoat?"

I clapped my hands. "Yes!"

Had Ava given her alibi to the police yet? She was the ringleader for the neighborhood coup. Did she think that after one or two neighbors backed out of supporting her, she might not be able to thwart Sylvia? Did she, as Shane suggested, think Sylvia's constant disturbances might make a difference in sales prices in the neighborhood, affecting not only Ava's livelihood but also her property value? Would Ava have risked everything to stop Sylvia?

Chapter 16

I THANKED BAILEY AND Tito for the information and, eager to contact Cinnamon to tell her about Ava's whereabouts and D'Ann's odd behavior on the morning of the murder, I punched the precinct number into my cell phone. Busy. I ended the call and tried again. Still busy. I repeated the effort while heading toward my car. Fruitless. Sheesh. Okay, fine, if I couldn't get through, I would drive there.

Except as I was passing a tent where vendors were selling barbecue, I spotted a man ahead—as tall as Rhett, dark hair, white-and-blue plaid shirt tucked into jeans. I ended the call and raced to catch him. Luckily, right before I tapped the guy on the back, I realized it wasn't Rhett. The guy was much taller, and he was wearing boots. Talk about eyes seeing what they wanted to see! Obviously I needed—wanted—to talk to Rhett and hash things out ASAP.

Continuing to move in the direction of my car, I dialed Rhett. I reached his voice mail. Drat. Wasn't anyone answering? I left a message and begged him—short of sobbing; I have a modicum of pride—to return to talk to me. When I accepted that he wouldn't answer as long as I was chatting on his voice mail, I hung up.

Rhythmic clapping caught my attention. I spun around and was surprised to see that a crowd had gathered, not to listen in on my conversation, but to watch the young woman who had given the rope-jumping demonstration on The Pier. She had cleared a spot in the parking lot and was teaching a new slew of people how to leap through the vertical loop.

I watched for a minute, imagining myself mimicking the steps in perfect time, but then my attention was drawn to a couple of onlookers who were eating barbecued ribs, not the dainty baby back kind but huge beef ribs. As they tore into them, barbecue sauce dribbled down their chins and onto their shirts. One of the eaters tried to rub the sauce off his T-shirt with his forefinger. Bad idea. A stain resulted and grew even bigger, the more he tried to get rid of it.

The action made me consider the steak sauce bottle cap found at the crime scene. Cinnamon and my father have often told me that it's the small things that come back to bite a criminal. Did Shane, for whatever reason, take a bottle of steak sauce to the crime scene? Or did the murderer know that Shane made the sauce and bring the cap to the site, hoping to frame him? It was a small clue to pin to a big crime, but maybe the murderer figured that the top was metal, and it would stand the test of fire. So would a cuff link.

"Jenna!" Our mayor, a squat woman named Zoey Zeller—or Z.Z., as she liked her friends to call her—scurried toward me. Garbed in a brown leather skirt and jacket, her hair frizzier than ever, she reminded me of an Ewok from *Star Wars*. She was carrying a foodie bag decorated with licks of flame and a fistful of napkins. "Super-duper-spicy ribs, hot off the grill!" She shook the bag. "Want one?"

"No, thanks."

"I called to you because I'm so sorry, dear. I haven't had a moment to breathe since the Wild West Extravaganza started, let alone stop into the shop and pay my condolences. Your father"—she gulped in air—"is innocent, of course, but I should have touched base with you and your aunt. How is she holding up?"

"She's doing her best to summon good vibes."

"And you?"

"The same. How is Dean Gump faring?" The mayor and the dean went way back.

"Not well. I've visited him a couple of times. He seems quite forgetful. He can't remember where he put his glasses, though they're on his head. He can't recall the last time he ate, either." She *tsk*ed. "I'm afraid the poor man misses Sylvia terribly. His niece Tina is attempting to bolster him, but well . . ." Z.Z. twirled her hand in the air. "You of all people understand. It strikes a blow when you lose someone you love."

Her words jolted me. I thought of David—no longer *lost*—and Rhett, possibly lost forever. What was I going to do?

"Do you know when Ronald plans to have a funeral?" I asked.

"I don't believe the coroner has released the body. Red tape." The mayor clicked her tongue. "Now, as for Shane Maverick, what do you know about him? I heard you used to work with him at the advertising agency."

"I did. He was a great salesman."

"Yes." She bobbed her head. "I can see that. He's slick. Too pretty for his own good, if you ask me. I like my men with character, not looks."

I did, too, though looks were a bonus.

"He reminds me of a snake oil salesman I once knew," she went on.

"You knew someone who sold snake oil?"

Z.Z. sniggered. "Heavens to Betsy, no. It's an expression, dear." She tilted her head and peered at me with a cagey eye. "You're teasing me."

"Yes, ma'am, I am. Why do you want to know about Shane?"

"Will he do right by Emily? That sweet girl deserves every happiness in the world."

"I believe he intends to follow through." What more could I offer? Shane never made a promise at Taylor & Squibb that he didn't keep. Did that alone exonerate him of murder? No. People changed; David had.

"Do you think he had something to do with Sylvia's death?" Z.Z. said.

"Why would you ask that?"

"I saw them together frequently a few months ago, and although I'm not your aunt, I do get otherworldly feelings." She fluttered a hand. "And what's going on with Ava Judge?"

"How so?"

"She was at Ronald's house the other day when I arrived. Not *at*, exactly. Nearby. In her garden. She always seems to be assessing something, do you know what I mean?" To demonstrate, Z.Z. squinched her nose and squinted. "When Ronald opened the door to allow me in, I feared Ava might swoop in and ask him to sell his house. Can you imagine doing such a thing when he's in such a fragile state? Has she lost her marbles?"

"But she didn't swoop."

"No, she held back. Ronald and I had a nice chat, and when I left, Ava was gone."

"Z.Z." A large woman near the bleachers tapped her watch.

The mayor jiggled her bag of barbecue. "I have to get going. I'm here with my sister. She can be a tad bossy." She chuckled. "We're scheduled to see another round of the pole-bending event. It's incredible, you know. In the first race, a girl, no older than my sweet Janie would have been, tipped so much to one side I feared she and the horse might go down. Boom!" Janie would have been sixteen now. Z.Z. lost her at the age of two. If that wasn't enough of a blow, a few months later, Z.Z.'s husband, overcome with grief, left town. Two months after that, he tragically dropped dead. How she managed to stay cheery amazed me. She thrust out the hand holding the barbecue bag. "But surprise! Lickety-split, she was back around the next pole. Fastest time so far."

"Z.Z., let's go!"

"Bye, Jenna dear!" The mayor scuttled away.

Driving back to town, I dialed the precinct again. Cinnamon was not available. This time, I left a message for her saying I wanted to talk. I didn't add that I had a list of suspects ticking through my brain. Where would I begin: with Shane, Ava, or D'Ann? And what should I tell her about David? Maybe my father, despite his promise, had clued her in about him already. In fact, maybe Cinnamon was at my cottage right now, grilling David and ready to send him packing.

I sped home to check on David. Cinnamon wasn't there. I tiptoed inside in case David was sleeping. He wasn't. He was watching a cooking show on television; Tigger was nestled in his lap. I gawped at the two of them—the poster picture for serenity—and I wished with all my heart that I could turn back the clock. That David wouldn't be a criminal. That he wouldn't be dying. That we could put our lives back together and make a go of our marriage.

But wishes weren't horses. And there was Rhett to consider. I loved him. I was certain.

I closed the door loudly. David spun around and smiled weakly at me. His eyes were red-rimmed as if he'd been crying.

"Did you talk to your mother?" I asked.

"Not yet."

"Your sister?"

"I couldn't."

Maybe that was why he had been crying. I didn't press. He released Tigger. The little rascal leaped over the back of the couch and darted to me, nose raised, sniffing. Could he smell my worry and David's despair?

David stood, shoved a tissue into the pocket of his chinos, and scratched his thighs roughly. He wasn't allergic to cats. Was the itching a side effect of his illness? "I'm hungry. Want to get something to eat?"

"I could make us something."

"You?"

"I cook now."

"No kidding."

"I'm not a gourmet, but I'm adequate. Lots of things have changed." I didn't mean for the words to hurt him, but they hit their mark.

He winced but recovered quickly. "Let's go out anyway. I could use the fresh air. I heard it's dance hall night at your café."

"Who told you that?"

"Your aunt came over to check on me. She said she was getting vibes from the house."

"Good vibes?"

"She didn't say." He winked. "I didn't press."

THE STAFF AT The Nook Café had transformed the place since I left. The waitresses were dressed as cancan dancers with big skirts supported by petticoats. The waiters wore black trousers with pinstriped shirts and bow ties. Katie had rented a player piano; I remembered her asking if she could budget for it. Scott Joplin's jazzy "Maple Leaf Rag" was cycling through.

David and I sat at a table by the window. A waitress delivered a flight of craft root beers in short tasting mugs. Soon after, Katie sashayed to our table and introduced herself to David. In all the times that I had brought David to visit Crystal Cove, they had never met. That was my fault. Katie and I had lost touch until I officially moved back.

In typical Katie great-gusto fashion, she personally shared her menu. Pride gleamed in her eyes as she ticked off items. "You don't want to miss the cowboy steaks. Forty-two ounces of prime beef cooked to a deep pink and topped with blue cheese. Or try the beef-and-black-bean chili. It's great, with just the right amount of kick, if I do say so myself. And for dessert, a Dr Pepper cake that will knock your socks off. I found the recipe in a cookbook called *Grady Spears: The Texas Cowboy Kitchen*. Moistest cake I've ever made." She was also offering a taster menu, which is what we decided to go with. A little bit of everything.

David's appetite wasn't what it used to be. He complained of nausea and nibbled a few bites. We talked about the weather, about the Giants, and about people he had known at Taylor & Squibb. He asked how the last campaign that I'd worked on before moving to town had gone. I admitted it hadn't been fun. It was for Jump and Pump, an adult-sized pogo stick. The company had wanted a daring *Don't try this at home!* commercial. We hired a dozen extreme-loving teenage boys and girls who agreed to jump through a fiery hoop on pogo sticks. Their bravado quickly waned when they realized how hard the task was. We ended up recasting with real stunt performers. The commercial never aired.

Throughout dinner, David scratched his arms. Occasionally his head would twitch. After we ordered tea and dessert, David asked about my father. Dad had not checked in on David, as my aunt had, probably because she reported back to him and told him David wasn't a threat. How could he be? He was so completely different than he used to be. His fight was gone. As intuitive as my aunt is, she would have picked up on that in an instant.

"Dad's doing okay," I murmured, "last time I asked. Not incarcerated. Yet."

David removed the tea strainer from his teapot and set it on a side plate. "Tell me about all these dead bodies you keep stumbling over."

"What do you mean?"

"You've made headlines, hon. I've read about you in the

newspaper and on the Internet. You're pretty good at figuring out who did what."

"Don't believe everything you read."

"Did you really nail one suspect with a dinner plate?"

My cheeks warmed.

"All those games of Frisbee paid off," he joked and reached for my hand.

I moved it into my lap and glanced at the cell phone that I had left on the table. No text message from Rhett. No voice mail.

"Expecting a call from that guy you're seeing?" David tilted his head. "I saw you with him at the sing-along, and I heard you necking on the doorstep."

My cheeks warmed again. "Yes, I'd like him to . . . I'm sorry. It's rude of me to keep looking, but he . . . we had a fight, and—"

"What happened?"

"He's not happy with your reappearance."

David offered a tired smile. "I think only Detective Dyerson is." He sipped his tea and murmured, "Call him."

"I tried." I explained how Rhett and I had left things at the pole-bending event. Correction: how *he* had left things. By leaving.

"Jerk."

"No, he's not."

"You don't walk out when the conversation gets dicey."

"You did. Permanently."

David grumbled and dumped two lumps of sugar into his cup. He hated sugar in his tea.

"Bailey's boyfriend, Tito—" I hesitated. "You remember Bailey."

"How could I forget her? A spitfire."

"Tito said men need a cooling-off period."

"He's right. Remember that book we read? We'd been married three years. What was the name of it?" He snapped his fingers. "Oh, right. *Men Are from Mars; Women Are from Venus.* By that therapist. He said you have to keep the rubber band taut between a man and a woman. The woman has to give a man space."

He was referring to the passage where the therapist suggests that a man, typically, retreats into his cave. A woman, thinking she has done something wrong, sneaks into the cave. She wants to see if he's all right and whether she can *fix* the situation. The therapist suggests that a relationship needs good, healthy tension, and that the woman, in order to maintain that positive tension, needs to stay outside the cave so the man will come back out. The message was pretty basic, but I got the point.

"I'm not sure I can do that," I said.

"Sure you can. You're a master of it!" David leaned forward and winked at me. "Trust me, I know. You're doing it now, and I want you so badly I can taste it."

Chapter 17

WHAT COULD I say? At that moment, it was clear to me that I didn't feel the same way. Yes, I cared for David, but I also pitied him, and I didn't trust him, and I would never love him the way I had before. Ever.

When we returned to the cottage, the tension between us was thick. I kept my distance, allowing him to clean up first and settle onto the couch. He complained of a headache and a stomachache. I asked if he wanted some medicine. He didn't respond. Poor Tigger seemed torn between the two of us. Having found his calling as a therapy cat, he seemed concerned about David, as if staying by his side would keep David healthy. Ultimately, however, Tigger chose snuggling with me on my bed, and I felt an odd sense of satisfaction.

The next morning, even though I had slept fitfully, I awoke energized and ready to attack the day. I skipped my morning exercise, put on a pink-striped shirt and white jeans, and checked on David. He was sleeping, his breathing shallow, his eyes puffy, as though he had wept during the night. Tigger leaped onto the couch and tucked into David. Quietly I tickled his chin and praised him for being such a good, sweet boy.

Next, I cut up some fruit and left a bowl of it and a sliced bagel on the kitchen table for David with a note:

> *Tea and honey are in the cupboard. Call me when you wake. ~J*

And then, before heading to the shop, I followed an impulse and drove to The Pier. Rhett hadn't returned my call. He hadn't texted me. When I arrived home last night, I didn't feel it was appropriate to call and wake him. Now, I wanted to see him in person. To apologize. To let him know I had made my decision. I was going to start divorce proceedings. David would have to comply.

Unfortunately, Rhett wasn't at Bait and Switch. The sporty saleswoman said Rhett had called in late last night. He went out of town for the weekend.

I left heartbroken. Had he gone away to decide how he felt about me, to find the words to end *us*, whatever *us* was? By choosing to allow David to stay under my roof, had I made it impossible for Rhett to reach out to me? I called his cell phone; the call went instantly to voice mail.

In a funk, I slogged to Mum's the Word Diner. I needed comfort food and a strong cup of coffee before I could face the rest of the day. Luckily for me, I had beaten the Saturday morning crowd. I slipped onto a stool at the counter, perused the menu, and selected a zesty western omelet packed with ham, cheese, and red pepper flakes.

"'Morning, Jenna." Ronald Gump was sitting two spots to my right, eating alone. A fedora sat on the seat beside him. His cane hung over the back of the stool.

"I apologize, sir," I said. "I didn't see you there."

"I'm pretty invisible."

"I'm . . . sorry for your loss." What else could I say?

He nodded thanks. He didn't look as pale as he had the last time I'd seen him—his skin was ruddier—yet he seemed dog-tired. He took a bite of what looked like a ham and egg sandwich. Some sort of orange-colored sauce dribbled down Ronald's chin and onto his checkered shirt. He chuckled softly and muttered, "Slob."

"I think the Wild West week is making slobs of us all," I said, giving him an excuse. "I can't imagine how people kept clean back in the day, what with beans and gravy, and well . . ."

My unconvincing argument elicited a tepid smile. Using a napkin, he blotted the stain, then pushed his glasses higher on the bridge of his nose. The move made me flash on his testimony. Could he have seen well enough with those bifocals to determine who was fleeing from the fire?

"Sir, I apologize for asking, but you told the police you saw my father running—"

"I did!"

"Are you sure it was him? I mean, was it possible you saw someone else, maybe someone about the same size as my father? What if the culprit"—I didn't want to be crude and say *murderer*—"was a woman? Maybe Ava Judge. Do you know what her alibi was? Or what about D'Ann Davis? She loves the color red. I'll bet she owns a plaid jacket. Or how about Shane Maverick? Do you think there's any reason he might have wanted to hurt Sylvia? I heard a barbecue sauce bottle top was found at the crime scene. Did Sylvia serve Shane's steak sauce recently on the property?"

Ronald leveled me with a cold stare. "Young lady"—he tossed his napkin on the counter—"I thought you wanted to chat, not investigate. Let me grieve in peace."

"Yes, of course. I only—"

"Don't say another word." He threw a twenty-dollar bill on the counter, snatched his cane and hat, clipped a sunglasses cover on his bifocals, and hobbled out of the diner.

I blew out an exasperated breath. What had I been

thinking? How could I have been so heartless? That wasn't
me. But with my father in jeopardy and David back in my life—

"Jenna?" Rosie sashayed up to me, her brown-toned skin
gleaming with perspiration. A glazed purple flower adorned
her uniform. Purple sequined hair clips glistened in her hair.
"What happened?"

"I scared off Dean Gump."

Rosie clucked her tongue. "Don't worry, sugar. He'll be
back. He loves his barbecue, and he loves his onion rings,
too. Ronald runs rings around Rosie." She leaned forward,
bracing her palms on the counter. "By the by, do you know
what he revealed a few seconds ago? Not that I'm spreading
rumors or anything."

"Of course not." I leaned forward, eager to learn a secret.

"His wife received a text that morning to meet on the
bluff."

"From whom?"

"It was anonymous, and get this, the text didn't come
through on Sylvia's regular phone. It was on a what-do-you-
call-it phone, the kind you can toss away."

"A burner?"

"That's it!" Rosie stabbed the counter. "Now why didn't
I see that mentioned in the newspaper?"

"I'd bet the police would like to keep that quiet." I put
my finger to my lips.

"Oh, of course. Shh." She mimicked my warning. "Do
you want my two cents? Ronald looks—"

"Better. Stronger."

"Yes, of course, but that's because of the makeup. He
shouldn't wear it, in my opinion. It makes him appear older,
don't you think?"

"He's wearing makeup?"

"On his cheeks." She tapped three fingers on hers.
"Didn't you notice? Rouge!"

Aha! That was why Ronald had appeared ruddier to me.
"I think he's trying to fool the community that he's on

the mend," Rosie went on, "but he can't put one past me. No, sir. He's exhausted. Look at him." She fanned her hand and stared out the front window.

I followed her gaze. Ronald hadn't traveled very far from the diner after being upset with me. He was standing at the foot of the stairs, leaning on his cane, chatting with a lady in denim.

"He's lost without Sylvia," Rosie continued, "and without her to inspire him, he's feeling quite *off.* I heard he's going to retire."

"I heard that, too."

"I hope to heaven it's not true. My daughter is a student at the junior college, and she simply adores him. She says he's always on his toes; he knows everyone's business. Why, the other day when she ran into him on campus, he knew her name right off the bat, and he knew her grade point average down to a decimal point." Rosie spanked the counter. "Can you imagine a sharp man like that quitting? No, sir."

I glanced at him again, and something started to eat at me. The woman in denim batted her eyelashes. Ronald smiled. Was he flirting or was he faking interest? With the clip-on sunglasses, it was impossible to see if his eyes were smiling.

A wild thought flew into my mind. Rosie said Ronald was lost without Sylvia, and the mayor had said something similar when we chatted at the pole-bending event, yet I recalled how horridly Sylvia had treated Ronald at the movie theater the other night. Had she pushed him too far? Did he kill his wife so he could move on?

No, I cautioned myself. I was grasping at straws. I had so many suspects and no clue why Sylvia was killed. The *why* mattered. In order to clear my father, I had to figure out the killer's motive.

MY AUNT HAD arranged for Fisherman's Village to sponsor a special day for families during the Wild West Extravaganza week. True, independent contractors like the rope trick lady had held their events in the parking lot throughout the week, but Saturday was our special day. Aunt Vera had hired a group to bring in a petting zoo and a small train. Each was set up within a fenced perimeter. She had also hired valet parking attendants to shuttle attendees back and forth to a lot farther up Buena Vista Boulevard so no one would be inconvenienced.

By the time I arrived at the shop, the fun was already in high gear.

"This is the cleanest petting zoo I've ever seen," I heard one mother exclaim.

"Almost on par with Disneyland," another said. "I swear, those animals don't poop."

Inside the fenced area toddler children, with their hands stretched in front of them, cautiously approached groomed goats. No food was allowed. That was what made the goats, you know, *poop*.

The choo-choo train, which was painted with an adorable assortment of horses, tooted with a loud neigh. Every time it did, children applauded and begged for more.

Aunt Vera met me in the lot looking regal in a burgundy caftan. "Isn't this a hit?"

"Absolutely."

"That Shane Maverick is a magician. He suggested it."

Speaking of Shane, I caught sight of his betrothed, Emily Hawthorne, and a towheaded five-year-old boy I knew to be her nephew. They were standing near Beaders of Paradise, waiting in a long line to board the train. Emily looked sweet in her typically Brontë-esque fashion. The boy seemed entranced by the train. He was resting his hands and chin on the perimeter fence. Emily saw me and motioned for me to join her.

"Coming?" My aunt hitched her head toward the front door. Her turban bobbled. "We have a wealth of customers."

"In a sec. I'd like to say hello to Emily."

"Don't be long. There are a few clients waiting for me to tell their fortunes." My aunt hated to make anyone wait.

As I approached Emily, butterflies took up residence in my stomach. What could she tell me about Shane? Did he kill Sylvia to keep his affair with her a secret?

"'Morning." I smiled. "How's that baby doing?"

"Kicking to get out," Emily said in her dainty, girlish voice. "I think he wants to be a soccer player like his uncles."

"You said you have four brothers."

"That's right but only one nephew. My sisters-in-law, according to my mother, have to get the ball rolling. She wants at least ten grandchildren, two per family. It's funny, really. When I was growing up, all my mother did was carp about the fact that she'd had too many children." Emily chuckled and stroked her nephew's neck again. "Jenna, is it true?"

"Is what true, about your mother?"

"No, silly." Emily offered an amused grin. "Are you investigating Sylvia's murder?"

I sputtered. "Investigating?"

"Your father stands accused."

"He's innocent."

"He hasn't been arrested?"

"No, he—" A prick of panic shot through me. Had my father been arrested? Surely my aunt would have said something. If only Cinnamon would return my calls.

"Have you considered Ava Judge a suspect?" Emily asked. "She was terribly jealous of Sylvia."

"Really? Why?"

Emily bobbed her pretty head. "Ava and Shane were involved at one time, but then he set his sights on Sylvia."

Smack me as the sucker. Emily knew about Shane's affairs? And Ava was pre-Sylvia? I had reversed that order.

Emily laughed. "Don't look so stunned. I'm not as stupid as I appear."

"I never thought you were stupid."

"Naïve, then. Looks can be deceiving." She winked. "Need I remind you, I've got four brothers? I had to play the delicate little flower to get heard around my house. My mother said I was wily." She batted the air. "Anyway, here's how it went down with Ava. She met Shane and, like every woman who has met him, fell hard."

I hadn't.

"She became super jealous when she realized he had the hots for Sylvia."

"How can I ask this tactfully? Were you in the picture yet?"

"Shane and I dated, pre-Ava, but we broke it off because he was always in and out of town, and I wanted something steadier."

Wow! Emily was way more worldly-wise than Shane or I knew.

"So he started up with Ava," Emily said. "She was obsessed with him. She gave him all sorts of gifts. But two weeks into their fling, he hooked up with Sylvia. That woman could make men act like lapdogs."

Honestly? I couldn't fathom that. Sylvia was not your typical femme fatale.

"Ava got mad at Shane and said she was over him, but she was lying. She wanted to get even."

"How do you know all this?"

"She wrote about it in her diary."

"How do you know she has a diary?"

"Shane told me. See, back then, when Ava said they were finished, Shane didn't believe her, so he peeked in her diary, and, get this, Ava wrote that she would kill Sylvia if Shane ditched Ava for her."

"Did Ava mention you in the diary?"

"Shane didn't say, but he saw the diary way before we started up again. Until now, he'd disregarded it. Men can be such idiots."

I quickly computed Shane's dating timeline in my head.

First Emily, followed by Ava, followed by Sylvia, and returning to Emily.

"Knowing what you know about him, why did you take him back?"

"Because, well, I was with child, and truthfully, I love him." Her eyes grew dreamy. "If I'd known I was pregnant before, we never would have broken up in the first place."

"Are you sure he's telling the truth about the diary?"

"As sure as there's going to be a beautiful sunset tonight." She swept her arm across the sky. "Have we ever *not* had a beautiful sunset?"

Okay, she was officially naïve again. I said, "Emily, if Ava killed Sylvia, you could be in danger."

She shook her head. "Ava's feud was with Sylvia, not me. I don't think she would hurt me."

"Haven't you seen the movie *Fatal Attraction*?"

Emily's eyes widened. Apparently she hadn't considered the whole picture, as in, a jealous woman might be eliminating all the other women in her path.

"Were any of the gifts Ava gave Shane cuff links with his initials on them?" I asked.

"How would you know about those?"

I described the single cuff link I'd found at the crime scene.

"You went there? Won't the police—"

"Could it be Shane's?"

Emily nodded. "Ava purchased them at Sterling Sylvia. Oh no. What if . . ." Her mouth started to quiver. "What if Ava stole the cuff links from Shane and took them to the crime scene to frame him?"

Call me cynical, but I couldn't help thinking what if Emily, furious with her intended and his roving eye, took them there to frame him?

Chapter 18

I HURRIED INTO THE shop, threw my stuff into the stockroom, and settled in behind the sales counter. Aunt Vera
had already racked up a number of hefty sales. While I
dialed the precinct—yes, I tried to reach Cinnamon one
more time—I restocked our bookmarks. Marketing Tip 101:
always have handouts with a website or contact information
on the sales counter.

A minute after I spoke with the precinct clerk, Cinnamon
came on the line. Hooray!

"Jenna, I miss you when I don't get a voice mail from
you daily. No, let me revise that, *hourly*." Her voice dripped
with sarcasm.

I ignored her and quickly related what Emily had told
me about Ava's diary. Granted, I wasn't sure whether Emily
was telling the truth, but I had to at least convey the information to the police, right? No stone unturned, as they say.

Cinnamon didn't scoff; she didn't scold. Acting like the

professional she was, she said, "I'll look into it. Thanks for the tip. Gotta go."

She didn't mention David; neither did I.

It wasn't until later that I realized I didn't tell her what Tito had said at the pole-bending event. Shoot!

For the next two hours, I pitched and sold a ton of books, focusing mainly on barbecue. After all, that was why our tourists had come to town, to experience the Wild West. The bestselling cookbook was called *Barbecue Biscuits & Beans: Chuck Wagon Cooking*, perfect for cowboy enthusiasts. I had learned about it on a blog I read. The book includes the history of the chuck wagon plus tasty recipes and preparation secrets from a pair of guys who have cooked for presidents and celebrities. I also sold a number of copies of a cookbook by Melissa Gilbert—the freckle-faced actress from *Little House on the Prairie*—called simply *My Prairie Cookbook*, which offers behind-the-scenes stories and photos, plus comforting family recipes. I had no idea how many of my customers were fans of the show. Some got teary when they saw I'd stocked copies.

As lunchtime rolled around, my father checked in with me by telephone.

"ESP," I said. I had been thinking about him for the past hour.

He muttered, "Pshaw," about having extrasensory perception—maybe he said something coarser than *pshaw*— and then asked how it was going with David. I gave him a quick recap and thanked him for not telling Cinnamon about the situation. "I promise David will be heading to San Francisco soon." *Sooner*, if I gave him no encouragement to stay, and I wouldn't.

"Good. Will I see you at the horse racing event this evening?"

"I'll be there." I ended the call, and a pang of regret swizzled through me. Rhett was supposed to have escorted me to the event. For a brief instant, I was mad at him for expecting more of me than I could give. Was he a cut-and-run kind of guy? Should I forget about him and move on? He didn't seem like the overly dramatic type. Maybe he felt by giving me space—a *lot* of space—I could make the wisest decision. Well, I had. *So come back, darn it!* If only *he* had ESP.

"Are you talking to me?" Bailey slung a stack of books onto the counter.

"No." Had I said the words out loud? Oops.

"You know that talking to yourself is a sign you might be crazy."

"I'm definitely crazy, bordering on loony."

Bailey pushed the books toward me. "Here. Want to wrap these up? They're for Gran." She hooked her thumb at Gran, who had returned for the fourth day in a row, this time with two of her grandchildren.

"More?"

"Yep. She must purchase enough items to cover our rent. We love this woman!"

As I tallied the total and inserted the books into a shopping bag, Bailey said, "Want to tell me why you were talking to yourself?"

I filled her in about my situation. "Am I being too hard on David? Or on Rhett?"

"Guys," Bailey said. "They're difficult to understand. They want to be tough; they want to lean on us. I'd give them both a long leash."

I thought of the cave analogy David had shared last night and decided that was the best advice. Let Rhett come back to me; encourage David to move on.

"I'm going to ask David for a divorce," I said.

"In his fragile state?"

"Wrong thing to do?"

"Right thing, and he should expect it. By the way, I know a lawyer who could handle that for you." Bailey winked. She was alluding to her mother.

"I'll contact her."

"Treats!" Katie bellowed at the top of her lungs. She paraded into the shop carrying a tray of mini quiches. Customers swarmed her. By the time she made her way to the sales counter, there were two samples left. Bailey and I each snagged one.

"Yum!" I exclaimed. "I love the peppery flavor. What's the cheese, cheddar?"

"Yep. Direct from Texas."

I hummed and said, "Can you make me my own quiche for lunch?"

"I'll see what I can do." She pivoted to leave.

"Katie, wait. I have a question. David is feeling sort of nauseous. What do I give him besides Alka-Seltzer?" I have never mastered the art of nursing.

"Ginger ale or club soda, and crackers, bread, or toast, anything to absorb the acid. Old Man Powers suffered from nausea, too." Katie used to cook for a widower; he died in his nineties. Afterward, she came to us seeking employment. Were we ever lucky. "Also noodles loaded with butter might help, but make sure you give him plenty of protein. You don't want him to faint from carb overload."

When she left, I realized I hadn't heard from David. Maybe I had been too hard on him last night. I called the cottage, but he didn't pick up.

By the end of the day, when he hadn't checked in, worry gnawed at me. I closed up shop and hurried home. Tigger met me at the door, a look of concern on his face. David was there, on the couch, sound asleep. I roused him. He looked like he had slept all day. The food in the kitchen lay untouched.

"Are you okay?" I asked.

He scrubbed his hair. "You care."

"Maybe. A little." I did; I couldn't fool myself.

"You look pretty in pink." He offered a drowsy smile.

I smiled back. He had always liked me in pink. "Thanks. Do you have enough energy to go out?"

"Where?"

"To a horse race."

"Sure!"

"But only if you eat something."

He offered a dopey pout. "Aw, Mom!"

BUENA VISTA BOULEVARD was closed to through traffic. Red, white, and blue banners hung across the road in a number of spots. Tinsel sparklers were jammed into the huge flowerpots set along the sidewalk. A few vendors hawked fast food and drinks. Garbage cans were positioned every thirty feet so no one would have to walk far to deposit trash. A red rope strung through chrome posts kept people from moving onto the pavement.

A horde of spectators was gathering on both sides of the street. Most shops were remaining open and benefiting from the foot traffic. I spotted Ronald and his niece Tina chatting with Shane and Emily. Shane seemed to be telling them a story. Occasionally he patted Emily on the back, thwacked Tina on the arm, or aimed a finger at Ronald. In other words, he seemed his normal, friendly self, without a care in the world. Hadn't Emily told him about our conversation? Hmm.

David and I pulled to a stop outside The Pelican Brief Diner. Music spilled out, thanks to the saloon-style doors. A fiddler was playing a rousing rendition of "Hot Time in the Old Town Tonight." I considered entering the restaurant and seeking Lola's counsel regarding a divorce, but now was not the time. David was smiling; he seemed energized; he wasn't yawning or scratching. Why ruin the evening?

I purchased two spicy chicken shish kebabs from a street vendor and handed one to David. "Eat."

He saluted and chowed down.

As we were throwing away our sticks, a crowd member said, "It's starting."

"Look!" Another pointed. "There's the mayor."

Mayor Zeller, a pip-squeak at this distance, rose to the top of a platform near the center of town and spoke through a microphone: "Welcome, ladies and gentlemen. The race will begin in a few minutes." She pointed to an oversized clock behind the platform, the kind seen at Olympic events.

A string of sleek horses and their colorful jockeys proceeded slowly along the boulevard. Some people *ooh*ed; others applauded.

"Once the race starts," the mayor continued, "there will be no crossing the boulevard, so get in your positions, and stay there." She descended the platform.

"Jenna!" a woman called from behind me.

I spun around.

Cinnamon, looking pert in off-duty attire—crisp chinos, checkered shirt, and a sassy red bandana around her neck—was heading for me. She waggled her cell phone with her free hand. "I've been trying to reach you."

I had resigned myself to the fact that Rhett wasn't calling and had put my cell phone on mute. "Why?" I asked. "Am I in trouble?"

"Nope."

Phew!

She drew near and beamed. "A witness came forward, a *reliable* witness, who saw your father arrive at the lake Wednesday morning."

"Really?" Excitement bubbled up inside me, but I tamped it down. "How is that possible? Dad didn't see a soul. The witness must be lying."

"He's not. He was there. He has a favorite spot, out of view of the rest of the lake. He took me to it. It's definitely a hidey-hole with lots of fish." She beamed. "Fishermen rarely like to share that kind of secret."

"Why didn't he come forward earlier?"

"He went out of town that afternoon and didn't return until today. When he learned about the murder, he headed straight for the precinct."

"So Dad is exonerated?"

"Yes!" She high-fived me, then regarded David. "Who's this?"

I cut a quick look at him. He looked scruffy with his five o'clock shadow. Why hadn't he shaved? "Um . . ."

"A friend," David said, offering an impish smile.

"It's complicated," I added.

"That's okay," Cinnamon said. "Don't tell me. Is Rhett—" She shook her head. "Uh-uh, don't answer. That's none of my business." Rhett and Cinnamon had dated for a brief time before he was run in for arson at the restaurant where he had worked as chef. He didn't commit the crime, but being a suspect put a wrench in their relationship. Cinnamon investigated; Rhett pleaded innocent. They became enemies for a long stretch, but they mended that fence once she nabbed the real culprit—the restaurant owner. "Do you know where I'll find your father?"

"I haven't seen him yet. Maybe he's inside the diner." I jutted a finger. Before she could leave, I gripped her arm. "Cinnamon, wait. Did you find Ava Judge's diary?"

She hesitated and studied David again.

"He's okay," I said. "If he breathes a word, I'll kill him."

"Not remotely funny," Cinnamon said.

"It wasn't meant to be humorous."

Cinnamon assessed me, then cracked a smile. "Okay. Yes, we searched. We didn't find anything."

"Did she put up a fuss?"

"She opened her home to us."

Why had Ava been so amenable? Was she innocent?

"Maybe Ava destroyed the diary," I murmured.

"Jenna, cut it out," Cinnamon said. "Stop. You're done. Your father is off the hook. No more theorizing."

"What if she burned it in the bonfire?"

"Maybe Emily lied about the diary," Cinnamon countered.

"To what end?"

Cinnamon jammed her hands into her trouser pockets. "Whatever the reason, let it go. Please. It wouldn't matter if we had found it. Written words of vengeance wouldn't prove that Ava killed Sylvia."

"Does Ava have an alibi for that morning? Tito Martinez said—"

"Stop! What am I going to do with you?"

"Sylvia had an affair with Shane."

"Which he readily admits." She smirked. "Yes, I've talked to him, and, get this, his fiancée knows about it. Do you think Emily is guilty of murder?"

"No. Not in her condition. And no way would Ronald Gump think petite, pregnant Emily was my father, not even clad in a bulky plaid jacket. What about D'Ann Davis? Did you ask her about the fabric found at the crime scene? You went and examined that, right?"

Cinnamon sighed.

"I told you before that D'Ann wears those hair thingies." I rotated my hand near the back of my head. "Like the weapon used—"

"That's it." Cinnamon held up a hand to cut me off. "I'm done. I have a list of viable suspects. Enough said."

"Aren't you frustrated?"

"Not nearly as much as I was when your father was a suspect. Now that he's in the clear, my team can bear down and get this killer. You, by the way, are not on my *team*." She offered a wounding grin and, without another word, spun on her heel and entered The Pelican Brief Diner.

David chuckled. "Hon, you haven't lost your ability to tick people off, have you?"

"Don't call me hon."

He threw his hands up. "Just saying. Have you forgotten that I lived through a few of your Supergirl quests at Taylor & Squibb?"

My boss used to say to me, *Jenna, my darling, you are like Supergirl, always on a mission. Cool your jets. Or should I say cape?* I didn't mind. In fact, I'd taken pride in the taunt. But now? I didn't mean to irk Cinnamon. I needed her as my ally.

"Occasionally you do try to wring blood from a turnip," David added.

"So?" I sniped, hating him for being right.

"Watch your adorable backside. You're liable to infuriate someone. Maybe even the killer."

Miffed, I swung away from him. I peered up the street and was surprised to see Shane and Emily staring at me. She looked downright peeved. Didn't she realize I would tell the police about the diary? It wasn't like she had sworn me to secrecy.

A few feet short of them, I caught sight of Ava. She waved, probably thinking I was looking at her, and jogged toward David and me, high heels clacking the sidewalk.

"Hello," she said to David as she arrived. She flipped her highlighted hair over her shoulder, flashed a brilliant smile, and thrust out her hand. "I'm Ava Judge." She sounded so professional, I expected her to whip out a business card. She was wearing a beautiful blue suit. Had she recently shown property? "And you are . . ."

"David," he said, no last name.

"David," she repeated. "You're new here. Planning to settle in town?"

"I'm visiting." He bit back a yawn and covered it with his fingertips. "Jenna, I need to lean against something." He moved to the wall of the restaurant.

Ava cocked her head. "Is he okay?"

"Tired."

"Hey"—Ava tapped my elbow—"I heard your father is cleared."

"Who told you?"

"My client is the one who cleared him." She pointed up the street to where she had been standing. A sixty-something man with a thick nose, crinkly eyes, and a bushy beard was gazing at us. He wiggled his fingers. "That's Mandy Patinkin."

"The actor in the TV show *Homeland*?"

Ava chuckled. "No, I'm joshing. That's not him. But he looks like him, doesn't he?"

He did.

"He's such a sweetie. A plumber. Hardworking as the day is long. This afternoon he bought the three-bedroom on Poinsettia." Ava licked her ruby red lips. "So who else does Chief Pritchett suspect?"

"She has a list." Even though Cinnamon told me to back off, curiosity was stampeding through my mind. "And you're on it." Cinnamon hadn't told me who was on her list, so it wasn't technically a lie.

Ava placed a hand on her chest. "How could I be?"

"You were seen in the vicinity of the Gumps' house on the morning Sylvia died. Right around dawn."

"Says who? Emily Hawthorne?" Ava huffed. "That girl has it in for me. Can you believe she hasn't even stepped foot inside the house she's going to live in? Honestly."

"Actually, no, it wasn't Emily."

Ava rubbed the underside of her nose. "Who then?"

"It was somebody else."

"Somebody with bad eyes," Ava hissed. "I wasn't there."

"He has excellent eyesight."

"In the waning morning light? Maybe he saw D'Ann or any number of neighbors. There are a lot of women in the area who are my size. In the dark, I would bet we all look the same." She jutted a hip. "Did he say I was wearing a red plaid jacket?"

I didn't deny or confirm. "He said you were traipsing around Shane Maverick's future house. That happens to be right next door to the Gumps'."

"I wasn't."

"Where were you then? Have you told the police?"

"They were at my house earlier."

Asking about her diary. "Ava, did you—"

A gun fired! Horses with riders tore down the boulevard. The crowd cheered.

At the same time, the swinging saloon doors flew open. A thin, short man hurtled between Ava and me and fell against the barrier rope. The stench of beer followed him. The chrome posts teetered. A few around us screamed.

The man regained his footing.

Another man, twice the size of the first, materialized in the doorway, fists raised. His beefy face was flushed. He growled at the smaller man, who shrieked and grabbed me. He positioned me in front of him as a shield.

"Let me go!" I ordered, my insides roiling with indignation. I stomped on his toe, but he didn't relent.

"Jenna!" David lurched off the wall and wrenched me out of the man's grip. He whirled me to one side.

"Break it up!" Cinnamon squeezed past the hulking man in the doorway and flashed her badge at him and his buddy. "That's it, fellas. You're cut off."

"Yes, ma'am" and "Sorry, ma'am" flew from their mouths.

By the time Cinnamon subdued the two men, I realized we had missed seeing the horse race.

And Ava had fled.

Chapter 19

A S I DROVE home, David kept asking me if I was all right. I was rattled by the ruckus, but I was more worried about him. He was doing his best not to let me see, but his hand was shaking. At the shop today, during a few spare moments, I had read up on chronic kidney failure symptoms; itching, nausea, and tremors were all signs of advancement.

When we entered the cottage, David said he was hungry, so I made a quickie snack using leftover hash. I had thrown together a batch a week ago and stored it in the freezer. Hash is so simple to make—only four ingredients; six, if you consider the spices. While I defrosted it, I baked twelve-minute biscuits. Easy-peasy and scrumptious. To me, there was almost nothing more soothing than warm biscuits slathered in butter. And I needed soothing.

Tigger ate his food and circled my ankles, expecting more.

I nudged him with my toes. "No way, Tig-Tig," I cooed.

"We don't want you to get so fat you can't chase the kiddies at the store."

After dinner, David and I didn't talk about the incident. We didn't discuss his symptoms. We kissed each other pristinely on the cheek and headed to our separate sleeping arrangements: me on the bed, he on the couch.

The resounding clang of church bells woke me early Sunday morning. One of these days, I would get around to visiting the Congregational church not far from my house. It was one of the loveliest I had ever seen with tall white spires and elegant stained glass. I'd heard that from inside one could take in the view of the ocean, which had to be distracting when listening to the sermon. On the other hand, perhaps it helped parishioners embrace the beauty of God's work.

I crept out of bed. My nightie had torqued around my midriff. I tugged it down over my thighs and checked on David. He was sleeping. Then I glanced at my cell phone: no message from Rhett. Drat!

Not hungry and in desperate need of a physical outlet, I put off my walk/run on the beach, donned shorts, tank top, and boots—a real fashion statement—and dragged the coil of rope and spurs from my VW. Yes, I was going to attempt the Texas skip wearing spurs.

For a brief moment, I wondered if the *clink-clink* of the spurs would wake David or the neighbors, but then decided the caws of the seagulls and the peal of church bells were way louder than I could ever be. I proceeded.

This time I was better at spinning the rope. It looped out and held fast about a foot above the ground. Like Bailey showed me, I slung it up and sideways, so that it became a loop large enough to leap through.

I recalled a jump-rope song I sang in the second grade and, though I felt foolish, started singing: "Down in the valley where the green grass grows, there sat Jenna—" I snagged the spurs on the rope and had to restart. Twirling, swirling.

"Down in the valley . . ." By the time I reached the phrase, "as pretty as a rose," I was doing well, passing through the loop without missing a beat. "She sang so high, she sang so sweet." Here was the part where the jumper added the name of the boy she liked: "Along came Rhett and kissed her on the cheek. How many kisses did she get? One, two, three, four."

I counted to twenty before I stopped. My heart was beating hard. I was perspiring. I took a breather and then did another round of the song. When I hit twenty again, I stopped and packed up the rope. Twenty kisses from Rhett would be nice, I mused as I removed the spurs and set them and the rope in the trunk of the car. Soon I would fix things with him—unless, of course, he was a stubborn dweeb who didn't deserve my adoration.

In the meantime, I looked in on David again. He was awake but sluggish. I made oatmeal drenched in brown sugar and cream and added sliced bananas. I poured him a big glass of water to keep him hydrated, and we talked briefly about his plans. He intended to head to San Francisco in two days. He wanted a little more time with me. No, he didn't expect to win my love or even my respect, but he was worried that there was a killer on the loose, and he, even though he was weaker than a slug, would defend me.

"If he finds out you've been poking around," David went on.

"He . . . or she . . . won't."

"You haven't been keeping your interest a secret, and that Ava Judge sure hightailed it in a hurry last night."

She had, and I'd wondered about that. Had the brawl scared her, or had I with my questions?

"Don't worry," I said. "I'll keep a watchful eye."

I washed the dishes and pointed to the bookshelves. "While you're resting today, read." David had always been an avid reader like me. "When I get home, we'll have dinner with my family."

He snorted.

"We always have dinner Sunday nights. You're coming," I said, not willing to budge. "Afterward, we'll pin down your plans." I would be sad to see him go, sadder to see him die, but I'd made my good-byes years ago. It was time to move on.

Keeping tears at bay, I dressed in an orange silk sweater, floral capris, and glossy orange sandals. Soon after, I scooped up Tigger and headed to work.

Bailey dashed to me as I was stowing my purse behind the register; she held a box from the stockroom. "I heard about your dad. Yeehaw! Cleared. I told your aunt."

Aunt Vera was in the children's corner, tying bandanas to the backs of the miniature chairs. A stack of white place mats sat in the middle of the table.

"What's she doing?" I asked.

"An impromptu art project for kids. A couple of mothers called in and begged for an activity." She gestured to the table. "The place mats have outlines of cowboys and cowgirls that the children can color. I think Vera also hired a guitarist to come in and sing songs."

Bailey set the box she was carrying on the counter. I peered inside. It was filled with cowboy-themed salt-and-pepper shakers. She lifted out a set consisting of a three-inch-tall white horse and black horse. "Check these out. They're magnetic. Isn't that cool?" She pulled them apart and let them snap back together. "I showed your aunt, but she thought they were silly. You don't think they are, do you?"

"Silly sells." I knew a girl in college whose mother had collected over one hundred salt-and-pepper shaker sets. She was a world traveler and had bought a pair on each of her trips. "Good morning, Aunt Vera," I called. She didn't respond; her mouth was moving as she continued her project. "Earth to Vera!" I yelled.

She startled and laughed. "Good morning, dear."

"Who were you talking to?" I teased.

"The usual suspects." She winked.

"When are the kids due to arrive?"

"Before noon." She wiggled a finger. "I put a stack of that adorable book called *Cowboy and Cowgirl Parties* written by that local author over there." She didn't have a free hand. She swung her chin toward the vintage table. "Set them out, will you?"

The local author, an effervescent woman with endless energy—she leads the PTA and most of the other child-related organizations in town—had put together a beautiful, self-published book with dozens of ideas for cowboy-themed parties: root beer bottles topped with tiny straw hats; cupcakes with gamblers' names scrawled in icing; recipes for tasty treats like Rio Grande Lemonade and cowboy potstickers; plus she shared a variety of ways to design and decorate cowboy- and cowgirl-themed cakes. She had begged us to sell a few of her books on consignment during the Wild West Extravaganza. How could we say no? She hadn't skimped on quality.

When I finished rearranging, Bailey said, "Now, help *me*."

I set a porcelain pair of kissing cow salt-and-pepper shakers by the fiction books and placed an intertwined pair of boot salt-and-pepper shakers on the round table filled with hardcover, pictorial books. The boots were silly, true, yet they were charming, and customers would be drawn to *charming* and then discover the nearby books, or vice versa.

While we orbited the store, Bailey said, "Tell me about last night. My mother said a man held you like a shield outside the restaurant."

"What?" Aunt Vera squawked from across the room. "Jenna, what happened?"

I explained the outbreak. "The littler guy didn't want the bigger guy to hit him. I think he figured I was taller, and he could hide behind me." Maybe he had nabbed me because I was the first thing he could grab, and female, and he figured his pal wouldn't hit a woman. "David saved me."

"Your hero," Bailey teased.

"Cut it out."

"Yes, do," Aunt Vera said. "No joking about that, Bailey. Now, dear, how is David?"

"Sicker," I replied.

"When is he heading north?" Bailey asked. "You are making him leave, right?"

"I've given him no encouragement to stay."

"And yet there he is. In your cottage. Did you mention the divorce?"

"Divorce?" Aunt Vera echoed.

"No." How could I? He had seemed so frail this morning, plus he wanted to stick around to defend me. "I will later today."

"And then you'll call Rhett."

"*Rhett*," I sniped. "The stinker." He had graduated from *dweeb*. "I've called him. He hasn't returned my calls."

"Because you haven't started divorce proceedings." Bailey scooped up the magnetic horse shakers she had placed beside the sugar-free cookbooks and waggled them in my face. "Those are the magic words: *I've filed for divorce*. I'm telling you, when Rhett hears that, he will come galloping back."

"I think he might need to hear it's final, not simply in process."

"Quickie divorces are easy if they're uncontested. You go to the courthouse, and—"

"I'm not so sure ours can be quick. David hasn't lived officially in the state for a long time." Before going to sleep, I had reviewed some Internet sites.

"Well, Tito said—"

"Hey, about Tito." I gathered the box and headed toward the stockroom, eager to end the discussion about David. When I returned to the register, I repeated, "About Tito . . ."

"What about him?" Bailey asked.

"Are you sure he saw Ava the morning Sylvia was killed?"

"Why?"

"She swears she wasn't in the area."

"You heard him. His eyesight is *perfecto*, and I believe him. When he took me big-game fishing—"

"You? Went big-game fishing? When?"

"A couple of weeks ago. Don't look so surprised." Bailey liked to sail, but she refused to work the rigging. She might break a nail. I couldn't imagine her handling one of the reels required for big-game fishing, which meant she was truly, hopelessly in love. "Anyway," she went on, "he could see the fish coming from a mile away. 'There!' he would shout, and *there* it was. He's very attentive. If he says he saw Ava, he saw her."

"Okay. Don't get snippy." I held up my hands.

Aunt Vera stopped decorating the children's corner and joined us. "What are all these questions about Ava?"

"Jenna knows something about Ava"—Bailey gave me the evil eye—"and it's not because she was seen near the crime scene. Spill, Jenna."

"I was asking her about her alibi when the fracas broke out."

"Why did you want to know her alibi?"

I mentioned the missing diary and how Ava had written that she wanted to kill Sylvia.

"According to Emily," Bailey said.

"Right, but before Ava answered, the guys started the brawl, the race got under way, and Ava vanished."

"Which means she's guilty."

"Or it means she didn't want to be taken hostage, too," Aunt Vera said reasonably.

I thought about touching base with Ava, yet a little voice in my head—that sounded distinctly like Cinnamon—was warning me to back off. It was not my fight. Dad was free.

"You need to find the diary," Bailey suggested.

"Me? No, the police do, and they *tried*, but Ava said it didn't exist, and Cinnamon believed her, and anyway, Cinnamon dismissed the idea that finding the written word would help."

"The written word would establish motive," Bailey said.

"Not necessarily," my aunt said. "For years, I've kept a diary. Believe me, it's not all true. Some of it is fantastical and filled with my hopes and my dreams."

I didn't know what was more astounding to me, to learn that my aunt wrote in a diary or that she was admitting that she wrote in one. She kept the details of her life close to the vest.

"Where do you keep it?" I asked. "Tucked beneath your mattress?" Maybe one day I'd sneak over and . . . *No. Nope. Never.* I couldn't invade her space. I treasured her too much. In time, she would tell all.

"Heavens, no. I keep it with me," Aunt Vera said, "so if I want to jot in it, I can." She twirled a finger at me like a wand. "And so people like you can't steal into my house and sneak a peek when I'm not looking."

Could she read my mind? Yes, I was pretty sure she could. I returned my focus to Ava. What secrets were in her diary? What could it reveal about her and Shane and Sylvia? If I told Cinnamon about my exchange with Ava last night—

Willpower, Jenna. No calling Cinnamon.

To distract myself, I concentrated on the business at hand: organizing shelves, restocking our gift bags, and packaging preorders that customers had made either over the telephone or via our website. By noon, I was ready for a good hearty meal.

As I made my way toward the café to find Katie and ask her what she had to eat, the front door burst open.

Lola bustled inside, hair askew, the flaps of her light-weave sweater twisted about her shimmery silver tank dress. She pressed a hand to her chest and blurted, "D'Ann!"

"She's not here," I said.

"I know that." She drew in huge gulps of air. Had she run to the shop? "She's at my restaurant. I'm worried about her."

"Why?" Bailey asked. "Is she stuffing her face? Actresses have to watch their weight. No fried foods. No heavy carbs. The potatoes at the diner are impossible to pass up."

"No." Lola glowered at her daughter. "It's not food. She's very strict about that. She's drinking coffee."

"I'm not following then," Bailey said.

I wasn't, either.

"Mom, spit it out," Bailey ordered.

"She's——" Lola glanced around. A few customers had trailed her in. Lola corralled us and moved us toward the stockroom. "She's mumbling to herself, and her eyes . . . they're wild."

"Is she on drugs?" Bailey asked.

"I can't tell. I've never been good at determining——" Lola worried her hands together. "I'm afraid she——"

"Might hurt herself?" I cried.

Aunt Vera moaned. "I knew there was something wrong." She stroked the amulet that was partially hidden beneath her bandana. "I was picking up bad vibes at her tarot reading."

I recalled how frantic D'Ann had seemed the other day, and yet after the quickie reading, she had left the shop looking triumphant.

"Lola," my aunt continued, "lead the way. Jenna, you're coming with us."

I balked. "D'Ann won't want me there."

"Three voices of reason are better than two for an intervention," Lola said.

"An intervention?" I yelped.

"I agree." Aunt Vera nabbed my arm, obviously not taking no for an answer. "Bailey, can you manage the shop on your own?"

"You bet I can."

THE PELICAN BRIEF Diner was one of my favorite places. Sawdust lay on the blond wood floors. Rustic booths lined the perimeter. Tables and chairs filled the center of the restaurant. A balcony, also set with tables, faced the ocean. A week ago, Rhett and I had sat out there enjoying a glass of wine and recapping our respective days. A pang of sadness zipped through me; I missed him. But right now wasn't about *me*.

Lola led the charge across the restaurant. She said, "That way," and surged forward. The hostess asked her if everything was okay, but Lola didn't slow down.

The place was buzzing with activity. Happy chatter abounded. For the Wild West Extravaganza, the diner was offering a dollar-a-shot whiskey tasting; a passel of men and women had congregated at the rustic bar to the right.

"There she is," Lola said.

D'Ann, dressed in a cherry-red silk dress, her hair in a knot on top of her head, sat by herself at a table for four. She was gripping a coffee cup and looking for all intents and purposes like the Wells Fargo stagecoach had been robbed with all her money on board. A red clutch purse lay on the table to her right. Beside it was a paperback culinary mystery that I had sold her. Unread. No bookmark. No dog-eared pages. Blithely, I thought if we could encourage her to peruse a few pages, maybe she could find the fun in life again.

Lola motioned for Aunt Vera and me to sit down. Aunt Vera settled onto the seat opposite D'Ann. I chose the chair to the left of her. Lola took the final seat.

D'Ann glanced up. Her cheeks were puffy and tear-stained. Her pupils were pinpoints. Was she high? When I'd worked at Taylor & Squibb, we had hired an actress for a lipstick commercial—a svelte older beauty; you would know her if I gave her initials. She showed up to the shoot as lethargic as a sloth. She could barely remember a line. And she wept, nonstop. It turned out she was addicted to pain pills. We had to send her home and recast. Talk about unhappy clients.

My aunt reached across the table and touched D'Ann's fingertips.

D'Ann pulled her hands into her lap. Fresh tears pooled in her eyes.

"Tell us what's going on, dear," Aunt Vera said.

"I—" D'Ann peered at Lola and then my aunt and me. "There are three of you."

At least she could count.

"Are you on drugs?" Lola asked.

"What? No!" D'Ann gasped. "Whatever gave you that idea?"

"You look . . ." Lola twirled a finger.

D'Ann pried open her purse, pulled out a compact mirror, popped it open, and examined her face. "Gawd," she moaned. "No wonder . . ." She blinked at us. "Is that why you're here? To talk me off the ledge? No, I don't have a drug problem, and I'm not contemplating suicide." Using a pinky, she wiped under her eyes, rechecked herself, and clicked the compact closed.

"What's going on, then?" Aunt Vera asked, her voice stronger, less delicate.

"If you must know, I'm broke. Flat broke."

I flashed on my Wells Fargo robbery scenario, surprised at how close I'd come to the truth. Maybe I did have psychic abilities. I said. "How could you be? You're a star."

"Star!" D'Ann moaned. "My last picture was a bomb, and I didn't take a salary. I opted for a piece of the gross. Vanity led me to believe it would be a smash hit. It was garbage." She offered a weak smile. "I came up here to sell the house—it's my second home—hoping the proceeds would get me out of debt. I had an all-cash buyer lined up, a budding Italian starlet. She was staying at the house last weekend. She wanted to make sure she loved it as much as I do. But then she heard Sylvia's party and watched me go ape, and she pulled out of the deal. *Finito!*" D'Ann brushed her hands together. "I was so angry at Sylvia. She knew . . . *knew* . . . I was selling. I told her I was in dire straits. She had that party on purpose, the vindictive—"

"And that infuriated you," I cut in.

"Yes!"

I recalled Gran's statement. She said D'Ann had warned Sylvia to *fix it*. Gran believed Sylvia had sold D'Ann paste. At the tarot reading at the shop, D'Ann admitted that Sylvia had sold her inferior goods. I had put D'Ann's motive on the back burner, but now . . .

I revisited my theory regarding Ava when I'd wondered whether Sylvia's disturbances might make a difference in sales in the neighborhood, thereby affecting Ava's livelihood. Had D'Ann suffered the same fate but on a much more personal level? After the neighborhood meeting on Monday night, did D'Ann work herself into a frenzy? Did she think that by killing Sylvia she could get her buyer back and convince the starlet it was okay to purchase the house? Though she was lean, D'Ann would have had the strength to overpower Sylvia. Anyone who has watched her in *Sinz of the City* would agree.

I said, "D'Ann, you were seen outside your house on the morning Sylvia was killed. You were tossing white things on the ground."

"So?"

"The person who saw you said it appeared to be a ritual."

"What are you getting at?"

"Were you performing some act to give you courage to confront Sylvia?"

D'Ann's gaze flew from me, to my aunt, to Lola, and back to me. "Are you implying that I murdered Sylvia? I didn't. What that person saw, whoever it was, was me preparing for a spiritual journey to the top of the mountain. Whenever I'm in town and I need rejuvenation, I go there before sunrise." She stroked her neck as if she were trying to rid it of wrinkles. "I needed to pray for a miracle. Another job. Something to bail myself out of the hole I'd created.

"That morning," she continued, "I wrote my regrets on a piece of white paper, and, as I always do, I tore up the paper and did a tap dance on the remains. It's nonsense, I know, but my guru makes me do it every time. It's a way to cleanse

my soul. To make me fresh. To make me sparkle." She fluttered her hands to illustrate *sparkle*. "Out with the old, in
with the new. You understand, don't you?" She chopped one
hand with the other. "If you're broke, you don't sparkle. You
appear desperate, and trust me"—she stabbed the table with
a finger—"there's nothing a director hates more than an
actress showing up to an audition looking desperate."

D'Ann met each of our stares. Her lower lip began to
quiver. "I promise you, I did not kill Sylvia. I was at the top
of the mountain by a quarter to six. I know because that was
when the sun rose that morning. It's true. You've got to
believe me." She covered her mouth with her hand and
gulped back a sob, and I recalled the first movie I'd ever seen
her in called *Get Real*. To make her costar believe what she
was saying, D'Ann had made the exact same gesture. Was
she acting now?

Chapter 20

MY AUNT SCOOTED her chair closer to D'Ann and said, "Jenna, dear, go back to the shop. Lola and I have this covered."

Did they? Was D'Ann snowing them? I didn't argue. Once my aunt laid down the law, I obeyed. I wasn't a pushover, just smart.

I left The Pelican Brief Diner and started toward Fisherman's Village, but I made a U-turn when I saw my father walking quickly along the sidewalk on the opposite side of the street. I dashed to him. "Dad!"

He didn't hear me and entered Nuts and Bolts, his hardware store. I hurried after him.

"Dad!" I called out as I raced into the long and narrow shop. As always, it was as neat as a pin. Streamlined shelves, each categorized with labels made from one of those label machines, held multiple boxes of screws, nails, and whatnot. I glanced at the plaque with the Seneca quote hanging on the wall behind the checkout counter: *The primary sign of a well-ordered mind is a man's ability to remain in one place and linger in his own company*, and I smiled. Yes, a well-ordered mind; that was what I needed. "Dad!" He had disappeared into the stockroom.

He came out scrubbing the back of his neck. "Hi, Tootsie Pop. What's up?"

"Congratulations, you're cleared!"

"I heard."

"Why aren't you doing a happy dance then?" I hurried around the counter and embraced him.

"Because it was to be expected, and as you know, I don't get overly excited about anything."

Did I ever!

"My highs are not too high; my lows are not too low," he said. "That's the FBI way. You should—"

I placed a fingertip on his mouth. "Celebrate. You're cleared."

He inhaled, then exhaled and sagged against me. I felt his chest heave, but he didn't cry. He wouldn't. We shared a long moment, but when the door to the shop opened and a pair of customers entered, my father pushed me to arm's length and whispered, "Get back to work. Love you." He hitched his head, signaling I should split.

I mock-frowned. "Heaven forbid you show a little emotion to those folks."

He chuckled. "Go. I'll see you tonight at dinner. And be glad I didn't ask for an account of David."

I shot a finger at him. "I'm handling it."

"Good."

As I exited, a crowd of people waving American flags nearly plowed into me. I tried the doorknob to Nuts and Bolts so I could retreat inside. Somehow it had locked behind me, and neither my father nor his customers heard me knocking. Swell.

Struck with a minor case of claustrophobia, I clung to the walls of the buildings as I moved with the swarm southward.

I heard someone call my name and scanned the throng. Tina, Ronald Gump's niece, was in the mix. So was Shane, who stood out, not just because he was tall but because his cowboy hat made him that much taller. He waved to me and shouted my name again. I acknowledged him and then ducked into the alcove of Artiste Arcade to wait out the onrush.

THE CROWD WAS following a mini parade on Buena Vista Boulevard that consisted of three cowgirl-attired women, each standing atop a brown-and-white pinto horse. Each of the horses was fitted with a beautiful red, white, and blue flower wreath. Each cowgirl carried an American flag.

Behind the trio materialized a pair of similarly dressed women, also standing atop brown-and-white pintos. Together, they held a banner announcing: *Come join in the Amazing Americana Bash at The Pier.*

While biding my time, a conversation in the doorway of the Sterling Sylvia jewelry shop caught my attention.

"You don't want to sell?" a woman asked shrilly. I knew the voice. "Fine. Good day." Ava, in an exquisite blue suit and Manolo Blahnik heels, was exiting. She hitched her purse higher on her shoulder.

"Wait!" a man yelled.

Ava pivoted and reentered.

I crept to the display window, which was gorgeously decked out with silver necklaces, earrings, candlesticks, and mirrors. Sylvia might have been a miserable woman, but she had such good taste. I peeked past all the lovely choices and spotted Ronald Gump standing next to the sales counter. His skin still appeared ruddy. His bearing seemed stronger. He had hung his cane on a rack by the register.

Ava strode to Ronald and ogled him. A hungry smirk grew on her face. What was going on?

"How much?" Ava asked.

"Five million," he said.

Ronald and Sylvia's house was worth around a million and a half dollars. They weren't talking about that. Was Ronald putting the shop up for sale?

"Five. That's not a steal like you promised, Ronald." Ava moved toward Ronald and stopped short. She tilted up her chin and grinned. "On the other hand, I've always had a fondness for this place."

Wow. I could understand Ronald wanting to divest himself of the asset, but why to Ava, Sylvia's nemesis?

Boldly Ava ran a finger along Ronald's jaw. She let it linger on his lips. He didn't bat it away. Was he interested in her? I wondered again whether he might have killed Sylvia so he could start a new life as a single man. The theory evaporated when he batted Ava's hand away and turned on his heel. He moved to a glass and mirror étagère at the side of the room and began rearranging a set of silver deer antler–style earring holders. Suddenly, he glanced over his shoulder toward the door.

I ducked to the side, out of sight. Had he seen my reflection in the étagère's mirror?

I didn't hear footsteps. He wasn't moving toward the door. I continued to listen.

Ava laughed. "This is quite an opportunity, Ronald. I feel so privileged that you contacted me."

He cleared his throat. "You called me."

"So I did," Ava said, her tone husky and alluring. Was she making a play for him? Maybe my assumption about why she would have wanted Sylvia dead was faulty. What if she killed Sylvia to clear the way for a union with Sylvia's husband? Did she write about *that* in her diary?

Aunt Vera said she always kept her diary close at hand. What if Ava lied to the police about not having a diary because it wasn't *in* the house at the time? What if she had stowed it in, say, her briefcase, which, when she's not carrying it, she typically leaves in her car? *Just the facts, ma'am.*

I scanned the store for Ava's briefcase. I didn't see it sitting on the floor; it wasn't on top of a display case.

Abandoning my eavesdropping venture, I jogged toward the alley behind Artiste Arcade where there were a few free parking spaces for customers. I wasn't going to break and enter Ava's car—I knew my limits—but if the briefcase was there, and if it was open and bulging with real estate material as it usually was, maybe I could peer inside and glimpse the spine of a diary. If so, I would call Cinnamon and suggest she interrogate Ava before Ava could do away with the diary. It was worth a shot.

Ava owns a black Mercedes CLS. She calls it her symbol of success. And there it was. Sun blazed down on the sleek car. I shielded my eyes from the glare and peered through the window into the front seat. The briefcase, as hoped, was sitting on the passenger seat and jam-packed: a wad of flyers; pens; pencils; a large measuring tape coiled into a silver case; an ultra fancy calculator, the kind Realtors use to assess mortgage rates; a wad of business cards held together with a rubber band; and, lo and behold, a red-spined book, about seven inches long, one inch thick. Was it a diary or an appointment calendar?

"Jenna," a man said.

I spun around. "Shane."

He approached quickly, the fancy buttons on his cowboy shirt reflecting the sunlight, his tennis shoes making no sound on the pavement. He looked *off*; his eyes were beady. A thin sheen of perspiration coated his upper lip and forehead. He rubbed it away with a fingertip.

"Fancy seeing you here," I said, my voice light though my body was tense.

"You heard me calling you," he said. "On the street. You waved."

Yes, I'd heard him, but I believed he was calling as a greeting, nothing more.

Furtively, Shane glanced over his shoulder and back at me. Call me crazy, but a frisson of fear skittered down my back. Was he Sylvia's killer, after all? Had he followed me because I was alone? Did he think I knew something that could point a finger at him? The alley was open at the far end. I could run, but in my sandals I would be no match for Shane with his long, muscular legs. He would catch me in an instant.

"Need something?" I said as calmly as I could muster. I gripped my purse handle while letting the strap fall off my shoulder. As heavy as the purse was, it might pack a wallop.

"Actually, I do." Shane licked his lips. "It's about Emily."

Relief coursed through me. "Is she okay? Is she having the baby?"

"No!" he barked, as in *heaven forbid!* He worked his lip between his teeth. "Sorry, that came out wrong. No, she's not having the baby. Not yet. She's . . . it's . . ." He shifted feet. "She's been acting weird."

"Weird, how?"

"Pacing at night and muttering to herself."

"Can you make out what she's saying?"

"I think she's saying *clinky jewelry.* What could she mean?"

When I spoke to Emily by the choo-choo train, we discussed the set of cuff links Ava had given Shane. *Cuff links and jewelry*, when slurred together, might sound like *clinky jewelry.* Was Emily worried that the police wouldn't come up with the same theory she had posed to me, that Ava had taken the cuff links to the crime scene to frame Shane? Perhaps Emily feared the police would conclude what I had, that she had taken the cuff links to the site herself. Or maybe, because of the cuff links, she knew that Shane, her beloved, had killed Sylvia, and she couldn't figure out how to turn the father of her unborn child over to authorities.

"Have you asked her what she means?" I said.

"Asked her?"

"I'm not big on relationship advice right now," I joked, "but most counselors will tell you that you have to talk. Communicate. Make sure—"

"What are you two doing?" Ava shrieked and ran toward us looking mighty ticked off. Her heels slapped the cement.

Uh-oh.

Shane surprised me by saying, "Later," and he hightailed it to the far end of the alley, veered right, and disappeared.

"Well?" Ava demanded.

"Well, what?" Embarrassment warmed my cheeks. The way Shane ran off, he gave the impression that we had been having a tryst. Would Ava write about me in her diary?

"I . . . Shane . . . we . . . no . . ." I sputtered, and then I had nothing else. No answers. My mouth went dry.

"What do you want, Jenna? Why are you hounding me?"

"I'm . . . I'm not."

"Were you and Shane collaborating?"

I shook my head. Words. I needed words! "I . . ." So often, I could be glib and quick-witted. Not now. What good was having a thriving career at an advertising agency where slogans popped out of me in the blink of an eye if I couldn't dredge up that talent when I needed it?

"The diary!" I blurted. Truth is powerful, my father tells me. "You asked about a diary last night."

"Yes." I pointed into her car. "Is that it?"

Ava screwed up her mouth. She glanced down the alley after the retreating Shane, and back at me. Her eyes skewered daggers into mine.

"The police asked you if you wrote one," I said.

"Not true. They asked me if I had a diary in my house."

Aha! I was right. She had evaded the truth by relying on the use of explicit language. How cagey of her.

"Did Shane tell you about it?" Ava asked.

"No." I wasn't going to bring up Emily's name.

She huffed. "Yes, I wrote a diary, and yes, there's some incriminating stuff in it."

What kind of incriminating? I wondered. Like how she would stab Sylvia with a hair stick and light her up in a bonfire?

"I like you, Jenna." Ava took a step toward me.

I retreated. The door handle scalded my skin through my

blouse. "I like you, too, Ava," I murmured. Until lately, I really did like her. I loved her energy. I enjoyed whenever she bought a cookbook and hugged it to her chest, so excited to try out a new recipe.

"Do you want to read my diary?" she asked.

Did I? Yes!

"Um, sure," I mumbled. I didn't want to appear too eager.

"Here you go." Ava flung open the car door—it hadn't been locked—and grasped the red-spined book. She thrust it at me. "Check out page ninety-two." I must have blinked because she said, "Don't look surprised. I can memorize entire legal agreements, and I'm very organized. I number my diary pages. I know which one you want to read."

I opened the book and thumbed to the correct page. She had written:

I'm so angry with Shane, I could kill him. Sylvia? Really? He wants her instead of me? I get why he used to like Emily. She's so sweet. So innocent. So syrupy. But Sylvia? That bloodsucking . . . She gets every man in town.

That drew me up short. Did Sylvia really attract other men? I had never seen her with anyone other than her husband, but I'd only been in town a short while. I continued reading.

Does Ronald know about his dear little wifey-poo and Shane? What would he do if I told him? Maybe I should get rid of her once and for all. Put all men out of their misery. I could start by pulling out every hair of her nasty little head. She wouldn't win men's hearts if she were bald. Or how about I poke out her eyes with a candlestick?

I paused. The crime Ava had concocted sounded nothing like the one that had occurred. I read on:

That's what I'll do. I'll use a candlestick right out of one of her ornate, overdone displays! Take that, Sylvia. En garde!!!

A date was written at the end of the passage. Six months ago.

Ava thrust out her hand. "You see? Yes, it's incriminating, but I didn't kill her. Shane saw what I wrote. We argued. He forgave me. When he told me he wouldn't continue with Sylvia, I believed him, but then Emily announced she was pregnant, and he did the honorable thing. He chose her and ended it with me. Yes, I still love him, but I would never break up a family." Ava huffed.

I started to flip the page, but Ava snatched the diary out of my hands.

"There's nothing else. That's all I wrote."

"Take it to the police."

"Why?"

"So you can be cleared."

"I don't need to be cleared," she snarled. It wasn't an attractive look for her.

"The police think you have motive."

"No, they don't."

"Do you have an alibi?"

Ava shook her head. "Dear, sweet Jenna. What am I going to do with you?" She nudged me out of the way, clambered into her car, and tore out of the alley.

Without giving me her alibi.

To make matters worse, as I passed through the alcove toward the street, I spotted Ronald standing in the doorway to Sterling Sylvia. Had he followed Ava to the alley? Did he spy the two of us arguing? He gave me the same disapproving look he had given me at the diner. I recalled what David had said to me, teasingly. Was I ticking off people? Should I be watching my adorable backside?

Chapter 21

WHEN I RETURNED to the shop, I headed straight for the vintage table. *Do not pass Go. Do not collect two hundred dollars. Do not join in the fun with the guitarist who is playing "Oh, My Darling, Clementine" for the passel of children. Do not engage with the parents*—who all seemed euphoric, by the way. Ah, Sundays, a day of rest for most. Not I. I needed to sort out theories in my mind. Ava, Shane, D'Ann. Who killed Sylvia? *Not your business*, that small voice—still Cinnamon's—crooned in my head. Was I trying to solve the mystery to avoid dealing with the problems in my own life?

Bailey was handling a group of customers by the foodie fiction display and didn't pay attention to me. My aunt, who was dealing with a customer at the register, shot me a come-here-and-talk-to-me, you-look-upset look. Apparently her ESP was working overtime.

No, I mouthed. I slumped into a chair beside the table and let my tote fall to the floor. A new puzzle displaying a

plate of sizzling barbecue ribs was in its box. I dumped the
pieces and started with the edges. A few minutes in, my
stomach grumbled. I peeked into the breezeway and saw a
couple of people hovering around the snack table. Katie had
set out an assortment of sliders similar to the ones she had
served at the foodie truck. Heaven.

I wedged between customers and nabbed a sandwich:
turkey with a savory barbecue sauce. Perfect.

As I was grabbing a napkin, my aunt sidled up to me.
"Are you all right?"

I was frustrated, embarrassed, and flummoxed . . . but I
was okay. I offered a curt nod.

"D'Ann is better," she continued, sotto voce. "We called
her assistant, who came and took her home. I think she gave
D'Ann a sedative. I told her I would check in later."

Flora Fairchild, a chatty woman who owned a handmade
giftware store called Home Sweet Home, drew near, her
apple cheeks flushed and her eyes riveted on us. "Hi, y'all."
Flora exuded charm, but she could be a bit of a nosy-nose,
and I was certain she was trying to pick up some gossip.
"By the way"—she pulled her long braid forward over her
shoulder and fiddled with the tip—"it was sweet of you,
Vera, to include my brother at your event."

I gazed at the adults milling about, trying to determine
which matched Flora. She had a twin sister who looked and
acted nothing like her. "Which one is he?"

"The guitarist, silly." Flora lifted a slider from the tray
and bit into it. "Num num." She swallowed and added, "He's
older than I am."

Really? With his angular face and short choppy hair, he,
too, looked nothing like Flora, and he appeared to be about
twenty years younger. A puppy.

"He's quite good," I said. I wasn't lying. I would hire him
again. His voice was melodious, and he was as animated as
a camp counselor. He was now singing a rousing "She'll Be
Coming 'Round the Mountain."

Flora polished off her juicy slider, blotted her fingers on a cocktail napkin, and said, "So what's this about D'Ann?"

"Nothing," Aunt Vera replied.

"I've been worried about her," Flora said, intent on inserting herself deeper into our conversation. "She's been on tenterhooks. Why, she was in the shop the other day, teary-eyed. Not good. Aging actresses can't afford to have that puffy look." Flora fluttered her fingers beside her eyes. "I sold her a lavender sachet."

"That was nice, dear." Aunt Vera took my elbow, steered me into the shop, and drew to a halt beside the puzzle table.

Flora, not getting the hint that our conversation was private, followed. "D'Ann is a regular Sister Teresa. Why, the other day, I saw her helping one of my neighbors, Nurse Noreen."

I know Noreen, a buttoned-down, never-a-hair-out-of-place woman who works the night shift at Mercy Urgent Care. She prefers nutritional cookbooks and nonfiction books.

"D'Ann was carrying Noreen's groceries into the house," Flora went on. "I think it was that morning."

"Which morning?" I asked.

Aunt Vera shot me a look, warning me belatedly not to engage.

"*That* morning. When Sylvia died."

"And she was where?" I asked.

"Near my house. I live at the top of the mountain. Before passing on, Daddy bought a house for each of his kids—Faith, Frederick, and me—up there."

"That's far away from the crime scene," I said to my aunt.

"I think D'Ann was out for one of her spiritual journeys," Flora continued. "She makes those regularly. She had her walking stick, and she was wearing some contraption on her face." She waved a hand in front of her face. "Have you seen it? It's horrid."

I said, "It's a hockey mask. She wears it because—"

Aunt Vera cleared her throat.

That message I interpreted in time. "Go on," I said.

"Right." Flora looked miffed that she wouldn't learn the whole story. "D'Ann saw Noreen struggling with those horrid reusable bags. Whatever happened to all-natural paper?" Flora *tsk*ed. "Being eco-friendly is so important these days. Nonetheless, D'Ann went inside. I was in my robe fetching my newspaper, or I would've helped. I think they had tea. Maybe D'Ann didn't. It would be hard to do with that mask on, I suppose. The two of them sat in the nook by the window and chatted for a few minutes." Flora's gaze swept from my aunt to me. "Not that I was counting, mind you."

"Are you certain of the time?" I asked.

"Of course. Is there some problem?"

"No, dear, it's wonderful news," Aunt Vera exclaimed. "A witness thought D'Ann might have had something to do with Sylvia's death."

Flora's mouth fell open. "You're kidding! D'Ann? No way. If only I'd heard she was a suspect, I would have come forward in an instant." She pushed her braid over her shoulder. "I'm glad I overheard you talking."

"D'Ann will be thrilled," Aunt Vera said. "She said she was innocent."

"Well, of course, she's innocent." Flora clucked her tongue. "I've never known a more delightful woman. And what an actress. I've seen everything she's done. I'll bet she was wearing the mask"—she twirled a finger in front of her face—"to prepare for a new role, maybe something dark and brooding." She looked to me for corroboration. I gave her none. "Or she wanted to be incognito. People hound celebrities something awful."

A notion caught me up short. What if D'Ann hadn't been the person in the mask? What if it was her assistant, doubling for D'Ann? And if it was D'Ann, why hadn't she mentioned helping out Nurse Noreen when Lola and Aunt Vera were questioning her?

Aunt Vera said, "Flora, dear, Jenna and I have some business to attend to. Enjoy the rest of the event." She flipped her fingertips toward Flora, as if shooing away a fly, and turned her back on Flora. Quietly, she said, "Now back to our previous matter. Where have you been? You came in looking frazzled."

"I went to visit Dad at Nuts and Bolts and, by chance, saw Ava at Sylvia's jewelry store. She was talking with Ronald. I think he's considering selling the place."

"To Ava?"

"I'll buy it," Flora said, crowding in beside me. "I love that shop. What a coup that could be! I could steer customers from that shop to mine and vice versa: homey things and high-end items. Perfect."

Aunt Vera glowered at Flora and gazed at me with resignation, knowing Flora was either unable or unwilling to take a hint. "How dreadful to think Ava might swoop in and take control of Sylvia's place if she . . . you know . . ." She didn't have to elaborate. I understood: if Ava killed Sylvia.

"I saw her"—I glimpsed Flora, whose eyes gleamed with intrigue—"doing . . . you know . . . that *thing* we were talking about earlier." I mimed writing in a diary. "You . . ."

Aunt Vera blinked that she understood.

"The part she wrote about Sylvia," I went on, "doesn't jibe with the you-know-what itself." The *murder*.

Flora watched us like a tennis match, back and forth. My stomach started to churn. I was never good at charades or Twenty Questions. Playing fill-in-the-blanks wasn't my forte, either.

"Did what Ava was"—Aunt Vera mimed *writing*—"show intent?"

Flora let out a little whoop. "I get it! Ava kept a diary. Do you think she killed Sylvia? Is everyone a suspect?"

"Flora," Aunt Vera said, "if you listen in one second longer, I will never offer you a tarot reading again."

Flora spluttered. "But . . ." She blinked at my aunt and me. She was a regular when it came to having her fortune told. Like I said, she wanted to know everyone's business, even her own. "But Ava couldn't have killed Sylvia. I saw her that morning, too."

"On top of the mountain?" I asked.

"No. Below. I was driving around checking out who was watering their lawns. You know we're having a water shortage crisis."

All of California was.

"She was outside the house that's for sale, the one the event coordinator is buying."

"Shane Maverick," I inserted.

Flora bobbed her head.

I flashed on my brief encounter with Shane in the alley but pushed the memory aside. Flora was corroborating Tito's statement.

"When did you see Ava?" I asked.

"Around six A.M." Flora smiled, enjoying being the center of attention. "I noticed her because Ava always dresses in a suit and heels, and yet there she was in jeans and an overcoat, her hair anchored with one of those Japanese hair sticks."

"Are you sure? A hair stick was used to murder Sylvia."

"Wow. I didn't know that. Not Ava's best look, by the way. She has too narrow a face. She should always let her hair hang loose. In any case, there she was, carrying a flashlight and a big duffel over her shoulder."

"A duffel?"

"If you ask me, she looked like she was ready to break into someone's house and steal the family jewels."

Or murder someone. "Why didn't you report her?" I asked. I couldn't imagine Flora not wanting a piece of the limelight.

"Well, she's a Realtor. At the time, I felt she belonged—"

The guitar music stopped. Applause rang out from the crowd.

"Oh, Frederick's done," Flora said, not finishing her thought. "Away we go! He has another gig. Sundays are his busiest days. Thanks again for hiring him. He needs all the jobs he can get. *Ciao.*" She flitted away faster than a hummingbird.

I fetched my tote and fished out my cell phone.

"What are you doing?" Aunt Vera asked.

"Calling Cinnamon to fill her in."

"With more hearsay?"

"With an eyewitness account, plus I should tell her about what I read in the diary." I dialed the precinct. "Busy," I muttered and stabbed End. "What is going on at that place?"

"I would imagine the police have plenty of disorderly calls to handle because of today's Amazing Americana Bash. There's free beer. Let's tell Cinnamon in person. Tonight. She's coming to dinner to celebrate your father's freedom."

"But that's six hours from now."

"Ava is not leaving town any time soon, and simply writing in a diary or being in the neighborhood—"

"Carrying a duffel."

"Carrying a duffel," she repeated, "does not convict her. In the meantime, breathe"—Aunt Vera hooked her arm through mine—"and come with me. I have something for you." She led me to the counter. She picked up a silver-wrapped, square box, about nine inches by nine inches. "This was sitting by the front door this morning. It's for you."

"Are you sure?" A few months ago, a secret admirer had left a rash of packages; none had been for me.

"Yes, I'm sure. Your name is on it."

"Who's it from?"

"No idea," Aunt Vera said, but she was smirking. Had she steamed open the tiny envelope that was affixed to the box? The devil. "Open it."

I plucked the envelope off the gift and withdrew the card:

Jenna, I'm sorry. I went off half-cocked. Forgive me? ~ Rhett

Tears pressed at the corners of my eyes. Of course I would. I never hold a grudge. Well, usually never. Once, back in high school, I did harbor a grudge after a frenemy hid a pile of springy paper snakes in my locker, which, when I opened the locker, leaped out at me and made me scream loudly enough to earn detention. And, of course, I was holding another grudge. Now. Against David for breaking my heart and reemerging in my life as if nothing had happened.

"Open it!" my aunt ordered.

I ripped off the wrapping and pulled off the top of the box. Wads of tissue paper. Lots of wads.

Bailey joined us and peered over my shoulder. "From Rhett?"

"Yes."

"Yay! Is it a ring?"

"A r-ring," I stammered. He wouldn't propose this way, would he, and not on bent knee, in some intimate place? Sheesh. I tossed the tissue right and left.

By this time, a crowd had circled us. Mostly mothers. The children were galloping in the corner; some had found hobbyhorses to ride. Where had those come from?

"Come on," Bailey urged.

"I'm going as fast as I can." When I reached the bottom of the box, I found nothing. Zero. Zip! "It's empty."

"Can't be." Bailey scoured through the wads of tissue on the floor. A few of the mothers helped out. "Got it!" Bailey chimed. She placed a small square of tissue in her palm and offered it to me solemnly.

I unwrapped the square and gaped.

"What is it?" Bailey asked.

It wasn't a ring; it was a lure. A fishing lure. A really pretty green-and-blue one with feathers and . . .

"Not a ring," I said. A pinch of sorrow nipped my heart.

The crowd offered a collective sigh.

Bailey signaled them to move on. "Shop! Buy things!" They obeyed. She whispered to me, "What does it mean?"

"I don't want to read anything into it," I said. And I didn't. Rhett left town. Maybe he went fishing. Maybe he wanted me to join him. Or maybe he was back in town. At Bait and

Switch. Perhaps he wanted me to come to the store. I glanced at the note again. The handwriting was a pretty scrawl; not his. The sporty saleswoman at the store must have written it for him.

"It's very cryptic," my aunt said. "Let me do a reading for you."

"No. Don't. I need space. I need time to think. I—" I sighed. "I'm going to get a cup of coffee."

Chapter 22

SITTING AT A table in the Nook Café kitchen with a cup of coffee and a big slice of chocolate fudge cake—one of Katie's specialties that melted in my mouth—I deliberated about the lure Rhett had sent me: its meaning, his intent. Coming up empty, I finally caved in and called him. The call rolled into voice mail, and I nearly threw my telephone at the wall. Why own a cell phone if you aren't going to answer?

Katie swooped into a chair opposite me. She pulled off a pair of oven mitts and folded her arms on the table. She didn't say a word. She could be agonizingly patient, so unlike me.

After a long moment of feeling her gaze on me, I spilled everything. My frustration with Rhett. My exasperation with David and the dilemma he had caused. My annoyance with Cinnamon and the precinct and their newfangled telephone system. She suggested I call 911. I replied that I wasn't about to be the person who clogged up that important line.

When I finished ranting, Katie said, "Life comes at us hard sometimes."

I gave her the evil eye. "That's a Dad-ism if I ever heard one."

She chortled. "Yes, it is. He was in a moment ago, picking up pies for your Sunday dinner dessert."

"Aren't you joining us?" I asked. When she did, she always brought sweets.

"Nope. I've got a hot date with Keller." She stacked one oven mitt on top of the other and fixed them so the fingers were pointing at me. "Do you know what I do when I'm irked about everything?"

"You never get irked."

"But when I do, I bake. Want to help me?"

"No."

"Sure you do." She pushed the mitts at me. "On your feet."

I spent the next few hours shadowing her while she created a dozen chocolate cakes. She never baked one huge restaurant-sized cake; she always preferred the individual size. *Better flavor*, she told me. First, she melted the chocolate in a double boiler. The aroma was heavenly. Then she whisked the eggs and milk and vanilla, moving seamlessly around her corner of the kitchen. While I watched, I considered giving myself a week's vacation so I could trail her and learn.

After she allowed me to ice one of the cakes—my swirling technique using a flat knife was getting better but definitely not restaurant quality—it was time to close up The Cookbook Nook. Surprisingly Aunt Vera and Bailey hadn't missed me a bit! With yet no message from Rhett—what was up with that?—I fetched my lure and sped home.

I found David lying on his side on the couch, sound asleep. Tigger was curled between David and the back of the couch. Had David fallen asleep on purpose to avoid having to join me for dinner and be subjected to my family's questions? Tigger lifted his head, his eyes wide. I put a finger over my mouth and whispered for him to lie back down, but he didn't obey. As if he knew David was faking, he dug his paws into him.

That got David's attention. "Yeow," he said. "Stop, kitty!"

Tigger pounced to the floor, mission accomplished.

David blinked when he saw me. "Hey, Jenna."

"Were you really sleeping?"

He sat up and stretched. Big fake yawn. "Yeah, sure." He glanced at his watch. "Whoa, is that the time?"

"Let's go. Dinner."

"No rest for the weary," he joked.

I was shocked that as sick as David was he had a sense of humor. Oh, the things I missed from our marriage, when we were happy and carefree. Was now the time to discuss our divorce? No, I didn't want to be late to dinner. We could talk later.

"Dad wants to see you," I said.

"Grill me, you mean."

"Rake you over the coals might be more apt."

"Touché." He rubbed his chin with the back of his hand. "I need to clean up, hon. I don't want your dad thinking I'm a bum any more than he already does."

While David went into the bathroom, I sat at my vanity and freshened my makeup. As I brushed through my hair, I heard my mother's voice in my head: *Fresh is as fresh does.* She always seemed put together and smelled of gardenias. Taking her cue, I switched out of my tired orange blouse and capris, threw on a cream-colored sheath, and spritzed myself with White Shoulders perfume.

Minutes later, David emerged, dressed in a striped shirt and trousers, his day-old beard shaved, hair brushed. He spread his arms and did a quarter turn. "How do I look?"

"Better." I didn't say good, although even sick and pale, David would always look good.

I retrieved two bottles of zinfandel from my mini wine refrigerator, my contribution to dinner, and, with David by my side, walked to my aunt's house.

"We're here!" I shouted as we entered.

The zesty aromas that met us were incredible. Aunt Vera had told me ahead of time what she was preparing for the meal: Tex-Mex, including fish tacos, tamales made with pinto beans, chicken enchiladas, extra-heavy on the cheddar cheese, and a crisp green salad with a savory chipotle dressing. My mouth started to water.

Aunt Vera poked her head out from the kitchen. "Hello, dear," she said in singsong fashion. "Hello, David. Nice to see you again." She acted as though he had never gone missing, which was quite miraculous when you consider how much she loved me and how his "death" had crushed me.

"Vera." He bowed his head in deference. "Lovely caftan."

She ran a hand along the seam of her gold-and-sea-green filigreed dress. "This old thing?" It wasn't old. She had bought it in January. "Thank you." She fluttered her fingers in the direction of the backyard. "The others are on the patio."

"Can I help you?" I asked.

"No, dear. I've got it."

The French doors leading from the dining room to the patio were wide open. As we passed through, I drew in a sharp breath. The ocean. So blue. So vast. When I first returned to Crystal Cove, I could barely look at the ocean without thinking of David and how he had died. Soon, however, I was able to draw strength and inspiration from the sea's steady ebb and flow. Now, with David standing next to me and my father glowering at us, I felt rattled.

Lola, who was sitting on the wicker settee with my father and looking radiant, as always, said, "Jenna, are you all right? You're as pale as your dress."

"I'm fine." *Regular breaths*, I reminded myself. *In and out. And from now on, always wear hot pink.* The color would reflect into my cheeks and fool everyone. "Here, Dad." I offered him the wine. If I gave him a chore, maybe his accusatory gaze would soften.

He moved to the wet bar to uncork one of the bottles.

While he did, he peeked at David. "You look fine, son," he said. Cold. Aloof. Lying through his teeth.

"I'm not," David quipped, no pity for himself in his tone.

"David," I hissed.

"You made me come."

"Stop, everyone," Lola said. "Let's all act civil. David, I'm Lola."

He said, "I remember. Jenna and I went to your restaurant once when I visited town."

"Yes, of course," she murmured.

"I loved the food. I ordered the fried shrimp."

"Our specialty."

My aunt's porch was set up in a cozy conversation style. Lots of chairs, each with a good view of the water. I sat in a wicker armchair fitted with cushions that were covered in a red Hawaiian fabric. David chose the blue counterpart.

Seconds after we sat, Aunt Vera arrived with a tortilla-chips-and-dip platter, the center bowl filled with a heaping amount of homemade guacamole.

"Ooh," Lola exclaimed.

"Ooh, yourself," Aunt Vera said. "Look at that." She set the platter on the coffee table and pointed at the horizon.

The sun hadn't fully set. Orange-tinged clouds filled the sky. Off in the distance, a group on the beach lit a bonfire. The blaze added to the ambiance.

My father crossed to me with a glass of wine. "David, will you be drinking?"

"No, sir. Water's fine."

"Vera?"

"The same. Water."

Dad poured each of them a drink from a pitcher on the wet bar, then poured two more glasses of wine, one for Lola and one for himself. He retook his seat beside Lola.

Silence fell over us.

I lifted a tortilla chip and scooped up a bite of guacamole.

"Mmm, Aunt Vera. This is tasty. Avocado, tomato, onion, a dash of lemon, and what else? White pepper?"

"Jenna, I'm impressed."

"Don't be. You gave me the recipe, and I make it at least once a week."

She laughed. "Clever girl."

"Where's Rhett, Jenna?" Lola sipped her wine.

My father cut her a look. My aunt did, as well. David, too.

"On a last-minute trip out of town," I said.

"Hello-o-o!" Cinnamon, dressed in an emerald-green blouse, white slacks, a cross-body white purse, and a pair of white strappy sandals—I couldn't ever remember her looking so trendy—emerged through the patio doors. She raised a bottle of California sparkling wine in the air. "Time to celebrate!" She noticed David and tilted her head. "Well, hi. You're the *friend*, right? It's"—she made quotation marks with her fingers without losing her grip on the bottle—"*complicated*."

"Good memory." He didn't elaborate.

"Got a name?"

"Call me Dave." Not David. "Can I call you Cinnamon?"

"Sure." She glanced at me.

Apparently, my father had kept his mouth shut about my husband coming back to life. I would keep quiet, too. The police in San Francisco had it handled, although I would bet the wheels in Cinnamon's brain were trying to conjure up how she knew "Dave." Perhaps she had seen his picture in the paper when she considered me a suspect in my friend's death and rummaged through my history?

I extended a hand for the sparkling wine. "Let me open that, Cinnamon. Aunt Vera, champagne glasses!"

My aunt shuffled into the house and returned in less than a minute with the champagne flutes I had given her for Christmas, each stem a different color, which made them perfect for a party. Nobody got confused which glass belonged to whom.

I peeled the foil wrapper off the bottle and tugged on the cork. *Pop!* Everyone cheered. Foam bubbled up the neck and threatened to spill over. Quickly I poured the frothy wine into the glasses. We each took one, even David.

Cinnamon raised hers in a toast. "To Cary!"

"To Dad!" I said and sipped my wine.

"And to our friendly fisherman with the hidey-hole," Cinnamon added. "Cary, for the record, I never thought you were guilty."

"Yeah, right," Dad gibed.

"I didn't," she pleaded. "I had to do my job."

"Good thing you have other suspects," I said. "You do, I assume?"

She nodded curtly, matter closed.

Not so fast. "Speaking of witnesses"—I took another sip of wine and eyed my aunt—"do you want to tell her what Flora said, or shall I?"

Cinnamon perched on the chair fitted with yellow pillows and set her drink on the coffee table. "Go on."

"Flora Fairchild was in the shop today," Aunt Vera said. "What she said clears D'Ann Davis of murdering Sylvia. D'Ann was busy helping Nurse Noreen that morning."

"D'Ann isn't a suspect," Cinnamon said.

"She isn't?" Aunt Vera peeked at Lola.

"Look," Cinnamon said, "I know D'Ann has a very strong motive. She's in dire financial straits, and she blames Sylvia for ruining her property value, but she was seen on her spiritual walk by two gardeners."

Well how about that! Cinnamon had tracked down witnesses that I'd suggested.

"On the other hand," I said, playing the devil's advocate, "I'm not convinced D'Ann is innocent."

"Jenna," my aunt cried.

"I'm not. D'Ann wears a mask when she walks. Cinnamon, are the gardeners positive it was D'Ann on that walk and not her assistant standing in for her? She and her assistant are about the same size."

Cinnamon cocked her head.

"You might ask Noreen," I said. "Flora said D'Ann and the nurse sat down to tea, but Flora didn't see D'Ann take off the mask. Flora only watched for a minute, so—"

"I'll handle it."

"Flora mentioned Ava Judge, too," Aunt Vera said.

"True," I said and explained that Flora saw Ava in the neighborhood at about the time of the murder. I mentioned that Ava had her hair pinned up with a hair stick. "Tito saw her, too."

"Martinez?" Cinnamon asked.

"Yes. I told you—" I halted. I hadn't related what Tito told me at the pole-bending event because Cinnamon had been unavailable, and when she finally did call me back, we discussed Ava's diary. Quickly I recapped how Tito was delivering newspapers that morning, covering for his cousin.

"Big deal," Cinnamon said. "Ava lives in the area."

"But why was she at the empty house that's in escrow, which is nowhere near her own house?" I countered. "And why was she carrying a duffel bag?"

"I'll look into it."

"That's not all." Aunt Vera signaled for me to continue. "Tell her about the encounter with Ava in the alley."

Cinnamon moaned and arched an eyebrow. "Jenna, what have you been up to?"

"Not investigating," I said defensively. Not on purpose anyway. "Earlier, I visited Dad at Nuts and Bolts, and when I was leaving, a crowd following the parade nearly swallowed me whole. I ducked into Artiste Arcade until the crowd passed."

Cinnamon folded her arms and leveled me with her gaze. "Go on."

David sniggered. I lasered him with a look. I was not

deliberately trying to tick Cinnamon off. He shrugged and nabbed a tortilla chip with some guacamole.

"I found myself outside Sterling Sylvia," I said, then repeated what I'd heard Ronald and Ava discussing.

"It makes sense that he would want to sell the shop," Cinnamon said. "It's too much for him to handle."

"So soon after the murder?"

"People don't always operate on reasonable schedules." Cinnamon worked her tongue along the inside of her cheek. "Tell me about the alley."

"The alley. Right." I swallowed hard. "See, I went that way to avoid—" I stopped myself. No more lying. Starting *now*. "I went that direction because I got to thinking about Ava's diary, and I wondered if she had snowed you by telling you she didn't have one in her *house* because she kept it in her briefcase, which she keeps in her *car*. I figured her Mercedes was parked in the alley, so—"

"You didn't break in?" Cinnamon cried.

"No, I didn't," I said, "but I thought I might be able to see the diary if it was in her briefcase, and I did. However, she caught me looking."

Lola choked back a laugh. My father frowned. David, to his credit, kept neutral.

"And?" Cinnamon asked.

"And she offered to show me the diary!" I threw my father a smug grin.

Lola and David exchanged an amused glance.

"And like Emily Hawthorne said," I continued, "Ava wrote that she wanted to kill Sylvia, but she didn't lay out the way Sylvia died. No burning at the stake. No stabbing her with a hair stick." I twirled a finger near the top of my head. "She wrote that she wanted to pull out Sylvia's hair, strand by strand, and poke her eyes out with a candlestick."

"Ew," Lola exclaimed.

Cinnamon unfolded her arms and splayed her hands. "So what are you saying? Is Ava guilty or not guilty?"

"I'm saying you should ask her what her alibi is. I asked her twice, but she dodged me."

"You asked her—" Cinnamon took a slow sip of her champagne.

"Tell her about Shane," Aunt Vera said, either not picking up on Cinnamon's annoyance or ignoring it. Probably the latter.

Cinnamon glanced between my aunt and me, then eyeballed my father. The corners of his mouth were twitching as if he were trying to suppress a smile. Was he—*heart be still*—on my side at last? Did he finally see that I was only after the truth and meant no harm?

Cinnamon let out a long sigh. "What about Shane?"

"He followed me into the alley."

"Jenna!" David barked. "Are you kidding? You know better. How many times have I warned you to look over your shoulder?"

"This time I didn't," I said, testier than I'd meant to be. He wasn't the boss of me.

"Sheesh," he muttered. "Pay attention. That guy has always had a thing for you."

"No way."

"*Way.* At a cocktail party for Taylor & Squibb, I remember how everyone was talking. He was raking you over with his eyes."

"Get out of here. Raking his eyes? What kind of phrase is that? Since when do you read romance novels?"

David grunted.

"Shane was not going to attack me in the alley," I stated, not admitting aloud that his appearance had given me the willies. I rushed to add, "He said he wanted to talk about Emily."

"Yeah, right." David sneered.

"Excuse me." Cinnamon was staring at us intently. "How do you two know each other again?"

"We're old friends," David and I hissed in unison.

My father coughed. Lola squeezed his leg. Aunt Vera unabashedly worried her phoenix amulet.

Cinnamon gave me a stern, authoritative look. When I didn't react, she said, "I'll check into Shane, Emily, and Ava, deal?"

"Do you know all of their alibis?"

"I don't, but I will."

"Before now, have you considered any of them suspects?"

"Let's stop talking about murder," Cinnamon said.

I held up a finger. "One more thing. Ronald."

Cinnamon glowered at me. "What about him?"

I recalled the uneasy feeling that had cut through me after the confrontation with Ava as I passed by Sterling Sylvia and caught Ronald watching me. "Have you questioned him since Dad was cleared?"

"Yes. He's adamant he saw someone in a red plaid jacket running from the scene."

"What if he killed Sylvia?" Aunt Vera asked.

Dad grunted. "Ronald? Nah. I told you before, he's losing it. His memory is lax. And, face it, he's fragile."

Cinnamon didn't say a word. Did she have Ronald on her radar, whether fragile or not?

"I like Ava as a suspect," Lola cut in. "She's a shrewd businesswoman. Cunning. She could have donned a red plaid jacket, knowing Ronald would think the killer was Cary."

"And," I said, building on that theory, "she could have put the cuff link at the scene to incriminate Shane."

"Unless it belonged to Sylvia," Cinnamon countered. "Remember I told you her maiden name was May."

"But it doesn't. Emily said—"

"What cuff link?" Dad asked.

"The one I found at the—"

"Fire!" David shouted.

Chapter 23

D AVID POINTED IN the direction of my cottage. Licks of red-yellow flame popped and crackled beyond the far end of it.

I leaped to my feet. So did everyone else.

Cinnamon pointed at Aunt Vera. "Call 911. Cary and Jenna, come with me." She charged down the rear steps and across the sand while pulling her cell phone from her cross-body purse.

Dad and I sprinted after her. David, too, but he lagged behind.

"Bucky," Cinnamon barked into her cell phone. "Fire! Jenna Hart's cottage. That's right. On the beach." She listened. "Great. Thanks." She yelled over her shoulder, "He's two minutes away."

"Do you see anybody fleeing?" Dad shouted.

None of us did, but that didn't mean anything. There were plenty of places beyond the cottage to escape unnoticed.

The people at the bonfire on the beach were racing toward us. One was carrying a bucket. We all arrived at the scene about the same time. The fire wasn't horrible. A thicket of scrub brush was ablaze, but the flames hadn't touched the house yet. Yes, left unattended, it could have blossomed into a huge fire. The word *lucky* sparked in my mind.

The wail of a siren cut through the night air, a mile or so away.

The bonfire guy carrying the bucket, a curly-haired man with a beefy belly, dumped sand on the flames. That helped lessen the fire but didn't douse it.

"I'll be right back," my father shouted and zipped around the corner. In seconds he returned carrying the nozzle end of a hose. Water sprayed from it. He quenched the remaining flames.

"Sorry," the guy from the beach said. "An ember probably flew on the wind. We'll be more careful."

A car door slammed. Seconds later, Bucky materialized, dressed in street clothes. He stood, hands on hips, studying the extinguished fire, then crouched down and ran his hands through the weeds. He rubbed his fingertips together and sniffed his hand. He rose to a full stand.

Another siren blasted through the air and quickly died. More doors banged. The fire department had arrived. A team of firemen in full gear barreled around the corner of the cottage.

"What do you think, Bucky?" Cinnamon asked. "A wayward ember?"

"Not likely. I smell accelerant."

A shudder scudded through me. *Accelerant?* Had someone set this fire on purpose, hoping I'd be in the cottage?

Bucky scanned the crowd. I followed his gaze. Everyone seemed concerned. No one seemed edgy or excited to see the fire. "Probably a teenage prank," he said, then clutched Cinnamon's elbow and led her away from the area while the two firemen did a more thorough dousing than my father.

David came up behind me and put a hand on my shoulder. "Are you okay?"

"I think so."

"I see footprints leading toward the beach."

"One set is mine," I said. "I thought someone was peeping in through the window the other day. I went out to investigate."

"You were right. It was me. But I see three sets."

I shuddered, realizing he was right.

"Is it possible someone is targeting you because you're poking into Sylvia's murder?"

"No," I said. "Uh-uh. That little fire?"

"To scare you. To make you behave." David wrapped an arm around my back. "Someone like Shane? He told me once that he was in the Boy Scouts. A scout would know how to build a fire."

CINNAMON ASSURED ME that whoever had set the fire would be caught, but I wasn't so sure. I heard Bucky talking to his buddies. There was no concrete evidence, nothing to tie a person to the crime. When they left, adrenaline was pumping steadily through my veins. Dad offered to stay and act as my sentry, but I told him to go home. David said he would pace outside and keep a watchful eye all night, but I refused to let him. The evening chill could make him sicker.

Instead, unable to sleep, I made a batch of cookies using frozen sugar cookie dough that I had thrown together last week. While they baked, I put on a pot of Earl Grey tea. When my nerves calmed, I put the tea and warm cookies on a tray and joined David on the sofa. No talk of divorce tonight. I'd deal with that tomorrow, in the light of day.

With the television sound set on mute so we could hear a trespasser outside, we watched an old Hepburn-Tracy movie. Around 3:00 A.M., I fell asleep leaning on David's shoulder.

At 6:00 A.M. Monday morning, the hum of my cell phone ringing in my purse on the kitchen table woke me. I nudged Tigger off my lap and peeled myself from David's shoulder—I could only imagine the creases in my cheek from his shirt seam. I rubbed the crick in my neck while hurrying to answer. David muttered something and curled into the arm of the sofa. Tigger scampered after me. He circled my feet, his tail an alert question mark.

Hurry, I urged myself. After four rings, it would go to voice mail. I rummaged through my purse and nabbed the phone. The readout read: *Rhett.* I pressed Accept.

"Rhett?"

"Jenna, are you all right? I heard about the fire. I—"

"I'm fine. It was nothing." At least I hoped it was nothing. The murderer had roasted Sylvia. I prayed I wasn't next on the menu. "Where are you?"

"In Napa. My mother took ill."

"I'm sorry to hear that." Bad, horrible me. Here I'd thought he had run out on me.

"No, I'm the one who should apologize. I should have called and explained. Splitting town without enlightening you was not my finest hour. Forgive me?"

"You were angry."

"Concerned."

I wouldn't quibble. "Is your mom going to be all right?"

"Yes. She had the flu. My sisters called me, frantic, because she had a high fever, and Dad was going nuts. He thought she was delirious. I'll be coming back tomorrow."

"Send my love."

"Will do."

"Now, tell me about the gift you sent me."

He chuckled. I adored the sound of his laugh. "Did you like it?"

"I'm not sure I caught the meaning."

"Really? I thought you of all people would."

"Nope."

"Way back when we first started dating, you shared a story about your dad and mom. She told him that when he finally broke down and asked her to go fishing with him, she would know he was serious about her—"

"Because fishermen relish their privacy," I finished.

"Yep."

My heart melted. How could I stay upset with a man who treasured my family memories as much as I did? "Thank you. It's a very pretty lure."

He grew quiet. After a long moment, he said, "How is your husband?"

I gulped. I would *not* tell Rhett I had slept beside my husband, no matter how benign the arrangement had been. "He's—" I glanced in David's direction.

He was rousing. He clambered to his feet, one hand gripping the sofa, the other on his forehead. Suddenly he slumped to the floor, grazing the couch on his way down.

"David!"

I dropped the phone and raced to him. Tigger tore after me and nudged David with his nose. David's eyes were open and fluttering. His face was puffy, his breathing ragged. He wasn't having a seizure, but he appeared dazed. I checked his pulse. Fairly strong.

"What . . . happ . . . ?" he rasped. His breath smelled like ammonia.

"You fell. Show me your teeth," I ordered, recalling the things to do to test for stroke. Smile was one of the first. He passed. "Close your eyes and raise your arms over your head."

He did.

"Good. Say: 'Sue sells seashells down by the seashore.'"

"Ha! I could never say that."

"Good enough." Any intelligible sentence would do.

"Can you sit up?"

"I think so." He did and propped himself against the sofa. He rubbed the back of his head.

"I'm calling 911." I hurried to my cell phone, said, "Gotta go!" and pressed End without waiting for Rhett's reply.

"Don't!" David rasped. "Authorities don't need to think you've got another fire or that you cry wolf." He inched into the sofa. "Take me to the nearest emergency room, and let's see if I'm dehydrated."

I didn't waste a second. I grabbed my purse and shuttled him into the car. We sped to Mercy Urgent Care, one of two decent-sized clinics in the area. Crystal Cove had its share of boating and surfboard accidents. David looked pasty and his breathing was labored, but, overall, he was handling the incident with aplomb. Luckily he had not passed out when he fell. The arm of the sofa had prevented him from striking his head on the floor.

A nurse escorted David through a door to take him to an examination room. Given his diagnosis, the emergency staff would put him through a battery of tests. She asked me to give my contact information to the receptionist. I did.

Only two other people were in the foyer with me. One standing at the check-in desk, the other sitting in a chair. Both were staring into their cell phone screens.

I crossed to the water cooler and filled one of those teensy paper cones with water and glanced at a few texts from Rhett. He was concerned about me. I relayed where I was and how David was doing.

"Jenna, is that you?" Emily was passing through the door that led to the examination rooms. She was wearing a frilly blouse with long sleeves and yoga pants. The sleeves of the blouse billowed as she walked toward me. She leaned slightly backward in order to balance her bulging belly.

"How are you?" I asked.

"Ready to pop."

"And Shane?"

"He's an absolute basket case, hovering around me like a mother hen." She hoisted her purse higher on her shoulder.

I noticed the cuffs of her blouse, which were attached with a pretty pair of gold cuff links, and recalled my encounter with Shane. "He and I ran into each other."

"When?"

"Yesterday." I wasn't about to reveal he chased me down an alley. "He told me he's worried about you. He said you were muttering something like *clinky jewelry*, which made me think of our conversation by the choo-choo train. Have you been wondering out loud about the cuff links?"

"I don't think so." She blinked rapidly; she was lying.

I crumpled my paper cone and tossed it into the trash can beside the water cooler. "Emily," I said in my best I-don't-believe-you voice.

"What?" Her mouth fell slightly open. She curled a finger around a lock of her long hair.

"Do you really want to do this while you're pregnant?"

"Do what?"

"Drop the pretense."

"What pretense?" Her voice sounded singsong and girly.

"You're savvy. You said so yourself. What's going on?"

Emily didn't respond. Her mouth quivered. "I . . ." She bit down on her lower lip.

"Go on."

"I put the cuff links there."

"I only found one."

"There should be two."

"Are you saying that you killed Sylvia?"

"No!" She glanced right and left. Neither of the others in the waiting room was paying attention to us. Between tight teeth, Emily said, "I. Hate. Ava. I went to the crime scene after the fact. I put them there to frame her."

After the fact? Why would she think that the police would search a second time? And why would she think putting the cuff links there would frame Ava, simply because she, *Emily*, concocted the notion that Ava had put them there to frame Shane? How mixed-up crazy was that! Talk about a plan that backfired.

I sighed. It didn't matter. Emily's confession would explain why Cinnamon and her team hadn't found the cuff links on the first pass.

"Did it dawn on you that by doing so you might also implicate Shane?"

"That wasn't . . . I didn't mean to . . ." She gulped in air. "I trust Shane. I do. But he keeps postponing the date for the wedding, so I've got to wonder if Ava is putting him up to that."

"I don't think he's involved with her any longer," I said. On the other hand, why had he flown down the alley when Ava showed up?

"Ava keeps delaying the close of escrow, too. Maybe Shane told her to do so. He said we're not getting married until we can move into the house." She sucked back a sob. "First, it was the sprinklers. They all had to be repaired. Then the roof. Now, who knows what? For all I know, Ava killed Sylvia so that every house that's for sale in the community will be in limbo. She enjoys being the savior who fixes up the messes." Emily said the last with such venom that spittle flew out her mouth.

I reached out to comfort her, but she shied away. She bumped into a chair behind her and flopped into it. She glanced up at me, looking like a doe caught in the aim of a hunter's rifle, and for a moment, I wondered if she was trying to build an insanity plea. Had she been as jealous of Sylvia as she apparently was of Ava? Maybe she killed Sylvia and was lying about going to the scene after the fact with the cuff links. What if she took them along to taunt Sylvia, to show Sylvia the gifts that Ava had given Shane, and to flaunt that she, Emily, had his heart now?

No. If that were the case, then why hadn't Cinnamon and her crew found the cuff links in their first search?

"Emily, have you talked to the police? They'll need you to confirm Shane's alibi."

"He didn't kill Sylvia."

"Where was he that morning?"

"He was at the office. He always gets there by six A.M.

Up and at 'em. The early bird gets the worm. He who hesitates . . ." She smiled. "That's Shane."

"And you were where?"

"At home. I . . ." Emily hesitated. Her eyes widened. "Oh my, you can't think . . ." She gasped. "You do. You think I killed Sylvia. I didn't. Jenna, I wouldn't have." She stroked her stomach. "I couldn't have. I'm telling the truth. I was home, sleeping. With the baby almost due, I need my rest. I . . ." She gripped my hands; she was trembling. "You have to believe me!"

Chapter 24

EMILY PLEADED WITH me for a full five minutes. Tears spilled down her cheeks. At one point a nurse asked if Emily needed a sedative. Was the baby coming? Did she need to lie down?

In the end, I believed Emily when she vowed she did not kill Sylvia. Was I the most gullible person in the world? Possibly.

I returned to the cottage, changed out of my now-reeking cream-colored sheath, and donned jeans and a three-quarter-sleeved, sky-blue sweater. I put on dangly seascape earrings, spritzed myself with perfume, and nabbed Tigger. We sped to the shop. Both of us could eat there.

For the first two hours, Aunt Vera hovered around me like a mother hen. She rubbed her amulet and checked my aura, which was plenty pink. Every so often, she asked if I was okay. I assured her I was. I was shaken but not stirred. She asked after David, too, and I told her what I could. He was in a doctor's care. He was stable. She said it had been good seeing him again, even though—her words—*the poor boy is definitely suffering.* According to her, his aura was black, which is not good. Black indicates illness and negativity. Not surprising, given the circumstances.

Midmorning, after setting out food for Tigger, I called the clinic. David needed to stay for observation. The doctor wanted to make sure there was no injury to his brain from the fall. I reminded him that David hadn't struck his head on the floor.

"We're being cautious," he told me.

I asked about David's ammonia breath.

The doctor murmured, "It's nothing," but I knew it was. I'd Googled it. David's single kidney was failing.

Aunt Vera swept past me and said, "Don't worry. I'll see that all expenses are handled for him." How did she know that the bills for his stay at the clinic could be an issue? I hadn't revealed that David had no insurance.

"Bless you," was all I said.

Around lunchtime, Bailey showed up with a plate of mini grilled cheese sandwiches and a side of barbecue sauce that she had scored from Katie. "Comfort food soothes the soul," she said.

I blessed her, too, and dove in. When was the last time I had eaten? Cookies at midnight?

Right before closing, while I filled six gift bags with copies of *Absolutely Chocolate: Irresistible Excuses to Indulge,* one of my favorite chocolate go-to books, with fifty-five full-color pictures and over one hundred mouthwatering recipes—a customer had purchased them for her cooking club pals; they were celebrating the club's tenth anniversary—Bailey joined me behind the sales counter and looped an arm around my shoulders. "How are you holding up?"

"I'm a wreck."

"Have you called Rhett since you hung up on him?"

"Oh gosh. Rhett! Where's my purse? I need my cell phone."

"I'll get it for you, and when you're done apologizing

profusely, come to the café's kitchen." She hooked her thumb. "Katie and I are making you dinner."

I finished the sale, closed the shop, and settled into a chair in the children's corner. Tigger snuggled into my lap as I dialed Rhett.

He answered after one ring. "As I was saying, how's your husband?" His tone was light, but I could hear the concern. Sound whooshed around him.

"Are you in the car?" I asked.

"Driving home. Let me roll up the window."

When he did, the quiet was unnerving. A shudder shimmied down my back.

"I'm so sorry for hanging up earlier," I said. Quickly I explained what happened: David's fall, racing to the clinic, the vague diagnosis. "Rhett, I haven't asked him for a divorce yet, but I'm going to. The timing . . ." I hesitated. "I know it's no excuse, but the timing hasn't been right. I intend to do it. I love you." The words flew out. Easily. Truthfully. "I love you," I repeated, "and I don't want you to think—"

"Shh," he whispered. "We're good. I'll touch base when I'm a few miles away." He blew me a kiss and hung up.

THE REGULAR KITCHEN staff—the sous chef and the assistant chef—tended to the meals that were to be served to customers in the main dining room while Katie prepped for our meal. The aromas were divine: grilled onions, crisp bacon, savory sauces. My mouth moistened with anticipation.

The chef's table, where once a week Katie treated her favorite customers to a specialty dinner, was located in the far corner and covered with a simple white tablecloth and preset for three, each with multiple forks, knives, and spoons, which meant—yippee!—we were having a tasting menu featuring mini morsels of goodness. Katie, true to her organized nature, had printed out a menu on white cardstock:

Watermelon margarita
Tomato-corn salad, seasoned with white wine vinegar,
lemon, and sugar
Mini filets, served with a peppery barbecue sauce
French fries topped with chili
Green beans with crunchy bacon bits and fried onions
Two choices of dessert: peach pie tartlets topped with
vanilla ice cream or apple pie tartlets with a wedge of cheddar
cheese

"Both of you, put on aprons," Katie said as she started slicing onions and adding them to a sauté pan laced with hot oil.

We obeyed.

"Bailey, you trim the string beans and set the bacon in the skillet. Jenna, take care of the margaritas. The potion is made. It's in that pitcher." Katie pointed to a two-quart glass pitcher standing on a counter next to a trio of martini glasses. "Rim each glass with a light dusting of salt." She showed me how to do the first glass by wetting the rim of the glass and dipping it into the layer of salt she had poured into a pie plate.

Katie let me have the honor of taking the first sip of the margarita. Sweet, salty, and oh so tasty. Just what the doctor ordered. Thinking of the doctor, I wondered how David was doing and called the hospital. A nurse said David was sleeping and shouldn't be disturbed. I asked for an update. She hesitated. I explained that I was his wife. I must have sounded iffy about that, because she put me off and said she would have the doctor call me. I hung up, slightly peeved.

Bailey squinted at me. "Don't go there."

"She thought I was lying about being his wife."

"Cut her some slack," Bailey said as she turned over the bacon using a pair of tongs. "The clinic is super busy. I heard there are a whole slew of injuries because of the Wild West events. A horse kicked someone. A wagon train rolled over a person's foot. Here, take over for me." Bailey brandished the tongs at me and handed me a pair of kitchen mitts.

I'd never fried bacon. Tentatively, I approached the sauté pan. The bacon was bubbling in its own grease. Nothing was spitting. The aroma was heavenly and reassuring.

Bailey continued, "By the way, speaking of the men in your life, did you get hold of Rhett?"

I quickly filled her in.

She smiled. "Glad to hear you've mended that fence. Don't fret about David right now. He's in good hands." She crossed to Katie. "What can I do next?"

"Dice the Roma tomatoes on the cutting board." She handed Bailey a serrated knife.

While Bailey did as ordered, Katie chopped green onions, cut fresh corn off the cob, and made her super-secret salad dressing. When she put everything in a bowl and started to toss, she said, "Jenna, turn off the heat, then set the bacon on that plate lined with paper towels while you tell me about the fire at your place."

I glanced at Bailey.

She shrugged. So much for secrets.

I enlightened Katie, from the moment David spotted the fire to the moment when the fire trucks left.

"And the firemen thought whoever set it did so as a prank?" she asked. "That it had nothing to do with you, um, investigating?"

"I'm not—"

Katie grinned and elbowed Bailey. *Gotcha.*

I huffed. "Cinnamon doesn't believe I'm being targeted, and most likely she's right. I mean, what do I know? Next to nothing. Sure, I went to the scene of the crime and found a few things like a cuff link and red fabric, and yes, I've seen Ava's diary, and I've learned all sorts of tidbits from Emily and Tito and even Mrs. McCartney, but I have no proof of motive for any of the suspects."

"Who's on your list?" Katie asked.

"Shane Maverick, Ava Judge, and D'Ann Davis, unless her alibi holds up, and then there's Ronald Gump, who seems eager to get rid of Sylvia's store and move on."

Bailey said, "Wasn't Ronald in bed asleep at the time of the murder?"

"According to him."

Katie said, "That Shane. He's a real looker, and he has a roving eye. At the food truck event, I saw him flirt with every woman who walked by. What's his motive, Jenna?"

"I'm not sure, other than hoping Sylvia would keep quiet about their affair."

"They had an affair?" Katie gawped.

"He's had a few."

"How long have you known him? Has he always been this way?"

I shrugged. "I don't remember him being a playboy at Taylor & Squibb, but then he didn't look like he does now."

Bailey said, "Me, either."

"Did Emily know about the affair?" Katie asked.

I nodded.

"Do you think, out of jealousy, she might have killed Sylvia?"

"She's shrewd," I said.

"*Downton Abbey* shrewd," Bailey added.

Katie clucked her tongue. She knew exactly what Bailey was referring to. She owned the boxed sets of all of the seasons of *Downton Abbey* and watched them repeatedly.

"Don't rule out Ava when it comes to jealousy," I said.

"Ava?" Katie plated the summer salads on gold-rimmed white porcelain plates and handed them to me. She hitched her head toward the chef's table, and then she retrieved a pair of kitchen shears and started cutting the bacon into small bits. "Why would she be jealous?"

"Because she's in love with Shane." I set the salads in the center of the table and returned. "They had an affair, too."

"Wow. Does Emily know about Ava?"

"Yep."

"What's Emily's alibi?" Bailey asked.

"Like Ronald, she claims she was in bed. It sounds reasonable. It was early. Shane had left for work."

"Speaking of Shane," Bailey said. "Jenna, you said that you ran into him near the crime scene."

"True, but he wasn't the one who was stalking me."

Katie raised an eyebrow. "Stalking you?"

"Do you remember how I was on edge and feeling like I was being watched? So, there I was at the crime scene." I described the *crackle-snap*; the rumble of the engines below; seeing D'Ann's assistant; running into Shane seconds later. "It turns out David was the one following me all that time. When he revealed that it was him on the hill, I put aside thoughts of Shane being a stalker."

"Until he chased you down the alley," Bailey said.

"What alley? When?" Katie's voice skated upward. "Sit. Talk."

We settled at the chef's table and dug into our salads. Each morsel was crisp and zesty.

In between bites, Bailey said, "Tell Katie what David said about Shane being a Boy Scout."

"So what if he can build a fire," I said. "That doesn't mean anything. Heck, I can build a decent fire. Any camping enthusiast can." My brother taught me at age eight how to build the perfect fire: constructing a tent-shaped structure over a pile of smaller tinder, then blowing the flame of a lit match onto the tinder without ever dousing the match. It only took ten matches to get the hang of it.

"But David's right," I said. "There's something off about Shane other than being a rogue." I forked a bite of salad. "I can't put my finger on it."

We ate the remainder of our salads in silence, and then Katie bussed our plates to the sink and prepared the rest of the meal by herself. "What's D'Ann Davis's alibi?" she asked while removing a tray of French fries from the oven. "Mind you, I enjoy her, so I'd like her to be innocent."

I said, "Flora Fairchild saw her at the top of the mountain before the sun rose. She was helping Noreen Nutting carry her groceries inside her house."

"Nurse Noreen?" Katie said. "I know her. She comes in here often for biscuits with a cup of chamomile tea. She is the sweetest lady in the world. She's the one who helped me out with Old Man Powers. She would never lie, so whatever she says goes."

"Good to know," I said. "If D'Ann was with her, then there's no way she could have killed Sylvia and made it that far in so short a time, especially since she was on foot."

Bailey said, "Did Cinnamon confirm with Noreen that D'Ann helped her?"

"I would imagine she's done so by now." I hope she had.

"What about Ava?" Katie asked.

"She's my main suspect for a couple of reasons. She loves that neighborhood. She would do anything to preserve it. If she believed Sylvia was hurting property values, she might have lashed out. If she was jealous about Shane dumping her for Sylvia—"

"'Resentment is like drinking poison and waiting for the other person to die,'" Katie murmured.

I mock-groaned. "Who are you quoting now?"

"Carrie Fisher." Katie smirked. "You know, Leia in *Star Wars*."

"She didn't say that in *Star Wars*," Bailey contended. Ever since she started dating Tito, she knew a lot more about movies. They binge-watched films together.

"I didn't say she did," Katie countered. "However, she's a celebrity, so she gets quoted for all sorts of things." She signaled for me to continue and moved to the stove to prepare the rest of our meal. "Back to Ava. Go on, Jenna. You said you had a variety of reasons to suspect her."

"Yesterday, I saw Ava in Sterling Sylvia talking to Ronald about buying the place. I wondered whether taking over Sylvia's business was her motive to kill Sylvia, but, get this, she also seemed to be flirting with Ronald."

"Was he flirting back?" Bailey asked.

I shook my head. "He was having none of that, but maybe he put her off because he spotted me in the reflection of a mirror."

Bailey said, "You don't know Ava's alibi. Does Cinnamon?"

"If she does, she's not confiding in me." I wondered if she had pinned down Shane's alibi yet. Would his staff corroborate his whereabouts?

Katie dished up the main course and sat at the table.

"Wonderful," I said after my first bite. The filets were grilled to perfection. The tangy barbecue sauce, seasoned with orange juice, garlic, and white pepper, gave them a nice kick. And I couldn't get enough of the green beans with bacon and grilled onions. Wow. Talk about a great combo of flavors.

"Five ingredients," Katie said about the beans. "You can make these. I'll write you out a recipe card."

"I'm afraid I'll overcook the beans."

"Not if you follow my instructions to the letter. It's all about giving them an ice bath."

An ice bath. Right. Like I knew what that was.

Katie pointed her fork at me. "You said you consider Ronald a suspect. Why?"

"When I was at Mum's the Word Diner, I chatted with him, and suddenly he got irked at me and shuffled off. Then Rosie . . . you know the waitress?"

Bailey and Katie nodded.

"She confided that Ronald would be lost without Sylvia. On the other hand, minutes later I saw him flirting with a woman—I think he was flirting; hard to tell behind sunglasses—and I thought about how horribly Sylvia had treated him, verbally abusing him and pretty much waving an affair with Shane in his face, and I wondered whether he might have offed Sylvia so he could start a new life as a single, eligible bachelor."

"But he's a little"—Bailey tapped her head—"off his game, don't you think? At least, that's what everyone says."

Including my father.

"Rosie thinks he's as sharp as ever."

"Maybe Tina would know." Bailey gestured upward, toward the art-house cinema upstairs where Ronald's niece worked. "She's been by his side through this whole ordeal, watching out for him. Why, she even came into the shop today. You missed seeing her. She was looking for a cookbook for him. She said he had never cooked for himself. I encouraged her to purchase that single men's cookbook, *Man Meets Stove: A Cookbook for Men Who've Never Cooked Anything without a Microwave.*"

"That's a perfect choice," I said. "I love that cookbook. What a hoot! In one section, the author gives men clever translations for measurements." I laughed remembering a few of them. A dash was a slight shake from a bottle; it was also slower than a run but faster than a walk. For a pinch, the author threatened to hurt the reader if he tried to measure out an eighth teaspoon. A number of customers had purchased the paperback as gag gifts.

"What about D'Ann's assistant?" Katie asked. "We don't know her. What if she—"

"Killed to please her boss?" I winced. "Ew."

"Mob guys do it all the time," Bailey joked.

I shook my head. "Get real. She's not in the Mob. I would rule her out."

That put an end to our discussion, and we ate dessert in silence. I devoured both tarts that Katie had put on the menu; I couldn't resist. Afterward, I collected Tigger from the shop and drove home.

On the way, I dialed the clinic. The attending doctor hadn't called me to give me an update on David. A different nurse—not Nurse Noreen, or I would have asked her a few pointed questions—informed me that the doctor was occupied, but David was awake, so she put me through.

"I have to stay one more night. For observation." He let go with a dry raspy cough. "Hold on." He drank some water, then added that he was sorry he wouldn't be able to attend the stagecoach races with Bailey, Tito, and me.

I assured him there would be more times to play, but when I ended the call, an emotion I couldn't put a name to caught in my throat. Would there be more times? I didn't love David the way I used to, but I cared about him, and to know he was suffering broke my heart.

Chapter 25

WHEN I ARRIVED home, I grabbed a hoe that was leaning against the side of the house and, holding the hoe
like a baseball bat, made a quick perimeter search. No tres-
passers, no one on the beach. I set aside the hoe, entered the
cottage, and proceeded to check all the doors and windows
to make sure they were locked. A half hour later, I climbed
into bed and did my best to put thoughts of David aside. If
I dwelled on his fate, I wouldn't sleep. I'd only had three hours
last night. I needed more.

As it was, I didn't nod off until after midnight because
images of suspects and fires and weird, evil masks cycled
through my mind.

Before my eyes closed, I wondered how Cinnamon was
faring. Had she pinned down anyone's alibi? Had she figured
out who was the killer? Was she on her way to apprehend
the killer now?

Or would the killer get off scot-free?

*   *   *

SIX HOURS OF sleep wasn't enough to keep my energy at
peak levels. I shunned exercise—it was, after all, Tuesday,
my day off—and I whipped up a protein-rich breakfast of
eggs scrambled with Parmesan cheese, spinach, and green
onions. I added a dash of Penzey's Barbecue 3001 spice,
which was a mixture of white and red pepper, ginger, nut-
meg, and so much more; it would add a lovely zing. Before
I sat down to eat, I scooped a can of protein-rich food for
Tigger. He, like all cats, was a carnivore and appreciated a
moist meal instead of dry kibble.

After a second cup of coffee and doing the crossword
puzzle in the newspaper, I checked in on David. He was
sleeping. The nurse said to try back later. I showered, lath-
ered up with sunblock, and threw on a pair of jeans shorts,
a crisp white shirt, and sandals. I added a cute red scarf for
color and for protection. Why protection? The stagecoach
event was being held at Midway Motocross, the same place
the pole-bending event had taken place, except the stagecoaches would travel the circumference of the property.
Viewing was standing room only—fans could bring foldable
chairs. Billowing dust was to be expected.

On my way out the door, I said, "Tigger, I'll be back by
the afternoon. Sleep well!" I blew him a kiss good-bye, and
hurried off.

Everyone in town seemed to be at Midway Motocross. As
I arrived, I slowed to watch a parade of antique stagecoaches,
each drawn by a pair of horses, entering the area. Red coaches
bearing a variety of logos for Wells Fargo; brown coaches
with wooden wheels; fancy black coaches with elegant let-
tering. Signs hung on a few of the stagecoaches stating their
type, like the Henderson Mudwagon or the Yellowstone
Coach. The drivers, each decked out in western gear, seemed
quite proud of their vehicles. The horses, too.

I caught up with Bailey, aglitter in a flashy T-shirt studded with silver sequins over equally snazzy jeans shorts. She was standing near the fried-chicken-on-a-stick truck, holding a succulent looking kebab.

"Delicious," she said, waving it like a wand. "Want one?"

The aroma was tantalizing, but I was full from breakfast. "Maybe later. Where's Tito?"

"Around. Probably getting a story and a few photographs. He's always *on*. David couldn't make it?"

"No. He's still at Mercy, under doctor's observation."

I didn't offer more; she didn't press.

"Well, now that you've arrived . . ." She beckoned me to follow her. "C'mon. We've staked out a place over here. Tito brought some foldable chairs." She moved a few paces and stopped dead. She threw a hand up, almost slapping me in the face, and swung around, a finger pressed to her lips. "Shh."

"What?"

"Look."

Shane and Emily stood about twenty feet away, both in silhouette. Shane was dressed in a black cowboy shirt, black jeans, black boots, and black hat. He had to be sweltering. No clouds blocked the morning sun. Emily was dressed in a frilly fuchsia-colored dress.

What must have caught Bailey's attention was that Emily's face was about the same shade of pink as the dress, and she was stabbing a finger into Shane's chest. I couldn't hear what she was saying, but I could read her lips. *You did it*, Emily said over and over, jabbing with each word. *You did it. You did it. You did it.*

Did what? I wondered. *Killed Sylvia?*

Shane shook his head while mouthing: *No, no, no.* Finally, he clasped Emily's hand and pulled her roughly to his chest. He squinted hard at her. He said something, his lips moving although his teeth were locked together. I couldn't read those words, but Emily's eyes widened. Had he threatened her? She jerked free of him and stumbled backward. He reached for her. She found her balance and hurried away. Shane started after her but stopped. He took off his hat and smacked it against his thigh. Dust clouded around it.

"Nice public display of emotion," a husky-voiced woman said from behind us.

I spun around. Shane's redheaded assistant, clad in a chocolate-brown cowgirl dress, her multiple braids laced with shimmery gold ribbon, joined us, except she wasn't looking at us. She was staring at Shane. Up close, I realized that she was even prettier than I'd thought. If not for the scrunched-up nose and lips curled with disdain, she would be gorgeous. Her name was on the tip of my tongue: Ude, Ulana . . . Ursula. That was it. *U* for Ursula.

"Are you wondering what that was about?" Ursula's voice wasn't husky from natural sultriness; it was raspy with anger. Her hands coiled into fists; her neck muscles drew tight. "What do you bet he admitted to his fiancée that he didn't have an alibi for the morning Sylvia Gump was killed?"

I gawked at her. "But he does have an alibi, Ursula. He was at the office. Emily told me—"

"Uh-uh. No, he wasn't. I happen to know because, when I arrived, the lights were out, and there was no aroma of him."

"No aroma?"

"You know . . . his scent." She tapped her nose with her fingertip. "And"—now she faced me—"the coffee wasn't made, either. Shane always makes a pot of coffee. Always! Extra dark. He needs three cups to get going. Plus"—she did that Egyptian goddess–type move, sliding her head from side to side; I could never pull that off; I would look spastic if I tried—"the printer was switched off. He turns on all those things himself. He hates when the office isn't up and running right away."

"Have you told the police?" I asked.

"I don't like to talk out of school."

Bailey rolled her eyes at me and mouthed: *Yes, she does.*

"I'm a nice person," Ursula added.

I wasn't so sure. Negativity was spewing off her, and even I, untrained at reading auras, could tell hers was as black as the night. Was her reason for being at the shop the other day to ask my aunt to cleanse her spirit? If so, it hadn't worked.

"But I don't think Shane should get away with murder . . . if he did it, you know what I mean?" Ursula didn't wait for our response. She pivoted, sending her braids out with a swoop, and strode away.

"We should tell the police," I said.

"And say what? That Ursula, Shane's paramour, because you know that's what she is or *was*, wants to rat out Shane because he dumped her? Can she be believed?"

I moaned. "Is there any woman he hasn't been with? Other than you and me, of course."

Bailey said, "I think we should find out what Emily and Shane were arguing about."

"She was saying, 'You did it.'"

Bailey's eyes widened. "How do you know that? Can you read lips?"

"Single-syllable words aren't that hard."

"What do you think he did?"

"I don't know." I glanced at Shane, who was frowning while viewing something on his cell phone. It was long, whatever it was. He kept scrolling down the screen. "Maybe I should talk to him."

Bailey bobbed her head. "He looks pretty pitiful. He could use a friend like you."

Over a loudspeaker, a man said, "Ladies and gentlemen, the race will begin in five minutes." A whoop let out from the crowd.

"Come with me," I said.

Bailey held back. "Uh-uh. You don't want him to think we're ganging up on him, do you?"

No, I didn't, and I did want answers. We were in a public place; I was safe. I dashed toward him. "Shane!"

"Hey, Jenna." He forced a smile, and his eyes lit up with charm. Talk about a polished salesman. He shoved his cell phone into his pocket. "Having a good time?"

"I am. How about you? Is Emily okay? She ran off."

"Swell. You saw that?" Shane's phony cheeriness dissolved. "Yeah, she's fine, but ticked off because . . . aw, heck, I lied."

"About?"

"About where I was the morning Sylvia was murdered."

Holy smoke! I couldn't believe it. He was going to confess. I needed Bailey to be a witness. I glanced quickly over my shoulder to catch her attention, but she had vanished. What the heck? A twinge of fear cut through me, but I pushed it aside. There were plenty of people milling around. Granted, none were looking in Shane's and my direction—most were moseying toward the viewing area—but I was not alone.

I swung back to meet Shane's gaze. "Where were you?"

"I told her I was at the office."

"But that was a lie?"

"No. Yes. I . . . went to the office but I didn't go in because Tina showed up."

"Tina, Ronald's niece?"

"Yep, and she wanted to watch the sunrise with me, and well . . ." He scratched the back of his neck.

Wow, did I feel slow on the uptake as memories of multiple sightings of them hovering near each other cycled through my mind: the two of them chatting near the food truck the other day; and again outside The Pelican Brief Diner; and a third time, following the parade right before Shane cornered me in the alley.

"But you're—" I stammered.

"Engaged. Yup."

"And she's—"

"So young. Yeah, I know."

"Not even legal drinking age," I quipped.

He had the decency to blush. "I can't help myself."

"Can't help—"

"It's stupid, I know"—he scuffed the dirt with his heel—"but I can't seem to get enough of Tina. That morning, she caught me as I was unlocking the door. How could I turn her down? We haven't . . . you know . . . slept together or anything like that." Emily had mouthed: *You did it.* Shane mouthed: *No, no, no.* "But I try to catch moments with her."

"Was Tina the reason you tore out of the alley? Were you worried that she would think you were seeing me on the sly?"

"No. Tina's cool. It was Ava. Even though she knows she and I are through—"

"She's vindictive. You thought she might blab to Emily." He nodded.

"How did Emily find out about you and Tina?"

"One of Emily's piano students must have seen us." Under his breath, he muttered, "I'm in love with Tina."

"What about Emily?"

"Emily is so nice, but . . ." He plopped his hat on his head and jutted a hip. "I'm a horrible person. I know."

I was thinking *cad*. "You've got to tell the police where you were that morning."

"Why?"

"Because you're a suspect in Sylvia's murder."

"Me? I don't have a motive."

Was he as dense as a cake donut? "Sure you do. You had an affair with Sylvia. Did she threaten to tell Emily about the two of you?"

"No."

"Did she threaten to tell the Wild West Extravaganza organization about your many liaisons? You were fired from your last position at the gym. Did Taylor & Squibb fire you for having inappropriate relationships, too?"

He guffawed. "Are you nuts? Don't you remember how

huge I was back then? Women didn't give me a second glance.
And, for your information, my previous employer didn't fire
me. The partners decided they wanted to stay private. I
wanted to expand. We parted ways amicably."

I shifted feet. "Did Sylvia find out about you and Tina?"

"Yeah, but—" His shoulders sagged. "Look, Jenna, I can't
tell the police where I was. That'll make them suspect Tina
of killing Sylvia, and right now they don't."

"Why would they suspect her?"

"Sylvia threatened to cut off Tina's allowance."

"Tina received an allowance from Sylvia?"

"No, from her uncle, but Sylvia ruled the roost."

Money. Always a good motive for murder. Especially for
a young woman who dreamed of becoming a chef. Culinary
school isn't cheap.

"Shane, if Tina is your alibi and you're hers, then you're
both in the clear."

He brightened. "Do you think so?"

A shot rang out. People cheered. The race had begun.

Shane said, "I've got to go. Duty calls." He pointed
toward the start line. "I didn't kill Sylvia, Jenna. Trust me."

"Contact the police."

He sprinted away.

As he disappeared from view, he glanced over his shoulder at me, and another notion struck me. What if he and
Tina had plotted together to kill Sylvia? What if he, thinking
I'd seen the two of them together, followed me into the alley
to stop me, once and for all, from prying? Had Ava's sudden
appearance saved my life?

Chapter 26

I OPTED NOT TO watch the stagecoach races and texted
Bailey that I was going to the shop. She responded in
seconds: Why? It's your day off. What happened with
Shane? I typed in: I can get a lot done when no one's there.
Tell you later.

Once I arrived at The Cookbook Nook, I called my father.
I wanted his advice. Should I contact Cinnamon or trust
Shane to do the right thing? Dad didn't answer; Lola did.

"Is he there?" I asked.

"No. He's doing a repair at Mrs. McCartney's house."

"You're kidding!"

"I'm not. Hell has, indeed, frozen over." Lola laughed.
"When a pipe bursts, and every plumber in town is busy,
who you gonna call?" She sounded just like a character from
the movie *Ghostbusters*. "Say, what's this I hear about you
wanting a divorce?"

"Bailey," I grumbled.

"She loves you like a sister."

"A sister with a blabbermouth."

Lola laughed again, low and throaty, like Bailey. "As long as David doesn't contest the divorce, we can get it done in a matter of days."

"He won't," I said, though how could I know for sure? We hadn't discussed it. And now he was under doctor's care. I heaved a sigh. What a mess.

While Lola was explaining the step-by-step procedures, Bailey whooshed into the store and motioned for me to hang up.

I ended the call after promising I would sit down with Lola and fill out papers in the next day or so. Then I glowered at Bailey. "Why did you ditch me?"

"I saw Tito signaling me. He snaps; I jump. Gotta fix that, by the way. I hate that kind of woman . . . or man. You didn't miss much, by the way. The stagecoaches tore off, kicking up so much dust that none of us could see a darned thing until the race ended. So . . . what did Shane say? I'm parched." She fetched a bottle of water from the stockroom and returned to the counter. She popped the top. It went flying. She scooped it up and tucked it into her pocket. "Spill!"

I filled her in.

"He's in love with Tina? Wow!" Bailey hooked a thumb toward the ceiling. "Hey, she's at The Cameo. I saw her taking the stairs two at a time."

"She is? Let's go up and verify what he said." I hurried out the door. Bailey followed.

No people stood in line at The Cameo. The next film showing wasn't until later in the evening. The front door stood open. I led the way inside.

The black-and-silver lobby was brightly lit. A young woman in jeans and a cropped *Cameo*-emblazoned T-shirt was cleaning the surfaces of the display cabinets that held retro candy, like Sugar Daddy pops and Hot Tamales. Another young woman, also in jeans and theater-logoed

T-shirt, was vacuuming the black-and-white-with-concentric-circles carpet. The few tables and chairs that usually stood in the center of the foyer had been moved against the walls.

We found Tina wiping down the specialty coffeemaker. Her hair was secured in a knot. She was wearing jeans with chic holes in them. Her cropped tee exposed about three inches of firm abdomen.

I strolled to the counter and said, "Hi, Tina."

She glanced over her shoulder and smiled. "What are you two doing here?"

"We wondered if you had a minute to talk."

"Sure. The boss is out. What's up?" She set the coffee grounds holder into a tub of soapy water and dried her hands on a paper towel, which she discarded.

"It's not our business," I said, and it wasn't, but curiosity is a powerful motivator, "however, I heard a rumor that you are seeing Shane Maverick."

Tina cut a glance at one of her coworkers. She hitched her head and moved to the far side of the lobby, close to the entrance to the ticket booth. We followed. While tightening her bun and pulling out wisps to soften the look, she said, "Why do you care? Did, like, Emily send you?"

"Emily? No."

"I don't believe you. She told that old battle-ax Pepper Pritchett to talk to me."

Pepper can be a nuisance and, yes, possibly a battle-ax, unless you win her over. I did a short while ago by whipping up some of her favorite homemade chocolate candies. Before that, she had been my sworn enemy.

"I told her to mind her own beeswax," Tina said. "I can and will date who I want, and Emily can't change that."

I remembered being Tina's age and feeling the same. Defiant. Entitled. *Don't tell me what to do.*

"Emily's pregnant, Tina. Try to understand where she's coming from."

"Like, maybe she should have been more careful."

Maybe Shane should have, I mused.

"Ooh!" Tears pressed at the corners of Tina's eyes. She flicked them away with her fingertips. "I know I should let him go. He's got obligations, but we have this connection that's so real."

Bailey said, "Are you sure? He dates a lot of women."

"He's going to stop."

Bailey snorted. She knew from experience that he wouldn't stop. Ever. Her history with married or betrothed men was behind her, but she had suffered.

"He will," Tina protested. "I'm the one he wants. He's going to support Emily, of course. He can afford to."

Could he if he lost his current job? Again I wondered whether Sylvia might have threatened to tell his employers about his multiple dalliances so they would fire him. Did that enrage him?

"He won't be a *deadbeat* dad," Tina assured us. "He won't."

"He travels a lot for his current job," I reasoned.

"Yes, but he'll be here primarily. With me."

Her energy was infectious, and truthfully, I could see her with Shane. They were close in height; they had similar features. Magazines often show how couples that have been together for a bunch of years start to look alike, as if they were meant for each other. Shane and Emily didn't have that same appeal. On the other hand, Tina was so young. Did she have a clue what she was doing? Did Sylvia warn her niece, and did Tina lash out and silence her once and for all?

"I told Uncle Ronald about Shane and me."

"Did he understand the dynamic? He has been acting a little addled lately."

"Uncle Ronald? No way. He's sharper than a carving knife. Like, for sure, he's been unsteady because he hated the idea of retiring. Sylvia put him up to that. She wanted to travel. But he has put in for reinstatement."

"Did your aunt know about you two?"

"Oh, man." Tina giggled. "Last weekend Sylvia found out, and she went at my uncle with her claws drawn."

"Why?"

"Because there we were, on the patio, my uncle in his robe, a bottle of Shane's sauce in his hand, and he started spouting Shane's good qualities. He said Shane was energetic and bright and he said young men like him go places. He said if Shane sold his steak sauce through proper channels, you know like through gourmet stores, it could bring in megabucks."

"Sylvia said, 'Big deal,' and Uncle Ronald said, 'It is a big deal if my niece is going to marry him.' Well"—Tina threw her arms wide—"Sylvia blew a gasket. She said Shane would never amount to anything, and she dove for the bottle. Ronald swiped it from her, and, *bloop*, the cap flew off. Sauce went all over Sylvia. And then to add fuel to the fire, Uncle Ronald drank the sauce straight from the bottle. Whewie!" Tina fanned her face. "Sylvia wiped the sauce out of her hair, smacked it on Ronald's face, and said, 'Listen up. If I don't get Shane, nobody does.'"

Bailey gasped. "She didn't."

"Yep."

"Were you shocked?" I said. "I mean, did Shane tell you that they, you know—"

"Had an affair? Yeah, I knew. When I found out, it took everything I had not to tell my uncle, but it was over. It only lasted a week, so why hurt him like that, right?"

I recalled Shane telling us at Bait and Switch that he'd overheard Ronald and Sylvia arguing on the porch Monday night. Ronald said something about love making the world go round. Had they been discussing Shane and Tina a second time? Did Sylvia rub it in Ronald's face that she and Shane had hooked up? Did Ronald lose it? No, Sylvia didn't die then. She died Wednesday morning.

I said, "Did you tell Shane what Sylvia said?"

"Yes but . . . No. Wait." Tina held up her hands. "Like, that didn't come out right. I don't want you to think that Shane—"

"Attacked Sylvia?"

"Yeah! Because he wouldn't. Besides, he was with me. Watching the sunrise."

That corroborated Shane's statement. I said, "Where were you?"

"On the beach."

"The sun rises over the mountains."

"We sat with our backs facing the water. Near the lighthouse." With her fingertip, she crossed her heart. "The sun is beautiful as it peeks over the horizon. A hint of orange, then golden-yellow. It warms your face. It's, like, magical." She aimed a finger at me. "Hey, what if Emily went after Sylvia? She didn't know about me yet. If she heard that Sylvia wanted Shane all to herself . . ."

"Who would have told her?" I asked.

"Maybe a neighbor who heard Sylvia yelling at my uncle?"

Bailey shook her head. "I don't buy Emily killing Sylvia. She purchases all-natural baby food cookbooks. She wouldn't want her unborn child around that smoke and stress."

I said, "Tina, what about your uncle? He must have been mad at Sylvia."

"No way," she cried. "He couldn't. I mean, like, he's the kindest man. Everyone at the college loves him. And haven't you seen him lately? He's so reliant on that cane. He took a fall a month ago that really wrecked him."

"He said he was in bed the morning Sylvia died, and he smelled smoke."

"Yeah, that surprised me. Usually he takes an early-morning constitutional. At five A.M. he's on that walk. Even with his cane. Like me, he enjoys a good sunrise. But he told me he had an upset stomach that day. That wouldn't be a surprise, living with Sylvia. She was a lousy cook." She tittered nervously.

The front door to the theater opened, and the owner, an arty woman with multicolored hair and a penchant for billowy smock dresses, entered.

Quickly Tina said, "I've got to get back to work. I can't afford to get docked. Shane didn't kill Sylvia, and neither did Uncle Ronald."

My cell phone buzzed in my pocket. I read the text from Nurse Noreen: Come to the clinic quick.

Chapter 27

"DEAR HEART." HELEN Harris, David's mother, met me as I entered the clinic and threw her arms around me. She held me in a smothering embrace. She never did anything halfway. Crying, for instance. Her eyes were red-rimmed, puffy, and bleary. And she must have been doing quite of bit of eating since I'd last seen her. She was carrying at least fifty extra pounds. "He's resting," she said and released me. She plucked at the hem of the perforated sleeves of her elegant black dress. No matter how her weight fluctuated, Helen always dressed tastefully. "I wish you had called me, Jenna."

"I'm sorry. David was going to—"

"I only found out that he was . . . *alive* . . . because Noreen discovered my business card in his personal things." Helen Harris didn't need a business card—she had never worked a day in her life—but she handed out cards to everyone.

"When did you arrive?" I asked.

"An hour or two ago."

Nurse Noreen, her white uniform perfectly starched and her white-blonde hair tucked in place, rounded the greeting counter and joined us. "Jenna, I'm so sorry. I only learned moments ago that you are David's wife or I would've—" Noreen's face was filled with compassion. "He's fading. Helen would like to take him home."

I was surprised the nurse was on a first-name basis with Helen, but then David's mother was probably more shell-shocked than I was. She wouldn't have allowed such informality otherwise.

"The doctor is allowing her to do so," Noreen continued.

"And then what?" I asked.

"I will provide twenty-four-hour care until he—" Helen pressed her lips together. She blinked back fresh tears. "I'm afraid by staying with you, David has impaired his chance of survival."

"He said he had no chance."

"One wonders," Helen said. Yes, she'd meant it as a barb, suggesting it was my fault David had given up on life the first time, and now it was my fault he was dying all over again. "A boy shouldn't be without his mother at this time."

A boy? I bit back a retort.

"I've already talked to the authorities," Helen went on. "They said, given the doctor's diagnosis, David could live out the remainder of his sentence at home."

A door burst open and a petite frizzy-haired nurse leaned out. She beckoned. "He's calling for you!"

"Me?" Helen asked.

"No, her." She pointed at me.

Nurse Noreen and I exchanged glances. At the same time, the front door of the clinic flew open. Rhett rushed in, hair tousled, eyes tight.

He crossed to me, bussed my cheek, and clasped my hand. "Bailey called me. How's David?"

"I don't know."

Helen eyed Rhett with outright loathing.

I frowned at her, warning her to be nice. "Helen, this is Rhett Jackson."

"A friend," he said, offering nothing more.

"Whatever." Helen barged past us and entered David's room.

Rhett pressed a hand to my back and nudged me in the same direction.

The top half of David's bed was propped up about thirty degrees. He was lying motionless, his head bolstered by a thin pillow. We entered single file, and he followed us with his gaze. His skin was pasty; his lips seemed dry, as if he had been licking them for days. A tube fed a clear liquid into his arm.

His mother hurried to his bedside, but she didn't touch him. Was she afraid he might break?

David stared at Rhett, but there was no hostility in his scrutiny. "Hey, bro," he rasped.

Rhett nodded.

"Take care of my girl."

Tears pressed at the corners of my eyes. "David, don't say that."

"Hon, face facts. I'm toast." He tried to smile but failed. His mouth stretched thin; he seemed haunted.

"Son, please," Helen pleaded. *Please* what? *Please don't joke? Please don't die?*

"Mom, what's done is done. I—" David shut his eyes.

"No!" Helen cried.

David opened his eyes slowly. He let out a long sigh. "I love you, Jenna. I always will. I—" He started to cough.

Nurse Noreen hurried to him and held out a cup with a straw.

He pushed it away. "I'm sorry. To you. To everyone. I—" More coughing. "I. Screwed. Up. Mom, give my love . . . to Sis." His sister was a renowned endocrinologist. David had always tried to measure up. "She should know that—" David's face went slack. His eyelids fluttered and closed.

"David." His mother clutched David's hand. "Sweetie? She should know what?" She sounded like a little girl. "Baby, talk to me." After a long moment, she released his hand and turned to me. Tears pooled in her eyes and streamed down her face.

I opened my arms. Helen swooped into them and wept for a long time.

I DIDN'T WANT to be alone that night. I was having a hard time wrapping my head around the fact that David had come back into my life and had left just as quickly. I asked Rhett to stay. Food held no appeal. Neither did liquor.

Doors and windows secure, I slogged to bed. Rhett joined me. We lay on top of the comforter, fully dressed, and he spooned me. We didn't talk; he let me cry. Tigger paced the cottage sniffing everywhere for David. Around midnight, he settled onto a stack of David's clothes. When the sun rose Wednesday morning, the sad sack renewed his search, mewing every few minutes, asking what was up. How could I answer him? David was dead. Helen would hold a funeral in a few days. In the meantime, I had to put my life back in motion. My sweet cat would have to do the same.

Rhett and I took a long morning walk, neither saying much more than that the day was going to be gorgeous and the weather was warm for the season. We drank strong coffee and ate power bars for breakfast, and then he kissed me pristinely on the cheek and left.

I showered and dressed in a white blouse and capris—I refused to wear black—and I went to work. On the way, I rang Bailey, told her about David, and asked her to bring her cat, Hershey, to the shop. He would distract Tigger. The two cats hadn't fared well the first week they met, but after an encounter where they joined forces against an enemy, they had become good buddies.

While Tigger and Hershey played tag, Bailey and my

aunt fawned over me, asking if I was okay, how I was feeling, and was there anything either of them could do. I asked for tea with honey—that was all I needed—and then I went to the stockroom by myself. As I disappeared, I heard Aunt Vera say, "You should call your father."

"Later," I mumbled, wondering why he hadn't called me back. Maybe Lola hadn't told him I'd called.

For an hour, I stoically picked through items I would use for next week's specialty theme: Beach Reads. An umbrella, sand buckets, seashells, colorful water bottles, tubes of sunblock, and sunglasses. The mayor was inviting book clubs to organize chats all over town: in coffee shops, in the park, on the beach. Everyone was encouraged to read a book, donate to the library, and honor literacy. At the shop, we were asking chefs from Crystal Cove to read aloud from a variety of cookbooks that included wonderful stories, like *The French Laundry* by renowned chef Thomas Keller. The beauty of reading from a cookbook is that there can also be show-and-tell. While one person reads, another can hold up the glorious pictures of food within. Delicious.

Midmorning, when the shop was at a lull and the latest satisfied customer had exited, Bailey and my aunt beckoned me to the vintage table.

"No tarot reading," I said.

Aunt Vera smiled warmly. "No, dear. We wanted to take your mind off David, so we thought we'd talk about other things." She nodded at Bailey. "I've made a chart."

"A chart?"

"To reveal who killed Sylvia." Aunt Vera pulled a piece of paper from behind her back. "Voilà!" She broke apart the completed foodie puzzle of crisp bacon, set the pieces in the puzzle box, and moved it aside. Dramatically, she placed the paper in the middle of the table. On it, she had written the name *Sylvia* in the center. Lines extended outward from Sylvia to a passel of names: Shane and Tina, D'Ann, Ava, and Dad.

"Cross off Dad," I said. "D'Ann, too." After David passed away, I spoke to Nurse Noreen for a brief moment. She assured me D'Ann had been the person who helped her with her groceries and shared a cup of tea. D'Ann had removed her funky mask. Why D'Ann had neglected to mention that when questioned was beyond me. I let it slide.

Aunt Vera X'd out the two names.

I peered at the chart and said, "You don't have Ronald Gump written down."

"Or Emily Hawthorne," Bailey chimed.

"Should they be on the list?" Aunt Vera asked.

"Yes." I tapped the chart in an open space, upper right. "Their alibis are weak. Both claim to have been sleeping. By the way, Tina"—I gestured toward the ceiling—"said that was unusual for her uncle. He goes for an early-morning stroll every day. Why didn't he go that morning?"

"Tina thought he may have had an upset stomach from drinking more steak sauce," Bailey said.

Aunt Vera's mouth fell open. "He drank what?"

"It's a long story," I quipped. "Ronald and Sylvia were arguing about Tina and Shane. They're in love, it turns out."

"Isn't he engaged to Emily?" Aunt Vera asked.

"Yep." I nodded. "*And* it turns out, Sylvia was jealous because she wanted Shane all to herself."

"She what?" Aunt Vera gaped. "But she's—"

"Married." I cocked my head. "Ronald did the only rational thing. He retaliated by drinking Shane's steak sauce."

Aunt Vera *tsk*ed. "What a soap opera. That Shane sure gets around."

"To his detriment," I said.

Aunt Vera continued to cluck her tongue as she wrote the newest additions on the sheet of paper and connected the names to Sylvia.

"Do we believe Tina, by the way?" Bailey asked. "Do she and Shane have viable alibis?" She said to my aunt, "They claim they were watching the sunrise." And turned back to me. "Did someone see them? There should have been witnesses. Lots of people stroll the beach at that hour."

Aunt Vera jotted the note by Tina and Shane's names.

"As for Emily," Bailey went on, "like I said before, I really don't see her being a killer, not with all the positive things she's doing to have a healthy baby."

"I don't, either," I said, "except she wants a house and a husband. She's been very clear about that. And she is about to lose both."

"Not to Sylvia," Bailey countered.

"True."

"Poor dear," Aunt Vera said, rubbing her amulet.

"Speaking of houses," I said, "I wonder whether Cinnamon ever found out what Ava's alibi was. Why was she at the house Shane is purchasing wearing dark clothes and carrying a duffel bag?"

The telephone at the sales counter jangled. Bailey hurried to answer. "The Cookbook Nook, how may I help you?" She listened. "Yes, Chief, Jenna's right here." Bailey beckoned me with a finger.

I cut a look at my aunt, who shrugged a shoulder. She wouldn't admit she had summoned Cinnamon with ESP, but I wouldn't put it past her. On the other hand, maybe Cinnamon had a touch of ESP herself and knew we were theorizing about the murder.

I took the telephone receiver from Bailey. "Hi, Chief."

"Jenna. I—" Cinnamon hesitated. The sound of a busy precinct hummed behind her. "I've been talking to your father, who decided it was time to fill me in. Your husband. David."

"I'm sorry. I should have told you, but—"

"No, Jenna, stop. I'm the one who should be sorry. I wish you had confided in me. I know why you didn't. You think I'm the Wicked Witch of the East, but I'm not green or uncaring, and—"

"West," I corrected. "The green one is from the West.

The Wicked Witch of the East is the one with the striped stockings. She died when the house landed—"

"Jenna!" Cinnamon snapped.

I sighed as energy seeped out of me. "I was conflicted."

"Please, in the future, turn to me. We're friends." Someone in the precinct interrupted, and she replied, "I'm ready. Jenna, I've got to go. Again, I'm so sorry about your husband. Let's get together soon and catch up." She ended the call.

I hung up the receiver.

Bailey knuckled me. "You forgot to ask her about Ava."

I dialed the precinct. The clerk informed me Cinnamon was already out the door.

Aunt Vera said, "Jenna, a twist of fate." She pointed to the parking lot. "Ava is right outside, farming, if that's the correct term. You can nail this down."

Chapter 28

ARMING TO A Realtor means concentrating all one's advertising and marketing in one geographic location. Ava considers the flats of Crystal Cove, which was anything along the long stretch of Buena Vista Boulevard, her area to get the word out. Dressed in a smart two-piece aqua-blue skirt suit and heels, she bustled from car to car. Her toned calves from playing tennis flexed as she stretched to secure bright yellow flyers beneath the windshield wipers.

"Ava," I called as I hurried toward her. Aunt Vera stayed in the shop with Bailey because four customers were entering as I was leaving.

Ava spun around and offered a big, hearty smile. "Jenna." Her joy wilted. "Oh, Jenna, I'm so sorry. I heard . . . about your husband." She embraced me, flyers in hand. "Wow, what a shock!"

What a gossip mill we had in Crystal Cove, and what a reversal from the way Ava had treated me in the alley. Isn't it amazing how one person's bad luck can make a hostile person sympathetic?

I pressed apart and said, "I was wondering if Chief Pritchett contacted you."

"She called me a couple of times"—Ava moved on to another car and slotted a flyer beneath the wiper—"but I've had to put her off."

Since when was Cinnamon so lax that she would let a suspect *put her off*?

"Ava," I said, trailing her. "You need to contact her."

"I will, but I've been running like a chicken with my head cut off. See, I listed D'Ann Davis's house last night, and there are already three offers coming in at dusk tonight. Plus I'm having an open house there in a bit." Ava shoved one of her flyers into my hands. It boasted, in big bold black letters: *DREAM COTTAGE FOR SALE. Open today 2–5 p.m.* An aerial picture of D'Ann's house was inserted below with the address. "It's like a feeding frenzy," Ava went on. "Celebrity heightens the sales value of any home. Have you seen it? It's so adorable. Red everywhere. That's D'Ann's color. And the porch has the most incredible view." Ava hiccupped out a laugh. "What am I thinking? Of course you've seen it. Her house is right next to your father's. I've gotta run. Again, Jenna, I'm so sorry about your husband." She scurried ahead.

"Ava, wait! I know what Chief Pritchett wanted to ask you."

"You do?"

"She wants to know your alibi for the morning Sylvia died."

"My—" Ava jutted a hip and leveled me with an icy look. "This is all your doing, isn't it? First, you set the police after me to find my diary, and now you demand they interrogate me? What did I do to deserve this kind of attack?"

"You didn't—"

"You're always sticking your nose into things, Jenna."

"No."

"Yes you are." Ava skirted around the front end of a

Mercedes and stuck a flyer on a red-and-white MINI Cooper. "I understood your curiosity the first time, months ago, when your friend was murdered, and even the second time when a second victim died right on your doorstep."

Actually, the victim to whom she was referring died right outside The Nook Café's kitchen door.

"This time," Ava went on, "I appreciated the fact that you were snooping because your father was a suspect, but he's been cleared, hasn't he? So why are you so interested now? Why are you targeting me?"

"You were seen in the area at the time of the murder."

"By whom?"

"Tito Martinez."

"Him." She grumbled while racing to the next car, "He hates me."

"Why would he hate you?"

"Because I won't advertise in the *Crystal Cove Crier*. I do this instead." She brandished another flyer. "I work my rear end off."

"He saw you, Ava," I said, not backing down, "at the home you're selling to Shane Maverick. Flora Fairchild saw you, too. What could she have against you?"

Ava balked. "Flora? I like Flora. She likes me. I sold her the darling house she owns. She hands out my business cards to her customers."

"Flora said she noticed you because you weren't dressed in a suit, as you typically are." I indicated her outfit. "You were in jeans and an overcoat and you were carrying a flashlight and a big duffel over your shoulder. In fact, she said you were wearing a Japanese stick in your hair. Where is that?"

"I—" Ava ran her tongue along her upper lip. "I wasn't wearing one of those sticks."

"She said your hair was up, and the style didn't suit you."

"I'm telling you my hair wasn't anchored with a Japanese stick. I hate those things. They never hold. I used one of these." She fished in her tote and pulled out a promotional hair gadget that involved a two-inch-square plastic card bearing her Realtor's logo impaled with a pen. Definitely not Japanese or lethal. "These are gimmicks I give out to female buyers."

"So you admit you were there? At Shane's house."

She pursed her lips, clearly disgruntled. "His future house, if I can hold the escrow together."

"Why wouldn't you?" I recalled Emily telling me that she thought Ava was stalling the sale on purpose.

Ava moaned. "If you must know, there are black widow spiders in the attic. Nests and nests of them. The owner didn't reveal that little tidbit. I went in the dark of night with the exterminator to check them out because I was worried that if Shane found out, he might back out of the deal, seeing as Emily is pregnant, and, well, spiders. Ick!" Ava flapped a hand, then continued. "And you know how it goes. If one buyer backs out, then another will, and another, and my reputation could be ruined."

"Did any buyers back out because of Sylvia's habit of causing a ruckus in the neighborhood?"

"Uh-uh." Ava shook a finger. "Don't go spinning that tale. Sure, she was a shrew and made everyone miserable, *me* in particular, but I didn't have one sale go bust because of her antics. I certainly wouldn't kill her, even if I had." She fished in her purse again and pulled out a business card. "Here. Call the exterminator if you want to confirm my story about the spiders. His name is Gus at Bugs R Us."

"Flora didn't mention seeing an exterminator's truck."

"That's because I asked Gus to park two blocks away. The company logo is a distinctive ugly cockroach. I'm not stupid." Ava tapped my arm. "Now, listen up. I paid Gus a lot of money to keep silent, but it's okay if he talks to you. Tell him I said that."

I RETURNED INSIDE the shop. Three of the customers that had entered as I exited were chatting among themselves by the culinary fiction table. Bailey was nowhere to be seen. I scooted around my aunt who was tending to a customer and, using the shop's telephone, called Gus the exterminator.

Gus, not believing Ava had given him the okay to talk to me, put me on hold and dialed her. When he came back on the line, he was more than happy to come clean about his pre-dawn exploration with her. He wanted to tell me about the size of the spiders they had discovered on their foray; I passed on the detailed information and ended the call, no wiser as to who killed Sylvia than when I had accosted Ava.

While making a mental list, Katie appeared at the entrance to the breezeway. "Yoo-hoo. Treats!" she shouted and did a U-turn.

"You are a godsend." I followed the amazing aroma to the table where Katie was setting the basket.

"What's in these? Corn and what else?"

"They're blueberry buttermilk corn muffins." She unfolded a checkered napkin that was keeping the muffins warm. "Try one."

I did. "Heaven. How I wish I could make muffins."

"You can."

"No way. Too many ingredients. My palms get sweaty whenever I see a recipe for one."

Katie set the basket down and planted a fist on her hip. "Jenna Hart, what is with you? Baking is like math."

"I did well in math."

"I know. Straight A's, if I recall. You intimidated all the boys. Here's the thing. Consider the wet ingredients are one ingredient and the dry ingredients are another ingredient."

"I'm not following."

"You set out two bowls: one large, one small. You put all the wet ingredients into the larger one and the dry ingredients into the smaller one. Now you have two ingredients." She pulled a stack of recipe cards for the muffins from her pocket. They were neat-looking cards with a Nook Café logo in the upper left. "Take a gander." With a finger, she outlined a portion of the directions. "See how the wet ingredients include only five things? That is one recipe. Make it.

"Now look at the second set, which only has five things. Make *it*." She underlined that section of directions. "They're in order in the ingredient list, so you can't mess up. Combine the *two* ingredients"—she curled her fingers in quotation marks for the word *two*—"and ta-da, you've made a complicated recipe simple. Yes, some chefs will give you grief and say you can't dump ingredients in all at once, but for a beginning cook, it's perfectly fine." She set the stack of recipe cards beside the muffin basket. "By the way, I printed these so customers can have a takeaway and think of The Nook Café for a quick meal."

"Great marketing."

"I'm learning." Her gaze softened. She placed a hand on my arm. "I'm so sorry about David. How are you holding up?"

Something snagged in my heart. "It hits me about every hour. Sort of like when he died the first time. I get busy and then there's a lull, and wham . . . David. Dead. Again."

"Here's the good thing. You know it will get easier."

My lips started to quiver. I pressed them together and nodded. It would get easier. With time.

"Jenna, dear." Aunt Vera peeked into the breezeway. "Your cell phone is humming. It's Rhett." She handed me the cell phone and said, "When you break free, tell me about your conversation with Ava." Then she moved to the sales counter to finish up with the customer.

I pressed Accept on my phone. "Hi." Tears pressed at the corners of my eyes. I needed to get past this fragile state. I hoped attending the funeral would help me. I hoped David was at peace. I hoped the SFPD weren't giving his mother any trouble. I would bet this time they wanted to do an autopsy to make sure David was dead. Ugh.

"Do you want company tonight?" Rhett asked.

"Yes. Come to dinner. I'll make muffins."

"Only muffins?" he teased.

"And roast chicken."

"I'll bring a salad."

"Excellent."

I returned to the sales counter; the customer had left. My aunt was organizing cash in the register.

I said, "Aunt Vera, we need to deconstruct the window display soon."

"Yes, the extravaganza is winding down, but never mind that right now. What did Ava have to say for herself?"

I told her about the spiders, adding Ava was worried that if word got out about them, she might lose the sale and one lost sale could snowball into more lost sales.

Aunt Vera visibly shuddered. "Spiders. Creepy. Have you called Cinnamon?"

"Ava is on her radar."

"Yes, but if you tell her, she'll have one less suspect to interrogate. I'm sure she'll appreciate the information. She's with your father at Nuts and Bolts."

"How do you know that?"

"Earlier, I was at Latte Luck Café, picking up a cappuccino. They were having their weekly coffee. From there, they were heading to the precinct and then to the hardware shop. It seems Cinnamon needs a one-to-one tutorial in home renovation. He's going to fit her with a set of tools."

Dad must have been the one who interrupted Cinnamon when she and I were talking.

Aunt Vera nipped my elbow with her fingertips. "Go. The walk will do you good. I'll tend the store."

"Where's Bailey?"

"She ran out with Tito while you were with Ava. It seems there's some glitch with their wedding venue."

Bailey couldn't be happy about that. Tito, either.

"Go!"

Chapter 29

THE DAY WAS warm. No clouds blocked the sun's glare. I was glad to be dressed in white. As I walked along Buena Vista Boulevard, I revisited Sylvia's murder. Something that Rosie told me at the diner niggled at the edges of my mind. What was it? I couldn't wrap my head around it. Dang!

When I arrived at Nuts and Bolts, a *Closed* sign hung on the door.

"Looking for your father?" Flora Fairchild waved from the doorway of her shop, the closest store in what I called our mini–San Francisco, an aqua-blue-and-white complex composed of eight narrow, two-story bayside structures, each with porthole-style windows. "He and Chief Pritchett"—she pointed down the street—"went to the smoothie shop."

I chuckled. Were they grazing through the morning; first, coffee, and then something more substantial, all so Cinnamon could learn how to renovate her home? I thanked Flora and made a U-turn.

In the lingerie shop past Home Sweet Home, the owner was already re-dressing her window with the Beach Reads theme: men's red robes hung on racks with red-hot thriller novels poking from the robes' pockets; ladies' red peignoirs and red-feathered satin masks were draped on top of steamy romance novels. I gave the owner a thumbs-up sign. She waved hello.

Continuing on, I negotiated my way through a knot of customers heading into Artiste Arcade. A For Sale sign hung in the display window at Sterling Sylvia. Ronald, looking ruddier and spryer than he had at the diner, was inside the shop chatting with a wealthy local dowager. The woman, who had oodles of money and way too much time on her hands, was taking notes on a legal pad. Was she considering buying the place? Ronald moved about the shop, gesturing gracefully to displays à la a Home Shopping Channel model.

Seeing the display in the front window gave me pause. In the time since I had last passed by, Ronald had created a memorial for Sylvia. A silver-framed picture of her stood in the center of a wealth of jewelry, and I was struck by how skinny yet stunning Sylvia had been with her silver-white hair and her fondness for the color silver: silver clothing, silver eye shadow, ornate three-tiered silver earrings, and—

I gasped. The photograph was old, dated. Sylvia's hair had been much longer back then. An exotic silver hair stick secured her hair high on her head. I imagined the weapon used to kill Sylvia. She couldn't have been wearing it; her hair was too short. In fact, I had surmised that she hadn't owned such a thing and decided the murderer must have brought it along. Could the hair stick used to kill Sylvia have been hers? The one featured in the photograph?

I felt eyes on me and looked around. Ronald wasn't engaged with his prospective buyer, who was texting someone; he was staring at me. He beckoned me inside.

My gaze moved from him to the photograph of Sylvia to the customer with her cell phone, and I had an *aha* moment.

I realized what was bugging me about my chat with Rosie. Ronald claimed someone had invited Sylvia to the plateau that morning by sending her a text message on a burner phone. Did the police know about that, or did Ronald reveal that tip to Rosie, hoping she would impart the information to me? Rumors breed more rumors.

Wait! Did Sylvia even own a burner phone? Was that a lie?

No, I was being cynical. The police must have possession of the cell phone; Cinnamon simply hadn't told me about it. Why would she?

Did Shane text Sylvia? During their liaison, did they meet on the plateau? What if Tina, aware of that tidbit, contacted her aunt while pretending to be Shane? What if Emily did?

The dowager snared Ronald's attention. As he sauntered toward her without benefit of cane, another *aha* moment hit me. I glimpsed his eagle-headed cane, hanging as it had the other day behind the counter. Did he really need it, or was he completely healed and keeping up the pretense with the cane to make it seem that he was incapable of murder? Maybe acting befuddled was part of his ploy, too. Rosie said he was as sharp as ever. Tina did, as well.

Ronald runs rings around Rosie.

What if Ronald had known about Sylvia's affair with Shane before last weekend? Let's say he decided it was time to kill his wife, but he wasn't quite sure how to do so. With premeditation, he purchased a burner phone just in case he wanted to generate a text message at some point to cover his tracks. At the crime scene, Cinnamon revealed that an anonymous caller had contacted 911 to report the fire, which compelled the fire department to act quickly. Did Ronald, after killing Sylvia, realize that if he didn't alert the fire department ASAP, the blaze could take out the entire neighborhood?

Ronald loves his barbecue.

Over the previous weekend Ronald and Sylvia had argued

about his niece's relationship with Shane. Ronald pressed the point that Shane was young and energetic, and he flaunted Shane's entrepreneurial skills. Sylvia went ballistic. She and Ronald struggled over a bottle of Shane's steak sauce. The cap flew off and sauce drenched Sylvia. Defiantly Ronald chugged down the sauce. Outraged, Sylvia blurted that if she couldn't have Shane, no one could.

The following Monday, Shane overheard Ronald and Sylvia quarreling. Ronald warned his wife to put down the canister of propane. Did that set-to inspire Ronald to roast her?

I peeked at the lingerie shop, and a series of images scudded through my mind in rapid succession: red robe; red brick; red fabric sticking out from the brick. Tina said her uncle was wearing a robe when he drank the steak sauce. Was it red? When the cap flew off the sauce, did Ronald retrieve it and put it in his pocket like Bailey had when the cap of her water bottle flew off? The morning of the murder, when I saw Ronald, he was clad in his pajamas. Was that because he had stabbed Sylvia while in his robe? He knew blood spatter wouldn't come out, so he ditched the robe. Did he bury it beneath the rubble of brick? Was that when the bottle cap fell out of the pocket?

I envisioned the scenario step by step:

Before dawn, Sylvia and Ronald went at it. Why? Maybe because he hadn't gone for his walk and she called him a lazy good-for-nothing. Did she lash out and slug him in the face? Rosie thought Ronald was wearing makeup. Had he put it on to cover up a fresh bruise?

No matter what, that was the last straw for Ronald. It was time for him to put his plan into action. *Enough with the belittlement*, he told her. *Enough with the bullying.* He ran at her. Sylvia, realizing he was no longer an invalid, fled out the back of the house. He grabbed a weapon from the dresser—Sylvia's exotic hair stick—and chased her down the steps.

But he was barefoot, so he squeezed his feet into a pair

of Sylvia's gardening boots that were sitting on the back
stairs and continued on. I'd noticed debris on them but
hadn't thought anything of it at the time. Did it matter? I
doubted the police could prove Ronald had worn them, and
whatever fresh shoe prints they had found at the crime scene
would have matched Sylvia's, not Ronald's. Besides, Cinnamon had probably ruled him out as a suspect because she
didn't think that he, in his condition, could have managed
the treacherous trek to the plateau.

But if he was fully mobile . . .

I glimpsed into the store again. Ronald was prodding the
dowager toward the door. Was he trying to get rid of her so
he could confront me?

As the woman dug in her heels, I bolted away. I caught
sight of Cinnamon and my father climbing into Cinnamon's
teal Camry, which was parked at a meter down the street. I
yelled, but neither heard me. I raced toward them while stabbing in my father's telephone number on my cell phone. He
didn't answer. Shoot. I tried Cinnamon's number. Also no
answer. What was wrong with reception in Crystal Cove?
There were no clouds. Were tourists using the same cell tower
signal all at once?

Cinnamon and Dad drove north on Buena Vista; neither
spotted me even though I was frantically waving my arms.
At the crossroad where the dolphins were tucked into the
stagecoach, they veered right, up the hill. Aunt Vera said
Dad was giving Cinnamon a tutorial in home renovation.
Cinnamon's house was located in the flats. Maybe they were
headed to my father's house; he had a veritable treasure trove
of tools.

While fishing my keys out of my purse, I sprinted to the
lot at Fisherman's Village. I scrambled into my VW.

My aunt ran out of the shop yelling, "Jenna? What's
wrong?"

"Call Dad." I switched on the ignition. The car sputtered
to life. "I can't reach him. He's not answering his cell phone,

and I can't call while driving; my Bluetooth isn't working. He's with Cinnamon. Ronald!" I shouted as I tore out of the parking lot. "He did it."

I had to catch up to Cinnamon, had to convince her to view the crime scene again. If she found Ronald's bathrobe stuffed beneath the pile of brick, she could arrest him.

CINNAMON'S CAR WAS standing in my father's driveway. The garage door was open, but my father and Cinnamon were not chatting in his workspace.

I pulled in behind the Camry and hopped out. "Dad!" I yelled as I sprinted to the garage. "Cinnamon!"

No answer. I tried the doorknob leading into the house. Locked. I pounded on it and called again. Still no answer. I whipped around, ready to climb down through the chimney if necessary, but I didn't get far. Ronald appeared in the garage, cane in one hand, a silver-hilted dagger in the other. His car blocked the driveway. Talk about stealthy!

"Hello, Jenna," he said, his voice soft and steady . . . lethal. "You ran off in a hurry. What did you see in the store window that transfixed you? Was it the jewelry in Sylvia's hair? Did that trigger a memory?" I must have blinked because he said, "Yes, I thought so. It was brazen of me to display it. Almost as bald-faced as lighting the fire outside your cottage. Oh, but the rush, the thrill. There's nothing like it."

Crazy. He was certifiably crazy.

He raised the hand holding the knife. I flinched. I had to defend myself. I glanced around the garage. Like Nuts and Bolts, the space was spotless. A pegboard affixed to one wall held a tool bench, a two-foot step stool, and a three-legged folding chair. Nothing I could wield easily. The vise on the six-foot-long tool bench was clamped down tight. All my father's man-sized tools were locked inside his floor-to-ceiling cabinets. Dang!

Stall, I urged myself. I needed to give my father and Cinnamon time to figure out I was here. "Nice cane, Ronald."

"I'm not here to exchange pleasantries, Jenna."

He hit the garage door button. The door cranked down fast. Dad must keep it well oiled with WD-40. At least darkness didn't consume us. Sunlight spilled through the side windows.

"Do you want to know what I think, Ronald?"

He leered. "I always like to know what my students think."

"You and Sylvia argued the morning she died."

"We always argued." He moved toward me, slowly, greedily, like a cat that had cornered its mouse and wanted to take all the time in the world to savor the moment. "What else do you *know*?"

"Sylvia abused you. Not just that morning. For a long time."

"That's putting it mildly, but there's more. Continue. C'mon, girl, use your brain."

A lightbulb clicked on in my head. *The steak sauce!* "You knew she had cuckolded you with Shane," I said, uttering the theory I'd come up with outside Sterling Sylvia.

"*Cuckolded.* A good choice of word."

"You knew way before last weekend when Sylvia made her declaration that only she could have him."

"Tina told you about that."

I nodded.

"Let's just say my wife was not discreet."

I snapped my fingers. "You touted Shane to Tina. You made it seem like you liked him, but in truth, you wanted to get back at both Sylvia and him. The steak sauce bottle cap didn't accidentally fall out of your pocket. You placed it at the scene of the crime to frame Shane for killing Sylvia. Two birds, one stone. My father in his red coat was a decoy."

"Aha. I knew you had it in you."

"A month ago, when you fell—"

"She pushed me."

"You recovered quickly. That's when you dreamed up your plan. When the Wild West Extravaganza came to town, you would make your move. You would pretend to be crippled, and no one would ever suspect that you were capable of murder."

"Very clever."

I wasn't sure whether he was complimenting me or himself.

"That morning," I went on, "you did something to taunt her. You wanted to be able to claim self-defense if necessary. What did you do? Eat something in bed and spill it on yourself?" I remembered seeing him that morning, trying to wipe something off his pajama collar while at the same time attempting to appear distressed about his wife's death. "Did she pop you in the eye? Did the bruise leak into your cheek? Is that why you're wearing rouge?"

His lips pulled back. His teeth were really white and really straight. He breathed heavily through his nose.

"To her surprise, you hit back," I went on, "and suddenly she realized you weren't going to take it anymore. She ran." I repeated the scenario I had envisioned moments ago: he grabbed the hair stick; he chased her; he realized he was barefoot and slipped into her garden boots. "When did you catch up to her?"

"At the fountain. She whirled around, fists raised. Too late. I plunged the stick into her cheating heart."

"You set the fire, except the fire department, which you called using a burner phone, showed up too fast, and the robe that you'd been wearing when you killed her and buried beneath the rubble of brick didn't go up in smoke."

Ronald grinned. "Ah, I get it now. I see why you came here. You want to show the police where I hid my robe. Too bad you won't get that chance." He lunged and lashed out with the dagger.

I dodged the thrust. He tried again. I dropped to the

ground and, with my right leg, kicked the heel of his cane. It flew from his hand. He spun around and jabbed the dagger toward my head. In the nick of time, I rolled to the side, grabbed the cane, and whacked the backside of his calves. He pitched forward but didn't fall. I let go of the cane, scrambled to my feet, and shoved him.

Ronald reeled into the tool bench. The dagger slipped from his grasp and skidded beneath the lower edge of a cabinet. Growling, he reached for it.

Using the momentary distraction to my advantage, I hit the garage door opener and scooted out before it fully opened. I dashed to my car.

Seconds later, Ronald was chasing after me.

Remembering the spurs and rope that I had stored in the VW's trunk, I fished the car key from my pocket and popped the automatic button. The trunk's lid rose.

I glanced inside. The spurs were trapped beneath the rope. Drat! I cut a look over my shoulder. Ronald was on me. He swung his cane. The metal caught me in the hollow of my knees. My legs buckled. I slumped forward over the rim of the trunk.

"Get up!" Ronald ordered.

"Sure," I said, but not until I'd gripped the strap of the spurs. I yanked the pair free and, as I swiveled to face him, swung up. The seven-pointed rowels struck Ronald beneath the jaw.

He screamed in pain and careened to the right. He tried to grip the rim of the trunk but missed. His body skidded along the rear-wheel fender; he banged on the door handle, which sent him spiraling to the left, giving me just enough time to knee him in the rump.

He toppled to the ground and howled in pain.

I raised the spurs to strike again.

He glanced over his shoulder and cried, "Don't hurt me! Please." His voice was pitiful, the look in his eyes that of a wounded, beaten animal.

Holding the spurs overhead, I said, "On your feet! Walk to the trunk of my car."

He obeyed. "Are you going to lock me in there?"

"No, sir." I reached for the rope, unwieldy and heavy, and tossed it on the ground. "Sit," I ordered.

Ronald did.

"Put your hands behind your back."

He was so readily submissive that I wondered what else Sylvia had subjected him to during their marriage.

I looped the end of the rope in a figure eight around his hands and tugged. The knot wouldn't hold a flea in place, but Ronald didn't seem to realize that. "Don't move," I ordered.

As I pulled my cell phone from my pocket, I heard footsteps.

"Jenna!" my father bellowed. In seconds, he materialized at my side.

Cinnamon showed up a second later and gauged the situation. "What's going on?" she asked.

I beamed. "Ronald is your killer."

Chapter 30

A FTER I'D GONE to the precinct to give my statement, my nerves were spent. I canceled dinner with Rhett, but he insisted that he come to the cottage. We watched reruns of cooking shows. Neither of us ate. Tigger settled onto my lap. He didn't budge until bedtime.

At seven the next morning, Dad called to check in on me. He had an update. Ronald had secured a lawyer, and the lawyer was trying to claim Ronald was mentally unstable, but Dad assured me he would be tried for murder. Cinnamon wouldn't relent.

At half past seven, David's mother called. She said she realized it was last minute, but she was having a memorial service for David later in the day. Could I attend? Of course I told her *yes*.

I ate sparingly, dressed in a black sheath and pink hairband—a small tribute to David's and my past—and Tigger and I headed to work.

For an hour, I straightened the children's corner.

Afterward, I moved back to the sales counter, where Katie had set a two-tiered crystal dessert stand filled with a variety of chocolates: truffles, buttery caramels, chocolate-covered nuts, and more. All taste testers. She'd had the brilliant idea to start offering a chocolate-making demonstration on the last Saturday of each month. It would be a nice treat for adults and could become a regular event for the Chocolate Cookbook Club. In anticipation, I ordered dozens more chocolate-themed cookbooks and fiction. We already had many set out for the town's book club–themed week, but I liked to be prepared.

Aunt Vera approached me. "Jenna, dear, why the black dress?"

"David's mother." I sighed. "She can't plan anything too far in advance or she gets headaches." I would grieve for David; I would not miss Helen.

"Would you like me to come with you?" she asked.

"No, thank you.

"Very well, but don't say I didn't offer." Aunt Vera took a chocolate caramel and bit into it. "Mmm. Scrumptious. By the way, I have a bit of news. Are you up for it?"

Bailey flew through the door, the skirt of her aqua-blue dress billowing. She skidded to a stop by the counter. "Sorry I'm late. You won't believe what I heard at Latte Luck Café."

"Me first," Aunt Vera said. "I was getting ready to tell Jenna that Shane lost his job with the Wild West Extravaganza group, and he and Emily aren't getting married. Emily doesn't want to move from city to city, wherever he might roam."

"Roam," Bailey snorted. "That's funny, seeing as Shane was a rover."

"What about the house they were buying?" I asked.

"Emily saw it and fell in love with it, spiders or no spiders. She's buying it with help from her parents."

"That's wonderful," I said.

"Okay, my turn!" Bailey cried.

"Not yet." Aunt Vera held up a finger. "As for Tina Gump, she slipped in before you all arrived and announced that she, too, is dumping Shane."

"Woot!" I chimed. Bailey echoed me.

"Poor girl," Aunt Vera said. "She's so upset with the news about her uncle. She loved him dearly, but she realizes she must plant both feet on the ground. I gave her a quick reading, and she made a big life decision. Knowing she has to take care of herself, and there will be no money coming her way any time soon, certainly not from Sylvia's will—Sylvia didn't appreciate Tina in the least—she's taking on two jobs so she can apply to culinary college. I asked her to work here part-time. Is that okay?"

"Wonderful," I said. "She'll get the hang of it right away, and none of us will feel guilty when we need to take an extra day off." I hesitated. "What about Sylvia's funeral?"

Aunt Vera nodded. "Tina will take care of that. She's not heartless. There are funds to cover it."

Bailey cleared her throat. "Now is it my turn?"

Aunt Vera opened both palms, ceding the floor.

"I was at Latte Luck Café with my mother, and D'Ann Davis joined us for coffee."

"Name dropper," I joked.

Bailey giggled and fluffed her hair. "Yes, *I* was dining with a star."

I swatted her. "Get over yourself."

"Okay." She dropped the façade. "Anyway, get this! D'Ann got a whopping big part in the next frat-boy comedy. She's going to be the hot, sexy housemother! She's so excited. She hasn't done a comedy in years. Plus, Ava sold D'Ann's vacation home at ten percent over asking price. Ava is doing a happy dance, and so is D'Ann. That will get her out of her financial hole."

"Bailey, sweetheart!" Lola, pretty in peach, hurried into

the shop, her arm extended. She was holding a bejeweled blue cell phone. "You left this at the coffee shop. I know how you hate to be without it."

"That's not mine." Bailey flourished her cell phone. "This is."

Lola blushed and glanced at the phone. "Then whose is this?"

"D'Ann's?"

"No, hers is red."

"Could it be a *burner* phone?" Bailey winked at me, knowing the whole town was abuzz that a burner phone was what nailed Ronald, the irony of the word *burner* not lost on anyone because of the fire. Bailey's phone jangled. She answered. *"Mi amor."* She turned her back on us, for more privacy. "You did what? Without me?"

Lola and I sidled around to face her. I raised my eyebrows to signal: *What was up?*

Bailey flapped a hand. "No, no. I—" She listened. *"Sí, sí, but—"*

"What?" Lola demanded.

"No, I did not say that, Tito," she said. "No, you listen—" She flinched and held the telephone at arm's length. "What the—" She gaped at me, tears moistening her eyes. "He hung up on me."

Lola slung an arm around her daughter. "Sweetie, can I help?"

Bailey wriggled free. "I doubt it. See, there was a glitch."

"With the wedding venue," I offered.

She bobbed her head. "Tito is there negotiating with them. He asked if I was sure this is what I want, a wedding at a vineyard. I told him yes. He said, *bueno*, because he is going to seal the deal for two years from now."

"Two years?" I said. "I thought you had it set for September."

Lola muttered, "Why, that no-good—"

"Mom! Stop! It's not his fault. It's the vineyard's fault. It double-booked."

"You want to get married this year, don't you?" I said.

"Yes!"

"Are you willing to give up having the ceremony at CC Vineyard?"

"Yes!"

Lola melted, raw maternal emotions flushing her face, and petted Bailey's arm. "Then call Tito back and tell him to stop what he's doing. You and your partner make decisions together, not unilaterally. Remember that. Now, I must go return this phone to . . . whoever lost it. Heavens!"

As she exited, I thought of David. Our wedding. Our vow to always be honest and to lean on each other in times of trouble. He broke the vow and crushed my heart. May he rest in peace.

I hugged Bailey and said, "Your mother is right. Tell Tito what you need. Don't be bullied. You are the boss of you, and together you and he are a great team." I kissed her cheek. "FYI, I might know another vineyard owner who can accommodate you."

"I love you!" She fetched her purse and flew out of the shop.

At the same time, Rhett strolled in, looking as handsome as ever in a dark pinstriped suit and soft pink shirt. The pink was a nice touch. He bounced a set of car keys in his hand. "Ready?"

I nodded. Today I was officially moving into phase two of my life with the new love of my life, and soon . . . I would refind my smile.

Recipes

From Jenna:

I like to use this sauce on chicken or steak. Use four to six pieces of chicken or steak. My dad taught me to always baste after the first searing of the meat. Otherwise the sauce chars too quickly. On the other hand, it works really well as a marinade for flank steak.

Balsamic Barbecue Sauce

(yield 1½ cups)

   1 cup balsamic vinegar
   ¾ cup ketchup
   ⅓ cup firmly packed brown sugar
  -1 garlic clove, minced
   1 tablespoon Worcestershire sauce
   1 tablespoon Dijon mustard
   ½ teaspoon salt
   ½ teaspoon freshly ground black pepper

Combine all the ingredients in a small saucepan and stir until the ingredients are incorporated and the mixture is smooth. Simmer over medium heat until reduced by one-third, 15 to 20 minutes.

From Katie:

*These aren't really muffins. They're biscuits stuffed with
goodness, but because they're baked in muffin pans, and
that kind of cooking is all the rage, I decided to call them
muffins. They are hearty enough for a meal. Enjoy! By the
way, you can go the simple route and use Pillsbury
refrigerated biscuits in the can, or you can make the
biscuits from scratch. I'm providing a gluten-free recipe, but
for those who can eat regular flour, swap out the gluten-
free flour with regular flour and omit the xanthan gum.*

Barbecue Muffins

(makes 10 muffins)

Ingredients for the muffins:

2½ cups gluten-free flour
1½ tablespoons baking powder
½ teaspoon xanthan gum
1 teaspoon baking soda
½ teaspoon coarse sea salt
6 tablespoons cold butter, cut into small cubes
¾ cup milk
1 tablespoon cider vinegar

Ingredients for the filling:

1 pound ground beef
½ cup ketchup
3 tablespoons brown sugar
1 tablespoon cider vinegar
½ teaspoon chili powder
1 cup (4 ounces) cheddar cheese, shredded

First make the muffin dough. (Or use Pillsbury refrigerated
dough; see below).

In a pastry blender, mix the gluten-free flour, baking powder, xanthan gum, baking soda, and sea salt. Add the butter and pulse until the mixture looks the size of peas. Now add the milk and cider vinegar. The mixture will quickly form a dough.

Remove the dough and divide into 10 equal portions. Set out a piece of parchment paper and, using a rolling pin, flatten each dough portion into a 5-inch circle. Note: I like to fold the parchment over the dough so it won't stick to the rolling pin. *[If you are using Pillsbury refrigerated biscuits, pull them apart into 10 portions.]*

Press each portion into a greased muffin cup, pressing down on the bottom and up the sides to form a "cup." Set aside.

Preheat the oven to 375°F.

Now make the filling. In a skillet, cook the ground beef over medium heat until it is no longer pink, stirring it and breaking it up into little chunks as it cooks. When done, drain and pat with paper towels to remove the excess fat.

In a small bowl, combine the ketchup, brown sugar, cider vinegar, and chili powder. Add the mixture to the cooked beef and mix well.

Using a ¼-cup measuring cup, divide the meat mixture among the dough-lined muffin cups. Sprinkle with 1 to 2 tablespoons shredded cheese.

Bake for 15 to 18 minutes, or until the dough is golden brown and the cheese lightly browned.

From Katie, a postscript:

By the way, I made a major mistake when I first created the biscuit portion of this recipe. I incorrectly made the milk mixture 1¾ cups. Oops! Well, guess what? The mixture started to really rise, and since I don't like to throw things away, I spooned the dough into popover cups just to see how they would turn out, filling the cups halfway. Ta-da! Perfect "popover" biscuits! I baked them at 400°F for 15 minutes. They came out incredibly flaky. Yield: 6 to 10 biscuits.

From Katie:

There's nothing heartier than a good chili. On a cool, foggy day in Crystal Cove, it's one of my all-time favorite meals. Make sure you cook it long and slow. The strong coffee adds a real kick to it. The toppings make it even more scrumptious. Personally I like to add all three of them. The cheddar should be really sharp!

Beef and Pinto Beans Chili

(serves 6 to 8)

    2 to 4 tablespoons canola oil, plus more as needed
    2 pounds boneless beef chuck, cut into small cubes
        (about ½ inch)
    2 cups chopped sweet yellow onions
    8 garlic cloves, chopped
    ⅓ cup chili powder, plus more if desired (*see below*)
    1 teaspoon white pepper or cracked black pepper
        (12 strong grinds)
    1 teaspoon dried oregano
    2 tablespoons tomato paste
    1 28-ounce can chopped plum tomatoes (do not
        pour off liquid)
    1¾ cups beef broth
    ⅓ cup brewed espresso or strong coffee
    4 to 5 cups pinto beans (*homemade recipe, see
        below*) or 2 15-ounce cans, drained

For topping, as desired:

Shredded cheddar cheese
Sour cream
Diced avocado

In a large pot, heat ½ tablespoon canola oil over medium-high heat. Pat the beef dry. Brown in batches, about 4 minutes each, adding more oil as needed. Transfer to a plate.

Pour off the beef juice.

Reduce the heat to medium and add 1½ tablespoons oil to the pot. Add the onions and garlic; cook, stirring, until golden, 5 to 6 minutes.

Add ⅓ cup chili powder and the pepper, oregano, and tomato paste. Stir and cook for 30 seconds.

Return the meat to the pot, and stir in the tomatoes with their liquid, plus the broth, espresso, and pinto beans.

Bring to a boil, then reduce the heat and simmer, covered, until the beef is tender, 1½ to 2 hours.

Divide among bowls. Top with cheese, sour cream, and avocado, as desired.

If you want to spice up the chili, add another 1 to 2 tablespoons of chili powder right before serving!

From Katie:

Let me share a wonderful trick on how to cook pinto beans!

First, slow soak: Add the beans to a saucepan and water, at a ratio of 2 or 3 cups water per 1 cup dried beans. Place the lid on the saucepan and soak a minimum of 8 hours. You can put this in the refrigerator overnight. So plan ahead!

Drain! Never cook beans in the water they have soaked in. Always drain and use fresh water for cooking. Also, *never* add seasonings or salt to the cooking beans. *Why not?*

Because this can change the cooking time and can toughen the beans. I found this out on the Internet. Who knew?

Now, get ready to cook the pinto beans. Add water at a ratio of 3 cups liquid to 1 cup dried (but presoaked) beans. So for a pound of beans, about 6 cups of water. Place the beans in the pot, then pour the water over them. The liquid should cover the beans by 1 to 2 inches.

Bring the beans to a boil. Reduce to a simmer and cook for 1½ to 2½ hours. Mine take 2½ hours! The beans are ready when they can be mashed easily. I remove a spoonful and test by pressing with a fork. Another thing I learned from the Internet: cooking time may vary depending on the size and age of the beans, the humidity and, well, other *what ifs*! It's nature, I guess.

Remove from the stove. Drain! They are ready to be used, or they may be stored in an airtight container for 2 to 5 days.

If you're using canned beans, remember to drain them in a colander. Rinse the beans under cold water to remove the liquid.

Use in the recipe as directed. Enjoy!

From Jenna:

This is so simple, even I can do it. I love corn any time of the year, but in the summer, when it's fresh from the field, it's incredible!

Barbecued Corn on the Grill

(serves 4)

    4 ears of corn, still in their husks
    Butter

Heat a barbecue grill to medium. Note: if you are cooking these with something like ribs where you are keeping the flame low, make sure you cook the corn longer—like 5 to 10 minutes longer! I like crisp corn, but I do like it better when it's cooked through.

Meanwhile pull the husks of the corn to the base of the ear. Be careful not to pull them off! Remove the silk from each ear of corn—there's not much, surprisingly. Put the husks back and place the ears in a large pot of cold water with 1 tablespoon of salt. Soak for 10 minutes.

Remove the corn from the water and shake off the excess. Place the ears of corn in their husks on the grill. Close the cover and grill for 15 to 20 minutes, turning about every 5 minutes, or until the kernels are tender. You can pierce with a knife or fork to test. Remove the husks. Serve hot with butter.

From Jenna:

You know I like easy recipes. I also like fresh, fresh, fresh. This crisp salad goes with anything: steaks, burgers, or a sandwich. And it's terrific by itself. Just don't be afraid to cut the corn off the cob. I was the first time. Big knife, slippery corn. It was a cinch. What a silly goose to be afraid.

Corn Tomato Salad

(serves 2 as a side dish, and 1 as an entrée)

    2 fresh tomatoes, sliced
    1 ear of corn, cooked, kernels sliced off
    1 celery stalk, diced
    ½ teaspoon white or black pepper
    1 teaspoon salt
    1 teaspoon fresh lemon juice

Mix the tomatoes, corn, and celery in a large bowl and add the pepper, salt, and lemon juice.

This may also be served as a salsa!

From Katie:

Hiya, cowboy cookie lovers! Yup, these have a lot of ingredients, so I know that makes Jenna really nervous, but for the daring bakers out there who take risks like I do, it's easy. Think: dry vs. wet. Put all the dry ingredients together first. See them in the list? They are at the top. Set them aside. Now focus on the wet items. At the end, you add the last three items that give the cookies their "grit": oats, Chex-type cereal, and chocolate chips. It's a snap! And for all you cookie lovers who don't need to eat gluten-free, just switch out the gluten-free flour for regular flour and omit the xanthan gum. Yup, it's that easy, pardner. Little side note: prepare the cooked oatmeal ahead of time. It takes 30 minutes.

Gluten-Free Cowboy Cookies

(makes 36 to 48 cookies)

2¼ cups gluten-free flour
1 teaspoon baking soda
½ teaspoon baking powder
½ teaspoon xanthan gum
½ teaspoon salt
1 cup plus 2 tablespoons shortening (see below)
1¼ cups firmly packed light brown sugar
1 cup granulated sugar
6 tablespoons peanut butter
3 large eggs

1 teaspoon vanilla extract
1 cup cooked steel-cut oats, cooked ahead of time
   (*see below*)
1 cup gluten-free Rice Chex–type cereal
1 cup semisweet chocolate chips

Preheat the oven to 350°F.

In a medium bowl, whisk the flour, baking soda, baking powder, xanthan gum, and salt. Set aside.

Using an electric mixer, in a large bowl, beat the shortening until creamy.

[Here's a tip for measuring the shortening, which can be difficult to measure because it's so sticky. In a 2-cup measuring cup, measure 1 cup of water. Add shortening until the water measures 2 cups. That means you have 1 cup of shortening. Pour off the water. Now add the extra 2 tablespoons of shortening.]

Gradually add in the brown and granulated sugars and beat well.

Add the peanut butter, eggs, and vanilla, and mix until all is combined.

Add the flour mixture, cooked oats, and cereal. Mix until blended. Add the chocolate chips. Stir well. The mixture will "puff" or aerate.

Drop the dough in portions approximately 2 inches apart on a parchment-lined baking sheet, using a 2-inch cookie scoop. *[If you don't have a cookie scoop, an ice cream scoop will do. Note: I only got 6 to 8 cookies on a sheet because they spread so much. They are definitely "cowboy-sized" cookies!]*

Bake for 11 to 12 minutes. The cookies should be nice and brown so they can get crisp. Cool on the baking sheets for 5 minutes.

Transfer to wire racks; cool completely. Store in airtight containers.

TO COOK THE OATS

In a 6- to 8-quart saucepan, bring 4 cups of water to a boil.
Add 1 cup uncooked steel-cut oats. Bring to a boil again,
then return to a simmer and cook for 30 minutes. Stir occasionally. Remove the saucepan from the heat and let the
oatmeal cool completely.

From Jenna:

*I will always remember my mother's meat loaf. She
served it every Friday without fail. I'm not sure if it
was because it was so easy and she had a busy Friday
or if she knew it was one of my father's favorite
meals. The apples give it a nice texture and flavor.
Whenever I have it, it brings back warm memories.
How I miss her!*

Jenna's Mom's Turkey Meat Loaf

(serves 6)

    ½ green apple, pared and sliced (about ½ cup)
    ½ cup chopped yellow onion (about ¼ large onion)
    ¼ cup Parmesan cheese, grated
    1 egg
    2 pounds ground turkey
    1 tablespoon bouquet garni (I use Penzey's)

Preheat the oven to 300°F.

Dump all the ingredients into a bowl. If you don't have
bouquet garni, make a mixture of equal parts thyme, rose-
mary, and basil.

Mush the mixture with your hands and press into a 5-by-9-inch loaf pan.

Bake for 1 hour, until nicely browned on top. Serve hot.

From Katie:

I have a friend who must eat low-sugar items. This recipe is not sugar-free. I use a sugar substitute that is sugar-free and I really like it for its consistency, but note that there is sugar in ketchup. So if you can tolerate a little sugar, this is a good sauce for you. It's so tasty! P.S.: You might be wondering why some sauces have a regional name to them. Well, they generally fall into four categories: vinegar and pepper, mustard, light tomato, or heavy tomato. This one is the vinegar-and-pepper kind. Enjoy!

Low-Sugar St. Louis Barbecue Sauce

(yields 1½ cups sauce)

1 cup ketchup
¼ cup water
3 tablespoons apple cider vinegar
3 tablespoons Swerve (sugar substitute)
1 tablespoon yellow mustard
½ tablespoon garlic powder
¼ teaspoon white pepper
3 to 4 pounds pork spare ribs

Preheat the oven to 300°F.

In a small bowl, mix the ketchup, water, cider vinegar, Swerve, mustard, garlic powder, and white pepper.

On a large baking sheet, place a long piece of aluminum foil. Rinse the ribs and cut them into portions. Set the ribs on the foil and brush both sides liberally with the sauce. Turn the ribs bone-side down on the foil. Top with more foil and pinch the foil tightly to seal.

Bake for 1½ hours. One hour "in," heat the barbecue to medium.

Remove the ribs from the oven, then remove them from the foil and set them on the hot barbecue, bone-side down. Cook for 10 minutes. Flip and cook another 10 minutes. Be careful not to let your barbecue temperature climb too high. You don't want to burn the sauce.

From Jenna:

I learned to grill chicken from my dad. He says to bake the chicken first in the oven to seal in the juices. Simply wrap the chicken in foil and bake at 300°F for 30 to 40 minutes. Then heat the grill to medium-low and grill the chicken slowly, 5 to 10 minutes a side, until the chicken is cooked through. Start basting after the chicken is seared on both sides. Baste and turn often.

Margarita Barbecue Sauce for Chicken

(makes enough for 1 whole chicken or 4 chicken quarters—leg/thigh or breast/wing combinations)

¼ cup Rose's sweetened lime juice
2 tablespoons honey
2 tablespoons tequila
1 tablespoon safflower oil
¼ teaspoon white pepper
1 teaspoon salt
2 teaspoons cornstarch
1 whole chicken or 4 chicken quarters

In a small saucepan, mix the lime juice, honey, tequila, safflower oil, pepper, salt, and cornstarch. Over medium-high heat, bring the mixture to a boil, stirring until the sauce thickens. Remove the saucepan from heat. Keep at room temperature.

Grill the unseasoned chicken as you normally would, brushing with oil so it won't burn.

After the chicken has seared, baste the chicken on both sides with the barbecue sauce. Grill for 2 to 3 minutes per side. Baste again. And again.

This is a light, sweet, but savory sauce.

From Jenna:

I'm graduating to more difficult recipes, it appears. Barbecue sauces can do that to a girl. There are so many spices, but Katie says, "Break a recipe into steps and it won't be overwhelming." She, like my dad, also likes to slow-cook ribs before barbecuing. She has taught me to tightly wrap the ribs in foil without sauce and bake for 1½ hours at 300°F. Then heat the barbecue to medium-low, baste the ribs, and cook for 10 to 15 minutes per side. Slow-cooking will make the meat fall off the bone. Be careful not to let your barbecue temperature climb too high. You don't want to burn the sauce.

Memphis Barbecue Sauce à la Jenna

(yields 2 cups sauce)

1 tablespoon vegetable oil
1 cup ketchup
⅓ cup water
3 tablespoons apple cider vinegar
2 tablespoons firmly packed dark brown sugar
2 tablespoons steak sauce

2 tablespoons Worcestershire sauce
1 tablespoon molasses
1 tablespoon yellow mustard
1 teaspoon salt
⅛ teaspoon white or black pepper, ground fine
½ yellow onion, diced
1 garlic clove, diced

Heat the vegetable oil in a medium saucepan over medium heat. Stir in the ketchup, water, cider vinegar, brown sugar, steak sauce, Worcestershire sauce, molasses, yellow mustard, salt, and pepper. Bring to a boil.

Add the onion and garlic, reduce the heat to medium-low, and simmer until the onions are tender, about 15 minutes.

Strain the sauce into a bowl through a mesh sieve, pressing a spoon on the onions and garlic to extract any liquid.

Baste your meat or poultry liberally with sauce while you barbecue.

From Bailey:

My mother loves serving this dish at The Pelican Brief Diner. It's savory and is a good side dish to just about everything. It has become one of Tito's favorite dishes. He likes things spicy, like me.

Spanish Rice

(serves 4 to 6)

¼ cup butter, cubed
2 cups uncooked white rice
1 can (14½ ounces) diced tomatoes with their liquid
1 cup beef broth, plus more if needed
1 medium onion, chopped

1 garlic clove, minced
1 bay leaf
1 teaspoon sugar
1 teaspoon salt
¼ teaspoon black pepper
⅛ teaspoon white pepper

In a sauté pan over medium heat, melt the butter. Add the rice and stir until lightly browned, 5 to 7 minutes.

Add the diced tomatoes with their liquid, beef broth, chopped onion, minced garlic, bay leaf, sugar, salt, black pepper, and white pepper. Bring the mixture to a boil. Reduce heat to low. Cover and simmer the rice for 25 to 30 minutes, or until the liquid is absorbed and the rice is tender. Add more beef broth if needed.

Remove the bay leaf before serving.

Isn't that easy?

From Katie:

I'm always searching for a new recipe for sweets. The patrons at the café don't want the same old, same old. They want new. And they seem to love spicy. For the Wild West Extravaganza, I decided that a hot, spicy fudge would do the trick. This is so easy to make. If you don't like it too spicy, omit the cayenne pepper, but keep the bacon. Chocolate and bacon are a superb sweet-savory combination!

Spicy Chocolate Fudge

(makes 32 large or 64 small pieces)

3 cups dark chocolate morsels
1 can sweetened condensed milk

    1 teaspoon vanilla extract
    1 teaspoon ground cinnamon
    ¼ teaspoon cayenne pepper
    ⅛ teaspoon white pepper
    4 tablespoons crisply cooked and crumbled bacon

Line an 8-inch-square pan with parchment.

In a saucepan, heat the chocolate and the sweetened condensed milk over medium-low heat until the chocolate is melted. Be sure to stir continually so the chocolate melts evenly.

Remove from the heat and stir in the vanilla, cinnamon, cayenne pepper, and white pepper.

[If you're worried about how hot it might be, cut back on the peppers and taste with the tip of a spoon.]

Pour the mixture into the prepared pan. Top with crumbled bacon and press the bacon lightly to affix to the chocolate.

Allow the fudge to set for at least 4 hours in the refrigerator. Slice into pieces using a hot, wet knife.

Grandmother's Spoon Bread

(serves 6-8)

    3 cups milk
    1¼ cups yellow cornmeal
    3 eggs
    1 teaspoon salt
    1¾ teaspoons baking powder
    butter, if desired

Measure the milk into a saucepan and bring to a boil. Add the cornmeal; reduce the heat to low. Cook and stir for several minutes, until the cornmeal has absorbed all of the milk. Remove the saucepan from the heat and allow the mixture to cool for about 1 hour. The mixture will be very stiff.

Preheat the oven to 375°F. Lightly grease a 1½-quart casserole dish.

Place the cornmeal mixture in a large bowl.

Separate the eggs. Stir the yolks, salt, baking powder, and butter into the cornmeal mixture.

In a separate bowl, beat the egg whites to soft peaks. Fold the egg whites into the cornmeal mixture.

Pour the batter into the prepared casserole dish.

Bake for 35 minutes in the preheated oven, or until the edges of the spoon bread become lightly toasted. Serve hot. This does not cut like a pie. Use a large spoon to dish it up.

Also from bestselling author
AVERY AAMES
writing as

DARYL WOOD GERBER

THE COOKBOOK NOOK MYSTERIES

Final Sentence
Inherit the Word
Stirring the Plot
Fudging the Books
Grilling the Subject

Praise for the Cookbook Nook Mysteries

"[A] witty, well-plotted whodunit that
will leave you hungry for more."

—Kate Carlisle, *New York Times* bestselling author

"[A] page-turning puzzler of a mystery."

—Jenn McKinlay, *New York Times* bestselling author

darylwoodgerber.com
facebook.com/darylwoodgerber
penguin.com